To my wife Beverley,
who always believed,
but now can't, quite.

INTRODUCTORY NOTE

The term "historical fiction" indicates that there is at least a framework of factual material involved in the story being told in a novel. It seems to follow, therefore, that everyone who reads historical fiction should have a right to know — or should be accorded the privilege of knowing — how much of what he or she is reading is historically correct and accurate.

The characters Caius Britannicus and Publius Varrus are fictitious, as are all their families, friends and relatives. They were all born of the author's need to answer the question, "How could this, or that, have happened or come into being?"

The events against which their fictional story unfolds, however, were very real, and the major imperial characters — Valens, Valentinian, Theodosius and Stilicho — lived and behaved as described herein. The time in which they lived, the latter part of the fourth and the early part of the fifth Christian centuries, was a period when world-shaking events took place; things that still affect our lives today, sixteen hundred years afterward, owe their beginnings to the ideas and events that were developing at that time.

The eighty-one-year period from 367 to 448 AD was among the most intense in the history of the province the

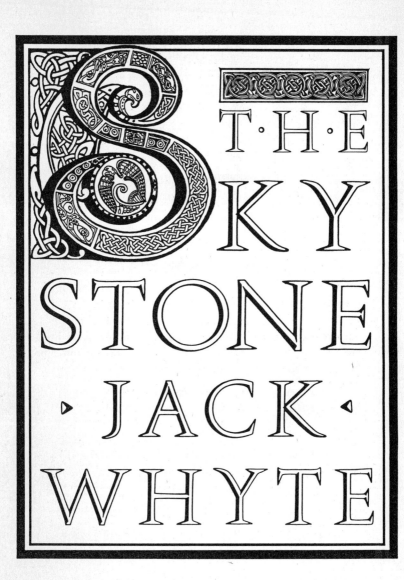

THE SKY STONE

JACK WHYTE

VIKING

VIKING

Published by the Penguin Group

Penguin Books Canada Ltd, 10 Alcorn Avenue, Toronto, Ontario,
Canada M4V 3B2

Penguin Books Ltd, 27 Wrights Lane, London W8 5TZ, England

Viking Penguin, a division of Penguin Books USA Inc., 375 Hudson
Street, New York, New York 10014, USA

Penguin Books Australia Ltd, Ringwood, Victoria, Australia

Penguin Books (NZ) Ltd, 182-190 Wairau Road,
Auckland 10, New Zealand

Penguin Books Ltd, Registered Offices:
Harmondsworth, Middlesex, England

First published 1992

1 3 5 7 9 10 8 6 4 2

Publisher's note: The Skystone *is based in part on actual events,
but all the principal characters are fictional.*

Printed and bound in Canada

Canadian Cataloguing in Publication Data

Whyte, Jack, 1942 –

The skystone

ISBN 0–670–84519–1

I. Arthur, King — Fiction.   I. Title.

PS8595.H95S58 1992   C813'.54   C92–094133–8
PR9199.3.W49S58   1992

British Library Cataloguing in Publication Data Available
American Library of Congress Cataloguing in Publication
Data Available

Romans called Britain. At the start of it, in 367, Britain was still firmly Roman, and the Roman authorities still maintained written records. By the end of it, however, the four-hundred-year occupation of Britain had ended, the entire Roman Empire in the West was in ruins, and Britain itself, the western Empire's richest granary, had been so thoroughly conquered by the Angles and Saxons that it would be known forever afterward as the land of the Angles — England.

In the space of those eighty years, civilized life, literacy, education and Christianity were stamped out and the Dark Ages settled on Britain. They would last for two centuries and more, so that by the time the light of learning returned to Britain, great changes had been wrought, and legends had been born. The English longbow was then a fact of life, and people talked on long, dark, winter nights of a great champion who had led his people valiantly in ancient times, armed with a magic sword he had received from a woman's hand. It was the beginning of what would come to be known, over the course of centuries, as the Arthurian Legend.

The Roman Army

The differences between the Roman army of antiquity and the modern army are differences mainly of names. The structures are comparable.

A modern Army Group, or a Brigade, made up of several regiments, is the approximate equivalent of a classic Roman legion. The officer commanding the modern Brigade is a Brigadier General, and he is assisted by an adjutant or deputy, plus a staff of senior officers made up of the Colonels and Majors of each regiment. These are assisted in turn by their company commanders (Captains) and subalterns (Lieutenants), who are backed up by their non-commissioned officers.

In the Roman army, the commanding officer of a legion was called the Legate. He was assisted by an adjutant or deputy called the Camp Prefect, and a staff of six senior administrative officers called Tribunes. The original function of the Tribunes was to spread the call to arms and ensure that the citizens rallied to the Eagles in time to march and fight. Later, the Tribunate became more of a political tenure, a training ground for young noblemen waiting to go into the consular or civil services. Whenever a Tribune chose to distinguish himself militarily rather than serve his time administratively and get out, his success was almost preordained.

There were normally twenty-eight legions in commission at any given time, and each legion was divided into ten cohorts. By the end of the third century, the first two cohorts of each legion had been expanded to Millarian status, which meant that each held 1,000 men and was the approximate equivalent of a modern battalion. Prior to that time, only the First Cohort had been Millarian. To the First and Second Cohorts fell the honour of holding the right of the legion's line of battle, and they were made up of only the finest and strongest battle-hardened veterans. Cohorts Three through Ten were standard cohorts of 500 to 600 men.

Each Millarian cohort was composed of ten maniples, and a maniple was made up of ten squads of ten to twelve men each.

The bulk of the legion's command was provided by the

Centuriate, from the ranks of which came the centurions, all the middle- and lower-ranking commissioned officers of the legion. There were six centurions to each cohort from Three through Ten, making forty-eight, and five senior centurions, called *primi ordines*, in each of the two Millarian Cohorts. Each legion had a *primus pilus*, the senior centurion, a kind of super-charged Regimental Sergeant Major. The *primus pilus* headed the First Cohort, the Second Cohort was headed by the *princeps secundus*, and Cohorts Three through Ten were each commanded by a *pilus prior*.

The Roman centurion was distinguished by his uniform: his armour was silvered, he wore his sword on his left side rather than his right, and the crest on his helmet was turned so that it went sideways across his helmet like a halo.

Each centurion had the right, or the option, to appoint a second-in-command for himself, and these men, the equivalents of non-commissioned officers, were known for that reason as *optios*. Other junior officers *(principales)* were the standard-bearers, one of whom, the *aquilifer*, bore the Eagle of the legion. There was also a *signifer* for each century, who bore the unit's identity crest and acted as its banker. Each legion also had a full complement of physicians and surgeons, veterinarians, quartermasters and clerks, trumpeters, guard commanders, intelligence officers, torturers and executioners.

Cavalry

By the end of the second century AD, cavalry was playing an important role in legionary tactics and represented up to one-fifth of overall forces in many military actions.

Nevertheless, until the turn of the fifth century, the cavalry was the army's weakest link.

The Romans themselves were never great horsemen, and Roman cavalry was seldom truly Roman. They preferred to leave the cavalry to their allies and subject nations, so that history tells us of the magnificent German mixed cavalry that Julius Caesar admired, and which gave rise to the *cohortes equitates*, the mixed cohorts of infantry and cavalry used in the first, second and third centuries AD. Roman writers also mention with admiration the wonderful light horsemen of North Africa, who rode without bridles.

Fundamentally, with very few exceptions, cavalry were used as light skirmishing troops, mainly mounted archers whose job was patrol, reconnaissance and the provision of a mobile defensive screen while the legion was massing in battle array.

Roman cavalry of the early and middle Empire was organized in *alae*, units of 500 to 1,000 men divided into squadrons, or *turmae*, of 30 or 40 horsemen under the command of decurions. We know that the Romans used a kind of saddle, with four saddle horns for anchoring baggage, but they had no knowledge of stirrups, although they did use spurs. They also used horseshoes and snaffle bits, and some of their horses wore armoured *cataphractus* blankets of bronze scales, although there is little evidence that this form of armour, or armoured cavalry, was ever widely used.

Until the fifth century, and the aftermath of the Battle of Adrianople, it would seem that almost no attempt had been made to study the heavy cavalry techniques used in the second century BC by Philip of Macedon and his son

Alexander the Great. It was that renaissance, allied with the arrival of stirrups in Europe somewhere in the first half of the fifth century, that changed warfare forever. In terms of military impact, the significance of the saddle with stirrups was probably greater than the invention of the tank.

Proper and place names

Most of the names used for characters in this novel would have been common in Roman times. The following is a guide to phonetic pronunciation:

Caesarius	[Cee-zary-us]
Caius	[Kay-us]
Claudius	[Klawdy-us]
Flavius	[Flavey-us]
Gaius	[Guy-us]
Luceiia	[Loo-chee-ya]
Plautus	[Plough-tus]
Quinctilius	[Kwink-tillyus]
Quintus	[Kwin-tus]
Seneca	[Sen-nic-a]
Tertius	[Tershy-us]
Theodosius	[Theo-dozy-us]
Valentinian	[Valen-tinny-an]
Vegetius	[Ve-jeeshy-us]

The land the Romans called Britain was only the land we know today as England. Scotland, Ireland and Wales were separate and known respectively as Caledonia, Hibernia and Cambria. They were not recognized as part of the province of Britain.

The ancient towns of Roman Britain are still there, but they all have English names now. What follows is a guide to phonetic pronunciation of Roman place names, with their modern equivalents. They are numbered to correspond to the map provided.

1	Londinium	[Lon-dinny-um]	London
2	Verulamium	[Verr-you-lame-eeyum]	St. Albans
3	Alchester		
4	Glevum	[Glev-vum]	Gloucester
5	Aquae Sulis	[Ack-way Soo-liss]	Bath
6	Lindinis	[Linn-dinnis]	Ilchester
7	Sorviodunum	[Sorr-vee-yode-inum]	Old Sarum
8	Venta Belgarum	[Venta Bell-gah-rum]	Winchester
9	Noviomagus	[Novvy-oh-maggus]	Chichester
10	Durnovaria	[Durr-no-varr-eya]	Dorchester
11	Isca Dumnoniorum	[Isska Dumb-nonny-orum]	Exeter
12	The Colony		
13	Camulodunum	[Ca-moo-loadin-um]	Colchester
14	Lindum	[Lin-dum]	Lincoln
15	Eboracum	[Eh-borra-cum]	York
16	Mamucium	[Mah-moochy-um]	Manchester
17	Dolocauthi	[Dolla-cow-thee]	Welsh Gold Mines
18	Durovernum	[Doo-rove-err-num]	Canterbury
19	Regulbium	[Re-goolby-um]	Reculver
20	Rutupiae	[Roo-too-pee-ay]	Richborough
21	Dubris	[Doo-briss]	Dover
22	Lemanis	[Leh-mann-iss]	Lympne
23	Anderita	[An-der-reeta]	Pevensey

The main towns of the Roman Province
of South Britain referred to in *The Skystone*

1   Londinium (London)
2   Verulamium (St. Albans)
3   Alchester
4   Glevum (Gloucester)
5   Aquae Sulis (Bath)
6   Lindinis (Ilchester)
7   Sorviodunum (Old Sarum)
8   Venta Belgarum (Winchester)
9   Noviomagus (Chichester)
10 Durnovaria (Dorchester)
11 Isca Dumnoniorum (Exeter)
12 The Colony
13 Camulodunum (Colchester)
14 Lindum (Lincoln)
15 Eboracum (York)
16 Mamucium (Manchester)
17 Dolocauthi
18 Durovernum (Canterbury)
19 *Regulbium (Reculver)
20 *Rutupiae (Richborough)
21 *Dubris (Dover)
22 *Lemanis (Lympne)
23 *Anderita (Pevensey)

* Forts of the Saxon Shore

The Legend of the Skystone

Out of the night sky there will fall a stone
That hides a maiden born of murky deeps,
A maid whose fire-fed, female mysteries
Shall give life to a lambent, gleaming blade,
A blazing, shining sword whose potency
Breeds warriors. More than that,
This weapon will contain a woman's wiles
And draw dire deeds of men; shall name an age;
Shall crown a king, called of a mountain clan
Who dream of being spawned from dragon's seed;
Fell, forceful men, heroic, proud and strong,
With greatness in their souls.
This king, this monarch, mighty beyond ken,
Fashioned of glory, singing a song of swords,
Misting with magic madness mortal men,
Shall sire a legend, yet leave none to lead
His host to triumph after he be lost.
But death shall ne'er demean his destiny who,
Dying not, shall ever live and wait to be recalled.

BOOK ONE

Invasion

I

Today is my sixty-seventh birthday, a hot day in the summer of 410 in the year of our Lord, according to the new Christian system of dating the passage of time. I am old, I know, in years. My bones are old, after sixty-seven summers. But my mind has not aged with my body.

My name is Gaius Publius Varrus, and I am probably the last man alive in Britain who can claim to have marched beneath the Eagles of the Roman army of occupation in this country. The others who marched with me are not merely dead; they are long dead. Yet I can still recall my days with the legions clearly.

I have known men who refused to admit ever having marched with the armies. Whatever their reasons, I regard their refusal as their loss. I remember my legion days frequently, with affection and gratitude, because most of my lifetime friends came to me from the legions and so, indirectly, did my wife, the mother of my children and sharer of my dreams.

There are times, too, when I think of my army days with an echo of incredulous laughter in my heart. I remember the foul-ups and the chaos and all the petty, human frailties and fallibilities that surface in army life, and my options are clear: laugh at them, or weep.

I remember, for instance, how I spent the afternoon of another summer day, more than forty years ago, back in '69. That day was my last as a Roman soldier, and I spent it leading my men, and my commanding general, up a mountain and into an ambush.

Traps are never pleasant spots to be in, God knows, but the one we sprung that day was the worst I ever encountered in all my years of soldiering. The heathens who caught us seemed to materialize out of the living rock. Savage, terrifying creatures, half-man, half-mountain goat, they took us completely by surprise in a high, rocky defile in the very centre of the rugged spine of mountains that runs the length of Britain.

We had been climbing for two days, picking our way carefully and, we thought, in secrecy through valleys and passes away from the major crossing routes. We wanted to arrive unannounced on the western side. The few officers with horses, myself included, had been on foot most of that time, leading the animals. We had just entered this defile and mounted up, thankful for the reasonably level floor it offered, when we were crushed by a torrent of massive rocks from above.

The three men I had been talking to were smashed to a bloody pulp before my eyes by a boulder that fell on top of them out of nowhere. They never even saw it. I doubt if any of the men killed in that first apocalyptic minute saw death approach them. I know I was stunned by the suddenness of it. It did not even occur to me at first that we were being attacked, for we had sighted no hostiles in more than a week and expected to find none there, so high in the mountains.

Those first plummeting boulders caused carnage

among our men, who had just bunched together on the narrow, rocky floor, exhausted after a long, hard climb. The mountains, which had until then heard only panting, grunting breath and muttered curses, were suddenly echoing with the roar of falling rock and the panicked, agonized screams of maimed and dying men. And then the enemy appeared, dropping, as I have said, like mountain goats from the defile walls above us.

Britannicus, my general, had fallen back from the head of the column only moments earlier to chivvy the men behind us, and as I swung my mount around, I saw his helmet's crimson plume about thirty paces distant, swaying as he fought to control his rearing horse. The cliffs directly above him were swarming with leaping men, clad in animal skins, and I began flogging my horse, willing the frightened beast to fly me over the men packed around me to a spot where I could organize some effective resistance.

It was hopeless. There was no room to do anything. In a matter of seconds, it seemed, the entire length of the defile was a mass of snarling, angry men locked in hand-to-hand fighting. This was a fight that, whichever way it went, would be won by brawn and guts, not by tactics.

I was using my horse as a battering ram, forcing my way through the struggling mass of bodies, stabbing right and left with a spear I had snatched from a falling man, but it was like one of those dreadful dreams when nothing works properly and everything slows down except the forces threatening you.

The narrow floor of the cleft we were in was bisected for a third of its length by a ridge of rock that was sharp

as a blade on top, and I reached one end of this ridge just
as my horse sagged under me, fatally wounded but unable
to fall immediately because of the press of bodies. I managed somehow to throw myself from its back before it did
go down and found myself standing on the ridge above
the struggle, unchallenged by anyone. I looked to my
right and saw Britannicus, his teeth bared in a rictus of
pain, less than a spear's length from me, an arrow in his
thigh above the knee. It was a red-flighted arrow, very
pretty, and it had pierced him cleanly, pinning him to his
screaming horse, which, like mine, did not have room to
fall. As I watched, a hand came up out of the press below
and grasped the protruding shaft, pulling it downward.
He screamed, and his horse lurched and went down on
that side, crushing his pinned leg beneath it.

I have no recollection of crossing the space between
us. The next thing I remember is standing on the
hindquarters of his horse, directly above Britannicus,
looking for a clear space to jump down into. The masses
parted and I leaped, only to take a spear thrust in the
chest in mid flight so that I fell backwards on top of
him. My breastplate had deflected the spear's point, but
I saw its owner set to try for me again. I tried clumsily
to roll to my right as he stabbed and this time felt the
point of the spear lodge between the plates of my
armour, beneath my shoulder. I rolled back again frantically, throwing my weight against the shaft, and managed to wrench it from the man's grasp as one of my
own men plunged a sword beneath his arm. He went to
his knees and died there, his eyes wide and amazed. As
he began to topple towards me, I was already on my feet
again, ignoring the spear, which had fallen beside me,

and drawing my dagger. My sword was gone. A hand grasped my left shoulder, tugging me violently around before I could find my balance. I swung blindly, finding a naked neck with my blade and falling again, hearing a voice inside my head cursing me clearly for not being able to stand up.

There was blood everywhere. I caught a glimpse of Britannicus beside me, staring, face pale as death, and then someone else fell on me, gurgling his own death into my ear. I lost all reason, panicking with the need to stand on my own feet. I reached and grasped and hauled myself up, throwing someone aside — whether friend or foe I'll never know — and managed to stand erect only to realize that I was weaponless and being pulled down yet again. I went to one knee and this time could not rise. A voice yelled "Varrus!" and a hand appeared from my left side, fingers extended to me. I clasped it and pulled myself up again, and as I did so, I clearly saw a bronze axe-head with a long, polished spike sever the helping hand cleanly from its wrist. Time froze. I saw the axe-wielder turn towards me, his weapon swinging to its height, and I knew the sharpness of that blade.

The details of that instant stand out clearly. The man was big, red-bearded, grinning in rage, showing black stumps of teeth. He wore a wolf skin across his naked chest and another around his loins, held by a leather belt into which was stuck a long dagger. He saw a dead man staring at him from my eyes. A voice in my mind agreed with him, and I was preparing for my death when that same handless arm, spurting its life, pointed itself at him, jetting its bright-red blood into his eyes and blinding him for the time it took me to throw myself forward, jerk the dagger from his belt as he reeled back from my weight and sink it to the hilt beneath his unarmoured ribs.

As he fell dying, however, he somehow found the strength to whirl his axe backward and down and around, and I felt the raking tear of its spike from knee to groin as it slammed jarringly up into the join of me. I dropped my head, cringing from the violence of it, to see the thick shaft, like a gross, wooden, impossible phallus, sticking from beneath my tunic. Pain exploded in me, wracking me with unimaginable fury as I fell into a whirlpool of screaming blackness, still clutching the severed hand of my saviour.

We won — how, I will never know. But that was the end of my career as a follower of the Eagles. By rights, it should have been the end of me completely. The spike had missed my testicles and had driven upwards into my left buttock, but it had damaged the hamstring behind my knee in passing and laid open my whole thigh to the bone. The medics wanted to take the leg right off, there and then, at the end of the fight, before taking me down out of the mountains, for they thought that I would never survive the journey. Thank God I recovered conscious-ness quickly! I squealed like an angry hawk, knowing the survival rate among amputees to be almost nil. But it would have done me no good had it not been for Caius Britannicus. He insisted that I be cauterized and sewn up to take my chances. I had saved his life more times than he could count, he swore, and if I were to die, then by all the gods in heaven, I had earned the right to die two-legged. I was his *primus pilus*, he declared, and a *primus pilus* was entitled to two legs, alive or dead.

He was absolutely correct, of course. *Primus pilus* — literally the First Spear — was the single most exalted and exclusive rank an ordinary soldier could attain within his legion. Rome had only twenty-eight legions in commission at that time, and each had one *primus pilus*. As *primus pilus* of my legion, therefore, I was officially recognized as one of the twenty-eight best professional soldiers in the imperial legions of Rome.

No man who ever marched behind the Eagles would ever deny that claim. Each *primus pilus*, down through Rome's thousand years of power, earned every single step of his promotion by being the very best among his equals at every stage of his career. Each progressed, without deviation or blemish, and frequently from the lowest ranks, up the ladder of honour, through the entire centuriate of the legion, to the ultimate post of First Spear. Everyone, including the political and appointed officers — junior legates, staff and tribunes — answered to the *primus pilus* in matters of tactics, discipline, troop dispositions and the daily administration of his legion's affairs. For his part, the *primus pilus* answered directly and only to his legion's commanding general — in my case, the Legate Caius Cornelius Britannicus.

I don't know how either of us survived the journey back down to the plains, but when we got there, Britannicus quartered me in his sick bay and I was tended by Mitros, his personal physician. We lay there on our cots, side by side, and waited to heal, and as we waited, each of us had ample time to explore his own thoughts — for me, I must admit, a novel experience at that time. I believe it may have been during those days that the idea of telling this story first entered my mind, but I cannot make that claim with absolute conviction.

Where does a man find the arrogance to contemplate the telling of a tale like the one I have to tell? "Inside himself" may be the most convenient answer, but in this particular instance it is both inadequate and inaccurate. My present determination to tell this story — and it is one that has often seemed stubborn and foolish even to me, in spite of the fact that I have been writing it for many years — springs from the fact that, in Caius Britannicus, I had a lifelong friend and mentor whose prophetic vision and moral integrity still awe me. Thanks to his strength of character, his powers of perception and evaluation and his insistence upon needing me, I was permitted to survive the ending of an entire world, and then to begin a new life at an age when other men were lying down to die.

Now that I am truly old, the fear of leaving that tale untold, and thereby consigning my friend to eternal anonymity, unsung and unrecognized, strengthens me to write. Having found that strength, I have struggled to find a beginning for my tale, the way a boy will search perversely for the centre of an onion, blinding himself with tears as he pursues his folly. There is, I now know, no real beginning. There is only memory, which flows where the terrain takes it.

Caius Cornelius Britannicus was not a good invalid. He resented being confined to bed, but until the hole in his thigh mended there was not a thing he could do about it. Regrettably, as a direct result of that, those first few days were the worst I ever spent in his company. I was grateful to him, but he was hard to take on an empty stomach, and since I spent most of those first days puking up the medicines Mitros was feeding me, my stomach was certainly empty a good deal. I would have been happier sharing those quarters with an angry leopard. He did eventually begin to settle down, however, and to accept his enforced inactivity with more characteristic philosophy. From that point on, we talked — rather, he talked and I listened, throwing my occasional copper contribution onto his pile of silver and golden ones.

From time to time, the monotony of our confinement would be broken when one or the other of us would have a visitor, but the men who came to visit me were awkward and uncomfortable in the presence of my august host and companion. To me, he was my Legate, my companion-in-arms for years, and a trusted friend. To my visitors, he was "Old Eagle Face," their commanding general, and therefore their nemesis and their god. They shuffled and whispered and fidgeted and couldn't wait to get out of there.

On one of those occasions, after a very brief visit by two of my subordinate cohort centurions, I turned to Britannicus and found him asleep, flat on his back, his high-ridged nose outlined against the light. The image brought back a surge of memories.

Africa, 365

You don't spend two years on active service in Africa without learning to get out of the sun during the hottest part of the day. I had been sheltered and reasonably comfortable, dozing quietly, when something startled me awake. I lay there motionless, holding my breath, my ears straining, and waited for whatever had made the noise to make it again. Then, somewhere behind me, just on the edge of my hearing range, a camel coughed, and this time the sound brought me to my knees, head down below the tops of the rocks that shaded me, as I tried to isolate the direction it had come from. A Roman soldier meets few friendly strangers in the desert; none of them ever rides a camel.

There were five men, four of them mounted on camels and wearing the long, black, stifling clothes of the nomadic barbarians who infested these desert lands. The fifth man walked between two of the riders, and something in his posture, even at that distance, told me he walked with his hands bound behind him; the fact that he was walking at all made it obvious he was a prisoner. They were about a mile from me when I first saw them shimmering through the heat haze, and they approached steadily and slowly until the walker fell to his knees, forcing the little procession to stop and wait for him to get back to his feet. Even from almost a mile away I could see that he was one of my own kind, for he wore a short, military-style tunic. I could see, too, that he was just about finished. I flattened myself to my rock, my eyes barely clearing the top of the small hill I was on, and watched the poor swine weaving and staggering as the group drew closer to my hiding place. They had him strung by the neck with two ropes, each one stretching to one of the riders who flanked him.

I had no worries about their finding me. They would pass close by to my left, heading directly to the water hole, the only water around for miles. I had been there at dawn. I had drunk my fill and replenished my water bags, and then I had looked around and chosen this boulder-strewn hill to hide on during the long day. Here, I was sheltered from the sun and from visitors by high rocks and a strategically hung cloak, and my horse was comfortable and well hidden. I had left no visible tracks for any casual or inquisitive eye to see. I was waiting for nightfall, when I would cross the five leagues of desert between me and the sea coast, and pick up a galley to take me out of Africa, home to Britain along the coasts of Iberia and Gaul.

I detest Africa. I loathe it from the bottom of my legionary's soul, and for the best of reasons, which I share with every other grunt who ever humped a military pack across its God-forsaken sands: I went there as a soldier. To me, it is a country with only two faces, one of which is false. The false face is a harlot's mask, painted to disguise corruption and decay. It is the face of urban Africa, gaudy with gross and exotic luxuries. It is the face most often seen by Rome's diplomats and wealthy, travelling merchants. Away from the flesh-pots and the palaces of its major cities, however, Africa shows its other face, its real face, to Rome's soldiers. That sneering face is twisted with hatred, toxic with hostility.

The soldiers who police Africa's lethal wastelands on foot have no illusions about its vastness or its mysteries; to them, Africa is Hades, a miserable, sweltering place of unpleasant duty, unbearable temperatures and unrelieved harshness. They know it to be peopled with alien, violent creatures whose feral natures reflect their environment. Its people are nomads — grim desert tribesmen whose lives seem wholly dedicated to strife in the form of never-ending local wars and vicious blood feuds. They call themselves Berbers, and the only common cause they ever seem to make is to war against Rome's soldiers. In consequence, the soldiers of Rome, down through the centuries, have regarded them with a mixture of awe and hatred and sullen respect, treating them as the most implacably savage warriors in the world, and convinced that the word "barbarian" was coined far back in antiquity to describe the Berbers of Africa.

These were the men at whom I was peering now. I felt sorry for their prisoner, but I didn't even consider trying to help him. There were four of those whoresons, and they had two free camels to string me between. I just crouched there, half standing and half leaning, hugging my rock, watching and waiting for them to pass by.

The prisoner fell to his knees again at about the closest point of their sweep by me, less than a hundred and fifty paces from where I watched. One of his two captors was not paying attention to him and didn't see him go down, so the rope joining the two of them together became taut and jerked the prisoner flat onto his face in the rock-strewn sand. I winced, imagining the stinging pain of the gritty impact, but it must have been insignificant beside the pain that followed it, for the rider cursed and slashed a long whip across the shoulders of the prostrate man. It did not provoke as much as a flinch. The prisoner was either dead or unconscious. With a disgusted curse, the fellow who had wielded the whip brought his camel to its knees and slid to the ground, approaching the prisoner and pulling his face up out of the sand by a handful of hair. The sand-caked mask gave no sign of life, but the man was obviously still alive, because his captor dropped him back to the ground and went to his camel, where he undid the neck of a water bag and splashed some of the liquid onto an end of the cloth that wrapped his head and hung down in front of him. Then, still clutching the water bag, he went back to the unconscious man, pulled his head up again and roughly wiped the caked sand from his face, so that I saw fair, sun-bronzed skin appear.

It took some time, but the prisoner eventually regained his senses, helped by a generous quantity of water that I knew was offered only because of the plentiful supply nearby. As soon as he seemed capable of standing upright again, the barbarian hauled him to his feet and left him there, swaying, while he climbed back up onto his camel. None of his three companions had either moved or spoken. I heard the guttural "Hut! Hut! Hut!" command to the camel and then, as they began to move again, just before he took his first staggering step, the prisoner turned, his face clean, his eyes screwed almost shut, and looked, unseeing, directly towards my hiding place.

That look had the effect on me of an unexpected plunge into icy water. My skin broke out in goose-flesh and my gut stirred in sheer horror. I knew him. And I knew, suddenly, that this time and this place had been preordained, that the whim that had brought me here had had a supernatural origin. I am not a superstitious man, and I was far less so then, but I knew that this was my destiny, my fate. I've heard a lot of men say that they relived their entire lives in one flash of time when they thought they were going to die. That wasn't quite what happened to me then, but I have never had a stranger experience than I did at that moment, when smells, sounds, feelings and sights assaulted me without warning from a time four years earlier.

I had been on campaign at the time, on the eastern borders of the Empire, but for all I knew as I struggled awake that day, I could have been anywhere. I was flat on my back, completely disoriented, with no knowledge of what had happened to me. And then a surging memory of battle, of being surrounded by screaming, barbarous faces, brought a swell of panic into my throat, and I started to scramble to my feet. And that's when my mind told me I had been killed, because try as I would, I couldn't move a muscle. I couldn't even scream — couldn't bite my tongue. The panic inside me rose to choking point, but then I heard my heart thumping like a drum in my ears, assuring me I was alive. I fought down the panic and willed myself to relax.

I lay there for a while, forcing myself to breathe slowly and deeply and to consider the evidence of the senses I had working for me. I could smell, hear and feel, for a fat fly had landed on my cheek and crawled into my open mouth. I tried to spit it out. Couldn't. Terror writhed in me again like a mass of maggots. I was afraid to try to open my eyes in case they were already open and I was blind as well as paralyzed. The fly flew out of my mouth; one second I could feel it on my tongue, and the next it was gone. I tried to open my eyes slowly. They were working, at least, but the light was blinding and I felt the muscles of my eyelids rebelling against my efforts. The rest of my body was dead. I could feel absolutely nothing below my mouth.

I have no idea how long I lay there, but eventually the bright light against my eyelids seemed to dim and I felt a coolness on my face, and then a solitary raindrop hit the bridge of my nose with a force and a suddenness that snapped my eyes open. I was lying on my back, my face directly towards a sky that was heavy with banked rain clouds. I had never seen anything so beautiful. Something was very close to my face and I swivelled my eyes downward as far as I could to try to see what it was. There was a dead man's face, horribly mutilated, within inches of my own. His skull had been shattered and grey brains leaked obscenely from the hole. The flies were so thick on the mess that they swarmed. I felt vomit surge in me and fought it down in terror, knowing that if I didn't succeed I would drown myself. The nausea passed slowly and I must have fainted.

I awoke again looking up at a man who towered above me, the hem of his tunic almost touching my face. It was almost dark now, and I thanked God fervently for sending him before nightfall. I tried to moan, to move, but nothing happened, and not a sound came out of me. Screaming inside, I watched in horror as his eyes moved over everything around me without approaching my face. I felt my eyes fill with tears. I was eighteen years old, stricken, somehow, in my first battle, and doomed to die here within inches of a man who couldn't see me! Through my tears I saw him look down and then stoop, suddenly, out of my line of sight. Then came a heaving grunt and my whole view changed with a lurch, and what seemed like millions of flies sprang into the air. I saw him straighten up again on the edge of my vision, and I knew that he had somehow moved me to my right. The movement had dislodged the corpse whose face had been so close to my own.

"Tribune!" His voice was low-pitched and deep. "I've found their standard. It was at the bottom of this pile."

He extended his arm, and I saw that he was holding the great silver eagle that I had been so proud to carry, perched on its staff above the SPQR symbol of the Senate and the People of Rome. Another, younger man stepped into my sight. He gripped the standard's shaft, looked up at the Eagle and then looked around him, shaking his head regretfully, his eyes coming to rest on my own. He looked just like an eagle himself, a powerful raptor with deep-set, blazing eyes of pale-yellow gold, a great, narrow, hooked beak of a nose and a mouth that was compressed into a lipless line over a strong, square chin. He was gazing directly into my eyes without seeing me, his mind focused on something other than what he was looking at. But then I saw his gaze sharpen. A furrow appeared between his brows and deepened as his attention concentrated on me. He took a step towards me and I saw his fingers, extended like talons, reach for my neck. His face, keen-eyed and predatory, came within inches of my own, and as the tip of one of his fingers touched the wetness of a tear on my cheek, I blinked. I was vividly aware of the crease marks around his eyes, which could only have been caused, I was convinced, by squinting into the sun, for even now, at the moment of my salvation, I was thinking that here was a face that could never smile or laugh.

"This man's alive! Get him out of there, quickly!"

Two more men loomed up behind him and he moved aside to let them dig me out of the great pile of corpses that I had been buried in. My relief was so great that I passed out again.

I recovered eventually from the paralysis that had gripped me — the result of a powerful blow of some kind to the base of my spine — and returned to my decimated unit, where I sought and received permission to try to trace the young officer who had saved my life. I never did find him, and his distinctive face had gradually faded into the stuff of my most hidden memories, forgotten until now.

Now those golden eyes looked my way again and reminded me of a debt unpaid. A strange kind of fatalism took hold of me then as I hid among my rocks and watched his captors drag him until they passed out of sight under the shoulder of my hill. By the time they were gone, I knew what I had to do, and I knew that my chances of success were slim at best against four of them, and practically nonexistent if they were bowmen.

As a boy growing up in my grandfather's home, I had been fascinated by a huge African bow that hung on one wall of his treasure room, so called because it contained all of the ancient and exotic armour and weapons he had collected in a lifetime dedicated to the study of such things. Grandfather Varrus was said to be the finest armourer and weapons-smith in Britain, but he was also known as an insatiable collector of antique examples of his art, and soldiers brought him curios and relics from all corners of the Empire, knowing he would be happy to pay for them.

Of his entire collection, that great bow was the apple of my eye. It was too big for me to pull, but that only added to my fascination.

Since coming to Africa as a soldier, I had acquired a similar, though much smaller version, and had amused myself by learning how to use it properly and well. All my long hours of practice now offered me my only chance to come out of this adventure alive, for I had perfected the art of rapid, accurate fire, plucking arrows from a row stuck point down in the ground and firing them faster than anyone else I had ever come across. But I had never had anyone shooting back at me while I performed the trick. I hoped this occasion would be no different.

When I was sure they were safely out of sight and hearing, I strung my bow, took eight arrows and set out to follow them, keeping low and approaching as close as I could to the water hole without being seen. They had stopped and were setting up camp. When I could go no closer, I dug myself into the sand and covered myself with my long, sand-coloured cloak. Now I had only to continue to wait for darkness to fall, as I had been doing all day. I had already given up hope of making it to the coast that night; I honestly doubted that I would be going anywhere after this encounter. To divert myself, I spent the time trying to ignore what was really on my mind by wondering about the eagle-faced prisoner and by debating with myself whether or not I had brought enough arrows. It was a pointless debate. If I needed more than two for each of my four targets, it would already be too late to use them.

Of course, I couldn't escape from what was really on my mind, so I gave up trying and let the old struggle start up again. I was a soldier, a soldier of Rome. I tried my best to be a good one. That was half of my problem, but the other half, the really troublesome part, was that I was also a Christian, and although I didn't try to be particularly good at that, I was, by childhood training and unwilling conviction, a believing one. I believed in the power and rightness of the Christian Commandments, particularly and frighteningly the one that says, unequivocally, "Thou shalt not kill." Ever. I had learned that incontrovertible truth at my grandmother's knee. She was a very devout old lady who was appalled by her husband's craft and his love of weaponry and things military, and she made it her duty to ensure that I would grow up aware of the sanctity of all life. I have never been grateful to her. Nor have I ever been free of guilt over being a soldier, a paid killer. The part of me that was shaped by my grandmother abhors killing. The part of me that loves soldiering enjoys the anticipation of violence and the fury of the fight. And, of course, I must fight. But after the fighting, after the killing, after the violence, comes retribution: self-hatred, revulsion, mental agony and physical sickness. Every time, without fail. But always afterwards, never before.

By nightfall, I was glad I had approached so close to the water hole during daylight, for these people had no intention of passing the night in slothful sleep. As soon as the moon rose, full, flooding the desert with silver light, they were astir and preparing to move out. I had been crawling towards their camp on my belly, hoping to surprise them asleep, but their sudden activity almost caught me instead. I froze where I was, within twenty paces of where the first one passed on his way towards the tethered camels. Two of the others were kicking and cuffing their prisoner, hauling him to his feet and checking the halters tied around his neck. The fourth man set out towards me and just kept coming. I had decided I was as close as I was going to be able to get, and had already lined up my eight arrows so that they stuck up from the sand like a row of palisades. He was within seconds of noticing them and me when he stopped, even closer to me than the camel-herder had been, and began to relieve himself in a loud gush of urine that died away gradually in a dwindling stream and a series of squirts.

I gathered myself, timing my move to coincide with his readjustment of his robes, and then rose to my knees and fired. My arrow took him clean in the breastbone from about fifteen paces, the force of it lifting him backwards off his feet while he was still looking down. I had my second arrow nocked almost before the first one hit and was swinging towards the camel-herder, expecting him to have heard the sound of his comrade's death.

He had heard nothing. All of his attention was concentrated on bringing the camel he had mounted to its feet. As his body swayed backwards, adjusting to the camel's ungainly lurch in rising, I released and saw my arrow bury itself to the feathers in the soft spot just below the peak of his rib-cage. He, too, fell over backwards without a sound, but his going was seen. I heard a raucous laugh, which quickly gave way to a questioning shout of alarm.

The moonlight was bright, but I was a long way from the two men remaining with the prisoner. They still had not seen me, but they split apart instinctively, throwing themselves to my right and to my left. I snapped a quick shot at the one moving to my right, but it was an arrow wasted, leaving me with only five. I scooped up all of them and ran to my right, for no other reason than that the man there seemed to be the closer of the two. There was a small hillock of sand, no more than a wave on the ground, but I dropped flat behind it, straining my ears for any sound that might betray someone moving. The prisoner stood motionless where they had left him, his hands tied behind his back and twin ropes trailing from his neck to the ground. There was nowhere for him to try to run to. As far as he was aware, I was just another desert nomad. If I killed his captors, I would probably kill him, too. I estimated the distance between us at fifty paces. Nothing moved anywhere. Now what?

The camels began to mill around, off to my left, and I was almost too late in realizing what that meant. I whipped my head around to watch them and was just in time to see a black shadow rise up from the ground at their feet and move to stand motionless among them, sheltered by their huge bodies. I sighted carefully at the part of him that I could see beneath the belly of the beast that was shielding him and released my arrow, hearing a shocked scream of pain and outrage as the black shape-less shadow I had pierced went flying. Three down. One left. I knew what to do now.

"Roman," I called, pitching my voice low. "I'm directly to your left as you stand now. Start walking towards me, slowly. I'll cover you. There's still one of your hosts alive out there. If he moves towards you, or if you hear anything at all, drop flat and leave him to me."

His head snapped towards the sound of my voice as soon as I started to speak, and he began to walk slowly towards me, as though he were taking an evening stroll. I stood up and kept my head moving, scrutinizing every shadow in sight, waiting for the fourth man to make a move, but nothing happened. When Eagle Face reached me, I let go of my bowstring with my right hand, holding the strung arrow in place between the shaft of the bow and the index and middle fingers of my left.

"Turn around." I drew my sword with my right hand, still looking around me for any signs of movement. "Stretch out your wrists." He did as I bade him, and I began sawing at his bonds, but it was impossible to keep watch and cut the ropes at the same time.

"Blast this," I said. "How's your eyesight?"

"Perfect." His voice was calm and cool.

"Good, then use it, while I cut these ropes properly, otherwise you're likely to lose at least one hand."

I laid my bow at my feet and stuck the arrow into the ground beside the other three, then cut through his bindings quickly, guiding my blade with the edge of my left index finger. He was tightly bound. "That's going to hurt like nothing on earth in a minute, once the blood starts to flow back," I told him. "Duck your head and let's get your collars off."

I don't know what it was that alerted me, but my military instinct took over. I pushed him off balance, yelling "Down!" as an arrow sliced through the tiny space separating our bodies. Even before the word was out of my mouth, I was on my knees, grabbing my bow in one hand and an arrow in the other. Then I rolled and kept on rolling, arms extended above my head as another arrow and then a third came looking for me. I saw the black shape silhouetted against the moonlit sky just as I rolled into a slight depression that deepened as I moved into it. Then, hoping that I was safe for a few seconds, I shrugged out of the cloak that was threatening to choke me, nocked the arrow carefully, pivoted my hips and came to my feet in a rolling lunge, drawing the bowstring to my chin as I did so. I was lucky again. I caught him in the act of aiming at Eagle Face, and by the time he had swung back to try a shot at me, my arrow was already travelling. It took him high in the right shoulder, and he staggered back and fell to one knee, his arrow flying off somewhere into the moonlight. I was running towards him flat out, fumbling with my dagger, when my foot came down on a piece of ground that wasn't where I had thought it was; I hit it with an impact that drove every vestige of wind from my body and sent me flying end over end. I was still trying to pull myself together when I heard Eagle Face's voice above me.

"Relax. Our friend has gone off into the desert. He won't be back. You are only badly winded and will recover. He's badly wounded and will not."

I looked up at him. He was massaging his right wrist and wiggling his fingers.

"You're right. This hurts like nothing else on earth."

I saw then that he was talking through clenched teeth, as he nodded backwards over his shoulder and continued.

"I can't hold your sword yet, otherwise I'd go over there and put that poor swine out of his misery."

Only then did I identify the horrible sound that had been assailing my ears. It was the sustained screaming that had to be coming from the man I had gut shot beneath the camel's legs. I lay there for a few more minutes, collecting my breath, and then I got to my feet and crossed to where the screaming man squirmed on the ground. I could see, without looking too closely, that I had shot him clean through the centre of his pubic bone.

This was the part I dreaded. All my ghosts came to haunt me as I dispatched him quickly, trying vainly not to get any of his warm, unthreatening, painfully personal blood on my hands. I straightened up slowly, my eyes full of the look on his face and my hands covered in his blood. Scooping up a double handful of sand, I used it to try to clean the sticky gore away, but the blood was congealing between my fingers already and I fell to my hands and knees, retching up my guilt in painful spasms.

After a while, I was able to get up and go back to Eagle Face, who was still rubbing his wrists and watching me with a strange expression on his face.

"Who *are* you?" he asked me. "How did you come to be here? And why in the name of all the ancient gods would you be foolhardy enough to risk your life against such odds for a total stranger?"

I grinned at him, shakily. "Not such a total stranger as you think," I said. "My name is Varrus. Publius Varrus. A ghost from your past, returned to pay a debt."

A tiny flicker of apprehension appeared on his face as he thought for an instant that I might be telling the literal truth, and then his face broke into a great smile and he held out his hand to me. I was aware of the strength in his fingers as they gripped my forearm. His right eyebrow climbed high on his brow in an expression I was to become very familiar with.

"Well, Publius Varrus," he said. "We are well met this night, although I know I have never laid eyes on you before. You mistake me for someone else, I'm sure, but I am glad of your mistake."

"No mistake, Tribune. You have laid eyes on me before tonight. And hands."

"When? What do you mean?"

"Just what I say. It was a long time ago, and there's no reason why you should remember it. It's enough that I do."

"If it caused you to save my life, then I thank God for your memory. Tell me about it."

I glanced over my shoulder at the shadows surrounding us. "I'll be glad to, but I think this is not the place. We had better move away from here. The water attracts too many visitors."

He looked around him. "You may be right, my friend, but I would dearly love to sleep for an hour before we move. I haven't had much rest in the past few days, and none at all since our friends took me, yesterday."

"Could you stay awake for another hour? I left my horse among some rocks on a hill about half a league from here. It's safer than this place. You can sleep all you want when we get back there."

"Half a league?"

"No more than that."

"Can you ride a camel?"

I grimaced. It was as close as I could come to smiling. "Can anyone? I've been up on one. Can't say I enjoyed the experience too much."

"It's better than walking."

"Tribune, in this country, anything's better than walking!"

During the ride back to my hill of rocks my stomach settled down again, finally, and along the way I told him about where we had first met. It pleased me when he remembered the occasion and proved it by recalling that he had noticed my tears first, and the fact that I had been a beardless boy.

"Beardless is right. And that's not all I was lacking," I told him. "That was my first campaign and my first battle. If you hadn't noticed me there, it would have been my last one, too." I told him of my search for him and my failure to trace him. "Where did you go? Why couldn't I find you?"

He shrugged his shoulders. "I moved on. I wasn't with your lot in the first place — just passing by on my way to join my own legion. Your skirmish was over when we happened along. My men handed you over to your own medics. But you were completely paralyzed, I thought. We didn't expect you to live."

"Nobody did, but the paralysis wore off after a while."

He shivered, and I noticed how cold the night had become. "Here," I said, "take my cloak. I have some extra gear and blankets with my horse, back there."

"Do you have any food? Real food, I mean?"

"Legion food. Dried meal and corn, nuts, raisins and dates. Some dried meat, lots of water I got earlier, and two skins of wine I was taking back with me."

"Thank the gods! You have a guest for supper."

Staying astride a camel was more easily said than done. It seemed to take years to reach the bottom of the hill where I had left my horse. We talked in quiet voices all the way back, for sound travels far on the desert at night, and I told him that I was on my way back to Britain to join the Twentieth Legion, the famed *Valeria Victrix,* my first posting in my homeland since joining the Eagle Standards some seven years earlier. He was interested in how I had managed to secure the transfer, and I pointed out that I had not had a major furlough in six years of frontier duty. That was all very well, he said, and I had certainly earned a long leave, but it hardly qualified me for intercontinental and inter-legion transfer. He was right, of course, and I felt no reluctance in telling him how I had managed to finagle it.

"I'm a centurion, Tribune. You know the breed. There's not much a centurion with seniority can't get, if he puts his mind to it. In my case, I was in a situation to perform a number of services for my commander. The kind of services he thought were worth rewarding."

He interrupted me, prompted, I would find out later, by the probity that was so much a part of his character. "I'm not sure I want to hear any more. It sounds to me as though the reward for you was a reward for himself, too. Safe back in Britain, you will be grateful, and unlikely to say anything that he could find embarrassing."

I caught his meaning and shook my head. "Not so, Tribune, with respect. There was nothing improper involved. My commander, the Legate Seneca, had a son who might have been a burden to him. I took the lad under my wing and saw him properly fledged. That's all there was to it."

He frowned. "Seneca? You are a friend of the Senecas?"

I shook my head, bewildered at the sudden hostility in his voice. "No, Tribune, I'm just a simple centurion. The Legate asked me to keep an eye on his son and straighten him around; make a soldier out of him."

"And did you?"

"Yes," I answered. "I did. He wasn't as difficult as he'd been made out to be. I just brought out the decency in him. The Legate was grateful, and here I am on my way home to Britain."

"Humph! You must be a man of great subtlety, to bring out the decency in a Seneca." His voice was heavy with irony and dislike. I felt a surge of anger.

"Well, Tribune," I snapped, "I grieve if I've offended you." He flipped his hand at me in an unmistakable order to be silent, and we continued for a while without speaking. When he spoke next, his voice was contrite.

"Forgive me, Centurion. I have no right to berate you, and no reason. You cannot be expected to choose your commanders. There has been a long and bitter enmity between my family and the House of Seneca. Blood has been spilled for it over the years, and there is no love at all between us, from one generation to the next."

There was nothing I could say to that. It was none of my affair, and I had no wish to be inquisitive. I accepted his words and passed no comment. After a time he spoke again.

"Home to Britain!" His voice sounded nostalgic. "All that greenery after all this sand. How much do you know about the Twentieth?"

I shook my head. "Nothing, except that they're famous. They've been called the *Valeria Victrix* since the days of Julius Caesar, and their legionary fortress has been at Deva, in Cambria, since Agricola's campaign, about three hundred years ago. Apart from that, I only know I'm posted to the Second Millarian Cohort as replacement for its *pilus prior*. Apparently the man they had was killed and there's no one really qualified to replace him from the existing crew. They have an acting cohort commander in place until I get there." I grimaced to myself in the darkness. "Frankly, I'm not sure what that means, so I'm expecting the worst, in the hope that anything less than that will be bearable. The only other thing is that I've heard they're not currently stationed in Deva — the Second Cohort, I mean. They're in the north-east, at Eboracum."

"The Second of the Twentieth, eh?" Even in the dark, I could see the smile on his face as he shook his head.

"What's so funny? What are you smiling at?"

He was grinning strangely to himself. "I was just thinking about our circumstances here," he said. "You are here because of my enemy, even though indirectly, and you have saved my life. Yet your mode of address to me is decidedly lacking in military respect, and I'm not sure what I ought to do about it."

I stiffened at the censure in his voice. He was right, of course. I was only a centurion and he was a Military Tribune, and my deportment had not been militarily correct. But somehow, because of our circumstances, it had not seemed necessary to defer to him here in the middle of a desert when there were only the two of us around. Now it appeared that I had been wrong in my reading of the man. He was more of a martinet than I had thought. He must have read my mind, for he swung his camel right around close to mine, a broad smile on his face.

"Relax, Varrus. We're going to get along, you and I. This meeting was obviously fated. My name is Caius Britannicus. I, too, was on my way to Britain when I was taken. To the Second Cohort of the Twentieth Legion. I'm your new commanding officer. Haven't I got a right to wonder what I'm going to do about you?"

II

For a period of weeks after the trap in the mountain pass, my whole world existed only in terms of the pain of my wound. Even now it is hard to describe. As a veteran, and the bearer of many scars picked up over years of duty in some savage places, I had thought myself familiar with pain. I was wrong. This experience of muscle and tendons and sinew shattered by the ripping spike of a hard-swung axe taught me just how little I had known. The pain I lived with had a wide range of intensity and textures, and I experienced it as a spectrum of pulsating colours, ranging from blazing white to a dull, harsh, throbbing red.

Of all the torments I had to endure, the worst by far was caused by the natural, waste-producing functions of my own body. They became my most bitter and treacherous enemy, scourging me with unimaginable agonies each time I had to accommodate them. Mitros was gentle in his ministrations at such times, but not always sympathetic. On one occasion — he was in a particularly impatient mood — he told me brusquely that women endured far worse in childbirth and I should be grateful I was alive to feel pain. But it was only his skills and his magical opiates that saved my mind from breaking during that first month.

Pain, however, like everything else in life, is transient. I began to mend, gradually, day by day, heartbeat by heartbeat. A time came when I could lie still and feel — almost explore — my pain, without wanting to scream like a baby. And a day came, much later, when I could lie on my back and think about things other than how much I hurt. From that point on, I began to mend visibly, and to talk, and to think rationally again.

I spent many silent hours reviewing and analyzing the affinity between Britannicus and me, and how it had developed and prospered after our meeting in Africa.

We had travelled back to Britain together, and by the time we disembarked at Lemanis in South Britain, each of us had a sound measure of the other's capacities. I was comfortable with the relationship we had established — one of Staff officer and trusted subordinate — and I felt confident that Britannicus was, too.

From Lemanis, we rented horses and made our way directly north to Londinium, the administrative centre of South Britain. There we reported to the Military Governor, to present our papers and gain official acknowledgement of our arrival. No one in Londinium had any time to waste with us. We were sent on our way — almost without rest — with a package of personal dispatches, a thirty-strong squadron of light cavalry under the command of a senior decurion, and an infantry detachment of one hundred and twelve replacements with six junior centurions. All of these the Tribune was instructed to deliver to the senior Legate in Deva, the fortress headquarters of the Twentieth *Valeria Victrix* for more than three centuries. We had expected to be sent directly to

Eboracum where the Second Cohort of the Twentieth had been stationed on temporary duty for several years. The official military mind, however, continued to function in its own peculiar way.

Deva lay in the hill country to the north-west, in Cambria. It had been built around 70 AD, during Julius Agricola's campaign to complete the conquest of Britain. Its site had been chosen because it dominated the territory where the lands of three warlike tribes — the Brigantes, the Deceangli and the Ordovices — came together. However, after three hundred years of the *Pax Romana*, Deva's original strategic importance had long been forgotten. Its location was now no more than damnably inconvenient. It took us five days of hard marching to make the journey there by road from Londinium.

As a fortress, Deva was impressive and seemingly impregnable, exactly as one would expect after three hundred-odd years of continuous occupation by one of Rome's proudest and oldest legions. We had less than one day to absorb it, however, before our orders took us back to the road again.

We learned immediately upon our arrival that our initial intelligence — acquired in Africa — had been accurate. The Second Cohort of the Twentieth lay at Eboracum, on temporary duty with the Second Legion, the *Augusta*, another three days' march to the north-east. The Legate who accepted our formal reporting for duty was surly and ill-tempered. He excoriated both of us mercilessly for having taken so long to get there — apparently we had been expected the previous week — and sent us on our way with ringing ears. My admiration for Britannicus grew as I watched the uncomplaining

manner in which he accepted the injustice and the ineffi-
ciency and inconvenience being heaped upon him by
incompetent superiors.

From the outset of our relationship Britannicus invari-
ably treated me with military correctness, slightly
warmed by courtesy and consideration. I found him to be
just, temperate, and dispassionate in his dealings with the
men under his command. But he could be awesome in his
wrath when provoked by incompetence or malfeasance.
A rigid disciplinarian, he was implacable once he had
decided that punishment was in order. And never, at any
time, did he show any capacity for suffering fools gladly.

In those days, Britain had been at peace for many years.
Legionary duties consisted, in the main, of road-building
and maintenance, policing the province, and maintaining
civil order. The army was, as it always was, the enforcing
power behind the law. Few circumstances called the
troops in Britain out to spill blood: occasionally, raiding
bands of Picts from Caledonia or Scots from Hibernia
would make incursions into provincial territory and
would have to be repulsed, or, much less common, unin-
volved units would be called out to put down an army
mutiny bred of anger, dissatisfaction, lack of discipline
and the tedium of garrison life. The Second Cohort's posting to Eboracum had come as the result of a mutiny. The
rebellion had been a deep-rooted one, and the thousand-
man Second of the Twentieth, the only uncontaminated
cohort in Eboracum, had been detained there by an apprehensive praesidium for almost two years.

Tribune Britannicus was ordered by the ill-mannered
Legate in Deva to take command of the Second Cohort,
get it out of Eboracum, and march it sixty miles south to

Lindum, to relieve a unit of the Fourteenth Legion posted there. So he and I came together into the life of the Second Cohort, the new Tribune, Caius Britannicus, and his new *pilus prior*, Publius Varrus. And together we began to reshape it in the image of Caius Britannicus.

It was fitting then, that almost two years later, we should be together when we first came face to face with the unthinkable — the opening action of a chain of events that was to alter all our lives, forever.

According to the official report, it happened in the hour before dawn on the first night of August in the year of our Lord 367. The frontier bastion known as Hadrian's Wall in the north of Britain was overrun by a federation of hostile tribes from Pictish Caledonia, aided in the east by a seaborne invasion of Saxons and in the west by a similar invasion of Hibernian Scots. That's all it says. Roman historians do not write eloquently of Roman defeats.

Be that as it may, the dimensions of the disaster were appalling. Hadrian's Wall was eighty miles long. At no point in that length was it less than fifteen feet high, and it was fronted along its entire length by a V-shaped ditch ten feet deep and thirty wide. It had a mile castle at every mile of its length, with two small, fortified watch-turrets between each pair, plus a series of sixteen fully garrisoned forts, spaced approximately six miles apart. It was defended at all times by a force of not less than three thousand — regular auxiliary infantry from time to time, depending upon local conditions and the availability of manpower, but mainly local conscripts, citizen farmers and mercenaries. Always mercenaries. And the whole thing collapsed in one hour on that black August night.

The scope, the timing and the co-ordinated swiftness of the operation are difficult to visualize, let alone describe. I only arrived at a perspective of my own — a very personal and probably flawed measure of the events — long afterwards, by comparing the eyewitness reports of the few survivors I met from time to time in the years that followed. Without exception, these men were still amazed, bewildered and confused, years afterward, by what they had encountered that night. Each was still surprised to have lived through it, and each could only recall reacting to the events and the immediate circumstances that affected him personally. Of all these men, the most articulate was Marcus Gallifax, a garrison centurion who escaped and managed somehow to join up with us later, as did a couple of others.

I spoke with Gallifax many times over the months that followed, and his recollections of that night were memorable and precise. They never varied either in detail or in delivery, so that, lying supine in my hospital cot, searching for ways to relieve the tedium of inactivity, I had no difficulty recalling either his face or his words. . . .

Hadrian's Wall, 367

It was his third tour of duty on the Wall, and he hated it more than he had on his first assignment. Marcus Gallifax held his cloak firmly across his lower face and leaned out between the battlements, his eyes screwed almost shut against the outrage of the wind as he scanned the darkness below and in front of him. He saw and heard nothing but blackness and the howling gale. The noise in his ears as the wind roared through the earflaps of his helmet made it impossible to hear anything else, but he couldn't even see the movement that he knew was out there: the writhing, whipping torment of the clumps of rank grass, bracken and gorse that carpeted the ground. His eyes teared rapidly and he grunted a curse and pulled back into the protection of the battlement on his left, wiping his streaming eyes as the frustrated wind howled by his shelter. The wind that seemed to blow endlessly from the north at this time of year had a malevolence, a concentrated hostility, that made it different from any other wind in the world. It came buffeting and blistering south out of the hills, its force twisted and compressed by their contours, and slapped hard against the fifteen-foot-high surface of the Wall, to be sucked down like cataract water into the ten-foot ditch below and then spewed back up and over and between the battlements with an erratic violence that could panic a man by snatching the air out of his mouth as he tried to breathe.

Gallifax made a virtue of his hatred, using its virulence to keep him on his toes so that his men were always, always vigilant. They thought he hated them and that he was always trying to catch them out in dereliction of duty. They were wrong. He didn't hate them. He hated that godless, savage frontier where nothing ever seemed to move except the demented wind that made progress along the Wall possible only in a series of leaps from one battlement to the next, the traveller having to brave each open gap and then huddle in the tiny protection of the next battlement before moving on. He leaped again, throwing his shoulders flat against the stonework, and made out the shape of a sentry huddled against the Wall less than four feet from him. The man had been expecting him, and Gallifax guessed at, rather than saw, the salute of greeting. A particularly fierce shock wave broke between them, and Gallifax waited for the gust to die down and then crossed to stand beside the sentry.

"How goes the night?" He had to yell into the man's ear to make himself heard, knowing that his words were being ripped away by the howling wind. "Anything to report?"

"No, Centurion. All quiet. But this is . . ." Gallifax thought he heard "a waste of time," but he could not be sure, for the man's words were further muffled by a heavy woollen scarf that was wrapped around the lower half of his face, against all regulations. The contravention did not disturb the centurion. He himself was wearing two pairs of long drawers beneath his leather breeches and long knitted socks on his legs and feet beneath his sandals.

He glanced up at the sky, looking for stars among the roiling cloud masses, but there was only blackness. The sentry was shouting something about snow. Well, it was cold enough for it. Gallifax nodded his head as though in agreement and then looked over to his right, where he could see a distant yellow glimmer of lamplight from the window of the watch-turret. "Thank you, Mithras, you soldier's god," he thought. "A man's needs are few and easily cared for on a night like this. Still air and warmth will make him feel blessed." The yellow light marked the end of the first half of his inspection tour. It signalled a cup of hot broth and perhaps a throw or two of the dice before he had to make the return trip to the mile castle. He clapped the sentry roughly on the shoulder and yelled in his ear again. "Watch is halfway gone, lad! Relief coming up at dawn!" He hitched his cloak up again across his left shoulder, tightened his grip on his vine-wood cudgel, the centurion's badge of rank, and moved on towards the tower. On a night like this, he could well see why a man might think guard duty was a waste of time. Each of the four poor whoresons he had inspected in the past hour might as well have been blind and deaf as well as cold and miserable. Every step of the last hundred paces towards that yellow lamplight was a fight for balance in the teeth of a wind that had now risen to maniacal fury, but at last he reached it, flung open the door and dived inside to the warmth and brightness.

What he found instead was horror and confusion. Trebatius, his friend of many years, was sprawled backwards across the table top, his face split in two by an axe. Herod, the young Judean mercenary, was squirming in a corner, pinned against the wall by a man almost twice his size who jabbed viciously and fatally with a dagger even as Gallifax's mind absorbed what he was seeing. Another stranger, equally big, had been in the act of lifting a steaming bowl to his lips with both hands when Gallifax burst in on them. He froze with shock, as did Gallifax, and for a petrified moment the two stared at each other in wild-eyed surprise. The centurion was powerless to do anything. Only his left hand was free. The other, muffled by his tight-wrapped cloak, was holding only the useless cudgel.

Gallifax was the first to recover his wits. He threw himself backwards out of the room again, pulling the door shut with his free hand. There was only one thought in his head: to raise the alarm. He was shouting at the top of his lungs as he ran back towards the sentry, but the man was gone. The wind was feral, a howling animal. In confusion, Gallifax stepped to the southern edge of the parapet, thinking the sentry might have been blown over. Then he crossed to the battlements and leaned out again. He had a momentary vision of someone standing close to him, on the outside of the Wall, fifteen feet in the air, and then fingers hooked into the back of his helmet and he felt himself jerked forward and over the edge as he thought, "Ladders! How did they bring up ladders?" He was still thinking that as he smashed to the ground at the bottom of the ditch, twenty-five feet below.

Thirty miles to the east of Gallifax, at precisely the same time, Lollius Malpax was in agony. There was no wind in his sector, but Malpax would have been oblivious to it anyway. Malpax had the runs, and he had had them for two days. His bowels were a water-filled labyrinth of twisting cramps and his total attention was given to timing the onslaught of his next bout of diarrhoea, so that he could get permission to leave his post in time to make it to the clump of bushes that he had been using as his personal latrine behind the Wall. Malpax was a Pannonian, from Hungary, and his squad commander was an Iberian who hated Pannonians. Malpax, after two days of suffering, had reached the point where he would have changed his name, his place of birth and his personal loyalties if he could have pleased the whoreson squad commander and been assured of some sick bay time, but it was not to be.

The commander kept him longer and longer each time Malpax asked permission to relieve himself, and he knew that one of these times he was not going to reach the latrine in time. He was correct, but for the wrong reasons. The squad commander released him and he ran, picking his way through the darkness in dim moonlight towards his clump of bushes, tugging at his clothes as he went. And then there was someone looming at him from the bushes, and a massive blow to his right shoulder that spun him sideways and threw him to the ground as he lost control and felt the warm foulness flood him. Years later he remembered thinking, just before he lost consciousness, that his squad commander had run ahead to lie in wait for him, just to get even with him for being a Pannonian.

Tetrino, a Sarmatian mercenary at one of the mile castles quite close to Gallifax, but to the west, remembers only regaining consciousness to see a crowd of bodies on the wrong side of the gate in the Wall, heaving and straining at the big bar that held the gate shut. He saw the bar give way suddenly, causing some of the men to fall, and then the gates were flung wide and Pictish chariots came through, the first of them crushing the bone in his leg with its iron-rimmed right wheel and hurling him back into blackness from the pain.

Apis Elpis, commander of the guard in a section far to the west of all of these, opened the door and stepped out of the mile tower to make his inspection. He found himself face to face, almost chin to chin, with a black-bearded stranger. In describing the encounter to me later, Elpis remembered thinking, "Who in Hades are you?" before his testicles were driven up into his belly by a savage kick. His brain seemed to explode and he went blind, probably squeezing his eyes shut in protest and denial of the suddenness of the agony, and he felt hands grasping at the shoulder straps of his corselet and lifting him effortlessly sideways to throw him from the parapet to the stony ground far below.

These were the lucky ones, the survivors, the only survivors of that night I have ever met. All of them recollect
that it was the middle of the last watch before dawn. None
of them had any warning or expectation of attack. None
of them knew what was happening, or had time to organize himself, let alone others. All of them lost consciousness and so lay as though dead. And all of them
were able to escape afterwards because the enemy made
no attempt to stay and destroy the Wall, or even to hold
it. They overwhelmed it simultaneously in an eighty-
mile-long wave, butchered the defenders and swept on
south into Britain. They were well organized, silent, effi-
cient and totally devastating. Hadrian's Wall, the vaunted
bastion of Rome's presence in Britain, was chewed up
within the space of an hour. The unthinkable had happened. Rome's most peaceful and prosperous colony had
fallen to invasion.

Britannicus and I, as luck would have it, were among
the very first to find out about it. We were about ten miles
south of the Wall just after dawn, headed north on a short
leave of absence to pay a visit to one of Britannicus's
friends, Antoninus, who was stationed at one of the mile
castles, and we crested a hill to be greeted by a spectacle
the like of which neither of us had ever seen. The valley
below us was choked with Celtic warriors, streaming
south. We sat up there for about an hour and watched.
There were thousands of them, and after the first shock
of what we were seeing had passed, we realized that this
was not just a big raiding party. It was an army.

We had no idea who they were, other than that they
were Celts, but we knew they could only have come
down from the north, and that meant they'd come over

the Wall. The fact that there were so many of them, and no sign of any opposition, meant that our garrisons on the Wall must have fared very badly. Even then, staring at them in their thousands, it did not occur to us that this could be anything more than a localized breakthrough. I looked at Britannicus to see what he thought of it all, and his face was like thunder.

We had left our cohort safely quartered about five miles away, and it was a good thing we did, too. Otherwise, we would have been surprised in our camp like sitting ducks, or caught on the march in extended order, not knowing anything had gone wrong. They say more than a hundred thousand came over the Wall that day. We hadn't even known there were that many people up there! Anyway, there were too many of them for us to deal with. Luckily, they were headed south through the valley down on our right, to the east of us. Our thousand-man cohort was dug in to the south-west of where we were sitting, so we got out of there and headed back to camp.

We tried very hard to be inconspicuous, but we were spotted by a group of charioteers — two horses to each chariot, and one with four — coming down to the west of us around the other side of our hill, and we were suddenly racing for our lives. Naturally, they were down in the valley where the terrain was fairly level for their chariots. We would be safe, we realized, as long as we kept high up on the hillsides.

We were shouting to each other as we ran; the fact of chariots on this side of the Wall meant that they had captured at least one mile castle and opened up the gates to wheeled traffic. That was not a pleasant prospect for the people living to the south, and the numbers we had already seen made it obvious that we would be unable to do much to help them.

I was trying hard not to notice the boulders and loose stones under my horse's hooves on the hillside; trying not to think what would happen if the horse fell; trusting that animal more than I'd ever trusted anyone or anything since my grandfather. We could hear them yelling below us, catching up and drawing level with us. As far as I could tell, there were three or four of them jammed into the four-horse chariot and two in each of the others.

We must have covered about two miles before I realized that we were on the wrong side of the valley. In order to get to our camp, we were going to have to go down, cross the valley floor and climb up the other side. Somehow, the sight of those hostiles on the wrong side of the Wall did nothing for my confidence in our Roman invincibility.

Britannicus must have realized the same thing at the same time. The hillside was starting to curve round to the east, away from our camp, and the valley bottom beneath us was narrowing dramatically, forcing the chariots into single file. They were now drawing slightly ahead of us, looking for some means of cutting us off.

"Come on, Varrus," he yelled, and he yanked his horse hard downhill to the right. My own horse stumbled as I followed him and nearly sent me flying, but he regained his stride and down we went, diagonally back the way we'd come and to the rear of the chariots. Rather than look where the horse was taking me, I preferred to watch the reaction of the chariots.

Our move caught them completely by surprise, and I could hear their curses as they tried to turn at full gallop without realizing how confined they were by the encroaching hillsides. One of the small ones spilled, throwing its riders flying. I heard the unmistakable scream of a horse.

The other two finally slowed right down and manoeuvred tight turns, whipping their horses hard and fast as they pulled around. We had surprised them and gained a lead, but we were headed down diagonally on a converging course with them, losing ground all the way, so that we were no more than thirty paces ahead of them when we reached the narrow valley bottom and swung left, hard, hammering up the other hillside and passing them again going in the other direction.

And then Britannicus's horse went down. I saw the Tribune literally somersault in the air and land on his feet, but his momentum kept him going and he rolled twice before I lost sight of him. Cursing like a demented Saxon, I reined in and turned. He was on his feet and running up the hill towards me, with the two chariots about twenty-five paces behind him. From the way my horse was blowing, I knew he would never take both of us up that hill, so I jumped off and drew my sword. There was a clump of big rocks to my right, less than ten paces from me, and I ran for it, dodging among the boulders as the Tribune joined me.

"Good man," he grunted, not even breathing hard. There was nothing effete about Britannicus.

By good luck, we had made the hillside work against them. They couldn't get near us with the chariots while we were among the rocks. One of them started shooting arrows at us, but his friends could smell blood — they wanted to finish this by hand. There were six of them, and they came leaping from their chariots and up the hill towards us as if they were on their way to the Colosseum to watch a slaughter. I had my ceremonial cavalry shield strapped to my back, and as I whipped it around in front of me I was wishing it was an old infantry scutum of wood and leather and solid metal. A man felt he had some protection behind one of those.

I don't remember much of the fight although I remember that each of us killed two men. At one point, Britannicus took a heavy blow on the head which put a big dent in his helmet, and down he went. I remember stepping astride him and ducking a slash from behind me, while the big Celt in front of me took a mouthful of the point of my sword. He fell sideways and I couldn't get my sword free. I heard a zipping noise close by my ear and I thought, "Well, this is how we end it." Then my sword was free and I swung around to see the heathen behind me falling, an arrow buried in his neck, and the only two of his friends still standing were staring up the hill, their mouths open.

I was blood mad. I went over the rock in front of me and tried to decapitate the man closest to me, swinging with every ounce of strength I possessed. It was a solid try, and I almost succeeded. My sword came free easily this time, but before I could reach the last of them, he was dead, too, his hands clawing uselessly at the javelin that had skewered him. I turned, and the hillside seemed to be alive with Roman soldiers. I dropped my sword and ran to see to Britannicus.

Titus Lautus, our adjutant, had sent out a hunting party to look for fresh meat. If they had arrived two minutes later, that's just what we'd have been. As it was, they'd seen us on the hillside on the other side of the valley, and although they didn't know why we were running so hard, they'd come down at the double.

Britannicus was unconscious, but he wasn't bleeding, except from the nose, and as far as we could tell he had only been knocked out by the force of the blow on his helmet. God knows the whoreson who swung it had been big enough! He was the one who had eaten my sword.

Two of the hostiles were still alive, but one of the new-comers soon set that right. I started to say something to the decurion in charge of the hunting party, but every-thing went red and I threw up. That was the one consis-tent result of my grandmother's efforts to keep me spiritually whole.

When I had finished, I returned my attention to the decurion. Thinking back on it later, I had to give all of them full marks for the discipline of their faces. Not one man among them gave any indication that he might have been surprised to discover that a centurion of their cohort could be human enough to be sick.

"How many of you are there?"

"Two squads, Centurion. Twenty, plus myself."

"Cavalry?"

"None, Centurion."

"Well, I'm glad you got here. Now we have to get back. How far are we from camp?"

"About two miles, Centurion."

"Good. The Tribune is in bad shape. Bring me that chariot with the four horses. I'll drive. Make the Tribune as comfortable as possible, and have one of your men collect our horses and walk them. Is the Tribune's horse all right?"

"It seems to be, Centurion. Nothing broken. Both of them are pretty well blown, though."

"They have every right to be. All right, let's get out of here as quickly and as quietly as possible."

The young decurion was frowning. "What's going on, Centurion? Who are these people? Where did they come from?"

I looked at him in surprise. He wasn't very old. "Where in Hades d'you think they came from, lad? They came over the bastard Wall, that's where they came from!" He looked stunned. "What's your name?"

"Strato, Centurion. Decius Strato."

"Well, Decurion Strato, the barbarian, the enemy that you've spent the last few years training to fight against, has come over the Wall in strength. In great strength. We're in the middle of a full-scale surprise offensive. An invasion. And we've been caught squatting. Do you understand?" He nodded as I went on. "The best thing we can do right now is get back to camp and hold it, if we can, until our Tribune here comes back to the land of the living." Many things I have been unable to remember about that day, but I remember seeing then in that decurion's eyes the realization of what I was talking about.

We placed Britannicus on the bed of the four-horse chariot and I drove. I aimed the four horses at the top of that hill and they climbed it at a walk, so that our infantry rescuers had no trouble in keeping up with us. We made it back to the camp without any further contact with the enemy.

Britannicus started to show signs of awakening shortly after we set out, but he was hurting badly and was in no hurry to regain consciousness. There was no great amount of room on the floor of the chariot, so I straddled him as he half lay, half sat in the body of the vehicle. When he began to come to, he started to thrash about a bit, and I think I kicked him once to settle him down. Anyway, he came out of it gradually and began to make efforts to stand up, and by the time we came in sight of the camp he was in command of himself again. When we rode through the gates, he was holding the reins.

Word of the attack had preceded us. The sentries spotted us while we were still a long way from the gates, and I could see from the activity that they knew what was happening. Flavinius, the second in command, had his wits about him, as always, and the entire garrison was standing to. Fully half the cohort, five hundred men, were hard at work strengthening the camp's defences, digging the surrounding ditch deeper and throwing the earthworks higher.

Britannicus was as white as death and must have had the earth mother of all headaches, but he called an immediate meeting of all centurions and officers, and informed everyone of the day's developments as far as he could. One of the first things he asked about, after informing them of the breakthrough, was the number of fleeing soldiers who had made their way into camp from the Wall. He was told there were none. He winced, dropped his eyes in thought for a minute and then shrugged, dismissing the thought, whatever it might have been, and got down to business. And Britannicus knew his business.

Because we were on the march, there was a detailed inventory of supplies on hand: the quantities and types of rations, weapons, wagons and all of the thousand details that keep an army unit functioning, no matter what its size may be. He reeled off allocations of supplies and detailed his orders for emergency procedures, including an intensified guard schedule that involved a four hours on, four off cycle for every man in the camp. He made every one of his listeners aware that the demands of the present emergency would mean that everyone must stand prepared to adapt at any time to new orders. He was dealing with defensive manoeuvres when the alarm sounded; a party of hostiles had been sighted by our sentries. He dismissed the meeting, calling on me as *pilus prior*, senior centurion of the cohort, to stay behind with his four senior officers.

He did not speak until everyone else had left the tent, and even then he stood silent, chewing reflectively on his top lip for long moments and ignoring us all completely. Finally he snapped out of his reverie and drew himself erect, after which he looked closely and searchingly at each of us in turn. We waited, making no attempt to second-guess him. Apparently satisfied with what he had seen in our faces, he nodded to himself and sighed noisily, blowing his pent-up breath out explosively.

"Gentlemen," he said, as though informing us of something he wanted attended to on parade the following day, "I have a feeling that what we are witnessing is only the beginning of something bigger than any of us have visualized. Something is out of kilter here, badly out of balance. This is not for discussion outwith these walls, but mark my words, we are going to be hard at this for a long time. This incursion is too big, too strong, to evaporate overnight." He turned his gaze fully on me. "For that reason, I intend to take some steps that might be described later as unique. I want a new maniple, Varrus, and I want it made up of the very best men in the Cohort. Your best, no less than a hundred of them — and more, a score more, if you can spare them. I want the fittest, strongest, ablest men you can muster, and I want them as quickly as you can get them together, you understand me?" I nodded, amazed, and he accepted my nod and turned his head to include the others in his conversation again. "These painted buffoons outside think they have beaten the Roman army. They don't know the difference between mercenaries, conscripts and regulars. They are about to be reminded of the standards that built the Roman Empire."

He stepped forward to his folding table and reached into one of its drawers, taking out a small throwing-knife, which he tucked up into the right sleeve of his tunic. Then he moved towards the doorway of his tent, and we made to follow him. Before we could take the first step, however, he had stopped and was speaking again, to all of us.

"This Cohort is the finest in Britain, gentlemen. I know, because I made it that way. Our discipline is two hundred years and more out of date. In the next few days we'll put it into practice and show these people that the Wall wasn't built to protect us from them, but to save them from us. Let's go!"

We walked out of his tent and into the two longest years of my life.

III

It galls me to admit it, but even today as I write this, the young men who make up our own forces here in the Colony are so involved with horses and cavalry tactics that they have little or no idea of the composition of the classic Roman legion. Consequently, I have to accept the fact that some explanation will be necessary if those who read these words in years to come are to understand what happened in those days to the Roman armies.

Before the growth of cavalry forces and tactics, the Roman legion was an infantry force made up of ten cohorts. Two of these Cohorts held ten maniples each, and the other eight each held five. A maniple consisted of ten, eleven or twelve ten-man squads, so that a legion at full strength numbered not less than six thousand men. In addition, each of the eight smaller cohorts had a squadron of thirty cavalry attached to it. Cavalry at that time were no more than mounted bowmen, skirmishing troops whose job was to provide a mobile defensive screen out in front while the legion was drawing up into battle formation.

The First and Second Cohorts of every legion were the Millarians, double cohorts of one thousand to twelve hundred men with sixty cavalry attached. Theirs was the honour and responsibility of holding the right of the line of battle. Only battle-hardened veterans were assigned to these cohorts, and their officers and warrant officers were the finest, having won their posts by exemplary conduct and outstanding ability.

Ours was a Millarian Cohort. Just before the start of the Invasion, as it came to be known, we had been on duty in the garrison town of Luguvallium, hard by Hadrian's Wall. Units of the Twenty-fourth Legion stationed there had fomented a violent, short-lived mutiny. Our task had been to eradicate the mutineers, using the experience we had gained in Eboracum. The exercise had been drastic and unpleasant, but we had completed it and were on our way to join up with two of our own auxiliary cohorts in Mamucium when the enemy came over the Wall. To this day nobody knows how many Roman soldiers died that day, and how many simply deserted into the hills, or even joined the barbarians. The invaders overran all of the north country and most of the south-east. There were even barbarians in Londinium! Ours was one of the very few units that survived, and we had Britannicus and his old-fashioned ideas — leavened with more than a bit of sheer military genius — to thank for it.

Britannicus was one of those rare officers who was like a god to his men. He was the toughest, most bloody-minded disciplinarian I'd ever served under, and the men would have marched into Hades for him. Once again, any future reader of these words may not understand that to be able to say that about any commander of Roman forces in those days was phenomenal in itself. The old days of the Republic and of Empire triumphant were centuries gone. By the beginning of the fourth Christian century, the eleventh century of Rome, senior rank was held, in the main, by horses' arses rich enough to buy it. And ninety out of every hundred of those leaders were afraid to antagonize the men they ostensibly commanded.

The average soldier in the armies of the Empire was a joke. Every one was a Roman citizen, by imperial decree. Black, white, yellow, brown or painted with blue woad, they were all Roman citizens. There were Germans, Numidians, Egyptians, Armoricans, Phoenicians, Greeks, Vandals, Huns, Thracians, Dacians, Franks, Saxons, Scots, Levantines and Jews. We taught them how to fight, instructed them in battle techniques and strategy, and equipped them, and then they deserted in their thousands to their home territories to organize resistance against the Roman succubus!

Everyone knew what was happening. We knew we were training our own adders to bite us. It was a fact of life, and it was aggravated by the fact that, while they were in the army, they all had their "rights." It had become normal for garrison troops to be excused from wearing breastplates and carrying shields at all times. They were too heavy for the men! The results were pre-ordained. The debacle at Hadrian's Wall was a microcosmic example of the state of the whole Empire.

Britannicus, following in the steps of his own father, would have none of this. He had a stony row to hoe at first, because his methods were as out of date as those of the Republic he admired, but he had the courage of his convictions and he was willing to lay his own balls on the line. He expected his men to make a twenty-five-mile march every week in full gear. That meant seventy pounds of helmet, armour, two spears, five javelins, scutum (the infantryman's heavy shield), leg greaves, cooking pots, rations, canteen and two palisades (long, pointed poles to be used in setting up the camp's defences each night).

Every night on the march, or on manoeuvres, the men built a fortified camp, surrounded by a ditch and palisaded walls and gates. Only then were they allowed to relax and eat their evening meal sitting down. Breakfast was always consumed standing or on the move.

Britannicus did everything he expected his men to do. He marched at the head of the column, on foot and carrying full gear. He could outmarch, outrun, outjump and outfight any man in his cohort at any time of the day or night.

When he first took command of the cohort, the men were appalled. By their own lights, they were already crack troops, second only to the First Cohort. By his lights, they were rabble whom he was determined to make into soldiers second to none. They hated his guts, and he fed them back their own vomit. He used the full authority of his rank and the Empire to punish them, harshly, every time they asked for it. Every time he so much as imagined defiance he ground their faces down into the dirt. And the more they hated him and resented him, the rougher he was. Eventually they discovered that if they were going to beat him, it would have to be on his own ground and by his own rules, so they tried that. And they failed. And then, somewhere along the line, they began to develop a pride in themselves, in their toughness, and in their rotten, whoreson, bloody-minded, miserable commander. And only then, and only very slowly, did they begin to realize that for every fault they could find in him, someone else, somewhere in the cohort, could point out something that was not too bad, or something that you had to respect, or something that you even had to admire.

They began to realize that they had no bad officers. At least, they said, not bad compared to what the other cohorts had to put up with. Britannicus had cleaned out his officer corps within weeks of his arrival, and now it seemed that any new officer in the Second Cohort was quickly made to shape up, or move out. No officer ever took advantage of an enlisted man in the Second Cohort; punishment was swift, severe and certain, but victimization was unknown.

The men discovered that they were always well fed — far better fed than the other units around them, where officers had other things to consider ahead of the diets of their men. Britannicus, it was observed, put the welfare of his men — their food, their equipment and their billets — above everything else.

The cohort had been under his command for two years when Aaron Flavius, *pilus prior* and thus my opposite number in the First Cohort, came to me late one afternoon and asked me to arrange an interview for him with Britannicus on what he termed "a personal and confidential matter." Too surprised to demur, I took Aaron's request directly to Britannicus. He had been in a foul mood all day long and was clearly uncomfortable with such an unusual request. His frown darkened to a forbidding scowl immediately, and he growled, "What does he want to see me about, Centurion?"

I spoke to a point in the air above his left shoulder. "I don't know, Tribune." We were being very formal that day.

"Are there no officers in his own cohort? And what about the *primus pilus*?" These were obviously rhetorical questions, so I said nothing. "Very well, send him in," he snapped. So in went Aaron Flavius, red-faced and ill at ease, but clearly determined about something. I was more than simply curious. This kind of thing was unheard of in the Roman army. I hung around outside, hoping to find out what was going on.

Flavius was in there for about a quarter of an hour, and when he came out, saluting at the door and whirling like a doll on his heel, I was waiting for him.

"What was all that about?"

He looked at me very strangely. "You'll find out," he growled, and then he marched out of there like one of my own men on defaulters' parade. I watched him go, scratching my chin as I wondered what was going on. The two men on guard duty, I realized, were watching me curiously. I rounded on them.

"What in blazes are you two gawking at? Hoping I'll take you into my confidence, are you? Get your minds on your work or I'll have you on latrine duty for a month."

I heard the door open behind me.

"Centurion Varrus."

"Tribune!"

"Join me, please."

"Yes, sir!" I withered the two guards with one last baleful glare and made my way into Britannicus's office, where I closed the door at my back, snapped to attention and saluted.

"Sit." The word came as a peremptory bark, more a command than an invitation. His face was turned downward in the act of reading something he had just written, so I could not see his expression, nor could I gauge his frame of mind from the tone of his voice in that one word. Reserving judgment on his mood, therefore, I sat on one of the two chairs facing his table and waited for him to get around to whatever it was he wanted to tell me.

He was in no hurry. He read the papyrus in his hand again, from top to bottom, his lips moving as he whispered the words for his own ears. Then he picked up a pen from an ink pot and signed his name to whatever it was he had written. That done, he turned his gaze on me, a wide-eyed stare I had come to know well. That particular expression meant he was looking but not seeing. His eyes seemed fixed on me, but his thoughts were elsewhere. I waited. Finally his gaze sharpened again and focused on me, and I knew he had arrived at a decision.

"Well," he asked me, "what do *you* think?"

I kept my face blank. "About what, Tribune?"

"About that nonsense," he said, waving his hand towards the door. "Your friend, Aaron Flavius."

Still I allowed nothing to show on my face. "What about him, Tribune? What nonsense?"

He was staring at me now with an expression of mild incredulity, and his next words came in a softer tone. "You really don't know, do you?" I said nothing, and he rose from his chair and began to pace around, undoing the buckles on his breastplate as he moved and spoke.

"I found it hard to believe that he hadn't told the *primus pilus*," he said, talking almost to himself. "I mean, Catullus is going to cut him a new anus for coming to me without going through him, bypassing the chain of command. But I didn't believe he wouldn't have talked it through with you at least, since he had to go through you to get to me. Here, help me with this, will you?"

I moved to help him with the last set of buckles beneath his right shoulder, the same ones I could never undo by myself. He shrugged out of the heavy leather cuirass and placed it on the floor by his feet, then stretched mightily and tugged at his tunic until it hung comfortably again.

"That's better! Now it feels like the end of a long, miserable day in garrison." He crossed to a wall cupboard and brought out two cups and a stoppered jug of wine. "Sit, man, sit, sit, sit in the name of Mithras and relax. You are now officially off duty, by my personal dispensation. I need your advice. Here." I took the cup of wine he offered and he sat across from me and raised his cup to eye level. "Let us drink to the health, although we may deplore the wisdom, of Aaron Flavius, *pilus prior* of the First."

I raised my own cup. "Gladly," I said, "but why? What's Aaron up to?"

"What's he up to? An excellent question. Would you trust him?"

The question confused me. "Trust him? I don't know, Tribune. It would depend on what was involved. Trust him with what? With my life, in battle? Certainly, of course I would. With my sister, if I had one? Probably not. I don't think I would be that big a fool. Trust is a relatively changeable commodity, Tribune."

"Hmmm, I agree, and a strange one, too." He slouched further down into his chair, his long, muscular, aristocratic legs stretched out towards the empty brazier in the corner of the room, and took a deep swig of his wine.

"He came to me in trust, and with a bizarre request, one that required tact, subtlety and diplomacy to a degree I'm not used to finding in centurions, apart from yourself." I held my peace and he continued. "He asked me to arrange a contest between our cohort and his own. He says he likes what he sees happening with our people, and he doesn't think much of his own Tribune or the performance he gets from his troops. That was where he had to be tactful, telling that to me. Anyway, as *pilus prior*, he believes the only way he'll ever be able to get his own people excited enough to smarten up is by having us challenge them, unit to unit. He thinks they're likely to see a challenge like that as insulting to their sense of priority. They are, after all, the First Cohort and therefore, by definition, the best soldiers."

"Ah, but by whose definition, Tribune? They're the senior soldiers, the most experienced, certainly, but the best?" I emptied my cup and he immediately filled it again. It occurred to me as he turned away that I could not think of any other officer who would ever be gracious enough, or sure enough of his own power, to serve a subordinate unselfconsciously.

"So who are the best?" He spoke over his shoulder. "Ours? What do you think of the challenge idea? Be truthful — this is just between you and me, man to man, out of uniform. Will it work? *Can* we challenge them? I mean, is it feasible that our men would back the challenge if we made it?"

I drank again and thought about the question before answering him. The wine was excellent; a far cry from the thin, sour vinum we drank normally. The question was a complex one. Finally, I shrugged my shoulders and admitted my ignorance.

"Truthfully, Tribune? I don't know. Had you asked me that a couple of months ago, I would have said no, it's not possible. Today, I honestly don't know. It may be possible, and our men might do it, if . . ." I stopped there.

"If what? What, Varrus?"

"If we — and I suppose that means you — approach it properly. Are we still man to man?"

"Yes."

"Good. Aaron Flavius is right. His Tribune, Cirrius, is a complete pig, hated by everyone, including our men. He treats his people like filth, and, as you probably know, he's had several of his rankers flogged to death for petty offences. Well, you may or may not be aware of this, but one of those men was Castor Liger, twin brother to Pollux Liger, our Eight Squad leader."

Britannicus nodded. "I knew that. Nothing I could do about it. What's your point?"

"Simply this. Although it's only a gut feeling, and I may be completely wrong, I believe that if *you* issue the challenge to Cirrius, personally and in public, one cohort commander to another, our people might just be bloody-minded enough to support you." I grinned at him. "After all, they've been cursing you and reviling you for two years, so they're due for a change, and this might be as good a chance as they're going to get. Cirrius is such a complete bastard that he makes you look good."

His grin matched my own, his whole face lighting up with the incandescence of his smile. "I'll have your arse for that remark, one of these days, my friend. You think we can beat them?"

"Repeatedly, Tribune, and *ad nauseam*."

"Should we set the date far enough in advance to allow them to prepare?"

I sat up straight and finished my wine. "Makes no difference, Tribune," I said. "They'll never beat the Second, no matter how hard they try."

Britannicus reached for the jug again and refused to listen to my protestations that I had had enough. When he had refilled both our cups, the jug was empty. He replaced it in the cupboard and returned to sit across from me. For a period of time, neither of us spoke.

"Well," he said, at last, "I'm going to make the challenge, and we'll see what happens. Win or lose, it should shake things up around here." He stopped again and looked at me quizzically, one eyebrow arched high on his forehead. "What about you? How do you feel about your life here? Are you content? Satisfied? Thinking of transferring out?"

"What? Why would . . .? No, thank you, Tribune. I am well here, and pleased with my lot. I've no complaints." I was slightly embarrassed by this turn in the conversation, but he pursued it.

"You could have . . . complaints, I mean. Some might say you should have. It hasn't been easy for you, has it?"

I was almost squirming now, feeling the blood flushing my cheeks, but still he went on.

"I want you to know I appreciate your loyalty, all the support you've provided for me over the past two years. It's a large debt, and I intend to repay it."

I cleared my throat and started to bluster something about having to leave, but he rode right over my protests, finally silencing me by standing up and holding out his right hand, palm towards me.

"Varrus, trust me," he continued, his face breaking into a grin. "I know what you're thinking. You're thinking your Tribune is losing his grip, losing his feeling for the fitness of things, and you don't want to be around him while he's falling apart. Forget it. I'm not going to embarrass you. But I am going to say what I have to."

He sat down again as I tried to breathe more easily. "We're very similar in many ways, you and I," he said then. "We are soldiers first and foremost, and we have a rigid and very fine code by which we live. We feel safe operating within that code. When we drift away from it, we lose that feeling of safety. We become embarrassed. But there are some things that aren't dealt with in the code, Varrus. I have some things to say to you that I cannot leave unsaid, and I feel this may be the best time to say them, so let's get them out and deal with them and have done with it.

"As I said a moment ago, I want to thank you, man to man, for the support you have given me over the past two years. It can't have been easy for you, being perceived as my man while everyone else was loving hating me, but you bore it stoically. I watched and listened and appreciated your loyalty. I have been tempted to say something to you long before this, but I guessed it might be better to simply leave you to your own devices. And it was, I think. The men accept you completely now, as one of them, and that is as it should be. And now there's something in the air, something I can't quite define, but I think we may be close to a breakthrough. Aaron Flavius focused my thinking, and I decided to speak my thoughts. There, I've finished, and I will never mention the matter again. But bear in mind, please, that I am in your debt. If ever you need a friend in the future, I will be glad to serve in that capacity." He smiled again, a small quirking of his lips accompanied by a rising eyebrow. "Now you may finish your wine and flee."

The following night, in the course of a well-attended dinner in the Officers' Mess, Britannicus publicly challenged Titus Cirrius, the Tribune of the First Cohort, to a match between his men and ours, man against man, squad against squad, formation against formation. The match would consist of athletic contests in the morning, and tests of military skill in the afternoon. The judging would be conducted by the Legate, assisted by officers from the auxiliary cohorts. Britannicus told me later that it was done in such a way that Cirrius could refuse neither the challenge nor the wager involved. Of course Cirrius, in common with everybody else, knew that his men had neither the training nor the discipline of ours, so Britannicus very nobly set the date for ten weeks in the future, around the Ides, the fifteenth, of October.

We whipped their tails, but not as easily as we would have done ten weeks earlier. Those lads made up a lot of ground in ten weeks of training; the word was out that there was gold riding on the match, and a lot of it was theirs. They drilled and marched and trained almost as hard as we did normally. In our cohort, all the jokes and sneers about our training rosters were forgotten and forgiven, and without anything being said, we stepped training up to a level that would have produced mass desertions a month earlier.

The magic had been performed. The Second Cohort had been transformed into a solid unit, pulling together for the honour and the gold they could win as a group, as a tight, disciplined, highly trained entity. A fighting force was born, and over the next few years it grew into one of the elite units of the garrison of Britain. The First Cohort kept on trying to beat us, but they didn't have a chance. We were too finely honed.

And, four years later, there we were — an elite fighting unit stranded in the field, in a fortified overnight camp, surrounded by God only knew how many thousand howling savages drunk on victory and spilling southward around us like wine from a broken barrel.

By nightfall that first day following the Invasion, we were no longer able to estimate the numbers of men drawn up around the camp, just out of range of our arrows. The first party who had spotted our camp and had been sighted by our sentries, causing the first alarm we heard from the Tribune's tent, had sent back runners to summon help. From that point on, they had gathered like vultures.

We watched the hordes that first evening from the safety of our parapets, wondering when they would attack us. We had no illusions about their fear of us. After Hadrian's Wall, our little camp must have looked like a pimple on an elephant's arse to them. The Picts, we knew, were dawn fighters. They would sleep during the night and come at us in massed charges with the rising of the sun. The Scots, we believed and prayed, were similar, so the odds looked good for a quiet night before Hades came to earth with the morning.

Britannicus, however, had other ideas, and they involved me. On leaving his conference, I had called a meeting of all the centurions in the cohort. There were twenty of them, not including myself. I asked each of them to pick the five best all-round soldiers in his unit of fifty men (the days when a centurion commanded a hundred men had been gone four hundred years). It wasn't quite that tidy, because some of them came up with six or seven, but within half an hour I had the names of one hundred and twenty of our very best.

I set the clerks to the job of drawing up a roster for this new maniple and chose two centurions to command it, sixty men apiece. I promoted ten of those men to decurion rank, retaining two who were already decurions, and then detailed ten centurions to assemble all of these bodies in full gear against the wall of the camp closest to my tent within half an hour. Having done that, I went to tell Britannicus that his "special unit" was being prepared.

He astonished me by having one of the smiths from the regimental armourer's quarters set up an anvil and a hammer at the assembly point. I stayed in his tent with him, sharing the briefing he was giving to young Cato, one of the subalterns, whom he had promoted to command the new maniple. When a decurion stuck his head into the tent to tell us that the men were all assembled, Britannicus himself came with us to address them.

The new 120-man detail stiffened to attention as we approached. The two centurions had them drawn up into their two divisions of 60 men each; ten ranks by six files. Apart from the far-off whoops and yells of the enemy outside the camp, there was utter silence. Britannicus eyed them and, cool as a spring breeze, inspected each of them. When he had finished his inspection he returned to the front and faced them, picking up the hammer from the anvil and swinging it over his head to bring it smashing down onto the flat surface. He knew then that he had everyone's attention.

"Watch the hammer!" He swung it again. "It bounces back from the surface. Watch it!" Again he swung, hard.

"The harder the blow, the more complete the rebound. And anything between the surfaces gets smashed. Now. Watch this." He took off his cloak and held it up in front of him, in his left hand.

"I could swing a hammer at this all day and it would be a total waste of time and effort." He did so, and the cloth slipped easily over the hammer head. But then Britannicus put down the hammer and began to fold the cloak again and again upon itself, until it was reduced to a compact wad of wool that he held high in his left hand, taking the hammer again in his right. He let the wad drop, swung the hammer and knocked the cloak a good fifteen feet.

"When it is folded, as you just saw, it becomes solid enough for me to hit it and move it." He paused, waiting for the message to sink in, and then continued, his voice never rising beyond an intimate but very powerful pitch, audible to all of the soldiers of the new maniple.

"There are thousands of bare-arsed hostiles just outside this camp dreaming of slitting our throats. They are a rabble, an undisciplined mob. But they love to fight, and they think they know how it's done. They don't! We are going to teach them how it's done. *You* are going to teach them how it is done. I have already taught you. You men are going to hammer these people until the concussion blinds them. You are going to hit them hard, compressing them and folding them back on themselves until the power of your blows is multiplied a hundred times by their density. Jam them together tightly enough, and you'll take away their power to strike back at you. Once you have them jammed together, compacted just like my old cloak here, you will hit them and rebound, just like that hammer head, ready to hit them again."

There was total silence in the ranks as he continued. "Before Julius Caesar reorganized his legions into cohorts, the maniple was the main striking force of the Legion. *The maniple.* A hundred and twenty men, just like you, fighting in twelve squads of ten men each. Each ten-man squad performed and manoeuvred just like a modern maniple, except that it was one-twelfth of the size." He paused and waited for his message to infiltrate the minds of the men listening to him. "Tonight, we are going to resurrect those tactics. Don't worry about it. You have been training for this for the past three years. You just didn't know it. Those heathen helots outside won't know what's hit them."

Another measured pause before he continued. "You will fight in three lines of four squads each, one behind the other, with gaps between the front line squads wide enough to accommodate the squads of the second line when it moves forward and the first falls back. As the front line falls back, the third line will advance at the charge to fill in the front line gaps. The first line, now in the rear, will then swing right and left to form the sides of a box, and you will then make a fighting retreat, protected by the mounted archers who will come out of the camp gates to cover your withdrawal. Nothing new — you've done it all before, in training. Just remember: Your purpose is to hammer. To deliver hard, unexpected attacks of short duration from any and all of the four camp entrances. Your intent will be to terrorize and demoralize the enemy.

"Remember, too, that your discipline makes you both unmatchable and unbeatable. The enemy fights in single combat. Every one of them is alone. You men, on the other hand, fight like a machine. There is little *human* about you. I expect you to get into their ranks quickly, hit them hard and then get back to the safety of these walls. Intact." His eyes moved from face to face.

"Upon re-entering the camp, you will rest for an hour and then hit them again from the other side." Again he paused before going on. "This is not an easy assignment, but each of you has been chosen as the best man in ten. You'll be tired by dawn, but you will be relieved of daytime duties. Remember, your prime purpose in this exercise will be to confuse and panic the enemy, to undermine his confidence." He stopped and looked them over carefully. "Is there any man here who does not want this duty?"

Silence.

"This is your last chance."

Nothing.

"Very well, then. Hammer them!" He spun on his heel and stalked off.

The new commander cleared his throat. Britannicus had not introduced him. The men were watching him. He coughed again.

"My name is Cato. I am now in command of this maniple. We will reassemble here in full armour half an hour before midnight. Centurion, dismiss the men."

I did, and they broke up gradually, talking among themselves. In five minutes I was alone, looking at the hammer and the anvil.

Well, Britannicus's plan for the hammering worked. It worked so well that first night that in four raids we lost only three men, all three wounded and none seriously. The men were exhausted and slept all morning, the company clerks having rearranged the duty rosters to free them for "special services." When the enemy attacked at dawn, the "Hammers" were already under blankets, and there they remained. The rest of the cohort had little trouble holding off the attacks; our walls and ditches were high enough and deep enough to discourage all but the most foolhardy attackers, and they were easy pickings for the bowmen on our walls.

The second night, about an hour before midnight, Britannicus split our cavalry into two groups of thirty and sent them off in opposite directions from the east and west gates of the camp, with orders to gallop at full speed through the enemy, keeping the camp walls within easy reach. The effect was magnificent. Each group charged out of the darkness, trampling bodies and creating chaos that hardly had time to settle before the second squadron arrived from the same direction. Each squadron made one and a quarter revolutions of the camp, re-entering by the gate beyond the one from which they had left. They lost four men.

No sooner had the peace begun to settle after that exercise than the Hammers went out through all four gates simultaneously, quietly and viciously, thirty men to a group. They stirred up panic on their own, hitting hard and drawing back before any resistance could be organized.

An hour later they went out again, through the north gate, in full force.

An hour before dawn they went back out again through the same north gate.

By the third night of the siege, the enemy was trying to kill the darkness with bonfires. But there is no wood on the high moors; in order to feed the flames, they had to work hard. We hit them with only one four-group raid from all gates that night, in the dark just before dawn.

Britannicus was banking heavily on the lack of discipline within the enemy ranks. They had numbers, but they had no co-ordinated leadership. No general. No Britannicus. And by the end of the fourth day they were leaving by the hundreds in search of easier targets.

When dawn came on the fifth day, we were alone and victorious on the moor. Thank God we didn't know that morning that we were the only fighting force of our size still active in the entire north of Britain.

Britannicus, however, suspected that things elsewhere had gone very badly wrong. His initial suspicion that this incursion might be a long and hard-fought affair proved to be depressingly accurate. On that first evening of the stand-off at our camp, he summoned Luscar, senior clerk of the cohort, and instructed him to keep an accurate record of everything that occurred, and to maintain the record as a daily log from that time on. That turned out to be a command that was easier for poor Luscar to accept than to observe. It took us almost a year to win back to a real Roman fort in Derventio, and we had to fight almost every step of the way. By the time we got there, we had eaten our oxen and our horses. We had one rickety handcart to hold our meagre supplies, and Luscar had used up every available scrap of papyrus in recording our odyssey. He carried hundreds of tightly rolled sheets in the pack on his back as we crossed the countryside haphazardly in a fruitless search for signs of Roman authority.

For almost a year we found nothing but ruined and abandoned villages, towns and military installations. The few local people we did see flocked to us in the begin- ning, thinking we could help them, but eventually, as our appearance degenerated and our condition grew more desperate, they avoided us, running into hiding as we approached.

We were assembling after breaking camp on a hillside, early on a July morning of the following year, when our look-outs sighted a squadron of Roman cavalry in the valley below us.

Of the eleven hundred-odd souls of the Second Millarian Cohort of the Twentieth Legion, three hundred and seventy-one were still alive, and forty-two of those were men we had found, survivors from different units. Besides myself and Britannicus, we had four more officers and twelve centurions.

I V

The cavalry patrol bunched up immediately as the sound of our cheering floated down to them from the hilltop. We saw the pale ovals of their faces peering up at us, and then, to our consternation, they swung their horses around and galloped away in the direction they had come from. Shouts of welcome and happy recognition changed in the men's throats to howls of outrage and disbelief, which lasted until Britannicus had claimed everyone's attention by climbing on to the boulder closest to him and facing them calmly. When the men had grown absolutely still, he spoke, in an almost conversational tone.

"*I* know you are soldiers." His emphasis produced frowns of confusion on many faces. We waited throughout a long pause as he stared at us before going on. "And *you* know who you are." He raised one arm and pointed down into the valley that was now empty of life and beginning to fill with the shadows thrown by the strengthening morning sun. "But those men have run for reinforcement. They have run to report the presence of a large band of hostiles and, depending upon how far away their camp is, they will return in strength, deployed for battle, in a matter of hours."

He paused again, allowing his silence to register his message, and then his voice grew stronger, and he hammered his words at us as though they were nails.

"When they return, be it in one hour or ten, they will find — *and they will see* — the soldiers of the Second Cohort of the Twentieth Legion."

As his meaning became clear, we began looking at one another, seeing ourselves for the first time as we had doubtless appeared to the patrol below. We saw men who bore little resemblance to Roman soldiers. What remained of our armour was dull, scarred, battered and long unpolished. Our tunics and cloaks were scabrous and tattered. Only our weapons were keen and burnished — our weapons and our Eagles.

One of the men, bolder than his fellows, raised his voice to point out to Britannicus that the riders below must have seen our Eagles, but he was cut short.

"Trooper," Britannicus snapped, "how many dead Romans have we seen in the past year? How many Eagles do you think might, across this entire country, have been captured by the Celts?" He broadened his address to take in all of us. "What those men down there thought they saw was a rabble of Celtic heathens carrying captured Roman standards . . . trophies of war! That is what they firmly believe. When they come back, they will find *us*, and by that time *we* will have found *ourselves*. We may not have the finery, the uniforms, or the trappings expected of Roman troops, but by the Living God, we have the pride and the discipline and the dignity to appear as what we are — soldiers of the Empire!"

The men agreed with him. I could hear truculence, grievance and angry shame in their murmuring among themselves — feelings that I shared, because I, too, felt demeaned and belittled by this lack of recognition.

Britannicus issued his next orders over the murmur of voices, and we moved in response down from our hilltop at the double, and spent the next hour and more in determined ablutions by the stream in the valley. By pooling the bits and pieces of armour that remained in usable condition, we were able to equip almost a full squad of men as recognizable standard-bearers, and these formed a vanguard behind Britannicus, myself and the other officers as the rest of the men assembled in disciplined ranks to await the return of the patrol and the forces they would bring with them.

We did not have long to wait. Only slightly more than an hour after we had taken up our positions at parade rest on the floor of the valley, before we really had time to grow uncomfortable under the strengthening July sunshine, our outposts signalled the approach of the Roman forces.

There were two full cohorts, more than a thousand men, in the battle force that came to meet us, and it took almost half an hour for their advance guard to draw close enough to make us out clearly. It quickly became evident that they were surprised by our positioning on the valley floor, and disconcerted by our obvious discipline. That they suspected some kind of elaborate entrapment was also obvious, evidenced by the protracted comings and goings of officers and messengers between the advance guard and the main body of the troops. We could not even put their minds at rest by signalling them with a trumpet, because we had lost our last surviving trumpeter and his instrument in a skirmish two months earlier. I heard Britannicus sucking air between his teeth in an almost silent expression of annoyance at the dithering we were witnessing, but he said nothing and we remained motionless.

Finally, in response to our own lack of activity, a small group of mounted officers, accompanied by a squadron of mounted bowmen, approached us hesitantly and drew up within hailing distance, whence they demanded that we identify ourselves.

Britannicus turned to me, his face fixed in an expression that masked any signs of disgust or disapproval. "Varrus," he murmured, "oblige me by walking to our friends and telling them who we are. I have no intention of shouting like a market huckster to allay the fears of a nincompoop."

I was grinning to myself as I walked forward, but as I drew closer to the newcomers I found myself becoming more and more conscious of the sorry figure I presented — unkempt and bearded and wearing the tattered rags that had once been my centurion's uniform. I looked nothing like a Roman centurion, and, as I approached them, I could see hostility and suspicion in the stares with which they catalogued and analysed my appearance. I eventually came to a halt directly in front of them, looking up at their shining splendour and having to remind myself forcibly not to salute them. I was no supplicant junior, I was a Senior Centurion, *pilus prior*, of the Second Millarian Cohort, and all of these youngsters were junior to me. I drew myself to attention and spoke.

"Publius Varrus, *pilus prior*, Second Cohort, Twentieth Legion, under the command of Caius Britannicus, who awaits your recognition." Their faces registered their confusion and their lack of knowledge of what to do next. I saved them the agony of deciding. "Who commands here?" I asked.

One of the young men, presumably the senior, nodded towards the rear, over his shoulder, in the direction of the advance party. "Tertius Lucca," he said. "He is senior tribune here. . . . We thought you were hostiles."

I grinned, asserting my seniority. "Don't let our sad appearance influence your judgment. We are Roman, and we're glad to see you. We've been searching for you for a long time. It's unfortunate that we ran out of clean uniforms before you came along — about a year and a half ago, in fact — but I suggest to you that our commander can be hostile if he puts his mind to it. You had better get Tribune Lucca over here to welcome us formally back to civilization, before Britannicus decides he is being insulted. I would also suggest that it might be politic for one of you to offer my commander the use of a horse. We had to eat his some months ago, and he dislikes walking."

The young man was still confused, blinking down at me like some kind of owl.

"What's your name?" I asked him.

"Placidus. Barates Placidus. Tribune, Third Cohort, Forty-first Legion."

"How long have you been in Britain, Tribune? I didn't know the Forty-first were here."

"Three months." He cleared his throat. We landed with the consular army of Theodosius, Count of Britain by the appointment of the Emperor Valentinian."

I made no effort to conceal my surprise. "Theodosius is here in Britain? And named Count of Britain? Why?"

The young man frowned. "Because the Emperor orders it thus."

I shook my head. "But what about the other military governors, the Count of the Saxon Shore in the south and the Duke of Britain? What happened to them?"

He blinked at me in astonishment. "They are dead, killed in the Invasion."

I looked backwards towards Britannicus and our men, and then returned my eyes to the young officer. "Invasion? The incursion was that big?"

"It was complete and almost totally victorious. The province was overrun by a conspiracy of Picts, Scots and Saxons. All of the northern and middle lands went down. Only the home base in Londinium was held. How could you not know this?"

I shook my head, trying to rearrange my thoughts. "We have been occupied in local fighting, trying to get back. We have had no contact with anyone since the day the Wall was overrun. So now you tell me Theodosius is here, to win back the province, obviously. He is already campaigning?"

"He is."

"Good. Successfully?"

"Of course."

"Of course." I was not being ironic. I had heard much of Theodosius and knew him to be no man's fool. I wondered what Britannicus would make of this news.

"Well, Tribune Placidus," I said, feeling light-headed, "you bring good news with the bad. I am going to return to Commander Britannicus and tell him that you are reporting our identity to your superior, and that he will be coming to welcome us back to the fold as soon as you have done so. Don't forget the horses. We have six officers." I saluted formally, and as I returned to Britannicus, I heard them wheel their mounts and gallop away behind me.

When Britannicus heard what I had to say, he frowned and bit the inside of his lip. I assumed he was thinking about the scope of the invasion, but I was wrong.

"The Forty-first Legion? Are you sure about that, Varrus?"

"Yes, Commander," I answered. "I didn't think they had been in Britain before the invasion, so I asked him, and he verified that they have only been here three months, as part of Theodosius's consular army."

"Aye, I hear you. A consular army of four, perhaps six legions, and we are rescued by the Forty-first. That is enough to make a man doubt the existence of God."

I blinked at that but said nothing, knowing from long experience that if Britannicus chose to explain himself, he would.

He glanced around him, checking quite obviously to see who was within hearing distance. Nobody was, but he inclined his head, indicating that I should walk with him. When we were far enough removed from casual hearing, he remarked, "Varrus, do you recall the night we first met?"

"In the desert. Aye, Commander, I do."

"We spoke of Senecas. Do you remember?"

"I remember. My old legate."

"Yes, your old legate. Well, unless things have changed in the past two years, the legate of the Forty-first Legion is a Seneca, too. The eldest brother of your former legate. His name is Titus Probus Seneca, and he is the senior of a brood of six brothers, so everyone calls him Primus."

He stopped and I waited, trying to make sense of what he had told me. I knew that there was no love lost between the families of Seneca and Britannicus, but I failed to see any traumatic importance in the identity of the legate commanding the legion that had found us. Britannicus, meanwhile, had fallen into a reverie and had forgotten that I existed. I coughed politely.

"I beg your pardon, Commander, but the significance of this is unclear to me."

"Significance? It has a vast significance, Varrus — to me, but far more seriously to you and to all our men. Primus Seneca is one of the two men in this whole world whom I can accurately call a deadly enemy. He hates me and mine, but the essence of his hatred is for me, in person. You know me well by now; I do not exaggerate. I have tried to kill him, and he has tried to kill me, and to have me killed, several times in years past. Only the benevolent interference of the Fates has frustrated both of us. We detest each other. It confounds me that it must be to him that I report today, in view of the fact that we have been absent from duties for so long. I have no fear of the man, but neither do I have an iota of trust in his humanity. I promise you, if there is a way for Primus Seneca to make trouble for me, and for anyone connected with me, he will not neglect it."

I could feel the confused frown etched into my forehead. "So," I ventured, examining my words carefully before bringing them out, "you think that this Primus Seneca will cause trouble for us? Now? How can he do that, Tribune?"

Britannicus smiled at me — a pitying, almost condescending smile — and gave his head a little jerk.

"Varrus," he whispered, "you are almost too innocent to be alive. Think of our situation. We have been absent, without leave or notice or communication with the army for more than a year. Missing, believed dead. Or perhaps, to some who are less charitable than you, missing, believed deserted." He brought his hand up quickly to forestall my shocked reaction. "No, wait. I am not saying we shall encounter anything like that, but it is a possibility, and I want you, at least, to be aware of it as such. What I *am* saying is that you should hold yourself prepared for anything, any kind of unpleasantness, and be equally prepared to inform our men as to what is happening, and why. That is all. I hope my suspicions are unfounded, and I know I am at fault in confiding them to you — that could be prejudicial to good discipline. I also know, however, the animal with whom I am shortly going to have to deal, and I want you to be aware of the political and the personal implications of what we are about to undergo. Do you understand me now?"

I shook my head, still unable to believe what I was being told. He raised an eyebrow at me, a half-smile on his face. "Come now," he said. "I speak only of possibilities, not of certainties."

I finally found my tongue, and my understanding. "I hear you, Commander, and I understand what you are saying, but ... "

"But what, Varrus?"

"Nothing, Commander. We can but hope you are wrong, and that the command of the Forty-first has changed hands."

"Exactly. Then we are in agreement."

"Yes, Commander. But ... what if you are correct?

What if this man is still in charge? And if he does decide to use this situation to personal advantage? What then?"

He looked hard at me for a long moment, chewing on his inner lip, before answering.

"Then, Centurion Varrus, we must hope that he is accompanied by others who can sway him to behave as a Roman legate and not as a vindictive Seneca."

"Is that likely, Commander?"

"I have no idea. But I suspect we will not have long to wait to find out. Here comes our rescuer." I turned to see the officers of the Forty-first returning, accompanied this time by their senior tribune, Tertius Lucca. We returned to the head of our command as they approached, and I had to bellow at our men to keep them properly silent in the ranks as their natural relief and excitement threatened to overflow.

Tertius Lucca rode ahead of his officers as they came towards us, and in response to some signal unseen by us, they reined in and held their position just over a hundred paces short of where we stood, leaving Lucca to advance in company with one other, the junior tribune, Barates Placidus, to whom I had spoken earlier. When these two had come half of the remaining distance towards us, they stopped and dismounted. I glanced sideways at Britannicus, but he gave no reaction.

"I think they are waiting for you to go to them, Commander."

"Obviously. Well, there seems to be little point in not doing so. At least they haven't shouted at us. Come with me."

I walked one pace behind him on his right as we made our way forward to meet our rescuers, and we stopped within three paces of them. Neither pair of us made any effort to salute the other. Lucca and Britannicus faced each other impassively, neither man's face revealing anything of his thoughts. A worm of dread squirmed in my gut. Britannicus had been correct; we were in trouble with our own people. I fought to keep my facial expression non-committal.

Tertius Lucca was a dark-faced, good-looking man in his late twenties, and his uniform seemed opulent next to our rags. He wore a corselet of burnished bronze plates, cunningly attached so that they overlapped to hang loosely and seemed to shimmer when he moved. His armoured skirt straps and his helmet bore the same sheen of expensive bronze, and his leather harness had that deep, glossed polish that only servants can produce. His cloak and his tunic were of creamy, white wool, decorated with a Greek border in dark green, and the crest on his helmet was of white egret plumes. I noticed, too, that he wore white leggings of the same rich wool beneath his sandals. It was he who broke the silence.

"Have you no salute for me?"

Britannicus shrugged. "I would have, gladly, if I thought you might return it, but I think you might not."

"You are perceptive." The Tribune pursed his lips. "And correct. I could not."

"Could not? On what grounds?"

"On the grounds that you have been found guilty of desertion and are hence beyond the recognition of a soldier."

"I see."

I was biting my tongue. I could hardly believe the coolness of Britannicus's voice.

"Desertion. Not killed in battle. Not presumed dead at all, even though no one has seen me since the fall of Hadrian's Wall. There is no doubt in the official mind, it seems. I did not die in battle. I deserted. With all my men. Look at me, man!" His voice cracked like a whip. "Do you believe I am a deserter?"

"What I believe or disbelieve has no relevance. You stand convicted —"

"*In absentia*!"

"*In absentia*, as you say. That state of affairs is not uncommon in cases of desertion."

"So," and still Britannicus maintained that calm, even tone, "what is your next step, Tribune?"

"I am unsure . . . " Lucca's eyes narrowed as he gazed at Britannicus and then turned his glance on me. "I know what it should be . . . what it should have been. I am guilty, even now, of wrongdoing in speaking to you like this, but this meeting, and the form of it, has been . . . unexpected." Britannicus held his peace and Lucca continued. "Had your men been deployed other than the way I found them upon our arrival, I would have joined battle instantly. I suspect you were aware of that?" Again, he received no answer. His next comment was unexpected.

"You owe this courtesy, small as it is, to one of your former officers, a friend of mine who served with you in Africa, years ago. Julian Symmachus. He is not here today, but I remember the fervour with which he defended your name and your honour when he first discovered you had been proscribed for desertion. He swore that you had to be dead, that you were incapable of desertion. He swore too loudly, fought too well on your behalf and made a nuisance of himself. He was transferred."

Britannicus was smiling. "I remember Julian well. I shall thank him for that. Where is he now?"

"He is dead. He was killed in a skirmish with a band of Scots."

There was no reply to this. Britannicus simply lowered his chin to his breast.

A large bee appeared from nowhere and began buzzing somnolently around Lucca's chin, attracted by the perspiration that coated his face in the growing heat of the summer sun. He flicked at it without looking, and so fast was his hand's speed that he actually knocked the insect away, whether to the ground or not I did not see. He undid the clasp beneath his chin and removed his helmet, resting it against his hip and wiping the sweat from his brow with his free hand.

"It was Julian's defence of you that I recalled today when Barates told me that Caius Britannicus awaited me. I determined then, right or wrong, to speak with you before taking action against you, and to do so, upon my own authority, with only one witness to our discourse. This was in tribute to Julian Symmachus only, understand. I have no wish to come to grief over you as he did, but neither did I wish to condemn you out of hand without even having tried to assess the accuracy of his judgment. Will you surrender yourself and your men to my authority?"

"As what?" Britannicus raised his head and looked Lucca straight in the eye. "Do you intend to treat us as deserters?"

"I have no choice. I must."

I heard again the sharp sound of my commander sucking air between his teeth, a sound that betrayed to me the perplexity he was going through.

"Do you believe, Tertius Lucca, as a professional soldier and a man of reason, that, being guilty as charged, I would present myself and my command so meekly to the wrath of Rome?"

"You might." Lucca was close to smiling, I thought. "Symmachus often talked of the various kinds of effrontery you have shown in the past, as a resourceful leader. A move such as this might be a master stroke of sheer duplicity."

The worm in my gut was whirling rapidly now, but Britannicus's next words astounded me. "What if I were to tell you I can prove total loyalty to Rome, on my own behalf and that of all my men?" He was standing fully erect, seeming to peer right over Lucca's head. "How would you react?"

"With amazement." Lucca was smiling openly now, but there was no malice in his eyes. "Can you do that? Can you prove your loyalty?"

"I believe I can, if given the opportunity. Even to Primus Seneca."

Lucca made a wry face. "I doubt that. The Legate has no patience with convicted felons."

"And even less with me. We are old enemies. Personal enemies."

"Oh. I was unaware of that. That is unfortunate."

"Will Seneca be my judge?"

"He will. He is the legate. He is God, on campaign. You know that."

"He could refuse to countenance my evidence."

Lucca nodded, slowly. "He could, and would be well within his rights. You stand condemned already."

I took advantage of the short pause that followed these

words to turn and look back at our forces. Every eye was fixed upon us, and I wondered what they were all thinking. Another bee hummed loudly in my ear and I swatted at it, uselessly. Britannicus spoke again.

"Where is the Legate quartered?"

"Officially? At Lindum, about thirty miles from here. But he is camped much closer today, in a fortified base camp about six miles from here. He has important guests in his train — a senatorial party from the Court of the Emperor, sent to inspect the progress of our campaign. He brought them out to visit the base camp yesterday. They return to Lindum tomorrow."

Britannicus raised his eyebrow. "Senators? Do you know their names?"

Lucca frowned slightly. "The senior is Flavinius Tesca. I do not recall the other names."

"Flavinius Tesca! I know him from better times. He is an honest and honourable man." Britannicus inhaled a deep breath and rose to his tiptoes, before rocking back on his heels. "Tribune Lucca, if you can guarantee to bring my men and me before the Legate Seneca while he has Flavinius Tesca in his train, I will surrender to you and rely on Tesca to see justice done on our behalf."

"I can guarantee nothing, Tribune." Lucca was frowning now, but all of us heard the honorific he accorded Britannicus. "It is my duty to take you and your men into my custody. If that is effected quickly and without strife, then I will deliver you today to face the Legate Seneca. But I must warn you that the Senator, Flavinius Tesca, has no authority over the Legate Seneca in matters pertaining to discipline and military law."

"I am aware of that, Tribune." The resolve in my commander's tone told me that he had made his decision. "But Flavinius Tesca is an imperial senator, and therefore a direct representative of the Emperor himself, here in Britain upon imperial affairs. If you will grant me one moment to address my men, who have no idea they stand accused, far less condemned, of anything, I will surrender them, and myself, to you. It seems ironic that my soldiers expect celebration and reward for having fought for, and maintained, their Roman pride, do you not agree? How eagerly would they have fought this past year, I wonder, knowing that they faced court martial and death on winning home?"

"Very well." Lucca sounded and appeared disconcerted. "Speak to them. While you do so, I will furnish you and your officers with horses."

"My thanks, Tribune." Britannicus caught my eye and we turned to leave, but Lucca stopped us, calling Britannicus by name. We turned back to face him again, seeing the wish to believe in his eyes.

"You really believe you can establish your innocence?"

"I have said so."

"You must know it seems impossible."

I agreed with Lucca. At that point, I was half convinced that, on returning to our own men, Britannicus would tell them what had happened and then try to fight his way out of this valley. But to where? My mind had not been able to stretch that far. I found myself staring at Britannicus, awaiting his answer as eagerly as Lucca was.

Britannicus looked at me and saw the lack of understanding in my face. He smiled at me and looked back at Lucca.

"Impossible? It would be, had I not decided the day the Wall went down to keep a daily record of our campaign. I have those written records, faithfully compiled day by day by our clerk, dated and signed by me. The written record of almost five hundred days, signed and dated by me each day. I began it on a whim; I maintained it out of habit and discipline; and it seems now I retained it and protected it by the will of God against this day and these charges."

Lucca's eyes had grown round in surprise, and he began to shake his head slowly in wonder. "That would be proof to me, if I could read," he said.

"My friend," said Britannicus softly, "it will be proof to Flavinius Tesca, no matter what the Legate Seneca may say."

The mention of his commander's name wiped the smile from Lucca's face. He stood to attention and snapped a salute, which we returned. "Tribune," he said, in a voice filled with strength and resolution, "you and your men may retain your weapons for the present. My cohorts will escort you, not convey you."

"Are you sure you wish to do that, Tribune Lucca?" Britannicus spoke in a low voice. "Seneca will not thank you for the failure to disarm convicted felons."

"Yes, Tribune, I am sure. The Legate will have my head for it, I think, but only if you fail to make your case." Lucca smiled again. "This is my tribute, a personal one, to Julian. I believe you, and I believe in him. Besides —" he turned his smile for the first time on his companion, young Barates Placidus "— it may be the only way to bring you into custody. Your men are hardened veterans, survivors, where mine are little more than unblooded recruits. Is that not so, Barates Placidus?"

The young man blinked. "Yes, Tribune."

"So be it," Britannicus murmured. "We shall not forget this, Tertius Lucca."

We returned to our own men, and Britannicus informed them of the conversation that had just taken place. Grimfaced, they listened in silence as he outlined the situation and emphasized the importance of the journal carried by Luscar, the clerk. He ended his address by reassuring them and making them laugh, in spite of the gravity of our situation.

"I have brought you here safely," he told them, "and I do not intend to abandon you now. I have spoken at length with each man among you several times since we began this odyssey of ours. You know that all of you are important to me. Trust me now. I will not let you down. But, for the love of God, look after Luscar for these next few hours. He is to be the hero of this day, but if we lose him now, we are all lost!"

Almost two hours later, we reached the camp. Lucca had sent word of our coming, and they were ready for us. Taking their direction from Britannicus, our men were solemn and unsmiling. The gates of the camp opened to greet us in silence, and beyond them we could see rank upon rank of legionaries standing stiffly. There was no sign or sound of welcome as we passed through the gates, and my belly was cramping with apprehension, terrified by what I was seeing.

The entire garrison was turned out and battle-ready, formed up in the hollow square into which we were marching. At the far end, opposite us, stood a magnificently uniformed legate, surrounded by his staff officers. Britannicus rode straight towards this group

and reined his horse in, holding up his right hand in the
signal for us to halt, which we did, coming to attention.
The silence in the square was absolute. I was aware of
the civilians in the background: three tall men and a
shorter one, all wearing amazingly clean, brightly
coloured clothing.

The Legate, a vision in silver and scarlet and black,
spoke in a high, neighing voice that dripped with dislike
and a kind of triumph.

"The prisoner will dismount!"

Prisoner? I felt the tension of the men behind me
increase immediately. Even my own skin broke out in
goose-flesh at the sound of the horrible word, even
though I had been expecting it and rehearsing the sound
of it in my mind. I swung around and barked, "Stand
fast!" over my shoulder. The few faces I saw in the brief
glimpse I had of my men were confused and incredulous.

"Stand fast, damn you!" I roared again.

Britannicus made no move to dismount. He remained
motionless and silent.

"Dismount, I say, or die." The Legate raised his arm in
a signal, and suddenly lines of archers swarmed up the
steps and along the platforms on the camp's parapets,
where they nocked arrows and aimed at us. Britannicus
turned from one side to the other and looked at the archers,
and then he eyed the assembled soldiers who hemmed us
in. His face was expressionless. Finally, he looked again
towards Seneca, in whose face I could see the resemblance
to his brother, my former legate in Africa.

"In the absence of criminals, I can only assume that
you are addressing me, Legate Seneca?" The expression
on Seneca's face was one of triumph.

"I see criminals aplenty, Britannicus. You, and your rabble."

I swung around again to still my men, but there was no need. They were white-faced, most of them, and straining to see over the heads of the men in front of them, but their eyes were on Britannicus, whose voice came again, hard-edged.

"You had better explain that, Seneca."

"There is no need. You and your rabble were convicted as deserters a year ago. No one expected that you would crawl back seeking clemency, but then your character is such that it does not really surprise me."

I could see the tension in every line of Britannicus's being, but his voice remained calm.

"On whose authority was I convicted? And for what cause?"

"For what cause?" Seneca scoffed openly. "For what cause? Is not the loss of a province cause enough? Your incompetence, and that of the others like you, caused the loss of almost the entire land to barbarian invaders, and in recognition of your culpability, you fled the Empire's justice to hide and cower in the hills. Now you have been starved out and come crawling back, hoping for clemency. Enough of this! Order your men to throw down their arms and surrender themselves, or I shall order mine to exterminate them and you."

Britannicus raised his voice. "Flavinius Tesca! Will you come forward, please? And Senator Opius?" There was an uneasy stirring everywhere as all four of the civilians at the back of the ranked soldiers began to move forward. Seneca was not pleased, and was obviously surprised by Britannicus's appeal.

"There is no need for that!" he snapped. "The Senators have no authority here in the field."

The civilians continued to approach, regardless of his words. When they reached the front they stopped, and the tallest of the four nodded to Britannicus, his expression non-committal. Seeing him do so, one of his companions also recognized the Tribune with a tiny nod. Britannicus spoke to the first man.

"Tesca, you are familiar with the situation between my House and the House of Seneca. Am I to be constrained and killed with all my men? For serving the Empire and winning back to civilization? Are we all to stand condemned? By a Seneca? In front of imperial senators?"

Tesca looked uncomfortable. "The condemnation is not Seneca's, Caius Britannicus. He is correct. You were convicted *in absentia* of desertion."

"Why? On whose word?" For the first time, Caius Britannicus allowed his voice to show anger. Tesca shrugged his shoulders. Britannicus kept his voice high, so that everyone in the camp could hear him.

"Flavinius Tesca, I appeal to you as one Roman of senatorial rank to another. Do deserters march into armed camps, under full discipline, to surrender as meekly as we have done? I wish to call one of my men forward. May I do so?"

"No! You may not!" This was Seneca.

Britannicus ignored him. "Senator Tesca? My appeal is to you."

Tesca nodded.

"Luscar! Step forward!"

Curullus Luscar, the senior and only surviving clerk of our cohort, marched forward and stood at attention.

"Produce your records, Luscar, and present them to the Senator."

As Luscar complied with the order, my eyes were fastened on Seneca's face, which registered suspicion and puzzlement. Luscar's pack was oversized, but it held few military contents. The entire space within his rigid, thick-sided leather pack was filled with the tightly rolled papyri on which, for the entire duration of our wanderings, he had kept his meticulous record of all our doings, making ink out of soot and urine, and filling the back sides of every document he had carried with his tiny, crabbed scrawl. Britannicus nodded to the piled papyri on the ground.

"I had Luscar keep a record of the events that followed the attack on the Wall last year. Since then, he has recorded everything, writing on the back of his precious records when he ran out of fresh material. He is a scribe by nature and by training, and I see now that God Himself had a hand in keeping him alive.

"I demand that these records be studied. They will attest to the loyalty of every man with me. The loyalty to Rome that brought us safely here after more than a year of struggle." He glared, defiantly, at Tesca, who cleared his throat to indicate his discomfort and then bent to pick up one of the tightly rolled scrolls. No one else moved. After a few moments, Tesca raised his head and cleared his throat again, turning to Seneca for the first time.

"Legate Seneca, the document I have here seems to indicate that an injustice may have been done." He held up his hand to forestall an interruption. "I only say 'may have.' This is a segment of a military log, dated eight months ago and signed by Tribune Britannicus as officer commanding the cohort." Seneca was spluttering, his face suffused with anger. "It's a trick, damn you, Tesca! Can't you see that?"

Tesca's face became flinty. "No, Legate, I do not see that! What I see seems militarily correct, if highly unusual." He turned and glanced up at Britannicus, and then at the rest of us, before continuing. "I wish to make a strong recommendation. A double recommendation: that the Tribune Britannicus surrender himself and his men, to be kept under guard, until I myself, with my three companions and four of your own officers, have had time to examine these — records — thoroughly."

"Are we yet to be treated, then, as criminals?"

Tesca's eyes went directly to Britannicus, without evasion. "In the eyes of the Empire, you *are* criminals. I do admit, however, that this —" he indicated the scroll he held, "— this record, as you call it, raises some doubt in my mind. In view of that, if you will consent to simple detention, you will be lodged comfortably, under guard, until we have had time to arrive at a decision, at this level only, regarding your guilt or innocence of the charges under which you stand convicted."

"What then?" Britannicus had lowered his voice again. "You said 'at this level.'"

"Then, if we are persuaded of your innocence of the crime of desertion, you will be taken to military headquarters in Lindum to face the Military Governor for formal exoneration."

"All four hundred of us?"

Tesca frowned. "Of course not. You and your officers and your scribe."

Britannicus sighed deeply and looked back to the bowmen on the parapets.

"Seneca," he mused, "your bowmen will have cramps for a week if they do not relax soon."

Seneca, his face suffused with rage and frustration, raised his arm, and I felt my scalp prickle, but he brought it back down slowly and the threatening arrows were lowered. I heard a susurration of released breath from the men behind me.

"That is far more civilized." There was almost a smile in Britannicus's voice. "Flavinius Tesca, I thank you for your level head. Centurion Varrus, pass the word for the men to lay down their weapons and to reassemble ... where would you like them to go, Legate, apart from the obvious?"

"Damn you, and them, Britannicus. They'll stay right where they are, at attention."

I didn't move. This was not yet over. Britannicus's voice dropped low, intended for one pair of ears only. "Seneca, my men are hardened. Yours are babies. I will not have my people stand in the sun to soothe your spleen. I will have them assemble outside the gates, and you can mount a guard around them, but by the Living God, if you try to vent your petty anger at me on them, then I'll turn them loose and very few men, yours or mine, will see tomorrow."

Seneca almost choked. "You threaten me? You dare, you gutter-dropped dung?" His voice was a venomous, choking hiss.

Britannicus swung to me. "Do as I command. Have the men assemble outside the gate. Go with them, and permit no break in discipline." He swung his leg over his horse's rump and slid to the ground. I looked once more from him to the others as two soldiers stepped forward to flank him, and then I turned to do his bidding.

The men spent the night and the better part of the next day under guard in a temporary horse stockade outside the camp. They were nominally prisoners, but they were well treated, and well fed, for the first time in months.

I spent the night in the camp, under guard, having washed with hot water and been issued with decent clothes that made me feel human again.

Late the next morning I was taken under guard to a gathering in the Legate's huge, walled tent. Flavinius Tesca, the three civilians and four officers had spent most of the night reading Luscar's diurnal record, and they were genuinely satisfied that we were guilty of no crime. In their eyes we stood already acquitted of any wrong-doing, and they agreed that our soldiers were to be released immediately. A senior centurion of Seneca's guard was dispatched to see to that, and Tesca called for wine to celebrate our salvation.

The Legate Seneca strode from his tent in a fury.

By late afternoon, Seneca's quartermaster was issuing new uniforms and equipment to our men, who would maintain their integrity as a unit under temporary officers, and Britannicus, with the rest of his officers, myself included, was on his way south for an audience with the Military Governor. A squadron of Seneca's cavalry escorted us, together with the four Senators whose presence in Seneca's entourage had been so fortunate for us.

V

Theodosius, the new Military Governor, turned out to be a grandiloquent and pompous pain in the arse, with all the charm of an angry viper, but he had a viper's strength and resilience, too, and he was, above all else, successful.

He was also something of a showman — had he not been a soldier and a politician, he could have made a rich living as a *lanista*, producing and presenting public spectacles for the amazement of the populace. This was brought home to me when Britannicus and I were ushered into his audience room at his headquarters in Lindum. Theodosius had not yet arrived, and we had to wait for him. Our escort, a tribune and two troopers, came to attention behind us, and two more guards stood stiffly at attention facing us, flanking a large table of polished wood in the centre of the chamber. One *cathedra*, an arm-chair with a high back, stood behind the table, and four *sellae*, traditional backless chairs, were ranged side by side opposite it. We made no move to sit.

On the table top, its naked blade almost glowing in the filtered light of late afternoon, lay Theodosius's sword.

This weapon was famous, justly renowned for its keen, silvery, intricately scrolled blade. When he was not wearing it, Theodosius kept it unsheathed, ostentatiously on display at all times for lesser men to admire. My breath caught in my throat the moment I looked at it and recognized its magnificence, and I was hard-pressed not to comment upon it. I did not dare to speak, however. We were still *de facto* criminals, condemned until Theodosius should formally repeal the proscription against our names. Until then we were forbidden to speak without permission.

Theodosius entered the large chamber only moments later. He listened to our case, presented by the Tribune who accompanied us, and examined our written record briefly. He nodded, then told us he had discussed our case at length with Senator Tesca and was satisfied of our innocence. He even congratulated Britannicus on his forethought, his leadership, his example and his endurance, and ordered the destruction of all evidence of any charges laid against us.

I found myself almost as fascinated by the man as I was with his sword. I was aware of his shortcomings, but spellbound by the aura of power his presence generated. He had landed in Britain with a consular army of four legions — between fifty and sixty thousand men, counting all personnel — just towards the end of the year 368, and had, in a matter of mere months, recreated the *Pax Romana* out of overwhelming chaos. He refurbished the diplomatic corps of the province, appointing a new *Comes Britanniorum,* or Count of Britain, to replace the incompetent Fullofaudes, the so-called *Dux Britanniorum*, or Duke of Britain, who had been killed in the invasion. He also appointed a new *Vicarius* of Britain, a civilian Roman Governor, to represent the Emperor in Londinium. Both positions were sinecures, and neither appointee made any mark during, or after, the brief period when Theodosius remained resident in Britain.

I met him personally shortly after our return and exoneration, when he summoned Britannicus, as one of the few surviving senior officers in the country who was not in disgrace, to attend a conference prior to the launching of his major campaign. The Emperor Valentinian had given Theodosius the title *Comes Rei Militaris*, Military Count, and as such, he was determined to make sure that everyone knew who he was. He was not a particularly pleasant individual, but he was a fine soldier and administrator, and his armies were spectacular. I suppose not everyone can be perfect. He was to be Emperor himself within ten years.

As Military Count, however, Theodosius did make several significant improvements to the province's general defences. He rebuilt and strengthened a number of badly damaged forts, and he greatly improved the defences of many towns — a major undertaking that he completed in an impressively short period of time.

The towns of Britain had stone walls, backed by earthen ramps and fronted by deep, V-shaped ditches. Theodosius ordered these ditches filled, and then added exterior towers to the walls, towers constructed expressly to hold heavy artillery — catapults of varying sizes that could hurl projectiles ranging from deadly *ballista* bolts and javelins, to massive rocks and stones, and blazing containers of oil. That done, he dug new, deeper, U-shaped ditches, this time sited far enough away to stop an attacking force short of the town's walls, but within range of the artillery on the new towers.

His most important and immediate contribution to the

welfare of the province, however, was an extensive refur-
bishment of Hadrian's Wall itself, including the regar-
risoning of the forts and mile castles along its length.

These were sweeping changes, and they involved an
intricate and convoluted redistribution of the military
forces under his command. The remnants of our old
cohort were split up and scattered among the new and
reformed legions, and Caius Cornelius Britannicus was
promoted to Legate, commanding one of these new
units. He took me with him as his *primus pilus*, his chief
centurion and second-in-command in all matters relat-
ing to the daily operations of the legion, as was his pre-
rogative. Things were never the same after the Invasion,
however. Britannicus had the reputation, but his new
men didn't have the balls to be anything great, and we
did not have the time to train them before going into
action. And then, in the closing months of Theodosius's
campaign, when we had the enemy well and truly on the
run, heading north to the Wall again, we walked into
that mountain trap and won ourselves a lengthy, if
unwelcome, respite from war.

Mitros, personal physician to Britannicus and now, by
association, to Varrus, began his daily arrangements to
lengthen my life by deepening my misery. Britannicus
was still asleep, and after the briefest glance at him
Mitros ignored him, and me, as he went about his work.
I watched him with a thin worm of fear churning in my
gut. I was already accustomed to the procedure he was
preparing for, but I knew I would never become inured
to the pain involved, in spite of the wondrous extent of
his healing powers.

Mitros poured white, crystalline powder from a phial into the pot already bubbling on his small brazier, and then removed the vessel from the coals almost immediately, pouring its contents into a shallow bowl to cool until I could drink it. The larger vessel on the big brazier contained a grey, viscous liquid that bubbled heavily, almost like the mud it resembled. Both mixtures, I knew, contained opiates that would dull my senses against the pain Mitros would shortly begin to inflict upon me. I would drink the mixture in the shallow bowl first, when it was cool enough. Even heavily flavoured as it was with fresh crushed mint, it tasted foul, but it was magical. Mitros had told me it was made from a substance rendered from the gum of poppies grown far to the east, beyond Byzantium. It conquered pain in proportion to its own potency. Each day Mitros made the mixture stronger, and each day my awareness of the pain diminished.

When the opiate had numbed me sufficiently, Mitros would undo my bandages and wash and clean the wounds that swept up into the centre of me, using hot water and astringent cleansers that I could not have tolerated without the assistance of the potion. Then, when he had finished, he would dress the wounds again, packing the inner bandages with an almost unbearably hot poultice of the foul-smelling, clay-like mixture from the big brazier. The poultice itself also held a painkiller, more powerful in its own way than the other, so that by the time the effects of the draught had worn off, the magic of the poultice had numbed my leg completely, leaving me able to sleep again until the following day.

Mitros tested the draught in the bowl with the knuckle of his little finger. It was evidently still too hot for me to drink. I swallowed a mouthful of saliva nervously, sniffed, and glanced towards Britannicus. He slept on, flat on his back, his great, hooked beak of a nose pointed to the roof of the tent. I remembered again his words to me on that first night we met, about having to decide what to do with me, and I grinned at the recollection. In the years that had elapsed since that night, Caius Britannicus had had more to concern himself with than what he would do with me. My grin grew wider, and I wondered what he might have done without me.

"Here, now we drink, and we grow well." Mitros was standing beside me, the bowl in his left hand as he reached with his right to support my head.

"Do we, by God? Well, Mitros, since we're doing it together, I've got an idea. Why don't you drink it today and I'll watch, the way you usually do? That way, we share the pain and the pleasure."

"Not amusing. Come."

I obeyed him, quietly and meekly, in the absence of alternatives. The concoction tasted awful. I can still remember the acidic bitterness of it, decades later.

When the bowl was empty, Mitros returned my head to the pillow and wiped my brow with a damp cloth. "There, now. Soon you will be asleep." And soon I would, but not immediately. Sleep drifted in very slowly after that draught, and sometimes it did not come at all; consciousness remained in a kind of dream state, where awareness still functioned but earthly problems like pain and discomfort disappeared completely.

Mitros had returned to his braziers, and now he lifted the other pot away from the heat, using a stout, wooden handling device to distribute the weight of the heavy vessel. He carried it to the sturdy table at the foot of my bed and left it there before crossing to the door of the tent, where he signalled for two soldiers to come and remove the braziers. I watched all of this in a kind of daze, eventually realizing that everyone had left the room and that I was alone, except for Britannicus.

Caius Cornelius Britannicus was a true Cornelian, a direct descendant of the pure, patrician stock of the founding families of the Roman State. During those early days of confinement, practically strapped to his bed and unable to influence anyone to change anything, Britannicus talked, sometimes for hours and hours, about his life in Britain as a citizen, rather than as a soldier. I remember I found that surprising at first, primarily because I had known him until then only as the military Legate Britannicus, the taciturn, professional commander who normally kept his company and his opinions to himself. As time passed, however, I discovered that I barely knew him at all. Whatever intimacies he and I had shared as companions in arms had exposed only a few small facets of the man's fascinating character and personality to me. Now, as he talked and I listened, more and more of the man inside him began to emerge. A paternal ancestor — his great-great-grandfather, in fact — had won his *cognomen*, Britannicus, through his efforts on behalf of the province in the time of Hadrian, more than a hundred and fifty years earlier, and his whole family had come to think of Britain as home over the intervening generations, although their primary allegiance remained always to Rome. For my part, I had been born in Britain and had grown to manhood without ever being really aware of it. I never thought of it as being an important place; it was simply Britain, the place where I lived. It took a few years in Africa, followed by years of enthusiasm on the part of Britannicus, to show me what Britain really meant to me.

He talked at great length and with real affection about his family and about their home, a villa close to Aquae Sulis, the famous hot water spa in the south-west. I heard the pride in his voice when he spoke of his wife, Heraclita, whom he evidently worshipped and whose imperial Claudian blood was as ancient and noble as his own. He spoke proudly, too, of his first-born son, Picus, who, like Caius and all his forebears, would join the ranks of the legions when he reached sixteen. The boy was eight now, almost nine, so there was no rush to find a place for him in the imperial ranks. For the next five years at least, young Picus would remain at home with his younger siblings: a sister, Meleiia, who was seven years old and the favourite of her doting father, and four-year-old twin brothers Marcus and Paulus. He talked of a sister called Luceiia and a brother-in-law called Varo, who owned an estate beside the Britannicus lands in the west and who acted as caretaker cum estate manager to the family in Caius's absence. Someday, he swore, when his duties were over and the Empire no longer required his services, he would return and assume stewardship of his own lands.

Early on in our association, Britannicus and I had discovered that we had both been born in Colchester, the oldest Roman settlement in Britain. His family had moved away early in his boyhood to live in the region south of Aquae Sulis, in the family villa, but he had always retained happy memories of Colchester. Traditionalist that he was, however, he always insisted on calling it by its original name of Camulodunum. Colchester, he maintained, was a bastard name, Celtic and Roman mixed, which stood only for "the camp on the hill." As a name, he said, it lacked character.

In the course of one discussion it came out that his father had had a friend in Colchester who had been a smith, and owned his own forge. This man's name had been Varrus, too. Britannicus didn't connect the name with me, personally, because no Roman citizen of his connection would have willingly worked with his hands. When I told him that this Varrus had been my own grandfather, his eyes widened with surprise, and he had wanted to know how Varrus the Elder had come to pursue a life of manual labour.

The answer to that was short and simple, and I had no worries about telling him the story of my grandfather, who had in fact been Varrus the Younger, youngest son of a minor branch of the famed Varus family. Over the course of centuries, our branch of the family had acquired an extra "R" in the spelling of its name and had, in the same process, lost almost all of the wealth associated with the one-R Vari. My grandfather himself had been brought up by slaves, which was not unusual in Roman households, but had become fascinated as a young boy with the smithy attached to the house. Drawn to the atmosphere of smoke and heat and the clanging of the smith's hammer, he haunted the place. The smith, for his part, took a liking to the young nobleman and taught him as much as he could about the art of forging and working with metals. It was a love that was never to leave the boy, and eventually, when he left the army, he set up a smithy of his own.

At first it had been a hobby, but as the smithy began to take up more and more of the young man's time, his father had become increasingly displeased. Arguments developed into open rifts, and the younger Varrus finally left home to realize his dream of working with metal. He had a little money from the sale of his smithy, and he made his way to Britain, where he set up another and began making tools and weapons to supply the army of occupation. Because he was Roman and an aristocrat by birth, and because he was a veteran of the legions, and because he made the finest swords available, he was able to build up a thriving business.

He married the daughter of a wealthy merchant, also of pure Roman birth, and produced one son who, in his turn, married yet another Roman and produced me. But my father was killed on campaign and my mother died of a fever the following year. From then on, my grandparents raised me, my grandfather completing the task alone after the death of his beloved wife. He died while I was stationed in Africa.

When I had finished my story, Britannicus lay looking at me for a few minutes before asking, "What are you going to do when you leave here, Varrus? Doesn't seem as though you'll be doing any more soldiering, thanks to that." He nodded towards my mauled leg.

I grinned at him. "Smithing, like my grandfather. I'm going back to Colchester to work the old forge. It's mine, now."

His patrician eyebrow arched in surprise. "Smithing? Isn't it a bit late in the day to be starting over? You're a soldier, Varrus. What in the name of all the ancient gods do you know about being a smith?"

I smiled at him, anticipating the impression I was about to make. "I probably know more about it than a lot of so-called smiths who are doing well by supplying the armies today, Legate. The old man taught me all he knew. I was as keen, and as good a student, as he had been. By the time I was thirteen, I could run the whole smithy. By the time I was fourteen I was making swords for local officers."

"Good God, I don't believe it!" But he did, I could hear it in his voice. "You mean to tell me you really are a smith? A worker in iron?"

I nodded slowly. "Yes, Legate. Believe it. I really am." I dropped my voice. "I even know the secret of white iron."

He raised his head from the pillow, trying to sit upright, "*White iron*? You mean the magical kind, the one men have lost the secret of making? You joke with me."

I shook my head. "No, Legate, may I die right now, I tell you the truth. To some of us, that secret was never lost — to the majority of men, however, it has yet to be discovered. You've seen Theodosius's sword."

"What about it?"

"Were you impressed by it?"

"Of course! Weren't you? It is magnificent. If I were superstitious, I'd be inclined to think it was made by Vulcan himself. I have never seen anything like it. It shines, almost, in the dark. And those patterns on the blade! I think they're Egyptian. At least, that's what Theodosius himself thinks they are."

I stretched a kink from my back and stifled a belch; then, when I was sure he thought I had no more to say, I added, "They're British, General, not Egyptian. The patterns are Celtic, from the mountains. And the blade wasn't made by Vulcan, it was made by Varrus. My grandfather made that sword for my father when he entered the legions. He had not quite finished it when my father had to leave, and so he kept it for when he would come home on leave. He never did. He died in Iberia.

"I played with that sword as a boy. Then one day some Roman officers saw it and wanted to buy it from my grandfather. It wasn't for sale. A week later, our smithy was broken open and the sword has never been seen again, until I saw it on display as the property of Theodosius himself."

"Good God, Varrus! Are you suggesting that Theodosius . . .?"

"No, General, of course I'm not. God only knows how it came into his hands. It's probably priceless. It may quite possibly be the finest sword ever made. A lot of men would give anything to own such a unique weapon."

We lay there in silence for a while, each of us thinking about the beautiful sword. Britannicus broke in on my thoughts.

"What makes it so different, Varrus? What makes it so much harder and sharper and cleaner than ordinary iron? And so bright?"

I thought about that one carefully before I answered him. "I don't know, General. I honestly don't know. I know how it was made. The old man taught me how to duplicate the process, and we made some fine blades of a light grey colour, but we were never able to duplicate that blinding brightness. My grandfather swore it was the skystone that made the difference."

"The what?"

"The skystone — a stone that fell from the sky." I smiled at the look on his face. "No, it's true. A shepherd who worked for one of my grandfather's friends heard a terrible noise in the air one night, followed by a crash that shook the earth. It almost frightened him to death and kept him huddled awake beneath his bed skins for hours. When he peeked out in the morning, he saw a great hole in the ground, close by his hut. At the bottom of the hole was a rock, almost buried in the ground. The shepherd tried to dig it out, but it was so heavy for its size that he could hardly move it. He was frightened to discover it was warm, too, so he left it where it was and reported it to his master, who examined it but thought little more about it.

"That afternoon, in the course of a conversation, he mentioned it to my grandfather, who sent my father to bring the rock to him. It was as heavy as iron. For some reason, he kept it for years. And then one night, intrigued by the weight of the thing, he decided to try to melt it down, to smelt it. It turned out not to be easy and he almost gave up the attempt, but just as he was about to abandon it, he noticed that it had developed a glazed texture, almost as though it had been starting to liquefy. So he kept trying. He had to use a far higher temperature than ever before to melt it down, whatever it was. Eventually he succeeded, and from it he finally forged the sword that now belongs to Theodosius, mixing some of the skystone metal with an equal amount of normal iron. When the blade was finished, he polished it with an abrasive stone and it developed the finish you find so admirable. Whatever that skystone was made of is the material that made the sword so bright."

When he responded, his voice was admiring. "Bright! The thing is unnatural! Have there been any more of these fabulous skystones found? I find it amazing that no one else has ever talked of them."

I indicated my own frustration on that score with a quick shake of my head. "Again, I don't know. If that one hadn't fallen where and when it did, it might never have been found. Who's to know how many others there are like it?"

"Hmmm. I see what you mean. But do you really believe it fell from the *sky*, Varrus? That's impossible. I mean, I believe that it fell, but it must have fallen from somewhere!"

"I know it seems impossible. My grandfather felt the same way. But it was still warm when the man found it, hours after it had fallen, and it did contain something that isn't known to smiths anywhere. He finished up believing that it truly did fall from the sky."

His eyebrow shot up and he shook his head. "Astonishing! Have you ever tried looking for any more of these phenomena? These skystones? I mean, how do you know there aren't thousands of them just lying around waiting to be found?"

"Lying around where, General?" I grinned at him, shaking my head at the foolishness of the thought that occurred to me. "A man could spend a whole useless lifetime just walking around, looking at stones."

He sucked air through his teeth. "Yes. I suppose you're right. But if ever one could find such a stone again, could you make another sword like that one?"

I considered that. "Yes, I could. I know how he made it. I'm sure I could make another."

Britannicus lay silent, thinking. He might have wanted to say more, but Mitros came in to change our dressings and he made us both take the sleeping potions that he believed were the secret behind letting the body heal itself. We slept.

The following morning, I awoke to the sounds of grunting and movement, to find Britannicus being hoisted into a sitting position by two soldiers whom Mitros had drafted for the duty. They made him reasonably comfortable, eventually, in spite of his cursing, which died away when the physician pointed out that this was part of the curing process. When they had all gone and left us alone again, I asked him if he was in much pain. He looked at me without responding for a few moments, then eased his leg slightly sideways with both hands and shook his head.

"No," he said, "doesn't hurt nearly as much as it used to. How about you?"

I smiled at him. "I feel no pain at all, as long as I don't try to move. 'Course, when I fall asleep, my body seems to want to move on its own. Then there's pain. I tend to wake up suddenly, very often."

He was watching me closely, frowning slightly. "Well," he growled, "at least you're beginning to look a little better. Those purple bags have gone from beneath your eyes and your face has started to fill out again." He cleared his throat, his frown deepening, then added, "Mitros tells me you should soon be functional again."

It was my turn to frown. "Functional? What, you mean I'll be able to walk again?"

"No, of course not. We know you'll be able to do that. You might have a limp, but you'll walk perfectly well.

No, I meant . . . functional — physically, sexually.'' He seemed embarrassed.

"Oh, that," I said, as a vision flared in my mind of the discomfort an erection would cause. "God, I prefer not even to think of that at this point."

He was looking at me strangely, and I felt myself flush under his gaze.

"What is it, General? What's the matter?"

He shook his head dismissively. "Nothing, nothing at all." He paused, and then continued. "You're an abstemious kind of a character, aren't you?"

"General?"

"Abstemious, fastidious. You're not much of a man for the womanizing life, are you?"

"I suppose not," I said, surprised and caught off guard by this unexpected departure from our normal style of talking. I added as an afterthought, "No less than any other normal man, though, if no more so."

"No, I don't think so." He shook his head again, an unusual, almost musing expression on his face. "I've watched you, you know, over the past few years, and I've been pleased by your temperance. It's one of the primary elements that make up exceptional soldiers."

He saw by the expression on my face that I was uncomfortable with his line of reasoning, and added reassuringly, "Oh, you are normal enough, God knows. It's simply that there's nothing excessive about you, in the vicious sense. You do everything in moderation, it seems to me, nothing to excess. You don't drink too much, you don't whore too much, you don't fight or even argue without reason. You are a fine example to your men."

"Gods, General," I said, "you make me sound too sweet to be wholesome."

"Ha! Far from it, but I apologize nevertheless." He was quiet for several moments, and I had closed my eyes again, wondering when the orderly would arrive with the hot water for my morning ablutions, when he spoke again. "Varrus, have you ever been in love?"

My whole body stiffened in the bed as I wondered what had come over him to provoke such unaccustomed intimacy. Britannicus never indulged in this kind of idle curiosity about anyone or anything. "Never, sir," I replied, hearing the awkwardness in my own voice.

"Never, Varrus? You have never been in love? Not once in your entire life?"

I thought about that, keeping my eyes closed, and as several errant memories chased each other through my mind, I felt a smile pulling at my mouth in spite of my earlier discomfort.

"Well, sir," I said eventually, "I have known a few young women, girls would really be more accurate, who set my heart a-pattering and my senses reeling from time to time in various places."

"Aha!" His voice sounded pleased. "And is there anyone in particular who still has power over you?"

My smile was easier now as I grew more at ease with our topic. "No," I answered. "Not today, not really. No one holds that power over me, and I could be sad about that, if I thought for long about it."

"Ah, Varrus my friend, then you are unfortunate. There is nothing greater than the love of a good woman. It can sustain a man throughout any troubles, for any length of time."

The silence grew and stretched until I broke it. "Aye . . . I've heard that said before, by several people."

"It's true." Britannicus's voice grew warmer and more enthusiastic as he honoured me with his confidence.

"Do you know, I can remember the day I first met Heraclita? I was about thirteen . . ." He broke off, then amended what he had said, "Well, I actually only saw her that first time, I didn't meet her. We didn't really meet for about another two years, but I had never forgotten her since that first time. You'll meet her some day, Varrus, and you'll see what I mean. She was — she still is — the most beautiful creature I had ever seen. I knew, even at that age, that my life would be built around her. We lived in different cities, so it was fortunate that our families were close friends. After that first meeting, however, our parents decided we would wed when we had grown, and we both approved. We became friends, I marched off to the legions, and years later we became lovers. But I had been in love with her since that first day I saw her, playing with a pet rabbit among the frosted sedge at the edge of a frozen pond, with her breath steaming in the cold air and her pink cheeks making her blue eyes seem even brighter than they were. And now we have been married for what?" He did a mental addition against the back of his closed eyelids and answered his own question. "Fifteen years. We were wed on my twenty-third birthday. She was twenty." His voice died away for a spell, his thoughts led inward by his words.

"My only regret about being what I am," he resumed eventually, "is that I have so little time to spend with my wife. I do my soldiering alone, and she stays at home and keeps my private world in order for me. She could come with me, but camp life is no kind of existence for a soldier's wife, and the family of a senior officer can have much grief, particularly if the husband and father is strict with his command. But love, Varrus, the love of a good woman is of matchless value." He turned his face towards me and shook his head in mild perplexity. "I really find it difficult to believe what you say, that you have never been in love."

"Believe it, General," I told him, smiling as I said the words. "I'm sure if I had been, I would remember."

The images in my mind right then were distracting and, for some strange reason I never really resolved, were causing me to feel some kind of guilt — perhaps because I felt I was, somehow, deceiving him. I was thinking of saying so, after which the conversation might have gone anywhere, but the medical orderly came in at that moment with the hot water for our morning ablutions, and the entire process of changing dressings resulted in a change of mood, which led in turn to our losing the desire to pursue what we had been discussing. Nevertheless, throughout the entire washing, cleansing, draining and changing of my dressings, I entertained and distracted myself by recalling the girl whose presence had been brought back into my mind by the way Britannicus spoke, the girl who had bewitched me the summer I joined the legions, when I was only fifteen. She was my spectral love, my special inspiration. I carried the memory of her with me, the physical, magical excitement of her, wherever I went in the service of the Empire, and the remembered sight of her face, the supple slimness of her waist, the deep, flashing blueness of her eyes and redness of her warm, sweet mouth, had nursed me to sleep many a cold night on campaign.

It was a wondrous time, that last summer of my boyhood, a time that would remain with me forever-more. I know now, or I strongly suspect, that my grand-father took special pains on my behalf that year, knowing that I would soon be gone into manhood and soldiery. He had a friend, a wealthy customer and patron, who lived in a superb villa close to Verulamium, and this friend invited my grandfather and me to spend the summer with him. We accepted, and I went to par-adise for eight long, golden weeks. The villa itself was magnificent, but it was nothing compared to the lands! The summer fields were heavy, lush with ripening greenness, and the air was filled with the scent of the grasses, mixed with the dryness of sun-hot dust, the smells of dung and flowers. My ears were teased by the buzzing of flies and insects, the song of birds and the rustling of long grasses as they brushed against my legs. I made new friends there, a Roman boy my own age called Mario whose father was an overseer on the farm, and a younger boy called Noris, the son of the Celtic thatcher who had roofed all of the houses and buildings for miles around. Among the three of us, we hadn't a care in the world.

And then one day, less than a week before my grand-father and I were to return to Colchester, we heard about a festival to be held at the next villa to the east. The son of the villa's owner had recently been married to a girl who lived far to the south-west. The wedding had been in the bride's home, and now the son was bringing his new wife home. Everyone was invited to the celebration. There would be musicians, players, a dancing bear, games, and food and drink for everyone.

The dancing bear was the biggest I had ever seen, but when I managed to approach close to it I was very disappointed. The poor thing was half starved and sickly, its skin broken and ulcerous from rubbing constantly against the bars of its tiny cage, and its coat dirty, matted and awful-smelling. I felt outrage for the helpless, obviously brutalized creature, and fury at the hulking, half-witted giant who was apparently its owner. I immediately went looking for my two friends, determined to enlist their help in freeing the animal that night after everyone had gone to sleep. I had seen them just a short time before, heading towards the stall where the pie-maker was finding it hard to keep up with the demand for his goods, and I set off towards them, cutting directly across the middle of the tree-dotted meadow where the festivities had been set up. And there, in the middle of the field on that hot, dusty afternoon, I came face to face with my future dreams.

I had just swung smartly around the bole of a good-sized tree, taking the shortest route to the pie stall, when my eye was attracted by a bright blueness that I saw to be a dress, worn by a tall girl of about my own age. She had long, straight black hair, an achingly beautiful smoothness of sun-browned face and skin, high cheekbones, a bright-red mouth and wide blue eyes that seemed to leap from her countenance. I saw her, all of her, in one flashing glance and stopped dead in my tracks, as completely stunned as though I had been hit with a heavy club. She was breath-taking. I had never seen anything so beautiful, anywhere. She was with three other girls, all shorter than herself, and they were all laughing at something one of them had just said. I knew the others were there — I could see them moving and hear their laughter — but I was aware of them only as shapes. The girl in blue held my eyes and my attention completely.

All four girls became aware of my attention at exactly the same moment, it seemed. They broke off their conversation abruptly and four pairs of eyes devoured every detail of my awkward, mid-step fascination, from the soles of my feet to the top of my head. Then, in that singular way that is unique to adolescent girls, they instinctively swung inwards, towards a common centre, giggling and chattering, convinced that somehow, by turning their backs on me and huddling together, they had disappeared.

The tall girl, however, distanced herself from her friends by simply raising her head and gazing directly at me. There was no smile on her face, no discernible expression in her eyes. She simply looked at me, and I at her, and somehow, across the ten paces that lay between us, I felt the warmth of her active, excited interest. My heartbeat sped up and my breath swelled and grew tight in my chest. I knew that I had somehow magically filled her universe as she had overwhelmed my own. Her eyes seemed to grow bigger and bigger as I gazed at her; they devoured me, filling my consciousness to the point where everything else faded away, and all I wanted to do was reach out and stroke the smoothness of her cheek. And then her friends were shouting and moving, pulling at her, urging her away. I had ceased to interest them and, miraculously, they had been unaware of what had happened between me and their beautiful friend. She went with them — unwillingly, it was clear to me — turning her head as she walked to keep me in her sight. Bereft of all memory of what I had been doing before, my own friends and the bear completely forgotten, I moved to follow her. She smiled and turned back to her companions, confident that I would not go far away.

I followed faithfully until the moment came — and I have no idea how it came or what led up to it — when we stood together, all others gone, the two of us alone, stranded in wonderful isolation among a throng of people who had no impact on us or our lives. I looked at her, speechless, and she at me. She smiled a perfect, pearl-toothed smile that made my chest constrict. I know we spoke, though I can recall no words, and then we walked together away from the festivities, away from the crowd, away from the eyes of people.

She was tall. She was lovely. She was mine. Neither of us doubted that, and there was no need to talk of it. There was no strain between us, no shyness, no false awkwardness. We touched each other gently, faces, ears and hair, with the awestruck, quivering fingers of reverent discovery. I touched a questing knuckle softly to the swelling, smiling fullness of her lips, and they parted, kissing my finger chastely. I felt the pliant slimness of her waist beneath my hand and almost caught my breath in panic as her face came close, close up to mine, and our mouths kissed. She was in my arms, filling my arms, enclosing me in her own, and I was overwhelmed by the closeness and the fullness and the softness and the clean, sweet-smelling scent of her, and we devoured each other with kisses, avidly, wildly, in the innocent need and fury and wonder of first love.

She told me to call her Cassie, short for Cassiopeiia, the constellation that rose in the evening sky shortly before we realized how late it had grown. She knew my name was Publius. I never learned her full name, nor she mine. By the time we rejoined the festivities, they had turned out to look for her and a stern father took her jealously in charge and out of my sight.

I had to return home to Colchester the following day and I never saw her again. But I never forgot her, either. She told me that her father was a soldier, a legate, and she herself an army brat, living the army life, moving from camp to camp and country to country with her father's command. Through all my travels with the legions I watched for her — and for her father — each time we visited a new town or garrison, but without a family name, I could not even begin to look systematically. And so she had faded, gradually, into my memories. I watched for her in each new town, even then, after fifteen years. And now that Britannicus had stirred up my recollections of her, I embraced them and used them to cushion me against the brute pain that even Mitros's gentle ministrations could cause my mangled flesh.

That particular day, and the discussion we had in the course of it, seems, in my recollection, to have been a turning point. During the next few weeks, we both began to recover more strongly, although Britannicus mended much faster than I did. A day came when he was able to leave the room and walk about outside while I still lay on my back. Within the month that followed that, he was exercising strenuously, getting into shape for his return to duty. Perversely, as he grew fitter, I grew more and more depressed. And then, one day, he was gone.

He visited me the morning he left and wished me Godspeed in my recovery, promising that if he ever passed by way of Colchester, he would find my smithy and visit me. We clasped hands and parted as friends.

I had been returned to regulation sick bay by this time, tended by the regular medics, and I suppose I was feeling sorry for myself. The fact that Britannicus had gone, however, made me face up to my problems. I could either languish and die in bed, or I could set myself to making the best I could of a crippled leg. I set out to beat my handicap, and I won.

Most of the physicians and surgeons who had examined my injuries — and there had been many over the months since I had been wounded — were of the professional opinion that I would never walk upright again. I was determined to prove them wrong, and I was intensely grateful that there were others, equally qualified, who did not share their opinions. One of the most scathing of these was Comius Attribatus, a brilliant surgeon of mixed Roman and Celtic blood who was also a grey-bearded veteran of thirty years in the army medical corps. There was nothing Comius had not seen in the way of wounds over three decades, he told me, and he swore that he had known men with wounds far worse than mine who had forced their bodies to conform to their will and learned to walk again, when reason and logic said they should have been cripples forever. I devoured his words, never able to hear enough of such stories, choosing to believe him because I wanted to more than anything else in the world. Under his close supervision I set out to retrain my cut and wasted muscles.

It was agonizing, lonely and frustrating work, and my progress was very, very slow. But I soon began to make visible progress, and even the most sceptical watchers came to believe I would win, and to lend their support to my efforts. I sweated off every trace of fat on my body, and gradually, shaking and quivering with sustained effort, I replaced it all with healthy, corded layers of muscle. My left leg had been shattered, of course, the muscles torn and poorly reconstructed, in spite of the excellent work of the physicians, and that was something I had to accept as a limitation. But after six months of exercise and effort, the leg worked. I could walk on it. It was a limping walk, hesitant at times, but it was real.

Eight months after the return of Caius Britannicus to duty, in the dead of winter, I arrived home in Colchester, looking as good as ever on horseback, but limping like a lame duck when I tried to walk.

BOOK TWO

Colchester

V I

My grandfather's smithy — now my smithy — was empty when I arrived. There were no fastenings on the doors, which hung limp and weary-looking in their frames. I inspected the premises and found nothing — no anvils, no tools — nothing. The forge itself lay cold, its grill thick with rust. Around the walls, dilapidated wooden shelves hung limp and empty, sagging wearily under a heavy coating of dust. The place hadn't been used in years, it seemed, although it had been my understanding that one of my mother's brothers had taken it over after my grandfather's death, just to keep it safe for my return. I closed the doors and made my way to my grandfather's house, where I found a family of cousins in residence.

To say that they were surprised to see me would be an understatement. To say that they were *glad* to see me would be an outright lie. They had thought me safely dead in the invasion, as were my uncle and his wife. Now here I was on the doorstep, alive and reasonably healthy, expecting to take possession of my house, which meant that they were dispossessed. Thinking back on it now, I might have been disposed to let them stay had they shown me any sign of welcome on my arrival, but they lacked even the civility to hide their disappointment at my survival; they seemed to go out of their way to antagonize me. I admit, however, that with the pain in my leg, the disappointment of finding the smithy abandoned and the long journey I had made, I was not difficult to anger.

Anyway, they moved out. Quickly. And I was home. The house was filthy, but I had good memories of the place. It was fairly spacious, in the Roman townhouse style, and I decided to hire a couple of servants the next day to clean it up and maintain both it and me in return for their keep.

I presented myself the next morning at the home of the local magistrate and quickly established my identity and my bona fide rights to the property left me by my Grandfather Varrus. I had taken the precaution of having Britannicus write a letter on my behalf in his official capacity as commander of the legion. Then, my identity and character legally established, I went back to the deserted smithy, to find it occupied now by three urchins, who were playing in the darkness inside the building. They fled at my approach, looking back over their shoulders at the limping deformity who had frightened them.

Deserted and abandoned as it was, I fancied that the walls of the place still held traces of the smells that had made it a magical place to me as a small boy. The sooty, smoky odour still lingered in the stones, and I leaned close to the wall behind the forge and sniffed deeply, recapturing scenes and images of my long-ago childhood. The very back of the smithy was floored with massive stone flags. One of them was a door, and beneath it was a room dug out of the earth. Within that room, whose existence was, I believed, known only to myself and my grandfather, were stored the treasures that he wanted me to have after his death. Deep in my soul, I was afraid that the secret room might have been discovered while the place lay abandoned.

I crossed slowly to the fire-pit of the forge. Only a few cinders lay forlorn on the bottom, fragments of the last embers of a fire that had once melted a skystone.

"Who's in there?"

The voice came from the doorway. I turned and saw the shape of a big man silhouetted against the bright light. Even without seeing any features, I recognized him and felt my heart lighten within me.

"I said, who's there? Who are you?"

I answered his question with one of my own. "Whose smithy is this?"

"What's that to you?" He took a step into the shop.

"I am curious. Whose smithy is this? Or was this? Is it for sale?"

"No. It's not for sale. It belongs to the family of Quintus Varrus."

"And where is the family of Quintus Varrus?"

I could see him now. My grandfather had always called him Equus, because he was strong as a horse. He had been a good friend to me as a child.

"Who wants to know?"

"I do, obviously."

"And just who in Hades are you?" He was starting to get angry.

"My name is Publius. Publius Varrus. Hello, Equus."

"Publius!" He was across the floor in one leap and had me lifted high in the air, into the light where he could see my face to be sure it was really me.

"Publius, by Minerva, it really is you! Where have you come from? When did you get here?"

I was laughing at his gladness. "Put me down, Equus, put me down. I'm not a child any longer. Think of my dignity — the dignity of Rome. I'm an officer in the imperial legions!"

"I piss on the dignity of Rome!" He stopped spinning me around. "But you are right. You have grown up. So I will put you down, and preserve your dignity and my own back. Publius! How are you? Are you well? Are you here to stay?" And on and on he went with a list of questions until I had to put my hand to his mouth to stop him.

"Enough, Equus, enough! I am here, I am well, although crippled by a barbarian axe, and I will be staying, at least until I can find out what happened to the smithy."

"Crippled? What happened? Show me!" His face was full of concern now.

"There's nothing to show. I stopped an axe with the wrong part of me. It nicked my leg, but I can still walk."

"Show me." He was frowning. I showed him.

"That's nothing! So you limp a little! You had me worried, then." He took my shoulders in his hands and grinned with delight into my eyes, almost devouring me with the welcome in his gaze. "By the combined crotches of the Vestal Virgins, you look wonderful, Publius! You're the double of your grandfather when I first met him, though he was a lot older than you before his hair turned grey. You're still not thirty, and your head is as silvered as an old fox! What have you been doing, boy? Where have you been since I last saw you? Minerva's nipples! Do you realize it's been eleven years?"

By this time we were outside in the bright sunshine. I looked back into the interior of the building. "How long has the place been shut up, Equus?"

He looked me in the eye. "About two years."

"Why?"

"Why not? The whoring Saxons were everywhere and your uncle was dead. I didn't see any point in leaving such a tempting target for looters, so I shut it down."

"*You* shut it down?"

"Who else?"

"And what happened to all the tools and equipment?"

"I removed them. Hid them. I didn't know if you'd be coming back, but I decided to give you five more years. If you hadn't returned by then, I'd have dug the stuff up and used it myself. I didn't think you'd mind, since you'd be dead."

In spite of the sudden lurch in my stomach, I felt a smile forming on my face.

"You'd have dug them up? You mean you *buried* them? Iron tools? In the ground?"

Now it was his turn to smile. "Publius, when they call me Horse, they're referring to my muscles, not to my resemblance to the rear end of the animal. I hid them. Underground. In your grandfather's secret vault."

"Under the floor?" I was incredulous.

He nodded his head, still grinning. "Under the floor. I couldn't think of any better place. Could you? I knew that if anything happened to me, and you came back, you would look down there sooner or later. And I knew that nobody else knew the room was there."

"How did *you* know it was there? Did my grandfather tell you?"

"Tell me? I helped him dig it out in the first place. We had to do it at night so no one else would ever guess it was there. When I decided to hide everything, I just packed all your grandfather's treasures more carefully and piled everything else in front of them. If you want to get down there now, we'll have to unload everything from the door inward, because the place is crammed full of stuff." He was almost hopping with excitement. "It's all there, every bit of it. If you're really here to stay, we can haul it all out tomorrow and be in business within the week. Come! See for yourself."

He lumbered over to the back of the smithy and crouched, fingers feeling for a hidden groove in the floor, scraping the dirt out of the crack, and then he heaved mightily and straightened his legs. The concealed stone door swung upwards easily on its counterbalanced hinges. I crossed to him and looked down. The hole in the floor was full of tools, anvils and assorted paraphernalia — the entire contents of a smithy. I grinned my delight.

"Equus, you're a genius and an honest friend!" I punched him on the shoulder. "Now, where's the nearest tavern? We have a double occasion to celebrate — my homecoming, and your partnership in the smithy!"

His face clouded in puzzlement. "Partnership? Was that what you said? How can that be? I have no money, Publius. I can't afford to buy half a smithy."

"Who said anything about buying? You've earned it, by keeping this safe for me. Haven't you heard the story of the faithful steward? Let's go drink some wine, Partner!"

We got gloriously, happily drunk together that night, and the next day we started unpacking the cellar. It was all there, everything we needed. By the afternoon of the third day, the fire was ablaze in the forge again and my spirits were soaring with the sparks from the red-hot iron under my hammer. The smell of the smoke set memories running and jostling in my head like boys released from their tutor, and I rediscovered the almost sexual tension that had once been commonplace in my life as I shaped living metal and made it bend to my will and my skill. The feel of tongs in my hand brought back knacks, mannerisms and old habits that had lain unused and forgotten for years, and the love and lore of my grandfather's craft brought his presence and his voice back into my head.

"Beware black iron!" he had told me, and it had seemed a pointless warning until the first time I picked up a piece of ordinary-looking metal lying beside the forge and discovered, painfully, that the redness had just left it. Recalling that day so long ago, I inhaled deeply, savouring the charcoal, the metal-flavoured smoke, enjoying the familiar, acrid bitterness of it, the stinging in the eyes and the pleasurable grittiness between my teeth.

I began by making nails, aware of the need to do something about the sad shelves that lined the room. The wood was dried and warped and split around the original nails, many of which were completely consumed by rust. I was struggling and grunting, biting my tongue between my lips as I concentrated on holding two angled pieces of wood together so that I could clamp them when I heard footsteps behind me. Assuming it to be Equus, who had gone to buy lamp oil, I did not even look around.

"Here," I grunted. "Hold this while I get this cross-piece in place."

A pair of hands materialized beside me, doing as I had bidden, but they did not belong to Equus. Surprised, I started to straighten up, but the stranger had already taken the strain of the load and nodded for me to go ahead. I acknowledged him with a half-smile of thanks, pulled the cross wedge into position and nailed it solidly with two big spikes.

"There!" I said. "That ought to do it, for a while, anyway." I straightened up and held out my hand to my helper, who gripped it. "My thanks," I said. "I didn't see who you were, or I would not have put you to work. I thought you were my partner, Equus. I'm Publius Varrus."

He smiled briefly and nodded. "They call me Cuno. Short for Cunobelin. I'm married to Phoebe, Equus's sister."

"Phoebe's husband? Then you are a king indeed. Cunobelin was a king, wasn't he?"

"Aye, long ago. Or so they say." His eyes were moving around the smithy, taking everything in. "So you're the grandson. Equus told us you were back and that you'd opened up the old place again."

He did not look back at me, so I took the opportunity to examine him. He was of medium height, broad-shouldered and barrel-chested, wearing a leather apron over work clothes, rough tunic and cross-wound leggings. His hair and beard were thick and blond — unusual in this part of the country — and filled with sawdust and tiny, tightly curled wood shavings. His clothes were thick with sawdust, too, and he had a way of blinking his close-set eyes rapidly, as though to keep them clear of flying wood chips.

"Did you know my grandfather?"

"No. I only came here about two years ago. That's when I married Phoebe. This place was closed down by then."

"What are you? A sawyer?"

He laughed, briefly baring his long, narrow, brown teeth. He was not a comely man, and he seemed to have difficulty meeting my eyes.

"No! Not by anybody's gauge. I'm a wheelwright. A wheelwright and a wagon-builder." That explained the small wood shavings; they were from turning spokes.

"A wheelwright, eh? You must be a good one. Judging by the shavings in your hair, you have work."

"Aye." The smile remained on his face. "I'm good. I have to be. Square wheels are hard to sell."

"I would think they are." In spite of wanting to accept this man as Equus's brother-in-law, I found myself instinctively disliking him, and I felt vaguely guilty, since he had offered me no harm. I have always been a believer in first impressions, and he impressed me as being untrustworthy, for some reason. I tried to dismiss the feeling, attributing it to the ill cast of his features, which were not his fault, and made a determined effort to be friendly.

"Look here, you are our first visitor, and I was thinking just before you arrived about a pot of ale. Will you have one?"

His eyes stopped roving the smithy and came back to me. "That's a fair offer. I will."

"Good." I poured two flagons from Equus's pitcher and we toasted each other silently before taking a good pull at the yeasty brew. I wiped some foam from the tip of my nose.

"Welcome to our smithy. Is there something I can do for you, or did you just wander in here by accident?"

"No, I came in on purpose, to say hello and see what you are doing."

I indicated the forge. "Not much, as you can see."

"Aye, but you have not had much time." He crossed to the forge and picked up some of the new nails that lay there in a pile. "You made these?"

"I did."

"You intend to make more?"

"I do." I was smiling, wondering where he was headed.

"Where will you store them?"

Now I was intrigued. "Store them? I'll sell them. No intention of storing them."

"No. Of course. What will you sell them for? Money?"

"What else? Isn't that normal?"

He flashed me his brown-toothed, rabbity grin again, tossing the nails he held into the air and catching them in one big hand. "I was thinking I might take some of them off your hands. But not for money."

It was my turn to smile, though I felt my eyes grow narrow. "For what, then?"

"For the good I'd be doing you, relieving you of the need to store them on these shelves." He was moving again, one hand stretched out to grip the edge of the nearest shelf. He tugged, and the old, dry wood creaked noisily and dangerously.

"Hey, careful! They're not that strong."

"So I see." He turned back and almost looked me in the eye, but his gaze slid away again, back to his flagon, just before contact was established. "I have a bargain for you," he said. "I have an order for six heavy draft wagons. For the army." The grin again. "The army still pays with money, but only on delivery."

I found myself smiling back at him. "So? What's your bargain?"

"Nails, and metal parts. I need good ones, and I need them fast. My supplier died a month ago, kicked by a horse he was shoeing. His two sons couldn't make a horseshoe between them. You fill my needs, on trust, and I'll rebuild all of your woodwork in here. Then, when the army pays me, I'll settle any difference with you, in cash."

I didn't even quibble. He was married to the sister of my partner. We spat on our hands and slapped palms to seal the bargain, and I had my first customer.

Equus himself walked in a few moments later and seemed surprised to see Cuno there. We made small talk for a while, and I was gratified to see that even Equus was not too fond of his brother by marriage. There was no overt hostility between the two, but Equus's distaste for Cuno was obvious. I mentioned the bargain I had struck with Cuno, and Equus merely nodded, neither approving the bargain nor condemning it.

Later, when Cuno had gone, I asked Equus about him and learned that he had drifted into town a few years earlier and worked for several months with the old wheelwright whose business he now owned. The old man had died without heirs, and Cuno had assumed the position of wheelwright to the town, marrying Phoebe shortly after that. He was good at what he did, Equus told me, but he drank too much and had beaten Phoebe cruelly on several occasions. Equus had posted warning, he said, of what would happen next time his sister appeared with a bruise on her fair skin. It was then that he told me directly that he could bring himself neither to like nor to trust Cuno. I asked him immediately if I had made a foolish bargain with the man, but Equus assured me that the bargain would be met and honoured. Money was scarce, he explained. Only the army dealt in cash. Equus believed that once Cuno had spoken to his neighbours about our arrangement, we would find more barter offers coming our way.

He was correct. The word spread quickly. Within the week we had a guarantee of a month's supply of fresh bread in return for four long-handled oven shovels; the bellows-maker down the street provided new bellows in return for short-shafted nails; and several local farmers had promised fresh produce and grain in return for iron tools. Business grew brisk, and within a surprisingly short time we found ourselves having to think and talk about hiring helpers.

In the interim, until such time as we could find suitably skilled workers and apprentices, Equus brought his sister Phoebe to help us out in the day-to-day running of things. She cooked for us at first, and devised a method of keeping inventory of our bartered goods, recording the goods and the services we tendered in exchange. Then, as she became familiar with our work and our requirements, she began to take a more active role as an intermediary between us and our growing network of customers. In a matter of mere months, she had made herself indispensable.

When Cuno had first mentioned Phoebe's name, I had not been able to recall her face. I knew instantly who she was, of course. I remembered, too, that I had liked her.

She was much younger than Equus — close to my own age, in fact, and even slightly younger — and she and I had shared much of our growing up. I remembered that she had always been able to make me laugh as a boy, no matter how black my mood. I also recalled quite clearly that, while not unpleasant to look at by any means, she was no great beauty. The casual association we shared in those days had been based on liking and a mutual, once-in-a-while need for companionship, not sexual attraction under any guise.

Nevertheless, it was heart-warming and gratifying to see the pleasure on her face as she greeted me on the first morning she appeared at the smithy, and I recognized her instantly. Phoebe had grown up well and turned into a handsome, red-haired woman with bold, appraising eyes, rounded, firm limbs and high, full breasts, and she had retained the sense of fun that had always distinguished her from the other urchins who had been her friends.

She astonished me one evening, as we were preparing to close up the smithy and go home. Equus was out somewhere, meeting with a customer, and I had just removed my apron and was washing off the day's accu-mulation of dust and grime. Phoebe had been stacking some small wooden boxes of nails on a shelf at the back of the smithy, and I had almost forgotten I was not alone. Her voice startled me.

"Did you ever find her, Master Varrus?"

I had begun to dry my face and I spoke through the towel. "What? Find who?" I put the towel down. "What are you talking about, Phoebe? Find who?"

"Her, your lost love, Cassie. Cassiopeiia. That was her name, wasn't it?"

I felt my jaw drop. "Good God, Phoebe, how did you know about that?"

She turned to face me, her own eyebrows arched in surprise.

"How? You told me, Master Varrus, you told me all about her. Don't you remember?"

"I told you? No, Phoebe, I don't remember. When did I tell you?"

"When you came back, that time you went to Verulamium. You were away all summer long that year, and it was the first time you had ever been away. And then when you came back, you'd changed. You'd fallen in love. You'd met her at a wedding feast and lost her the same night. Don't you remember?"

Her voice had changed subtly, slipping back, almost imperceptibly, into the voice of the Phoebe I remembered, accented with the slow, steady, comfortable stolidity of the local Celts. I did remember, now that she had brought it back to me with her gently slurred words, but I was amazed that she should, and I told her so.

"Well," she said, "'t'wasn't so much that I remembered as that I was reminded, if you know what I mean."

"No, I don't know what you mean. Tell me."

"Well, it's right here." She nodded towards the wall in front of her. "Right here where you wrote it, don't you remember? You taught me to read it and it was all I could read for years and years."

I stepped forward, my ears deaf to what she was actually saying, and stared in amazement at what she was looking at. Two letters, a P and a C intertwined, were incised on the plaster surface of the wall, their edges faded and smoothed but still legible, even after almost a decade and a half of exposure to smoke and soot. Now I could remember carving them in the plaster, watched by Phoebe, and telling her of my undying love for the beautiful girl in blue with the long, black hair. I could not believe, however, how completely I had forgotten doing so. I reached out and touched the letters, tracing them with the tip of one finger as I felt a hard, unaccustomed swelling in my throat for the boy I had been, and the hopes and dreams and fancies that had prompted me to carve a tribute to a girl who I knew only as Cassie. In truth, I didn't even know that Cassie was really her name. We had been flirting with each other, having fun, teasing each other with never a thought for reality and the lives we had to live with others.

Phoebe was watching me closely.

"No, Phoebe," I said, sighing, "I never did find her. I looked for her every place I went, but I never saw her again. It's funny how I forgot doing this, though, carving her name here, and telling you about her. I forgot the reality."

Phoebe sniffed and turned away, bustling over to where she had left her shawl and her bag. "You'll find her again, you wait and see."

I laughed aloud. "Phoebe," I scolded, "listen to yourself! It's been almost fifteen whole years! She is most definitely married long since and mother to a brood of brats. Her beauty, great as it was, will have faded long ago . . ." But even as I laughed, my voice died away.

"And? What would you do, Master Varrus, if you turned around one day, tomorrow maybe, and found her looking at you, faded and fifteen years older, surrounded by her children? What would you do?"

I was silent, visualizing the tall, blue-draped girl Cassie, trying in vain to add fifteen years and the effects of them to what I remembered. Phoebe's voice drew me back to where I was.

"Master Varrus?"

"Phoebe, my dear, I wish you would call me Publius. You and I have been friends for too long for any other nonsense."

She smiled and bowed her head, "Thank you, but I feel more comfortable with Master Varrus. You will find somebody else, you know. It's in you, the love. What you felt for that girl was far too strong to be allowed to rot or go to waste, you mark my words. And I should be home by this time. Cuno likes to have his meals on time. Good night, Master Varrus."

After she had gone, I sat by the banked, slowly smoking forge for a long time, thinking about my life and the changes I wished I could make in it. One of those changes, by itself alone, would be an absolute necessity if ever I were to meet the girl in blue again, or any other like her I had not achieved conscious erection since being wounded. Paradoxically, I had had regular nocturnal emissions, so I knew my body was still working, somehow, but lust was alien to me in my waking hours.

I rose, eventually, and made my way back to my house.

It became clear to me very rapidly that Equus and Cuno had both been correct when they told me that only the army dealt in cash in these parts, and so I set my mind to laying my hands on some of it. That I was able to do it quickly was due more to luck than to planning.

A name overheard in a tavern where I sat one day with

Equus after closing the smithy led to my presenting
myself at the entrance to the local military headquarters
at the start of my second month in Colchester, in the first
week of March. The two young soldiers on duty at the
gate looked at me with the mute, almost insolent indifference that their kind reserve for civilians, even when
those civilians are obviously veterans. I stood firm, gazing back at them without rancour, waiting for one of them
to address me. I was not dressed in the manner of a smith,
but neither was there anything about me to mark me as
an officer or as a man of noble standing.

"Well? What do you want? This is a military camp.
If you have business here, state it and be done. If not,
move on."

Almost word for word what I had expected. Now I
spoke, letting them hear the iron in my voice.

"Pontius Aulus Plautus. Your *primus pilus*."

They glanced at each other warily, wondering if they
had been over surly to one who spoke their senior centurion's name with such authority. The one who had
addressed me spoke again, his voice less abrasive, more
conciliatory, more uncertain.

"What about him?"

"Tell him there is a stranger at the gate who wonders
if he still flavours mutton stew with camel dung."

There had been three of us, junior centurions together
in North Africa, and one very unpleasant tribune who
had suffered long and painfully from chronic stomach
upsets. Only the three of us ever knew why. The hint
of a good story got them, as I knew it would. One of
the soldiers spun on his heel, his eyes wide with
mystification, and disappeared through the judas gate.

Minutes passed. The remaining sentry did not look my way again but stood spear-straight, his eyes focused on infinity. Then came the sound of hobnails on cobblestones, the judas gate opened again, and a vision in polished leather and burnished bronze stepped through and looked at me from deep-set, heavy-browed eyes, his frowning face a mask of displeasure.

"Publius Varrus." The voice was as I remembered it — deep, low-pitched, gravelly and capable of inspiring fear in officers as well as raw recruits. "You gutter-dropped son of an Alexandrian whore! I thought you were dead."

"No, Plautus, just avoiding you, as always."

He crossed the space between us in two strides and threw his right arm round my neck, starting to pull me down into a headlock, and then he remembered who and where he was and he turned the move into an embrace, holding me tightly to his breast, wordlessly, as seconds drew out into minutes. The clean, well-remembered scent of him took me back years to more carefree, if not happier, times. Finally we released each other and he held me at arm's length to look at me, letting me see the tears that had spilled from his fierce eyes.

"I did think you were dead, you know," he muttered, and then he hawked and spat and spun around to face the staring sentries, his arm across my shoulders.

"Look at this man, you two. Mark him well! He is responsible for all your grievances. This is Gaius Publius Varrus, the kind of whoreson soldier puling little turds like you will never be. This man has hauled my arse out of more tight spots and saved my worthless life more times than I can count. Next time you find yourselves cursing me, curse him instead, for without him I wouldn't be here to plague your worthless souls. And if you stay in this army long enough, you might, some day, find a friend as good as him. You might, I say, but I doubt it."

That day stretched into a long, drunken night.

The following afternoon found me seated in the office of Antonius Cicero, a direct descendant of the golden orator, and legate commanding the military district of which Colchester was the hub. I knew him of old, too, for I had served under him in Africa and with him, after my promotion, in North Britain. He was a close friend of Britannicus's and newly appointed to this command by Theodosius. With us in the room were Trifax, the garrison armourer, and Lucius Lucullus, the paymaster, both of whom I had known and liked in pre-invasion days. Plautus was there, too, standing stiff against the wall, uncomfortable in the informal company of staff officers. It was gratifying to be so well remembered and so obviously welcome in their company, and I was relaxed as I spoke to them, telling them what I was doing now.

Cicero waited until I had finished and then spoke. "So you are here in Colchester, operating as a smith?" I heard the edge of incredulity in his voice, in spite of his well-bred attempt to disguise it.

"Aye, Legate, that is correct."

"Amazing. What do you do, exactly?"

I looked at each of them and then stood up. "Let me show you." I unbuckled the belt from my waist and laid it, with the short-sword and dagger it held, on his table. "A sample of my work." They all leaned forward as Cicero drew the sword and examined it closely.

"You made this?"

"Aye, and the dagger and scabbards. It's a matched set."

"Yes, I can see that." His voice tailed away, then, "These are very fine, very fine." He was at a loss for words, unsure of my purpose, and he feared he might offend me. I waited as he passed the sword to Trifax, the armourer, and the dagger to Lucullus. "Let me understand this, Varrus. Are you offering these for sale?"

I grinned at him. "I am. These, and as many others as I can get orders for. That is my business."

Poor Cicero was out of his aristocratic depth. He looked at Trifax. "What do you think, Trifax?"

Trifax was as blunt as a rusty dagger. "Don't have to think, General. This sword is flawless. If I could get my own people to turn these out, I'd be a happy man. But I can't. I'll buy as many of these as I can requisition. Lucullus?"

The paymaster shrugged his patrician shoulders. "I only pay the money. I'll take your word on the quality, although for once I can see it for myself." He looked at me. "Quality taken for granted, Publius, what about quantity? Can you produce enough of these to justify the paperwork?"

"If you want a hundred a day, starting tomorrow, no, I can't. If, on the other hand, your expectations are reasonable and your settlement of accounts prompt, I'll keep you supplied with weapons of that quality."

"Be specific. As you are set up now, how many of these could you turn out in a week?"

"Right now, two a day. Within a month, eight a day. I can expand to meet your needs with no loss in quality if, as I say, you pay me promptly. Expansion costs money."

He nodded. "We pay promptly. What about the smiths' guild? You have their approval?"

"For what? I belong to no guild."

"Oh! I see. That could be awkward."

I frowned. "How? I don't see what you mean."

He cleared his throat. "The law, Publius. We are required by law to deal only with civil suppliers who are in good standing with their guilds."

"Horse turds for that!" I stood up, sudden anger welling in my throat. "You must excuse me, gentlemen. I seem to have been wasting your time. I belong to no guild, as I have said. Nor did my grandfather. I didn't need the approval of the smiths' guild to lay my balls on the line for the Empire and I'll be damned if I'll ask their approval to earn my bread."

"Sit down, Publius." Cicero's voice was bland. He spoke directly to his paymaster. "Are you serious? You mean we cannot buy Varrus's swords because he does not belong to some ridiculous civilian tradesmen's organization?"

Lucullus cleared his throat again. "That is the law, General."

"How do we get around it?"

"We cannot, General."

"And horse turds for that, too!" The profanity sounded strange, uttered in Cicero's cultured tones. "I want Varrus's swords for my men. Are you telling me I cannot have them?"

Poor Lucullus was looking very uncomfortable. "No, General, not I. All such contracts have to be arranged through the office of the Procurator."

"Ahh! The office of the Procurator. I begin to see. No

doubt the Procurator's 'department' gains a commission on the services involved?"

A short pause, then, "Yes, General."

"How much?"

"Ten to fifteen percent, depending on the size of the contract."

"Blatant theft." Cicero turned to me. "Publius, if our excellent Lucullus here can find a way around this nonsense, legally of course, would you be prepared to surrender the required *per centum* 'tax' to the Procurator?"

I was smiling now. "Of course, General. I'd be happy to." Particularly since we had not yet negotiated my price, which I had just raised by 20 percent.

"Excellent! Lucullus, can that be arranged?"

Lucullus was no fool; he looked at me and smiled a tiny smile. "I'm sure it can, General."

"Wonderful. By the way, Lucullus, that reminds me. When must we submit our budget to the Procurator?"

"Next month, General." His expression tacitly added, "As you well know."

"Well, Publius Varrus, it's good to know we will be well armed and well supplied in future. A jug of wine would be appropriate now, I believe."

My feet hardly touched the ground on the way home that night, and within the month we had an iron-bound contract to supply arms to the local garrison.

VII

It was on Midsummer's Day that I finally allowed myself to open my grandfather's treasures and gloat over them. I had waited, month after impatient month, until I felt that I had earned myself the reward of spending time to examine these wonders that were now legally and rightfully mine.

From the way I have been speaking of treasures, anyone reading this will probably have imagined a hoard of coins and jewels. That is not quite correct. My grandfather had been an armourer — a master sword-maker and also an earnest historian and student of weapons and weaponry. During his early years with the legions, he had picked up several assorted examples of the armourer's craft and the metalsmith's art that had caused him excitement and given him great pleasure. In later years, while he served as armourer to the various legions stationed in Britain, he had encouraged legionaries to pick up other examples for him. The end result of forty years of this was a collection of antique and esoteric weapons the like of which existed nowhere else that I knew of. These were my grandfather's treasures, each individually wrapped in protective cloth and many stored in cases that he had made specifically to house them. Every piece was accompanied by a scroll outlining the history of the item as far as it was known by the old man. Where the history of the piece was obscure, he consulted all available sources and made some very shrewd guesses.

Some of the shapes I remembered from boyhood, and I felt like a boy again as I opened them one by one. There was one particular piece that chilled me to my bones with awe. It was a face-protector of dull, black iron, shaped to fit the forehead and muzzle of a horse, with flared eye-protectors. It had been crudely decorated with a drawing of a mounted man charging with a long, heavy spear balanced over his shoulder, and beneath the drawing, the Greek word meaning "companions." The lover of history in me had to swallow hard as I looked at this piece of armour, because I knew it had protected one of the horses of the Companions, the hand-picked friends of the King, who had ridden into battle at the side of Philip of Macedon and later with his son the great Alexander, fully seven hundred years before I had been born. The Companions! How often had I dreamed of them as a boy, imagining myself winning glory under the greatest military commander of ancient times.

To keep company with the faceplate, there was the badly rusted remnant of a *sarissa*, the sixteen-foot-long spear carried by the Macedonian cavalry. It had a long cross-piece attached below the blade, presumably to stop the entire spear from going through the body of whoever was skewered, and to give the rider at least a chance of pulling it out again as he galloped past his victim. My grandfather had really studied this weapon in his youth. Like the one in the drawing on the horse's faceplate, the *sarissa* was carried point down, the shaft over the rider's shoulder, and was used with a downward thrust. It was originally left in the body of the first victim, and the rest of the fighting was done with swords. The victorious cavalry — Alexander's cavalry were always victorious — would return later to collect their *sarissas* from the bodies of the men they had slain in their charge. The crosspiece, added later, meant they then had a chance of retaining the spear for a second victim.

In a large, long case that I remembered well, there was a collection of original Roman *pila*, the fighting spears of the ancient legions. Seven feet long, the shaft of these original spears was of wood for half its length, the other half being a metal rod with a wicked head. Embedded in an enemy's shield, the rod, of soft iron, would bend, and the cumbersome weight of the thing dragged at the shield until it became useless to the man trying to shelter behind it.

Another carefully wrapped package contained the great African bow that I had marvelled over as a child. It was composed of alternating layers of wood, animal horn and sinew, and it was truly a mighty weapon the like of which had never been seen in this part of the world. I laid it aside for closer examination later.

There were several items that I had never seen before, and a parchment wrapped in deerskin, addressed to me with the instruction that I should read it carefully at my leisure and study the contents and methods described in it. Intrigued, I laid this package, too, carefully aside. A second, new-looking package contained a magnificent shirt of soft leather, onto which had been stitched, with the most astonishing precision, thousands of tiny metal rings in overlapping rows, in the fashion of our own Roman plate armour, but in a form much lighter and far more supple. The accompanying note said that it had been brought back from the country north of the Danube and was the kind of armour being worn now by many of the Germanic and Saxon chiefs.

The last package was a magnificent box of rich, oiled wood no more than a foot long by a hand's breadth wide by about half of that in depth. At first I could not even find out how it opened, but eventually I discovered that the top and bottom had been carved to fit one over the other into matching grooves. I knew this package was special, from the way it had been hidden away at the back of the hoard. I was trembling slightly in anticipation as I opened it, but I almost dropped it when I saw what it contained. It was a knife. A dagger. But such a dagger! The blade shone like polished silver, and in fact I took it to be that at first; the hilt looked to be of polished gold. The entire weapon was covered with a slight sheen of oil.

I picked it up reverently. It felt alive in my hand. I tested the blade with the ball of my thumb and drew blood! Gaping at the blood in amazement, for I had barely used any pressure, I carried the knife upstairs and out into the sunlight, where it blazed in my hand like a torch. I heard footsteps behind me and Equus stood by my side.

"I see you found it. I've been dying of impatience! Thought you'd never go down there. Boudicca's buttocks, man, sometimes I think you're not human! How could you not go down there for all this time?"

I didn't even bother to answer him. I was too busy staring at the wonder in my hand.

"He was sorry it couldn't be a sword, but that was all of the skystone metal he had left, and he didn't want to pollute it with ordinary iron the way he did with the sword he made for your father. He didn't know what it was, but whatever it was, he thought it was fitting that it fell from heaven. It holds an edge like nothing in this world. It'll shave the hairs off your arm. Try it."

I did, and the tiny hairs of the back of my wrist gathered in a small clump on the edge of the blade.

"Have you ever seen the like?"

I simply shook my head, hefting the knife in my hand. It had an unusual hilt, slightly cruciform, the arms of which protruded for about an inch above and below the blade.

"Why the cross-piece?"

"Extra weight. And balance. You can throw it. It flies as though it had wings, like magic."

"Is the handle solid gold?"

Equus shook his head. "No. Gold-dipped, though. Underneath it's brass. Gold was too heavy. And too soft."

"And too expensive. It looks like one piece — the hilt, I mean. How did he make it?"

"He poured it." Equus grinned at my wide-eyed look. "Did you find the scroll he left for you? It's all in there. The old man thought it was an entirely new technique, revolutionary, he said, if it's properly used."

"How did he get this finish on the blade, Equus?"

He shrugged his massive shoulders. "He didn't. It was there already. All we had to do was polish it . . . and polish it and polish it and polish it. But it was worth it. And the brighter it got, the easier it became to polish. We put the oil on it to protect it against rust, although we didn't know whether or not the skystone rusted. Better to be safe than angry."

I held the beautiful thing up to my eyes. At the top of the blade, just below the cross hilt, my grandfather had inscribed a tiny "V" for his name and mine: Varrus. I felt a lump swell in my throat and swallowed hard.

"Equus, I'm going to take the scroll, and this, and go home. Will you see to shutting everything up?"

He grinned again. "Thought you might do that. Of course I will. Go home. Go!"

VIII

"How bad was that wound of yours?"

Plautus and I were sitting in one of the local taverns frequented by the garrison centurions, waiting for Equus to come and join us and watching the antics of some of the other customers in the place. His question was unexpected.

"Bad enough. Why d'you ask?"

"Just curious. I was watching the slut with the big tits across there, and something about her reminded me of the bitch who used to run that big old brothel, over in Alexandria. You know the one I mean. The big one."

"The big brothel, or the big bitch?"

He laughed. "Both."

"You mean Fatia?"

"That's the one! Fatia. What a whore that one was. She could suck the pommel off a sword! Hello! What's going on over there?"

I turned to look at the commotion that had erupted in the back of the tavern. Somebody had been caught cheating at dice and there were naked blades being waved around. The quarrellers were civilians, however, so Plautus had no need to get involved. We were too far away from them to see any of the details, but a sudden scuffle and a scream told us that blood had been spilled before the tavern owner and his enforcers could reach the scene. They were there within seconds, however, restoring order with heavy hands and clubs.

Plautus sat back in his seat. "God-cursed civilians, they make me sick. Not a one of them fit for military service, but they cause more trouble in one night in this place than all the old sweats who come in here. If the place was mine I'd declare it off-limits to all civilians."

"That's nice. Then I wouldn't be able to come here."

Our beer was gone, and I signalled to the serving girl to bring us more. We both watched her in silence as she swung her fleshy body towards us, slopping ale from the jugs she held in one big hand. As she leaned over the table I could smell her — warm and sweaty and slightly sour. She leered at Plautus and he reached to tweak one of her prominent nipples as she laughed and swung away.

"She stinks like a goat," I said. "What is it about her that reminded you of Fatia? At least Fatia was clean."

"Aye, clean, but voracious. What a mouth!" He shook his head in nostalgic wonder. "What a mouth that bitch had."

"Plautus, are you drunk?"

He blinked at me. "No more than usual at this time of night. Why? Are you?"

"I don't think so, but you're not making sense. You asked me about my leg and then started prattling about Fatia. I don't see the connection."

He hitched himself around in his seat and looked me straight in the eye. "You used to be a bigger whore-chaser than I was. You introduced me to Fatia's place, remember? Now we've been back together again for, what? Two months? I haven't seen you as much as look at a woman in all that time. It just occurred to me that you might . . ." His voice faded. "You know . . ." I stared at him in amused surprise. He was embarrassed! "Your wound — I thought perhaps . . . damnation, I think I *am* drunk."

I smiled gently. "I've still got all my equipment, if that's what you're getting at. It was a close thing, though. Missed by an inch."

"An axe, you said?" He looked fascinated.

"Aye, with a spike on the back. It was the spike that got me. The whoreson swung it underhand, up into my crotch."

"Aiee!" His face puckered up in sympathy and horror at the image. "It hurts just to think about it."

"You should try it from where I sit. I still wake up at night in a cold sweat, dreaming about it."

He shuddered, but he couldn't leave it alone. "You didn't lose anything?"

I smiled at the worry on his face. "I told you, no. Apart from the ability to walk straight. Everything's still there, and it all works. I pump myself dry regularly in my sleep, so I know. But otherwise . . ." I sighed, resigned to telling him, but looking around first to be sure nobody else was listening. "I don't know, Plautus. It just doesn't seem to work while I'm awake. I can't get it up. I don't even have the urge anymore. I haven't had a woman since it happened, and that's been over a year now."

"Have you tried?"

I laughed, a short, bitter laugh. "No, I can't really say I have. As I said, I've lost the urge."

"Maybe if you bought a whore you'd be all right? I mean, if it works for you in dreams it should work when you're awake, too, shouldn't it? I mean, if you get the urge when you're sleeping, you must be able to get it at other times."

I nodded my head slightly. "You'd think so, but it doesn't seem to work that way."

"'A'ssamazing," he slurred. He was definitely getting drunk. "That's . . . amazing. A shame, too. I think we'd better get you fixed up, Publius."

"Perhaps. But not tonight, Plautus."

"No. Not tonight. Too late. What's the time?"

"Almost curfew."

"Time I was getting back. Wonder what happened to Equus?"

"Oh, he'll get here, sooner or later. You'd better go. I see your friends over there getting ready to leave. I'll sit here and have another beer and wait for him."

"Isn't this ridiculous? A man my age having to be back in bed by midnight?"

"That's the army, Plautus. If I hadn't shown up back here in town, you'd stay in the barracks every night."

"That's true. It's a good life. Well, I'd better get going." He stood up, swaying slightly, and grinned down at me. "Tell Equus he's a pissy-arsed civilian with a pissy-arsed civilian's bad manners, breaking an appointment with a *primus pilus*. Good night, my friend. Don't worry about your cock. We'll get it fixed up. Just you leave it to old Plautus."

I bowed, still sitting. "I'll be glad to. When I die, it's yours."

He blinked again, missing the comment completely, and threw me a salute. I sat there smiling, watching him leave with three other centurions, who waved to me as they went out.

I had another beer, wondering what was keeping Equus. He should have been there an hour before at least. Two beers later there was still no sign of him, and I was surrounded by an evil-smelling crowd of late-arriving revellers. My gorge rose at the stench of them. Being a Roman has its disadvantages at times, and the constant expectation of cleanliness is one of them. I left my drink unfinished on the table and made my way unsteadily to the door, where the cool night air revived me enough to let me get my bearings, and I set out to walk home.

I was drunker than I had thought, and it proved to be a long, weary walk, on a night that was unseasonably cold for the time of year. My route took me past the smithy, and I told myself, on a drink-inspired impulse, that Equus was probably in there, working late. In fact, it was long past midnight, and it was no more than maudlin, drunken sentimentality that took me in to the smithy's womb-like warmth instead of to my bed. I found the key under its stone, easily enough, but it took a lot of fumbling in the dark before I could insert it in the padlock.

As soon as I entered the smithy, however, locking the door conscientiously behind me, I knew someone was there. A lamp burned on one of the benches, and there was a feeling of presence in the place.

"Equus? Are you here?"

There was no response, and yet I knew I was not alone. I am not a superstitious man, but the smithy was obviously empty, and when I realized that I had had to unlock the door to let myself in, I felt the tiny hairs stirring on the back of my neck. I crossed to the lamp, peering around me into the shadows as I went, but saw nothing to alarm me. And then, as I picked up the lamp, I saw a disembodied face staring at me with enormous eyes from the floor in the corner by the forge. I leaped with fright and almost dropped the lamp, but even as I reacted I recognized Phoebe. She was lying on the floor, wrapped in a dark blanket that blended with the heavy shadows in the corner.

"Phoebe," I said, trying to disguise the fright she had caused me, "what in the name of all the gods are you doing here? And at this time of night?"

To my horror, she started to weep, placing me immediately at a disadvantage. I stood there mute, gazing at her in consternation as her sobs grew and expanded to fill the whole room. I can handle most situations, but the tears of women have always left me helpless. I could do no more than wait until she settled down, which she eventually did, and then, amid a succession of sighs and choking sobs, her story came out.

Cuno had been drinking again. A four-day bacchanalia had ended in a rampage of violence during which he had tried to kill her. She had escaped from him and run here to Equus for protection, and Equus had calmed her, given her some blankets, locked her inside the smithy for safety and gone looking for Cuno. She had cried herself to sleep and had not been aware of my entrance until I spoke, startling and frightening her.

Somehow, during the telling of her story, I found myself seated on the floor beside her, comforting her with an arm around her shoulders as she whispered her tale, with bent head, into the region of my armpit. Had I been sober, I would have been upset by her story. As it was, I listened with no great feeling of shock until she had finished, when I said "Hmmm," or something equally intelligent.

Her sobs were growing less frequent now, and it seemed natural to remain where I was until she grew completely calm. I was staring like an owl at the crown of her head, seeing the white scalp beneath her hair, when I became aware that she was no longer sobbing, no longer moving. I felt my eyelids starting to droop and blinked them rapidly, holding them wide open by an effort of will. I was feeling extremely comfortable there, with the hard wall at my back and the hard floor beneath my buttocks and the soft warmth of Phoebe's body against my chest. She straightened slightly beneath my arm, raising her head to look into my face, and her voice was a gentle breath in my ear.

"Can I stay, then?"

Could she stay? Of course she could stay. I had not raised my head with hers, and I now found myself looking down the bodice of her smock, imagining the warmth emanating from the full, heavy white breasts that nestled there, soft and vulnerable, exposed to my eyes. Suddenly, with no warning, the hand that had rested so casually across her neck, cupping her shoulder, let my mind know that it was full of female flesh. Shoulder flesh, certainly, but that was just a start, for I knew, equally suddenly, that I could have her, there and then. She was spurned and beaten, vulnerable and available, and she would even be grateful. The knowledge frightened me back to awareness of who and where I was. I withdrew my arm guiltily and sat up straight.

"Stay here? Of course you can stay here." I heard the bluster in my own voice. "Equus will be back soon, or he may have finished with Cuno already and be waiting until morning to let you get some rest. You just settle down there, and get back to sleep. You'll see, everything will be fine, come morning." I was struggling to get back up to my feet, but my traitorous, crippled leg was betraying me. I had no feeling in it at all. I threw both arms out against the wall behind me for support and levered uselessly with my sound leg.

"What's the matter? Can't you get up?"

"My leg. The bad one. It seems to be asleep. No feeling in it."

"Here, let me help you." In a second she was up, out of her blankets and pulling me upright. She was a big girl, and I was grateful for her strength. Erect, I let go of her hands and reached behind me again for the wall's support, feeling myself sway slightly.

"Thank you, Phoebe. It'll be all right now. Get back into your blanket. It's cold."

"No it's not. It's warm in here. Are you sure you're all right?"

"Yes, fine. My leg just goes strange from time to time, if I sit the wrong way. It sort of stiffens up."

"Does it hurt much?"

"Not usually."

"Now?"

"No, not now. It's just numb."

"Can you walk on it?"

"I will in a minute, when the feeling comes back into it."

"That's happened to me a couple of times. It's a strange feeling. Like being pricked all over with needles."

She was standing close, watching my face with a peculiar expression, her arms folded beneath her breasts so that they swelled up visibly in the scoop of her neckline.

I looked away. "There," I said. "That's better." I bent my knee and flexed it and then stepped away from the wall and fell sideways. She caught me in her strong arms, my face against her breasts, and hauled me upright again, leaning me back against the wall, where I remained, feeling weak and foolish and remarkably sober all at once.

"It's not better at all, is it?"

"No." I shook my head, smiling foolishly. "Not yet." But then it started to get "better," and the sudden, brutal, unexpected ferocity of it made me suck in my breath with a hiss as the torn muscles in my thigh knotted and cramped and I felt myself falling again. She took my whole weight in her arms and half carried, half dragged me to the only chair in the room, into which she dumped me unceremoniously. I was beside myself with pain far worse than any I had felt before. My entire leg, from the buttock down, was a howling, twisted knot of agony. Through the fog of it I heard her voice, urgent and demanding, hissing in my ear. "Stop writhing, or I can't help you! Lift up! Up! Stay still, damn you!" And then, eventually and gradually, over the space of what seemed like uncountable aeons of time, the awful, dementing pain began to recede, displaced by a firm, rhythmic, soothing motion and the kneading of strong fingers that worked on the muscles of my leg, relaxing them, easing the tightness out of them and gentling their spastic tremors until they disappeared altogether. I opened my eyes, conscious of sweat drying on my skin.

I was lying on the floor of the smithy, beside the overturned chair Phoebe had thrown me into. I had no remembrance of falling. Phoebe knelt above me, straddling my bad leg, her hair hanging down over her face as she concentrated on the action of her hands on my thigh muscles. I could feel a sensation that was unusual, pleasant, somehow familiar, yet unplaceable. And then I recognized it. It was the cushioned warmth of naked thighs around my bare foot. I froze with shock. She felt me stiffen and knelt back on her haunches to look at me, pulling the hair back out of her eyes with one hand. The movement brought the astounding heat of her centre down on my toes, but she seemed unaware of it.

"Bad," she said. "That was bad. Does that happen often?"

I shook my head, mute, my thoughts fastened on what my foot was feeling, wondering how this had happened. She kept her eyes on mine, her face full of concern.

"Does it feel better now? Still hurt?"

I shook my head again and swallowed, clearing my throat. "No," I whispered. "Thank you."

"I'm glad I could help. I had to do something. I thought for a while there you were going to die."

"Was I that bad? I don't remember."

"Be grateful, then. You were out of your head with pain. Look, where you gripped me." She showed me her right arm, ringed with the inflamed marks of my fingers. "You're a strong man, even for a smith."

"Did I do that? Really?" My throat was parched and sore. "I'm sorry. I don't remember."

"I know. I told you, you were out of your head for a while. I had to hit you over the head. Does it hurt?"

"No. Where?"

"There." She touched the side of my head and suddenly, where she touched, there was pain. It hurt, but nowhere near as badly as the cramps in my leg had hurt.

This pain was no more than a mild annoyance. I touched the spot, cautiously, and felt a huge lump.

"What did you hit me with?"

"A piece of wood."

She dropped her head and I felt her fingers begin to knead again. She leaned forward to get more purchase, tightening her knee grip on my leg and lifting her body clear of my foot, so that I felt relatively cold air on my toes. Her thumbs dug deep and I flinched.

"Ow! Where did you learn to do that?"

She looked up at me again, her fingers and thumbs still busy. "I'm a masseuse, or used to be before I got married. I worked in the women's bath house, by the main barracks. Officers' wives, mainly."

"You speak very well." I realized what I had said, the arrogance of it. "I mean . . ."

"I know what you mean, but thank you. Yes, I speak well. I had a tutor. Paid for him myself, out of my earnings at the bath house. I decided there was no use remaining illiterate."

"Illiterate?"

"Yes. I can read and write, too. Why not? It hasn't done me any harm. Any good either, for that matter."

"I see." I was longing to bend my leg, to bring my foot against the heat of her again. She dropped her head back to her work, and I realized that her face, which I had always thought plain and uninteresting, was anything but. I searched for a question to make her look up again.

"Does Cuno read and write, too?"

That did the trick. "My husband? Cunobelin? The descendant of kings? Hah! He can hardly even talk. Prefers to drink, and beat me."

"Then why do you stay with him? Leave him."

"Leave him?" Her voice had scorn in it. "That's easy to say." She dropped her head again, her fingers working swiftly, with agitation, moving up my thigh, so that she had to move forward on her knees, gripping my thigh tightly between her own knees to hold it steady. "Run from the brute. Where would I run? And to do what? Where?"

I gasped again as she found a knot. "Do what you're trained to do. Anywhere. There are other towns. Go to Londinium. You're a masseuse. You'll find a use for your skills there. He wouldn't follow you. You have no children, have you?"

Her fingers stopped kneading. "No. I have no children." She settled back again, bringing the fire of her centre onto my leg once more, but differently this time, so that my bent knee fitted wholly into the softness she had there. I saw the startled widening of her eyes as she realized the immodesty of the physical contact. Her withdrawal was instinctive and would have been total had I not stopped her with an involuntary "Don't!" She froze.

"Don't what?"

"Don't stop. Not yet. There's still some soreness there."

"Where?"

"There, in my thigh. A tightness. Lower down, just above the knee."

Even in the dimness of the single lamp's light, I saw a flush steal up over her neck. She had been in the act of jumping up, and one of her legs was no longer touching mine. Slowly, kneeling still, she moved backwards, the sides of her knees sliding down my leg, and I felt her skirts tugging at my toes and then the gathering of her front hem as she pulled it down along my leg. Her fingertips clasped me lightly, probing above my knee.

"Where is this tightness?"

There was a different quality to her voice, now. A huskiness — almost a whisper. I raised myself up on my elbows and saw that my legs were bare, my tunic pulled down decently to cover my sex. Her skirts were rucked, baring her white, round knees on either side of mine.

"There," I said. "Where your thumbs are." She dug deep, and I gasped.

"Lie back. Here." She reached for my discarded breeches and wadded them into a ball. "Put this below your head."

I did as she told me, my thoughts in confusion. I wanted this to go on, far more than I wanted it to stop, and yet I was afraid. I should have been aroused, rampant, with what was going through my head and the tension in my guts, but my manhood lay still and flaccid. Her fingers probed again, deep into the muscles above my knee. There was no tightness there, but the sensation was pleasurable and I was, after all the pain, still a little drunk.

She spoke again in that same husky whisper. "Relax your leg. Let it relax completely." I tried. "Can you straighten it at all?"

I shook my head. "No. The hamstring was damaged. It shrank. I can't extend it fully."

"Can you flex it? Bend it? Try."

I bent it slowly, further than I had intended to, until I felt the back of her skirts fall from my toes, leaving my foot free within the tent of her clothing. I could feel a pulse beating in my neck.

"That's good. Now straighten it again."

I did, feeling the sole of my foot against the rough material of the inside of her skirts. Was she aware? If she was, she gave no sign. She was breathing deeply, causing her breasts to show against her bodice.

"Now," she said, and went to work in earnest, gouging and digging, kneading and squeezing, at one point moving slightly backwards again so that again I felt the heat of her, but not direct contact, and the sensitive skin of my foot felt a hint of tickling, wiry hair.

I lay and luxuriated in the sensations she produced in me until she stopped suddenly.

"That's enough! I'm getting tired. I have to get up."

"No. Please don't."

She sighed. "What do you want of me, Master Varrus? It isn't lust. You show me no desire."

"I'd like to, Phoebe, but I can't. Yet I enjoy your warmth. Your touch."

"Can't?" She paused for what seemed to me a long time, then, "Is it your wound? These scars? Did they unman you?" There was only tenderness in her voice.

"Aye. It seems they did, in some ways at least."

She sighed again. "Poor man." Her hands resumed their movement on my thigh, but now it was her palms that caressed me, and after a few minutes she sank down again onto her haunches, this time open and quite deliberate in laying her vulva, scalding hot and bare, against my foot.

I felt no shame, only contentment and acceptance as her hands moved up my thigh and into the join of my belly. Her fingers moved to brush my flaccid sex, but then I stirred my foot against her nakedness, feeling its yielding softness, and she bore down against it, moving herself against the boniness of my arch. She leaned forward slowly and laid her face in the junction of my thigh and belly; the warmth of her breath tickled me as she continued to rub herself slowly against my foot, one hand cupping my buttock and the other my sex. I laid my hand on the smooth nape of her neck and my foot felt the moisture of her readiness. Then, suddenly, there came a stirring of desire in my own loins. I held my breath, not daring to move, and felt myself stirring to life in her gentle grasp. And as I grew and grew, she stopped her movements and stared in silence at the sight before her eyes, and then she said, "Oh, you beautiful liar," and moved quickly to straddle me and slowly to impale herself on the new-born miracle she had achieved.

That was a grand and passionate coupling, the like of which I have never again experienced. I felt as the blind man cured by the Lord Jesus must have felt, and the ecstasy of my release was indescribable, enhanced as it was by the regaining of what had been lost to me. Useless to try to describe the thoughts and sensations that transported me. It was as though a dam had broken somewhere inside me, and the juices that swirled through the breach were almost inexhaustible. I was insatiable, rising time and again with almost no recovery time required. When Phoebe, hours later, whispered, "No more, no more. I hurt. I can't take any more," I believed her implicitly. We had moved back to her blankets by the forge, and it was almost dawn. I rolled away from her and got to my feet.

"Where are you going?"

I stooped and kissed her. "Home. Equus may come here any minute. But I'm coming back, don't worry."

I crossed to the quenching trough and splashed icy water over my face and head, drying myself with a rough towel that lay on the bench, and then began to struggle into my tunic. I didn't see her approach me until she spoke close by my ear, in a small voice.

"Master Varrus? Are you angry?"

I looked at her in amazement. "Angry? With you?" And then I saw the look in her eyes, the apprehension and the uncertainty, and I smiled at her and drew her into my arms, hugging her close and whispering into her ear. "My beautiful, beautiful Phoebe, how could I possibly be angry with you, ever? You have given me back my manhood. I had believed that I would never lie with a woman again. Never plough another furrow." I kissed her, feeling the cushioned softness of her love-swollen lips. "No, I'm not angry with you. Don't ever think I could be. But your brother will be here soon, and he might bring your husband with him. It would do you no good to be found here with me, so obviously sated. Would it?"

She was looking at me with narrowed eyes, gauging my truthfulness, and now she smiled, a wicked smile. "Sated? That's a word for people who know what it means. My husband would see nothing. He's never made me feel this way, so he wouldn't recognize my pleasure." Her hand fell to my crotch again, and she squeezed, gently. "I'm glad I helped him back to life. You be good to him, now that he's well again."

I grinned at her. "I will, Phoebe. I will." I squeezed her breast. "But you just finished telling me that you couldn't take any more, and now you're teasing him."

"Oh, I wouldn't want to tease him, he's too good for that."

She moved her belly against me, rising on tiptoe, and I pulled her against me, slipping easily up into the lubricated heat of her just as Equus came to the door of the smithy. We froze, not daring to move or make a sound, and I almost giggled, thinking how ludicrous we would look to Equus, standing there like a statue of fornicators. I heard him fumbling for the key, but I had brought it inside with me. Phoebe tried to pull away from me, but I gripped her buttocks tighter, holding her impaled, shaking my head. I leaned to her and whispered in her ear, "It's locked. I have the key. He can't get in." Her eyes grew round and we listened to Equus grumbling to himself. Then came his voice. "Phoebe? Phoebe, let me in. It's Equus!" I shook my head at her, warning her to make no sound. He called again a few times, and then cursed in disgust, and we heard his retreating footsteps as he went home to look for the key.

When he had gone, Phoebe giggled. "Poor Equus. He'll be so angry."

"Aye, and he'll soon be back. I have to go. But listen to me, now. I am going to bring you back a bag of money. Gold. Don't say anything!" She had been about to protest. "Just listen! It's a gift, from me to you. I have no need of it. You do. You have given me back a life I thought I had lost forever. I want to do the same for you. You understand? A life for a life. Use it to get out of here and away from that husband of yours. You deserve better. Equus will be here when I get back. When he comes, don't lie to him. Tell him I came looking for him last night and found you here, and that you told me what had happened. Then say no more. He would never think that I stayed. I'll hand you the money when he isn't looking.

Don't argue. Take it." I cocked my head, looking at her intently. "You will, won't you?"

She was staring at me with round eyes filled with tears. She nodded slowly, and then emphatically. "Yes. I will. And God bless you."

"He might, but I doubt it. You have. Let me know where you go to, will you? Perhaps we may see each other again." She nodded, tears spilling from her eyes. "Good," I said. "Now, where were we? I was enjoying that. I've never known a better cure for a thick head."

She smiled at me then, slowly and lazily, leaning back into my palms, and her hand reached down between us as she raised herself on her toes.

"I think," she whispered, grasping me gently, firmly, guiding, "if I remember it all correctly," a pause, intense with concentration; delightful, tactile movement, probing and positioning, ". . . that you were just . . ." minor, maddening adjustments, ". . . about . . ." a long, slow, scalding slide, ". . . there!"

I returned within the hour with the money for her flight, as I had promised, and managed to transfer it to her without Equus being any the wiser. The man was distracted, having spent the main part of the night searching fruitlessly for Cuno, the delinquent husband. But Cuno, apparently, had not been too drunk to remember what Equus had sworn to do to him if he ever maltreated Phoebe again. He had vanished for good, and he never did return to Colchester. We presumed that he had fled to escape Equus, but were unable to prove anything, and no one was inclined to dedicate valuable time to searching for the fellow.

Phoebe departed, too, within the week, leaving a letter for her brother explaining why she had gone, but making no mention of her destination other than that she would send him a message to let him know that she was well once she had settled in her new life. She spent the night before her departure with me, and wrote me thereafter several times from Verulamium, where she had settled. Equus was upset by her departure, at first, but he settled down once he had heard from her and knew that she was well. He never suspected my complicity in her flight.

I X

It was a blazing hot day in midsummer and I was unhappy, cooped up in the darkness of the smithy doing last-minute work on a neglected order of pike-heads for the German mercenaries of the local garrison. It was a consignment that had given place to other priorities and now required emergency attention. The inside of the smithy seemed as black as the pit, although the truth was that I was simply feeling lazy, having no stomach for work that day. I finished hammering a cooling pike-head and plunged it into the quenching trough, looking through the cloud of steam towards the doorway as I did so, and there sat Britannicus, high on a magnificent white horse, his full-dress uniform a glory of scarlet, white and gold. I dropped tongs and hammer and ran as fast as my bad leg would allow me to the doorway, where I stopped, suddenly overcome with shyness.

He looked at me sardonically, his eyes taking in my beard, my sooty face and arms, and my leather apron.

"By the divine Augustus! Vulcan in person! Tell me, fellow. I'm looking for a friend of mine, probably your owner. Varrus the Roman. Where will I find him?"

"Vulcan was lame from birth," I said. "I got my limp just recently, wasting my time in trying to help out an ungrateful colleague."

His face broke into a great grin. Then he swung his leg over his horse's back and slid to the ground, his arms open, with the apparent intent of throwing them around me. I jumped away in horror. One touch of me and my soot would ruin that dress tunic forever. I held up my hand to keep him off.

"For the love of God, General, don't touch me! You'll never get clean!"

He stopped just in time and stood, looking me up and down, still smiling widely. "You may be right, old friend, you may be right. You do look rather . . . sooty. But at least I can take your hand!"

We shook, as Romans do, arm to arm, looking each other over in delight. It had been almost two years since we had parted company. He looked in top fighting condition, even though he must now have been forty-one years old. He was lean and bronzed and strong-looking. His scarlet cape and plume and his gold helmet and armour made the rich white wool of his military tunic look like damask.

"What brings you to Colchester, General? And why so formally dressed? You are a sight for sore eyes. You look marvellous!"

"Thank you, Varrus, so do you. But Colchester? I thought I was in Camulodunum."

I grinned at him, having forgotten the archaic compunction that made him insist on calling every place in Britain by its original Roman name, rather than by the Celticized names used by the people.

"How are you, Varrus? Is life dealing well with you? Are you happy?"

"What's happiness, General? I have a good life and a

place to live and a place to work. I'm content. What more could a man want?"

"How's the leg?"

"It's fine." I glanced down at it. "It'll never be straight again, and it aches in the winter, but I can walk on it, as you can see."

"Excellent!" He glanced around the yard. "Do you have a jug of wine to offer a thirsty man?"

"No, but I have something better." I looked back into the darkness of the smithy. "Equus! Come out here. I want you to meet someone."

Equus came out into the sunlight, wiping his hands against his tunic. I introduced him to Britannicus as my partner and asked him to pour us some of his home-brewed ale. There was a bench in the yard; as we made ourselves comfortable on it, Equus went to get us a drink.

"You didn't answer my question, Commander. What's the occasion for the finery?" I nodded at his uniform and he shrugged disparagingly.

"It seems that all of Britain is fully at peace. I am on my way to Verulamium with Theodosius. Tonight we dine with Antonius Cicero and the garrison here. We arrived this morning and held a full-dress review of the troops at noon. I came directly here after the ceremonies."

"Ah, so that's what all the commotion was about! I heard the trumpets, but I was busy and didn't pay much attention. I knew if it was important Plautus would tell me about it soon enough. Will you be staying in town tonight?"

"Yes. And leaving tomorrow at first light. I came to invite you to dine with me tonight at the fort. Will you come? You know several of the officers."

I blinked in surprise. It would be a formal officers' dinner. I reviewed my entire wardrobe in half a second. I had nothing suitable for a banquet.

"Can't, Commander," I said. "Sorry, but I've got nothing even remotely suitable to wear to an affair like that. I've bought no new clothes — no stylish ones, at any rate — since I came here. I have no need of them, normally."

He shook his head. "Not good enough. Too easily remedied and too weak as an excuse. Not acceptable at all. I'll have my man supply you with some of my clothes. They will fit, and I have far too many for my own needs. We'll bathe together in the evening and see if the army masseurs can get the soot out of your pores with steam, water, perfumed oils and muscle. You must stink like a goat!"

I laughed aloud. "Commander, the dirt's no more than a disguise. I do bathe, from time to time."

"Thank God for that!"

He had removed his helmet when he sat down, and now he unhooked the fastening of his military cloak, allowing it to fall unheeded behind him as Equus arrived, carrying two enormous flagons of the cold beer he brewed in his own home. We always kept a cask of it down in the coolness of the cellar and it slaked a thirst in a way no other beverage could. Britannicus accepted his with a smile of thanks and put it straight to his lips. Equus stood and watched him drink deeply for a few seconds and then turned and left us.

After what seemed like minutes, Britannicus stopped drinking and wiped his lips with his forearm, breathing deeply.

"This stuff is delicious, Varrus! Did Equus . . . Equus?

Is that his real name?"

"It's what he's called. I don't think even he knows his real name. He forgot it years ago."

"Did he make this?"

"Yes, Commander. He's very proud of his ale."

"He should be." He drank again, then, "How many slaves do you have working for you, Varrus?"

It was my turn to shake my head. "None, Commander, as you well know. Slavery is non-productive."

He smiled gently. "Ah, yes, I remember your personal heresy. Slavery built the Empire, Varrus."

"That's horse turds, Commander, and you know it. The free farmers and the citizens of Rome itself built the Republic, and the Republic became the Empire, and slavery finished both of them."

Now he was grinning hugely. "That's treason, Varrus. Valentinian would have your tongue cut out for voicing such thoughts. How can you deny the benefits of slavery?"

"Same way I did the last time you brought it up. It's plain common sense. What I find surprising is that any man with a brain in his head can defend it."

Britannicus stood up and walked away to look at the riot of hollyhocks growing wild in the corner of the yard. He stood there for several moments, deep in thought. I spoke to his back.

"I know you agree with what I'm saying, in principle. I've heard you say so. I'm not stupid enough to think that all slaves should be freed, or could be. But I really believe that depriving a man of his humanity is a certain way to deny anyone, including him, the benefit of his living. A slave has no incentive to improve. That's why there were never any slaves in the legions. Go back to the days of the Republic, when Rome was the strongest it has ever been. All the best ideas, the finest decisions, the greatest steps forward in knowledge, in strategy, in deployment, in whatever you want, were developed and put into place by free men. None of them came from slaves. Not one. That's all I'm saying. I don't care if other people have slaves. My point is that any man who works for me or with me will better his own life and the conditions of his life by doing so. I'll make it worth his while to do the best he's capable of."

He had turned around and was looking at me. "What about the Greek city states?"

"What about them, Commander? We've been through this before. They prove my point."

"Not so, Varrus. In Athens, a slave state, the human mind was lifted to its greatest achievements ever."

"Aye, and they still died out! They had to! Commander, how can you be a Christian and believe that God made man in his own image, and still maintain that any man has the right to own any other man?"

"Religious philosophy? From you, Varrus?" He was smiling again.

"That's not philosophy!" I felt the blood rising to my face. "That stuff's too deep for me. The democracy of Athens was built on a basic fault: only citizens were allowed to think, and only slaves were allowed to work. The slaves had no life at all to speak of, but they were expected to produce everything the parasitic thinkers needed to live on. It was bound to fail. It bred hatred on the one hand and laziness on the other."

Britannicus crossed back to the bench and picked up his flagon, and I saw another illustration of my point.

"That ale you're drinking — where do you think it came from?"

His eyebrow went up again. "You told me. Equus brewed it."

"He did, but out of what?" I read the amusement in his eyes. "We know a farmer, General, who supplies us with the materials from which Equus makes his beer. Equus supplies me with his beer because I supply him with the workshop to make the nails and the tools with which he pays the farmer for his crop. If the farmer stops growing his crops, or if I deprive Equus of his workplace, or if he stops making his nails and tools, that chain will break down. The farmer will go somewhere else for his goods, or Equus will seek another farmer to supply him with hops. In the meantime, I'll have no ale. Somebody loses."

He smiled and half nodded, his eyebrow arched in what I took to be derision, but I carried on.

"It may seem like a contrived example, but it's not. It's not. It's simple and real, like life. There has to be something produced before anyone can consume it, and I believe no man has a right to live if he does not produce something. Parasites are destructive. Yet our society, our Roman state, has never seen any need to encourage its people to produce sensibly or to govern their own production! That's all I'm going to say. Otherwise I'll get angry."

He smiled at my vehemence. "Enough! Sorry. Show me your workshop."

"I'll be glad to. But tell me why you got me onto that topic as soon as you arrived? That's almost exactly where we left off talking two years ago."

He grinned. "That is correct. It was exactly where we

left off. I was simply curious as to whether or not you would remember your own eloquent argument, although I never seriously doubted for a moment you would.''

I led him inside, and we spent the next half hour going over work in progress. Britannicus asked a lot of intelligent questions and I tried to provide him with intelligent answers. He seemed impressed with the way we were set up, and I felt pleased. Then, after standing for a while watching Equus, who was finishing the last of the pike-head order, he pulled the sword from the scabbard by his side and extended it to me, hilt forward.

''What do you think of this?''

I took it and examined it. It was not a good weapon, in spite of the jewellery and inlay work on the hilt. The blade was plain and ill balanced. I hefted it and weighed it in my hand.

''Well?'' He clearly wanted me to evaluate it and I did not want to hurt his feelings.

''Where did you get this, Commander?''

''Never mind, for the moment. Would you buy it?''

I looked him straight in the eye. ''No, Commander, I would not. The blade is ill weighted, the metal won't hold an edge for any length of time, and the tang is starting to work loose inside the hilt.''

''Hmmm! There was no looseness inside the hilt when I bought it last year. What would cause that?''

''It was probably made by a slave.'' I couldn't resist the jibe. ''No self-respecting armourer would allow such a shoddy piece of work to leave his hands. I would venture to guess that it was bought cheap by a jeweller, who made it look fancy and sold it for its decorative value rather than its usefulness.''

He shook his head ruefully at my candour and took the offending weapon back, slipping it into its ornate scabbard. "Do you have any swords for sale?"

I shook my head. "No. Not that I would have such a ceremonial piece for sale at any time. These things are made to order. I do have one sword, but it's an experimental type that I've been working on for some months. It's not been proven yet."

"May I see it?"

I went and fetched the sword for him. He ran his eyes over the lines of it and hefted it for balance, transferring his gaze immediately to the hilt.

"How have you done this? It's bronze, isn't it?" I nodded. "But it's solid! No seams. How?"

"A new technique, or rather, an adaptation of a very old technique. I think it's going to work very well. The entire hilt is poured in one piece and bonded to the iron of the tang."

He swung it in a series of sharp, jabbing cuts. "Will you make me one like this?"

"Happily. I'd give you that one, but I'm still not satisfied with the weight and balance of it. I'll make you one that will be perfect. Not fancy, Commander, but as close to a perfect weight for you as I can achieve."

He placed the sword flat on the bench. "Do so, my friend, and name your price."

As we walked back out into the sunlight, I was half smiling at the thought of charging Caius Britannicus for using one of my swords.

His horse was cropping the grass growing between the flagstones of the yard, and he stopped with his hand on its neck. "Varrus, have you ever heard of the Bagaudae?"

I thought for a moment. "Weren't they the rebels in Gaul who turned bandit about a hundred years ago? Stirred up a hornet's nest of trouble for the administration over there for a long time, if I remember correctly. What about them?"

He was stroking his horse's muzzle gently. The big white animal whickered softly and pushed its muzzle against his shoulder.

"You have a good memory, my friend. That's exactly who they are. I'd hardly call them bandits, but they are nominally rebels. They are still active, and the legions over there do nothing about them. Fascinating people, Varrus. They've held virtual rule over a major part of southern Gaul for almost a hundred years."

I stared at him. "What do you mean, rule?" He simply shrugged his shoulders. "You mean they *govern* the province? And the legions *let* them? I find that hard to believe. Why haven't we heard more about them? Why haven't they been stamped out?"

He shrugged slightly again. "Cowardice, Varrus. Sheer cowardice."

"On whose part? The legions'?"

"No. The Empire's."

I could feel myself frowning. "Commander, you're not making sense."

"Oh yes I am, Varrus. I'm making absolute sense."

"Not to me, you're not."

"That's because you were born and bred here, Varrus, sheltered by the army and by the seas around this island. The real bureaucracy of the Empire never really established its stranglehold here in Britain the way it has everywhere else. Take yourself, for example. Do you know that neither you nor your grandfather would have been allowed to live and work the way you've always done if you'd lived in any other part of the Empire? The regulations and restrictions would have killed you."

"You mean the guild rules? Yes, I've encountered those."

His eyebrow went up again. "You have, have you? And what was the result?"

"I'm still here, and I will not join the guild."

"Good for you. I should have known. It's not just smiths they affect, you know, the guild rules. They're everywhere. They're killing trade throughout the Empire. Britain is about the only place where there have always been ways of getting around their regulations — of staying free, in the sense of a merchant being free to conduct his own affairs without interference. But you know all this, don't you?"

"Some of it. Most of it. What are you getting at, Commander?" I was utterly confused.

"This, Varrus: the Bagaudae in Gaul rebelled, a hundred years ago, but they are not bandits. They are ordinary but courageous people who decided they could not continue to live under the Empire's rules, even then."

I frowned. "For example?"

"Examples? Try crippling taxes, unjust and self-serving laws, constant inflation, corrupt officials, restrictive regulations governing the way they lived their lives and constant government interference."

I had nothing to say to this, so he continued. "They walked away — out of the Empire. Away from their homes, from their businesses, from their employment. Away from the taxes and the duties and the burdens. They

walked away to the hills and the forests and they refused
to go back. They built huts and they lived on whatever
they could grow and hunt for themselves." His voice was
almost a monotone. "It started as a trickle at the end of
the third century and it grew into a flood. We're now at
the end of the fourth century and it's still going on. For
over a hundred years now these Bagaudae have paid no
taxes, obeyed no Roman laws and spared the lives of no
Roman soldiers who came after them. Most of them live
communally on huge villa farms and settlements. Each
man contributes to the life of the commune with his own
skills and abilities. They have no use for money; they
barter. And among their numbers are physicians, magistrates, architects, lawyers, administrators and a large
number of professional soldiers."

"That's incredible," I said. "And the Empire does
nothing?"

He spread his hands wide in a gesture that was purely
Gallic. "What can the Empire do? The bureaucrats are
afraid that the story will spread. The official policy is to
do nothing that will attract attention to the problem. To
ignore it, in the hope that it will go away. Rome leaves
the Bagaudae in peace, because the alternative might stir
up a furore that could breed an Empire full of Bagaudae."

"How do you know all this?"

He smiled at me. "I read, and I talk, and I ask lots of
questions of lots of people. How would you like to come
and be the smith in my Bagaudae community?"

The unexpectedness of the question made me laugh
aloud, but he cut me off before I could make any reply.

"There's not a slave in the place, Varrus."

He was serious, I could see, but I had no idea of what

he was getting at. I know my incomprehension was showing on my face.

He continued, in a low voice, "Think on it, Varrus. I am very serious. You would be a great asset to my plans for the years ahead. I want you with me."

I shook my head. "What plans, Commander? I have no idea what you're talking about. Your farm is where? By Aquae Sulis? That's over a hundred miles from here. Why would I want to close down my business and move out there, other than just to be closer to you? What purpose would it serve? I'm known here. My work is here, and it's going well. I may never be wealthy, but as long as I have my health I'll never lack for anything."

"Is your mind closed on the matter?"

"No, of course not! But I wish I knew what you are driving at!"

The wide smile I knew so well flashed again. "Some day, Varrus, I'll explain myself completely. In the meantime, I should be getting back to the fort. Will you come now?"

I glanced behind me to where Equus was still working away on his own. "No, Commander, I still have a few things to attend to here, and after that I shall go home and change into something that will get me past the guards at the gate. I'll meet you at the bath house in about two hours."

"So be it. I'll have my man ready with some finery for you. As a hero of the legions, you should look as good as we can make you, although with that face of yours . . ." He punched me on the arm. "So be it, my friend, till later. It's good to see you again."

I stood and watched him as he vaulted onto his horse and cantered out of the yard, a vision of military splendour in scarlet and gold. A hero of the legions, he had called me. I wondered what I had done to deserve that? Mind you, I'd had my leg carved up and had survived, which was unusual in itself. Perhaps that did qualify me for junior hero status. I laughed at my folly and went about my business.

X

The dinner that night was a typical officers' formal banquet, very masculine, in spite of the fact that there were more girls there than I had seen in one place at one time for years. Plautus was there, officially supervising the guard and surreptitiously eyeing the girls.

Theodosius was present, of course. He pretended to know who I was when Britannicus brought me to his attention, but I could tell that he had absolutely no memory of me, or who or what I was, and he cared even less. I didn't let his bad manners upset me; he had always been a horse's arse and he was consistent in this behaviour at all times.

I had no doubt, however, that the Legate Primus Seneca recognized me. We came face to face with him shortly after entering the banquet hall, before I'd had time to adjust to the finery of the garments the Commander's servant had provided me with. He turned away, ignoring Britannicus completely, but not before he had swept me from head to toe with the iciest, most venomous glance anyone had ever thrown in my direction. I looked at my host, my eyebrows raised in a query, but he merely smiled a small smile and continued towards the centre of the room as if we were the only two people present.

We accepted two goblets of wine from a passing legionary and stood in companionable silence for a few moments, taking stock of the other people in the large and crowded room. One of the brightly caparisoned officers looked vaguely familiar, but I couldn't place him in my mind. Britannicus must have seen me watching him and read the slight frown on my face correctly.

"Umnax," he said. "Tribune in the Forty-second. Seneca's factotum. Known as 'The Smiler' because he never does."

"Hmmm," I grunted. "He's an ugly son of a whore, isn't he? I remember him now. I'm surprised it took me so long." I glanced at Britannicus before returning my eyes to Umnax. "Did you know they were going to be here tonight, General? Seneca and his people?"

"Yes, of course. Why?"

"Oh, no reason in particular." I cleared my throat. "Have your paths crossed recently?"

He smiled. "Frequently. I have been able to do several things to cross him in his planning. The man is a spider, Varrus. A malevolent, scheming spider, constantly spinning webs."

"How do you mean, sir?"

"I think it's about time you stopped calling me sir. My name is Caius, and we have been friends long enough for you to use it." I felt a wave of discomfort sweep over me, but he kept on talking. "Seneca and his family seem to have no other purpose in life but to extend their wealth, which, as I am sure you know, is already fabulous. They are totally unscrupulous about doing it, too. Last month I was able to use my influence to thwart his latest plan to grow fat from the armies. His cousin, Quinctilius Nesca, tried to take over as Quartermaster of the armies — do you know him?"

"No." I shook my head, hoping he would not notice I was unable to call him by his name.

"A toad. Fat, greasy, greedy and non-human. A disgusting creature." He broke off to smile at a beautiful young woman who had approached us, declining to sample the array of sweets in the tray she offered. They looked wonderful, and I helped myself to a tiny pear made of the paste of almonds. As the girl moved away, he continued. "Primus almost managed to have Nesca win the contract, too. Can you imagine? Quartermaster General! That would have meant that everything supplied to the armies would have passed through his sweaty hands, and suffered thereby, while he and his family grew richer. Luckily I found out in time and was able to avert it. Our dear Seneca has been most unhappy ever since."

I grinned and glanced at Seneca himself, to find his baleful glare full on me. He knew we were talking about him. From that point onwards, whenever I encountered Primus Seneca's gaze, his cold eyes were fixed on either me or Britannicus, and each time he saw me look at him he directed his eyes elsewhere. There was no doubt in my mind that Primus Seneca had broadened his detestation of Caius Britannicus to embrace Publius Varrus.

The evening progressed, however, and I forgot about Seneca as the proceedings grew noisier and more abandoned. There were wrestlers and gladiators and dancing girls from all over the Empire. The wine was plentiful and the food was impressive, and as both of these made their mark on the diners, everyone relaxed and a mood of conviviality quickly developed. I enjoyed myself hugely.

Several of the junior officers became involved in trials of strength with the wrestlers, and one brash young man even challenged a gladiator to combat. Wooden training swords were produced and the two of them went at it in a space that had been quickly cleared in the middle of the room. The young officer did remarkably well. He was no fool with a sword and there were times when he seemed to have the professional gladiator working hard to protect himself. The betting grew fast and urgent as the odds swayed to favour first one and then the other of the contestants in this ritual Roman combat.

Eventually, however, the professionalism and experience of the gladiator began to tell, and the young officer grew visibly tired. It was clearly costing him more and more of an effort to keep his sword arm extended. Those who had bet against him were already counting their winnings when suddenly, and quite brilliantly I thought, he released his shield and threw himself forward in a rolling dive to the floor, catching the gladiator by surprise and whipping his feet from under him with a sweeping kick. The man went down and the officer's sword was at his throat in the blink of an eye. The place went wild as winners and losers screamed praise and abuse at the young victor. Arguments on orthodoxy sprang into life instantly; there was haggling everywhere as some tried to get out of their wagers because of the way the fight had ended.

The gladiator, in the meantime, was watching closely as his conqueror showed him how he had got the better of him. It was clear that he was impressed with the move and intended to keep it in mind for future reference.

There was a trumpet blast from the head table and silence fell instantly throughout the room. Theodosius stood, arms outstretched.

"My friends! Let us bear in mind that we are here this evening to comport ourselves in dignity and fellowship. I myself have lost a wager in this event, and I like to lose as little as anyone. But the objective of armed conflict, any armed conflict, is victory — personal survival and the overthrow of one's opponent. That is what we have seen here. I declare Tribune Drusus the winner and declare all wagers in his favour valid."

There was a renewed chorus of cheers and jeers, but it was short-lived. For my part, I was pleasantly surprised that Theodosius had taken the decisive step he did, and I had to admire him for it, considering that he could have won his own wager by declaring Drusus's move a foul.

Later in the evening, Britannicus introduced me to three men, two of whose names have long since gone the way of the majority of casual introductions. The name of the third man, however, I do remember. He became one of my closest, lifelong friends. His name was Alaric and he was — and still is — a Christian bishop.

I had never heard the name Alaric before that night, but nowadays, as I write this forty years later, it ranks among the foremost names in the world. Another Alaric, a warrior and leader of the people called the Visigoths, threatens today to ring the final knell of Rome and write *satis* to the legend of the Empire invincible.

Bishop Alaric's two companions that night were also bishops, and it was their triple presence more than anything else that was keeping the whole evening from degenerating into an absolute saturnalia.

I liked Bishop Alaric immediately. He was dressed simply, in a white, toga-like robe, and he carried himself like a soldier. He spoke with a total simplicity and clarity that seemed to me like a different language — no rhetoric, no exaggeration, no flowery phrases. The man considered what he wanted to say, and then he said it in an absolute minimum of words. The strange thing about this was that it made you listen very carefully. I know, because we talked together for a long time. Britannicus had been commandeered by someone else as soon as he had introduced us, and we were left alone together.

At first, knowing that this man was a churchman, I thought it was going to be difficult to make conversation, but nothing could have been further from the truth. I found him fascinating. He talked about the problems he and his people were having in carrying the Word of Christ to the barbarians, and to the ordinary people of Britain, who were still predominantly pagan. From there, he went into an analysis of the reasons underlying the recent surge in pagan and idolatrous worship in Britain during the past thirty to forty years, and of the disastrous effect this was having on the faith of the Christians who still had to live with it. He told me honestly that there simply were not enough priests available to fight this renaissance of paganism effectively. The peasants were the ones who seemed most taken up with reversion to the old ways, he said. Their counterparts in the towns and cities, seemingly more sophisticated or at least more enlightened, were far less impressionable and far more orthodox in their adherence to Christianity.

I asked him what he saw as the solution to the problem, and he assured me that paganism could not hold out against the slow, patient instruction and enlightenment offered by the Church. Listening to the quiet confidence and conviction in his voice, I had no difficulty in believing him to be right.

I asked him if he had ever had much trouble with the Druids. Weren't they the priests of the old religion? He was amused by my question and told me that he had great hope for the Druids. They were a gentle people, he said, far removed from their bloody and brutal origins. They still existed in the mountainous areas of Britain, but they were followers of Light, easily convertible to the teachings of the gentle Christ.

From that point, the conversation drifted naturally to the various customs of the tribes he had encountered earlier in his priesthood on his travels throughout the Empire. He mentioned that he had spent a number of years in Gaul, and I immediately asked him if he had had any dealings with the Bagaudae. From the way he looked me in the eye and smiled, I knew that I had asked the right question of the right man, and for the next quarter of an hour he explained to me why he thought that the communal farm system favoured by these remarkable people — that's what he called them — was destined to become the rural social unit of the future. Of course, as he talked about it, I could see that such a unit would provide the perfect vehicle for the propagation and survival of the Christian faith, but a lot of what he said emphasized and supported what Britannicus had been saying earlier in the afternoon. I was surprisingly disappointed when one of his fellow bishops came over to remind him that they had to leave.

As soon as the three Churchmen were off the premises, and after Theodosius, Cicero and the other senior officers had withdrawn to their apartments, the decorum of the evening degenerated quickly. I would have been happy to stay and sample the wares of some of the outrageously beautiful dancing girls who seemed to be preparing to get down to the serious business of the evening, but I left with Britannicus, who, apart from being a senior officer and therefore *persona non grata* at this stage of the night, was always fastidious to the point of fanaticism concerning women. He came home alone with me, having dismissed his escort, and we sat talking long into the night. It was during this long conversation that I casually produced the skystone dagger in its case.

"What do you think of that?" I handed him the box and, like me, he could not immediately figure out how to open it. I let him work it out for himself and he had it in a few minutes. When he saw what it contained, he made no sound and gave no sign of emotion. He took the knife from its bed and laid the box on a nearby table, and for the next two minutes he said nothing. Then, "Did you make this, Varrus?"

"No. My grandfather again. Do you remember the story of the skystone?" He nodded, not taking his eyes from the dagger. "That was made from the last of the metal from that skystone. He used it as it was. Didn't want to pollute it with ordinary iron as he had the sword he made for my father. It will shave the hair from your arm."

"Varrus," he whispered, "this is incredibly beautiful. It is enough to make a man believe in magic. I have never seen a blade so pure, so exquisite. Nor a hilt so flawless, though flawless is a word usually reserved for blades. This makes the sword of Theodosius seem tawdry." He replaced it reverently in its box, shaking his head in awe and leaving the lid off so that he could continue to look at it. "That is a weapon fit for an

Emperor." He looked at me and grinned. "Sad that there has never been an Emperor fit for such a weapon. What makes the blade so silvery?" He held it up so that it reflected the flame of the lamps.

I stared at it, shaking my head. "I don't know, General, but I think there's another metal in there besides iron."

He glanced at me sharply, his interest caught at once. "What kind of metal? What is it?"

I shook my head. "I don't know, General. I have no idea."

He took the knife from its case again, holding it with its point towards me, a puzzled frown on his face. "You must have some kind of an idea! Can't you even make a guess?"

I smiled, more for myself than him. "General, if I had any way of knowing that, I'd be a very rich man."

"Publius, in the name of all the Caesars, there aren't that many metals, are there? You should be able to pin-point one of them!"

I shrugged my shoulders and gave voice to a thought that had lain unspoken in my mind for some time now. "Yes, you'd think so, and I'd have to agree with you if I were convinced that there aren't that many metals. But I'm not convinced. I believe that there could be hundreds of metals that we simply have not yet discovered."

"Hundreds?"

I shrugged. "Well, perhaps not hundreds, but dozens. We know of gold and silver, lead and zinc, copper and tin, and iron. Perhaps a few others."

"What about bronze and brass?"

I was surprised at the naivety of the question. "Those are alloys, Commander, mixtures of the metals I've just named."

"Oh, yes, of course they are. I knew that. Can you name no more?"

"Not offhand, no. Iron is the most recently discovered of these."

"Iron? It's been known for centuries."

"Yes, it has. But we're still only learning how to work with it. It is the hardest of all metals, of course. Or all the ones that we know."

His face was creased in a slight frown. "I'm not sure I know what you are talking about, Publius."

I smiled. "Neither am I, Commander, but I have a half-formed theory on the hardness of metals. The harder they are in themselves, the harder they are to find. Harder to smelt, in the first place."

"Smelt? Like melt?"

"Same thing. Except smelt means to melt out of the raw rock."

"Fascinating! Tell me more about iron, Publius."

"What do you want to know?"

"Everything."

I laughed aloud while the lamp on the table between us flickered, indicating that more oil was needed. It had been full when we sat down. I nodded towards the guttering flame.

"Some other time, I fear, General. It's very late, and I would have a lot to tell you. Didn't you say you are leaving at first light? You'll have no sleep tonight."

"That will be nothing new. I really would like to hear about your theories on the hardness of metal, iron in particular."

"Very well, then," I said. "On your own head be it. But first I have to replenish the lamp."

I was marshalling my thoughts as I brought oil for the lamp and fresh wine for ourselves, and by the time I sat down again, I knew what I wanted to say. I nodded towards the skystone dagger lying on the table.

"Let's suppose that what I postulate is true. Whatever that stuff is — the metal in that blade — it's not iron. 'Fine, then,' we say, 'it's something else — but what?' " I squinted at him, then leaned forward to stir the coals in the brazier. "Do you understand what I mean?"

He blinked at me. "No."

"What do we call it, if it isn't iron?"

"I'm sorry, Publius. I don't understand."

"Then I'll show you. Wait here, please. I'll be back in a minute."

I came back several minutes later, lugging a heavy wooden box. He watched me, wordlessly, as I spread its contents — three roughly uniform iron bars as long as my forearm and as thick as a finger, and one plain sword blade — on top of the table by his side.

"What do you see?" I asked him, resuming my seat.

"Three iron bars and a sword blade."

"You see any differences between the bars?"

"No, they all look the same."

"Right, now watch this." I picked up the first bar and bent it easily in my hands until it was almost the shape of a horseshoe. I dropped it on the table top, picked up the second bar, and bent it, too, but not as easily, and not as far as the first. Britannicus watched closely, saying nothing. To bend the third bar, I had to place it on the edge of the table and push down, hard, with both arms. The sword blade flexed slightly and would not bend at all.

"They're all iron, but they're all different. The first is what we call wrought iron. It's pure iron — recently smelted and unworked — soft, as you saw, and malleable. The second one's been heated and beaten a couple of times. The third has been in the fire and under the hammer more often. And the sword blade's been heated in an air-fed, charcoal forge and beaten into shape, then edged, then re-heated and quenched in water while it was red hot. It's the hardest of all. That sword will be worn by one of the garrison soldiers, when it's finished. Now watch."

I picked up the sword blade and used its point to gouge marks in the three bars. As before, the resistance varied from bar to bar. Then I used the bars to try to make an impression on the iron of the sword blade. None of them even scratched it.

"Now do you see my point?"

"I think so." He still looked bemused. I picked up the sword blade again.

"This metal, this blade, is the hardest iron I can make, Commander, and I don't know anyone who can do better. In all the world, to the best of my knowledge, you'll find no harder iron. Except in the sword of Theodosius, and in this." I picked up the skystone knife with my right hand and laid the sword blade between us with my left.

"Hold that end firmly. Don't let it move." I then bent over the blade, bracing my fist and the end of the skystone knife against my shoulder, and dragged its point down the length of the sword blade. It cut deeply, even curling a shaving of iron. I straightened and held the knife's point out for Britannicus to inspect.

"Look. Not a trace of damage."

"Good God!" He took the knife and gazed at it as I continued talking.

"That's not iron, but until I know what it is, I'll call it iron. And here's the theory you wanted to hear about: I know that high heat smelts iron from the ore-bearing rock. Once we have the pure iron, higher degrees of heat, and variations in the way we apply the heat and treat the iron, produce harder iron. And iron's the hardest metal we know. Every other metal is softer, easier to melt, and easier to work with. I think the amount of heat we can generate and apply has much to do with the hardness of the metal. The fires we work with today, fuelled by charcoal and heated by bellows, are the hottest smiths have ever worked with."

I took the knife from his hand. "Grandfather Varrus had to work harder than he ever had before to smelt this, whatever it is. And I never saw the skystone. Maybe it wasn't even the ore-bearing rock we know. Perhaps, if I had seen the stone, I would be able to recognize others like it, who knows? But this I do know: there's a secret here, in this metal, that's waiting to be discovered. If I could find the secret of whatever it is that makes this . . . iron — I have to call it iron — so different, so far superior to the iron we know, then men would call me a magician when they saw the blades I could produce. And I would be, too. . . . Magic, after all, is no more than the product of knowledge others don't share."

Britannicus was shaking his head in amazement, his shoulders slumped in dejection.

"Publius," he said, "I believe every word you have said. But where on earth can we find another skystone, and how will we recognize it?"

I stood up and began to throw the pieces of iron back into the box. "There's the pity of it, Commander. I think I have as much chance of finding another skystone as I do of finding a wife at my age."

We had little more to say to each other that night, and Britannicus left shortly after that, walking straight and tall in the light of a full moon, promising to visit me again in the near future. Depressed and dissatisfied, I made my way to bed, where I intended to remain shamelessly until midday.

It was not to be. I had barely climbed into bed when I heard an approaching clash of hooves outside, preternaturally loud in the silent night. Even before they had clattered to a halt outside my house I was out of bed, filled with a sense of impending disaster.

It was Plautus, unkempt, dishevelled and out of uniform.

"Is Britannicus still here?"

"No. Why?" I was still pulling on my clothes, my sword belt in my left hand. I had snatched it up without conscious volition.

"When did he leave?"

"About five minutes ago. What's wrong?"

"Which way did he go? One of my men tipped me. There's a plot. They knew he was here and they're out to get him."

"Damnation! Which way did you come?"

"Direct, but I didn't pass him. But he could have taken the other street at the fork back there."

"Go back and check it, Plautus. I'll go the other way."

I didn't have to ask who "they" were. I cursed myself for not noticing which way Caius had gone. Either direction, right or left from my gate, would have led him eventually back to the fort. We split up, Plautus, mounted, to the left and myself, on foot, to the right.

I had developed a technique of running that allowed me to make the most of my bad leg. I progressed in a series of bounds, launching myself off my good limb and using the bent one merely as a balancing point. It worked well and allowed me to cover ground quickly in short bursts. On this occasion, however, the sustained effort and my anxiety tired me quickly. Darkened tenements hemmed me in on either side before I had run two hundred paces, and as I turned one corner a frightened cat leaped, hissing, from my path, the suddenness of it almost causing me to fall. I stopped and listened, but I could hear nothing except the pounding of my heart and the rasping of my breath. I stood there for the space of twenty heartbeats, forcing myself to calm down before I ran on, cursing the fact that every street in this town sloped upwards towards the fort on the hilltop.

I passed one junction where two streets crossed, glancing left and right as I ran through the intersection. The pale light of the full moon allowed me to see that both streets were empty of life. I had gone about halfway up the next length of increasingly steep street when somebody tried to kill me.

My lopsided style of running saved me. The increasing gradient and my growing fatigue had me progressing by this time in a bobbing, dipping series of lurches. As I hunched into one lurch, the tip of a sword blade hissed by my head, slicing into the lobe of my right ear. My instincts and training took over immediately, and without thought I allowed my bad leg to collapse under me. Rolling forward and away from my assailant, I maintained my momentum and drew my own sword as I rolled. I whipped the blade up in front of my face just in time to counter another swinging slash that almost disarmed me. I turned it aside desperately and managed to unbalance the black-cloaked figure that loomed above me. Then, spinning myself on my rump and putting all my weight into my lunge, I slashed at the one glimpse I had of a bare knee and felt the edge of my blade bite deep, grating on bone. I realized at the same instant that this might be Caius Britannicus, treating me as a potential attacker.

It was not Britannicus, and I knew that as he fell, cursing me in a high-pitched whine of agony. We grappled together there on the edge of the cobbled street. I was glad of my smith's muscles as I forced his arms down and slipped the point of my sword into the soft flesh beneath his chin, ramming it quickly upwards through his skull so that he died suddenly, his frantic liveliness turning to dead weight in a moment of spastic shuddering.

I regained my feet and freed my sword, shaking like an old man with the palsy and fighting hard to get fresh air into my lungs. There was no one else in the street — just myself and my dead attacker. And then I heard the ring of iron and the sounds of a struggle coming from an alleyway I had run past before being attacked. Ignoring the corpse on the ground, I ran towards the sounds and saw a knot of fighting men about halfway down the alley.

Britannicus had his back against the wall and faced five armed men. I yelled something as I threw myself towards them, and they turned to see who I was. As they did so, the Commander slashed one of them, who fell to his knees and then keeled forward onto the cobbles.

Then I was among them, hacking and slashing with my sword in one hand and my dagger in the other. I must have been a threatening sight, because the first man facing me panicked and turned as if to flee. I jumped at him and got my left arm around his neck, pulling him back into me and on to my hard-stabbing blade. I felt him arch and die and I thrust him forward, towards his companions and off my sword. As he fell away from me, I felt my shoulder being grabbed and pulled, and then, for the second time within minutes, I was scrabbling around on the ground again, fighting for my life against a large, unknown enemy. A fallen sword clanged on the ground by my head as I struggled, and then my assailant, who was above me and about to finish me, went rigid and collapsed on top of me. I heard running feet and then the clatter of hooves and much shouting and yelling, and I discovered that I did not have the strength to push away the body that lay on me.

Plautus had arrived, with others, and two of our attackers were taken alive. Britannicus helped me to my feet and I leaned against the wall, exhausted, trying to catch my breath while a confusion of voices rattled around me. I heard Plautus say, "Five of the swine. They were determined to get you, Legate."

I had to hawk and clear my throat before I could raise my voice. "Six," I said.

"No, five of them. None got away, Varrus. There were five."

"Six," I said again, my voice weak and my stomach heaving. "There's another one up there in the street above us. He jumped me as I ran by." I turned to the wall behind me and vomited.

"Lars and Pector, get up there and check. Bring the body back here." I felt Plautus's hand on the back of my neck, cold and strong. "By the Christ, Publius! I never knew anyone like you for puking after all the fun is over. Are you all right? Are you wounded? I can't see you for blood. Is any of it yours?"

I managed to shake my head, but of course, as I later discovered, some of it was my own. My cut ear was bleeding heavily.

By the time I had regained my self-possession, the two men Plautus had sent to search for the body in the street above had returned, dragging the corpse between them by the heels. Another of the soldiers had found a handcart and the rest of the bodies were thrown onto it. As they threw each body onto the cart, Plautus examined the dead faces by the light of a lantern. "Well, well," he said. "Look what we have here."

The last man, the one who had been dragged back from the street above, was "The Smiler," Primus Seneca's factotum tribune. None of us was surprised, and no one said anything. The others were all unknown to us and obviously street ruffians hired for the occasion. The two prisoners were set to work pulling the loaded handcart back to the fort. I walked between Plautus and Britannicus, both of whom were unhurt.

Needless to say, Caius Britannicus did not leave Colchester at first light. He made a formal report of the incident and brought a formal charge against Seneca as the instigator of the assassination attempt. No one, including Theodosius, had any doubt of the veracity of the charges levelled, but nothing could be proved against Seneca. His defence was that his subordinate, in a rage of misguided loyalty to his principal, had decided on his own initiative to revenge what he took to be a series of insults to his Commander and had hired assassins to carry out his orders. The assassins themselves had dealt only with "The Smiler." They were executed that same day, and in the absence of conclusive evidence, Seneca was legally exonerated of any complicity in the matter.

By the time Britannicus did leave, twenty-four hours behind schedule, the love between him and Seneca had grown no deeper. In the meantime, I had managed to have my ear bound up and to get a good night's sleep.

X I

The mother of my house servant died about a month after Britannicus's visit. The event had no significance for me personally; I would not remember it at all were it not for the fact that I had an unexpected visitor on the first night I spent alone at home without my servant and his wife. My leg had seized up on me again that day, with far less ferocity than on the previous occasion but still with sufficient malignity to send me home for the day from the smithy. I had spent the afternoon reclining on a couch with my leg supported on a pile of cushions, reading the scrolls that my grandfather had left to my attention. The one dealing with his newly perfected method of pouring solid metal sword hilts fascinated me, and I was rereading it for about the tenth time when I heard someone at the door of my house. I got up from my couch, pleased to notice that my leg felt fine again, and went to the door, where I stood blinking without recognition at the tall shape that faced me, silhouetted against the late-afternoon sun.

"Publius? Master Varrus? Do you not know me?"

I squinted against the glare, tilting my head to one side, and recognized him.

"Bishop Alaric!"

I ushered him inside and led the way to the chamber I used as a dayroom. "I didn't recognize you, standing against the sun the way you were. I certainly didn't expect you. Sit down, please." He seated himself in one of the big, padded armchairs my grandfather had loved. "Will you drink some wine with me?"

"Yes," he said, smiling, "I would like that."

After I had served the wine, I sat opposite him, wondering what his visit could be about. We drank in silence for a few minutes as I searched for something to say that would not sound too foolish or too curious. He saved me from embarrassment by speaking first.

"I enjoyed our meeting last month, Master Varrus, and I have been thinking of you, intermittently, ever since."

I was intrigued. "You have?" I said. "Why? Why should you think of me? Or even remember me?"

He smiled. "Why should I not? Do you believe yourself to be unmemorable?" I gave him no reaction and he continued. "I remembered you because of your calling, first of all, and then because of some of the things Caius Britannicus told me about you on our journey to Verulamium following the attempt on his life. You are a craftsman in metal, he told me. More than a simple smith."

It was on the tip of my tongue to say something modest and self-effacing, but then I recalled what I had so admired about this man — his simplicity of speech. "Aye," I said. "You could say that, almost. I am a craftsman in iron."

"Only in iron?"

"Mainly in iron. It is the metal I prefer above all others. I work from time to time with bronze and brass, too, and copper. But I prefer iron. I find it has more . . ."

"More what?"

"Character, I was going to say, but I think challenge would be more accurate."

"You enjoy challenge?"

"Aye, doesn't everyone?"

He smiled again. "No, Master Varrus. Not everyone does. What about silver?"

"Silver?" I indicated my disdain with a small shrug. "A fine metal, for jewellers. What about it?"

"Have you worked with silver?"

"No. Silversmithing is a craft all on its own. It's more art than discipline, if you know what I mean. He said nothing, obviously waiting for me to continue. "Silver is too soft, too malleable to appeal to an ironsmith. It has a delicacy, a fragility, that sits ill with the kind of strength and directness the ironsmith brings to his craft. Why do you ask me about silver?"

In response, he reached inside his long robe and produced a sheet of folded papyrus.

"Have you ever seen the likes of this before?"

I took the sheet and opened it to find the inner surface covered with a delicate tracery of curves and swirling, intricate shapes.

"These are Celtic," I said. "Beautifully done. Who did them?"

"I did." He took the papyrus back from me and I watched his eyes follow the designs inscribed on it as he spoke. "I copied them from a number of sources while I was in the west, in the mountains there."

"Why would you do that?"

"For the pleasure it gave me. This is the artwork of the Celtic peoples of Britain. I am a bishop of the Church in Britain. I have decided that I would like to have a plain, pectoral cross in silver, decorated in this, the Celtic fashion. A vanity, I suppose, but a more practical vanity, or at least a less pretentious one, than this."

He reached inside his robe again and pulled out a gold cross, studded with red and green jewels, which he handed to me. I took it and examined it, conscious of the surprisingly solid weight of it and of the craftsmanship that had gone into the making of it.

"This is magnificent."

"It is barbaric. Sybaritic. I find it gross."

I scratched it with my thumb-nail, feeling the richness of it. "Where did you get it? May I ask?"

He looked at it musingly. "In Rome, last time I was there. It is eastern, made in Constantinople."

"Yes." I turned the thing over. The back was covered with oriental scrollwork. "I've seen this work before, but never in a cross."

He snorted. "The Church is growing wealthy. It has become the accepted fashion for bishops to wear such things."

"But you find it gross."

"Yes. I do."

I handed it back to him. "Was it a gift?"

"It was."

"Why did you accept it, if you find it so distasteful?"

He looked at me as if I had lost my wits. "Because of its value, of course. I saw its worth. I intend to sell it in Londinium. The price I get for it will aid me in my work."

"God's work?"

"The two are the same." There was no hint of censure in his voice to counteract the cynicism in mine.

"I see. When were you in Rome?"

"Three years ago."

"Why haven't you sold it before now?"

"I did not have to. Now I need the money."

"For your work?"

"For my work."

I cleared my throat, deciding the man was telling the absolute truth. "Tell me about this silver cross you visualize. Why do you want that?"

He pursed his lips. "As a token. A symbol."

"Of what? Forgive my bluntness, but I do not understand. Why should you need a symbol? Of what? Your faith? Your position?"

"Both of those, but more." He picked up his cup of wine and looked into it, and then he got to his feet and began to move about the room, sipping occasionally at the wine.

"I see the Church here in Britain, Master Varrus, as lacking an identity, a local flavour if you like, that would make it more acceptable to the people here. The pectoral cross is an excellent badge of office. I have no doubt of that. It is large, easily visible and unmistakable. The garishness of that gold one, and of the others I have seen, however, suggest a foreignness and a preoccupation with worldly wealth and power that offends me. You see? I spoke of vanity and here I am, in my own vanity, decrying the vanity of others. Anyway, my thought is that a plain, silver cross, stark and simple, adorned only with inscribed Celtic designs such as I have shown you, would serve the double purpose of defining my function to my people here and dedicating their art, their traditions and their abilities to the glory of God. Does that make sense?"

I picked up the jewelled cross again from where he had left it on the arm of his chair. "Aye, Bishop," I said. "It makes sense, I suppose. But why silver? Why not plain gold? Why not wood, for that matter?"

"Why not? I understand what you are saying. Let us just say that there is a modicum of vanity involved. Wood does not appeal to me. Silver does. It has a beauty, a purity, that is unique. It is pristine."

I raised my hand, palm outward. "I can't argue with that." I handed the cross back to him again and this time he replaced it inside his robe. "But why have you come to me? I'm not the one to make your cross for you. There are silversmiths by the squad in Londinium, any one of whom could do that in his sleep."

"No, Varrus. There is your error." He placed his empty cup on the table. "I'll take no more of your time, but let me leave you with this thought. You may never have worked with silver, and you may care little for its delicacy, as you say, but you are a man who respects integrity, whether it be in a man or in a metal. I have been asking people about you. You are also, by your own admission, a man who responds to challenge. I am on my way to Londinium. While I am there I will convert this golden bauble into money. If you will, please think about what would be involved in making this cross for me, respecting the integrity of the metal, of the design of the cross itself, and of the decoration you would add to it. Consider, too, the challenge of the silver. I will return within the month. If you tell me then that you do not want this commission, I shall respect your decision. Is that fair?"

I shrugged my shoulders, bewildered. "Aye, I suppose it is. I'll think on it. But I make you no promises."

"I want none. Now I must go." He made a move to rise, and, on an impulse, I stopped him. He waited, looking at me in silence as I struggled with the question that had risen, unbidden, to the tip of my tongue. After several seconds had passed, I found the words to frame it; more accurately, I found a minor question that would allow me to work towards the question that concerned me.

"Please," I said, "if you can spare me a few more minutes, I would like to ask you something about the Tribune, Commander Britannicus."

He settled back into his chair and crossed his hands on his stomach. "What would you like to know, Master Varrus?"

"Nothing that will embarrass either of us to discuss, Bishop, but I could use some enlightenment on a thing that has been bothering me. Have you known the Tribune long?"

He nodded. "All my life. His family and my own are close and have been for many years."

"I thought so. Are you Roman born?"

"No, I was born here in Britain, as was Caius."

"What can you tell me about the enmity between him and Primus Seneca? I know it is deep and bitter, but I have never been able to discover the cause of it."

"Have you asked Caius?"

"Commander Britannicus? No, I have not. He has spoken of it, but I have asked him nothing. Our relationship is not one that would allow such intimacy."

Alaric smiled. "I think you are wrong, there, Master Varrus, but I appreciate the reason for your thinking that way. You would regard such a question as impertinent, but Caius Britannicus would not. He regards you as a friend, not as a subordinate. I think he would gladly tell you the story himself, were you to ask him."

I thought about that for a second, and then responded, "I could not do that."

Alaric smiled. "All right. Theirs is a blood feud — a family feud, the origins of which have been forgotten while the virulence remains and seems to grow."

"All the Senecas hate all the Brittanici? Is that what you are saying?"

"Almost." He was frowning slightly now, thinking. "Caius Britannicus is the next-to-last of his line. He has a sister, Luceiia, a son, Picus, of whom he is very proud, and three other young children. There are no other members of the family Britannicus left alive, not even cousins bearing the same name. The Senecas, on the other hand, are a prolific breed. Primus is the first of seven brothers, all of whom are soldiers save the youngest, who is a ne'er-do-well. The family is fabulously wealthy, you understand, and has been since the days of Julius Caesar when Seneca the Elder, the banker, was estimated to be the wealthiest man in the world." I nodded, to show that I was aware of the Seneca legend.

"As I said," Alaric continued, "no one knows when this war between the families began, but it has grown like a weed, and it has blighted both families, particularly the family of Britannicus. Caius had an elder brother, Jacobus, who was murdered, along with their parents, almost twenty years ago in Rome. The circumstances surrounding the crime pointed towards Primus Seneca as the instigator, although nothing could ever be proved. The case was taken to the Senate, but there was nothing to be done in law.

"Caius thought otherwise, however. He was a very young man at the time, with more than his share of youth's hot-headedness and lust for revenge. He challenged Primus Seneca, accused him publicly of the crime, and they fought, each employing a number of mercenaries to their cause. The affair created a scandal. There was open warfare in the streets between the adherents of both families, and there were many deaths. Public sympathy was with young Caius, but there was no proof of Primus's guilt, and so the authorities stepped in and put an end to the fighting by transferring the two men — both soldiers, remember — to opposite ends of the Empire." He sighed, deeply and disgustedly. "That solved the immediate problem, of course, but in fact it resolved nothing. The Seneca family continued to live in Rome, and in Constantinople, and Luceiia, Caius's baby sister, was sent to live on the family estate here in Britain, where she remains to this day."

"Is the Commander wealthy?"

"Extremely. You have obviously never seen his villa in the west."

"No." I shook my head. "But I think he would like me to go there and live as one of his Bagaudae."

"Ah yes, his Colony. I believe he will establish it, you know. I sincerely hope he will."

"Why? Do you mind my asking?"

He smiled. "Why should I mind? Caius is a man who needs to be occupied. He has a mind that is capable of greatness. You know he foresees the death of the Empire in the near future?"

I was stupefied. "What are you talking about?" I asked, my surprise audible in my voice.

"Just what I say. Caius believes that the Empire, as we know it, is doomed."

"Rome? Doomed? By what?"

"By its own excesses."

"That is nonsense! It's impossible. It's . . . it's an obscene thought!"

"Is it? Really? I wonder. Our own Lord foretold that He would return after a period of time for the final Judgment of mankind, and that when He did, the world would end. He died to redeem the souls of men. To give mankind an opportunity to grow in spirit, and to put away the things of this earth. It seems to me that the Empire is of this earth. There is little heavenly about it."

I sat blinking in confusion, my head reeling. "You must forgive me," I said. "We have come too far, too quickly in this conversation. I am beyond my depth. We started out talking of the Commander and his enemies, and suddenly we are dealing with metaphysics and the end of the Empire. I am not qualified to talk of these things."

He grinned at me. "It is I who should ask forgiveness, Master Varrus. You asked only about the feud. My personal convictions led me astray. But let me summarize my own thoughts on Caius Britannicus and the Senecas in a way that will not take me far from what I have just been saying, and yet might make my thinking clear to you. I know you do not doubt the coexistence of Good and Evil, and no man could doubt the strength of the Empire, on the surface at least. In my mind, Master Varrus, Caius Britannicus, and men like him, represent all that is good in the Roman way. Honour, honesty, integrity, probity and the respect for law and order, both spiritual and temporal, are their watchwords. The other face of the coin is represented by the excesses, the venality, the corruption and the disregard for humanity and divinity that characterizes the worst elements, and, unfortunately, the most powerful elements in the Empire today. White and black. Right and wrong. Day and night. Britannicus and Seneca. I will say no more, for now I must go. Thank you for your hospitality, and I will speak to you again on my return from Londinium within the month."

My thoughts that night were drawn in two different ways: one, to the sheet of papyrus Alaric had left lying on my table, and the other, to the frightening and apparently impossible scenario to which he had referred, and to which, it seemed, Commander Britannicus subscribed. The end of Rome. The end of the Empire. My grandfather's parchments were put away and, for the time being, forgotten.

My mind could not encompass the appalling implications of this new thought. No man can visualize the end of the world in personal terms, and Rome was the world. The barbarian states outside the Empire's frontiers were *Ultima Thule* — so far away as to be beyond imagining. I tried to ignore the terrifying thought of it, without much success, and without making any progress towards gaining a rational perspective on how our lives here in Britain would be affected by the end of Rome. I finally duped myself into accepting the impossibility of the premise and into accepting the thesis that this was simply an eccentricity of Caius Britannicus. Every man, I reasoned, is entitled to one personal folly.

After a week, I found myself buying silver ore and familiarizing myself with the properties of the metal.

After Alaric's return — within the month, as he had promised — I found myself spending endless hours in the study of proportion and of Celtic art.

After that time, I was never free of a compulsion to fashion silver crosses of all shapes and sizes.

About a month after Alaric's return from Londinium, on an evening when I was working on the design of the first pectoral cross I was to make for him, my servant came to tell me that there was a soldier at my door wishing to talk with me, and I bade him bring the man in.

I saw immediately from his trappings that my visitor was an aide to the Military Commander, Antonius Cicero. He drew himself to attention as he entered my room.

"Centurion Publius Varrus?" I nodded acquiescence. His salute was crisp and perfect. "The Legate Cicero sends his compliments, sir. This scroll was delivered to him today by military courier with a request that he forward it to you."

I thanked him and took the scroll he proffered, immediately conscious of the weight of it. As the soldier left, I noticed that it was already dusk. I lit several lamps against the gathering darkness and then decided to forage in the kitchen while there was still enough light to see by. I loaded a platter with bread, cold meat and some pickled onions, poured myself a flagon of Equus's brew and went back to examine the weighty scroll. It was sealed with the signet of Britannicus. Surprised, for I had never had any such communication from him before, I prised the seal open gently with my thumb-nail, being careful not to break the wax, and unrolled the missive. I was even more surprised then to discover that the thick parchment was only the wrapper for four sheets of fine papyrus covered with Britannicus's neat, characteristic script. Forgetting food and drink for the moment, I pulled a lamp closer to me and began to read.

Caius Britannicus
to:
Publius Varrus

Greetings — This for your reading only:

I have been remembering the story of the sword your grandfather fashioned for your father, who died abroad without ever seeing it. I hope the fact that you are now making one for me is not ominous.

It always surprises me to learn again that the affairs of Empire proceed irrespective of our petty affairs here in Britain, and that the Powers who command the destinies of men and peoples remain aware of the minor functionaries in the provinces. I am commanded by the Senate and the People of Rome to proceed immediately to Rome, and thence to Constantinople, where I will be granted the Consulship of Numidia by the Emperor Valentinian himself, and be provided with the means and the authority to execute all of the appropriate consular functions within the Province of Numidia in the proper style and fashion.

The appointment, which is generally regarded as the supreme military achievement, is of course a great honour, and I suspect that Theodosius had a deal to do with the bestowal of it. Had it occurred even five years ago, I would have been delighted. Now, however, I perceive it as something of a mixed benison, a blend of inconvenient duty and dutiful inconvenience. You, however, and my wife are the only two souls to whom I could ever confide such a viewpoint.

Five more years under the sun of Africa! The prospect does not appeal to me. Five more years of dealing with the fractious and contentious nomads native to the land appeals to me even less, particularly since mine will be the head on which will fall the odium and opprobrium if all does not go well under my care during my term of office. When have things ever gone well in Africa for five consecutive years? Only Scipio ever emerged from there with true glory, and the Consular Army that won him his title "Africanus" was made up of four real legions! My soldiers will be conscripts and mercenaries.

That, however, is the pessimistic view. The other side of the medallion presents a different face. At the conclusion of my term of office, I will be free to retire with full military and civil honours to the province of my choice — to return home, in other words — with all the pecuniary stipends concomitant with senatorial and consular rank. That means, dear friend, that at the age of fifty I will be a retired landowner, and wealthy enough to indulge my whims and realize my dreams. Remember my request of you!

Another advantage, I am told, of proconsular status is that I may transport my family and keep them with me in comfort and luxury. I am still unconvinced of the wisdom of such a course, but Heraclita is adamant. She is tired of staying behind, an uncomplaining victim of the military life, and she believes it will be good for my son Picus to see Rome, Africa and the Emperor's Court at Byzantium. (Constantinople is too new a name for such an old city!) I find myself inclined to bow to her wishes in this, in spite of what a small voice tells me is my better judgment.

Should you have reason to travel to the west while we are gone, you will be welcome in my villa, close to Aquae Sulis. It will be tended in our absence by my brother-in-law, Quintus Varo. You will find him amiable and a useful friend, should you have need of one. He owns the villa next to mine and our lands are contiguous. I have told him of you. He will make you welcome, as will my own sister, Luceiia, who was married to his wife's brother.

I have written these lines mindful of my promise to visit you soon. Alas, it will be longer than we could have anticipated. Keep my new sword safe for me, and find me a skystone while I am gone.

Your friend ever,
Britannicus

Proconsul of Numidia! I was elated for him, and at the same time worried by his accurate diagnosis of the problems that would face him there. However, I was confident, overall, that he would do well. I reread his letter several times then, thinking that five years without seeing him would be a long and lonely time. He and I had been comrades now for longer than that, and these past two years were the only time we had been parted. Five years! My natural pride and pleasure at the honour done my friend gave way to despondency, and I found myself staring sightlessly at Bishop Alaric's Celtic scrolls. I started to eat the food I had prepared for myself but it tasted like sawdust, and even Equus's ale was flavourless. Thoroughly depressed, I threw on my cloak and set out to find Plautus, to drown my sorrow with him in a tavern.

XII

There was a spirit of resurgence, of renewed optimism in Britain in the years that followed Theodosius's campaign against the invaders, and Equus and I profited handsomely by it. Our business grew rapidly; we had to more than double the size of our premises, and hire new workers regularly. By the end of our fifth year of operations, we had four apprentices, one of whom was Equus's own oldest son, Lannius, and six smiths in addition to ourselves. Equus had shown a natural aptitude for running our affairs, maintaining a tight but flexible production schedule and handling the day-to-day administration. My major function was now finding new contracts for our services and maintaining cordial relationships with our existing customers, the major one being the army of occupation. Life had been good to us.

My friendship with Alaric, Bishop of Verulamium, had deepened so much over the years that I had come to regard him as I did Equus and Plautus, almost as a brother. I seldom thought of him as a man of God, except when the work I did for him reminded me of his calling. The first cross I made for him had been exactly what he wanted, and in the making of it I had fallen in love with silver, taking great pleasure in the working of it — its ductility, its purity, its texture and its lustrous richness. It was a love that did not detract from my love of iron, but rather reflected it, for only in the polished newness of silver could I find a resemblance to the brilliance of my skystone dagger.

Plautus, showing the real mind that lay beneath his abrasive, rude-tongued public persona, took great pleasure in my silverwork and believed the tale of the skystone without reservation. He, too, asked me whether there might be other such stones lying around, and received the same response that I had given Britannicus. Undeterred, Plautus took a pragmatic approach. Without giving any reasons for his demand, he ordered his patrols to ask questions everywhere they went about strange noises, explosions, falling stones and the like, whether they occurred day or night. In response, we heard some outlandish reports, two of which took Plautus and me off together in the hopes of finding another skystone. In one spot we found a massive oak tree, long dead, sundered by some cataclysmic force in the distant past, and in the other no more than an enormous pile of jagged rocks that had split from a high cliff and obliterated a valley at the foot of it. Plautus's orders stood, however, and the inquiries continued, for which I was grateful.

On a warm evening, in the spring of my sixth year in Colchester, I sat alone in the small garden at the rear of my house, examining the latest in a series of silver crosses I had made for Alaric and waiting for Equus and Plautus to arrive for dinner. My crosses were growing more and more artistic, and this one was certainly unique. I was not quite sure whether I liked it at all, now that it was finished.

I had taken a fancy the previous year to combine the cross upon which Christ had died with the other symbol of his degradation, the crown of thorns thrust on his head by his Roman tormentors. The end result had been a beautiful but quite impractical piece, for the tines of the realistic silver thorns caught so often and so badly on the clothing of the wearer that the thing could not be worn at all. It was decorative, but useless, so I had melted it again to reuse the silver. Now, months later, I was looking at its successor. I had represented the crown this time as a plain, wide circle of silver, cut into quadrants by the arms and uprights of the cross, and into the circle I had engraved a graphic representation of the interwoven thorns, using an adaptation of the stylized bramble work so common in Celtic art. To balance the centrality of the circle, I had then widened the extensions of the cross into wedge shapes. The effect was different from anything I had seen before, but, as its creator, I could only hope that Alaric would like it. I was prepared to let my own judgment wait upon his.

As I sat there musing, the sky, which had clouded over unnoticed by me, opened suddenly in a torrential downpour. I scrambled to the door and stopped under the eaves to watch the effect of the heavy rain on the growing things in the garden. The weight of it was so great that the young, new flowers reeled beneath it, flattened to the ground. I stayed there until its force abated, and then I remained there, staring at something I had seen before. It was something anomalous that had nagged at me in an undefined way for all the time that I had lived in the house since my return, yet something I had never really paid proper attention to. It was one of a pair of military pikes that my grandfather had nailed diagonally to opposite walls of the garden for decoration. Looking at them now, their rusted heads streaming with rainwater, I had a flash of recognition. They were very old and rusted; at least, the heads were very old. The shafts looked comparatively new. By rights, these pike-heads should have been with all the other old weapons in my grandfather's collection, protected from further deterioration. Why, then, were they here, out in the open, exposed to the weather, mounted as useless, almost frivolous decorations on a wall?

My skin broke into goose-flesh as I realized that they must be there for a purpose, for I suddenly knew beyond a doubt that it was totally out of character for my grandfather to treat old weapons this way. But for what purpose? I knew only that it concerned me — that it had to concern me. There was no other explanation possible.

Excited without knowing why, I stepped out into the falling rain and crossed to the nearest pike to examine it more closely. It was as I had thought: the head was almost rusted through in places, but the wooden shaft looked strong, brand new, in fact. I tried to prise it off the wall, but it had been nailed securely by three big, double-pointed, U-shaped nails. Sure now that I had a mystery on my hands, I went and found a crowbar and levered the nails carefully from the wall. The pike fell heavily to the ground as I sprung the last one. It was at least ten times heavier than it had any right to be; I could hardly lift it from the ground. Astonished, I knelt down on the wet grass and drew my dagger and with its point I soon solved the mystery.

The shaft was made of strips of wood bound together over a central tube of tin. As soon as I realized this, I made short work of the outside cladding and bared the whole tube, which ran the entire length of the shaft. Impatient now, I hacked at the soft tin with my dagger blade — and exposed the gleam of gold. I rose to my feet, placing the ball of one foot against the middle of the hollow shaft, and wrenched the end upwards. The soft tin split at the point where I had punctured it and a shower of golden coins cascaded to the wet grass. I stared at them in disbelief and then ran to the other wall and tore off the second pike to pour out a similar rain of golden pieces. I was rich! I stood there in the rain, blinking vacuously at the golden pile at my feet. Then I turned and slowly went inside.

Equus was coming towards me from the front door as I entered. He frowned as soon as he saw the expression on my face and asked me what was wrong. I shook my head, unable to speak, and pointed a thumb over my shoulder to the garden. Still frowning, he stalked purposefully to the door and out of sight. The expression on his face as he passed me struck me suddenly as being very funny, and I began to laugh. My laughter grew to painful proportions when he came back in from the garden, his face as blank and shocked as my own must have been. I was hugging my middle, choking on my mirth by this time, and the incredulity on his face drew away the remainder of my strength, so that my legs gave out under me and I fell to the floor. His expression changed from incredulity to incomprehension, then to bewilderment, and finally to weak, uncertain laughter. By the time Plautus arrived several minutes later, we were both rolling helpless on the floor, and his face unmanned us even further.

Eventually, inevitably, sanity returned, and we took Plautus outside to see what lay there glistening among the long, wet grasses. In all, there were more than four thousand gold *auri*, each of which, pure and unpared, was worth a cartload of silver *denarii* at current values. Most of the coins dated from the days of the early Caesars. Some bore the head of Claudius and some of Nero, although most of them were Tiberian, but there were others that bore the head of Augustus himself. There were also more than two hundred newer coins, dating from very recent Emperors.

All three of us were stunned at the richness of the hoard, but it was Plautus, pragmatic as ever, who began asking questions.

"Why would he hide them there, like that?" he asked me, and I had an answer for him.

"That was my grandfather. What better place could he have chosen?" I said. "He left the pikes there knowing that sooner or later I'd be bound to notice something wrong. He knew that I knew him well enough to understand that he would never profane an old weapon like that without a reason. All I had to do was look at it and think about it."

"But you might never have noticed it!"

I was not to be gainsaid, however. "Plautus," I said, "I would have, sooner or later. Believe me. Today is the first time I have been in this garden when it rained, and I saw it."

It was Equus's turn to ask a question. "What would have happened if you had not come back from the wars?"

"What do you think? My uncle would still have lived here, or one of my cousins. It would not matter who lived here, in fact. The tin base of the tubes would have rusted out in another two or three years, and the coins would have fallen out onto the ground of their own weight. That's why they were mounted diagonally. If I hadn't come home, someone would eventually have benefited. I believe that's what my grandfather intended. That's the kind of man he was."

"But where did all this money come from in the first place?" This was Plautus. "Wouldn't he have left you some explanation, somewhere?"

"He probably did. I haven't even looked." I picked up one of the broken tin tubes and there, tucked into the top of it, was a tightly rolled parchment. I unrolled it and read it aloud.

" 'Reader, I hope you are Publius Varrus. If you are, then you have solved my riddle, justified my faith in you and earned the reward you must now be contemplating. The coins are yours by right. A few of them I earned throughout my years here, working in my smithy. The others, the older coins, I came by honestly, unearthing them by accident when I started to excavate the cellar under the forge.' "

I looked at Equus inquiringly, but he shrugged his shoulders and made a face indicating that he had known nothing of this discovery. I continued reading.

" 'The most recent of the hoard were minted during the reign of Claudius, so I assume they have been hidden in the earth here in Colchester since the days of his reign, when Colchester was built upon the ruins of Camulodunum. If that is so, they have lain hidden for almost three hundred years. Use them as you will. I have no use for them. If you are reading this, then you are safe and my prayers have been answered. Live long and happily.' "

I felt my eyes mist over as I read these last words, and none of us spoke for several minutes. Then Plautus spoke again.

"What are you going to do with them?"

"What? The coins?"

"Aye, the coins. There's more money here, lying around unguarded, than there is in the rest of Britain. This is an invitation to robbery, Publius."

I looked at the hoard piled haphazardly on the table top. "You're right. We'll have to do something with it. But what?"

"Bury it again."

"Where?"

"What does it matter? Just get it out of sight."

We finally poured the coins into a large amphora as an interim hiding place until Equus and I could fashion a strong-box to hold them. It took the combined strength of all three of us then to move the amphora into my study, where I sealed the neck with wax later that night. In the meantime, I threw each of them a leather pouch full of coins and then spent an hour or more convincing them to accept them. How we managed to pass that evening without the servants realizing what was going on is beyond me, but they never suspected anything. They were used by this time to the three of us carousing together at least one evening each week, and I think they were glad to be relieved of the need to dance attendance on me and happy to tend to their own affairs.

It took me a long time to appreciate that I was now a wealthy man, and it took another man's death to bring it home to me.

I was walking with Plautus one morning from the fort, where I had been meeting with Lucullus, the paymaster, and we were passing the main gate of a large and luxurious townhouse, more like a villa than anything else, when we heard loud screams and cries of grief coming from the other side of the walls. Curious, we stopped and looked inside the gate, and Plautus began asking questions. It turned out that the old man who had lived there for years, a retired general, had been found dead in his bed that morning. The howling was coming from his servants, more out of fear for themselves than out of grief for their master, I suspected, for the old man had died without heirs.

Plautus took over, since the dead man had been a general, and went back to report the matter to the military authorities and initiate funeral arrangements. I continued homeward and forgot the incident until that evening, when Plautus turned up unexpectedly on my doorstep. I saw immediately that he had been drinking. He poured himself a large cup of wine and flopped into a chair.

"Well, that's that! Got the old fellow off to the barracks for burial. Your health!" He swallowed deeply and went on. "No point in leaving him there at home, poor old catamite. According to his servants he doesn't have a relative left in the world, nor any friends to mourn him. You know, Publius, a man can live too long."

"What do you mean?"

"Just what I say. That poor old son of a noble Roman whore outlived all his contemporaries. All his friends. He just died alone. That's no good at all. I hope I die young."

"Young? You?" I laughed at him. "Plautus, you're an old man already! Besides, he might never have had any friends. Perhaps everybody hated him."

"No." He shook his head drunkenly. "His servants didn't, and if they didn't hate him he must have been all right. They're knee-deep in their own dung over what's going to happen to them now."

"What d'you mean? What's going to happen to them?"

"Nothing, but they have to move out, tomorrow. They're finished. Can't stay there. 'S not their house, so out!"

"They'll find somewhere else, Plautus. It's not the end of the world."

"It is for them. Who's going to take them in?" He snorted. "They can't even rob the place. The Procurator's people moved right in today."

"Why would they do that?"

"To take inventory. They have to. The old man had no heirs. Everything goes to the State."

"What will the State do with it?"

He shook his head. "I don't know. Sell it, probably."

"To whom? That's a big place. Who could afford it? I can't think of anyone in this town who could."

"I can." He smiled, pleased with himself. "Why don't you buy it?"

I stared at him in amazement. "Me? Why in the name of all the gods should I buy it?"

He grinned at me. "Because it would suit you, and you can afford it. You'll get it for half price, too, 'cause you're right. They won't be able to sell it t'anybody else and they don't need it."

I was half interested. "Why do you say it would suit me?"

He was still grinning. "Because, my friend, there is one room in that place that will make your eyes fall out. That old man was rich. Very rich. He took one of the small interior courtyards, you know? A courtyard? Open to the sky? Covered the whole thing with glass! Real glass! The whole thing. Must have cost a fortune. What's there now is a big room, bright, like outside, with a glass roof . . . 's daylight, bright daylight in there all the time. 'Cept at night, of course. Whole place is filled with plants. As soon as I saw it, I thought, Here's the place for Publius's treasures. It's perfect. It would be like having them outside, in daylight, except that they'd be inside in daylight, if you see what I mean, all warm and dry.''

I was staring at him. "I think I do," I said. "At least, I . . . hmmm . . . I'd like to see this room. Can you arrange it?"

The following day, because I fell in love with that one room, I tried to buy the house. Because of legalities, I was not permitted to, but, thanks to the influence of Antonius Cicero, I was permitted to rent it for an outrageous amount. The terms of rental were excellent; for all intents and purposes, in every sense except outright ownership, the house was mine. It was explained to me by the Procurator's people that, should the Emperor ever decide to come to live in this part of the Empire, in this particular town, I would be expected to vacate the premises.

I began to live the way I imagined a wealthy man should live, although I sometimes felt that I rattled around in the huge place like a lonely pea in a dry pod. Having made my bed, however, I was determined to lie in it, and I counterbalanced the pleasure I took in the treasure room against any regrets I had of my impulsive decision to assume the tenancy of the house.

XIII

Old age is a fascinating phenomenon, and a man's perspective on it changes rapidly as he accumulates winters. I am now at that stage of life where my grandchildren prove that people may legitimately think of me as old, but I am still young in my own head, and I anticipate with pleasure a long chain of satisfying, busy years before I grow old enough to die.

It was not always so. When I was younger, decades younger, I endured a period of terror, barely admitted even to myself, of growing old before I had time to live. I suppose all men must know that fear at some time, but keep its nightmares deep-hidden. I was not yet forty at the time, and the torsion of the mental fluxes I was going through brought out, from time to time, a rashness in me — an impulsiveness and, infrequently, an intransigence that I had not suspected of myself.

About three months after I moved into my new home, at the height of a magnificent summer, an event occurred that introduced the stench of the Senecas to my nostrils in a way that made me wonder why I had not been able to smell it before. I know it was my fate to behave as I did on that day, and I would do the same again today. I merely reacted to specific stimuli, without thought of long-term consequences.

It had been a long day, the second of what was to have been a week spent on the road, at leisure, with Plautus, who was on furlough. Ostensibly, we were on our way to Verulamium to visit Alaric and deliver yet another silver cross, this time a large one for public display during his services. We had left Equus in charge of the smithy and set out to make our way slowly to the south, prepared to make a three-day journey out of one half that long. We carried leather legionary tents, arrows and bows for hunting and barbed, iron-wire hooks for fishing. The weather was glorious. I was thirty-seven years old and had believed myself twenty in my mind until that morning, when we had met two young women in the fields. Plautus, three years my senior but with black, close-cropped hair and a clean-shaven face, had prospered with his choice. I had not. The chit that I had been attracted to looked at my greying hair and grizzled beard, and at my limp, and treated me as though I were her toothless grandfather, laughing at me and bidding me be ashamed of my almost incestuous designs. She made me feel old, and the beauty of the day had withered around me.

Now, in mid afternoon, we were seated in the front yard of a prosperous *mansio*, separated from the main road by a low wall with wide, open gates. We had enjoyed a meat pie, with fresh vegetables, new-baked bread and sweet, luscious plums, and Plautus had finally stopped crowing over his conquest of the girl that morning. I was still in a foul frame of mind, my memory stinging from the cruel injustice done my years.

The owner of the hostelry, a veteran of the armies, had just brought a fresh jug of wine to our table and was passing the time of day with us when we heard raucous voices in the distance, and all three of us looked idly for the source of the sounds. There were several men in the distance, grouped around two chariots, each of which was harnessed to a trio of horses. I noticed our host's face darken as he saw them.

"Who are they?" I asked him. "Do they live around here?"

"No, sir." His eyes had a worried look as he went on. "At least, they do, but not all the time, thank the gods. They visit nearby from time to time."

"Their presence doesn't fill you with happiness. Who are they?"

"I know only two of them. Nephews of Quinctilius Nesca, the commercial money-lender. He has a large villa to the south of here. The others are their . . . friends."

Quinctilius Nesca. Where had I heard that name before? It was familiar, and I had heard it only recently. Before I could comment on it, Plautus spoke up.

"They have done damage to you in the past?"

The *mansio*-keeper looked at him wryly. "Damage? Aye, sir, you might say that. Sometimes. In truth, almost always. They are very wealthy, and spoiled. They know no discipline. They seem to think they need none, with the people around here, anyway." He was still watching the small, distant group. "I beg your pardon, sir, but I must make preparations." He hurried away, and I turned to Plautus, who was eating one of the few remaining plums.

"We should get going. Are you about ready?"

He spat out the plum stone, stretched himself and broke wind loudly. "For what? There's no rush, is there? It's a beautiful day, the sun's hot, we've still got a jug of wine, and I don't feel like moving."

I grinned at him, momentarily forgetting my bad humour. "Plautus, you're a pig sometimes. Look at you — you're unshaven, unkempt, and you fart and scratch and belch and spit as though you'd never seen a parade ground. If your recruits could ever see you off-duty, out of uniform, all their fears of you would drown in laughter."

He farted again, deliberately. "That's what furloughs are for, friend, to give a man the opportunity to cleanse himself of all the rust that builds up through disuse."

"That's what I said. You're being a pig."

He belched, and I laughed aloud as he went on.

"Well, at least I'm a placid pig, and I pay for what I eat and drink. I wouldn't want to be our host and have to depend on those bucks to do the same."

He nodded sideways, and I looked to see the two chariots come racing towards us. They clattered across the road and right into the front yard where we sat, and their occupants, six of them, spilled out shouting at each other and laughing and yelling for someone to look after their horses. They made a lot of noise. Or rather, five of them did. The sixth, who remained in the chariot, stood out from his companions in every way. He was taller than all the others, broad-shouldered and heavily but cleanly muscled, with thick, fair hair and a tanned, handsome face. He stood silent, and I thought at first he was smiling, for he showed white, shining teeth and very bright blue eyes. But he was not smiling. There was no humour in his face, and he was staring hard at Plautus. I felt a stirring of misgiving in the bottom of my gut.

"Come on," I said to Plautus, who was unaware of the stare. "Let's drink up and move on. We'll take the jug with us. It's not going to be quiet around here for a long time now."

"Relax, man. They're just spoiled rich brats. They'll get bored and move on soon enough. Won't bother us if we don't bother them." He was looking at them as he spoke, and the silent one knew he was talking about them. He flicked his reins and walked his horses forward, right up to our table. Suddenly his five companions were silent, watching. Neither Plautus nor I reacted in any way other than to look at the three white horses that now stood within arm's reach of us. The chariot tilted as the driver stepped down, and I saw his sandalled feet approach on the side closer to Plautus. Plautus looked at me, his eyes expressionless, and took a mouthful of wine without swallowing, holding it behind pursed lips.

"You! Take care of these horses." The words were spoken in a flat, ominous tone filled with the threat of violence.

Plautus washed the wine around his teeth, swallowed it and grimaced, smacking his lips and then sucking them in to bite them between his teeth. The triple leather reins landed on the table between us. I raised my eyes and looked at the speaker, who ignored me completely. His eyes were fastened on Plautus, who sat immobile, side on to him, still looking at me as though the two of us were alone.

"I gave you an order, dung pile." No change in the tone of voice. None of the other five moved to approach, but now one of them spoke.

"Thrash him, Deus."

Deus? I looked more closely at the fellow they were calling God. At this proximity, he was even more impressive than he had appeared from a distance, but there was something in his face that told me he was older than he looked, and his expression recalled to me the junior tribune who had eaten Plautus's dung stew so long ago in Africa. It was that same look of intolerant, autocratic harshness, of implacable arrogance and intractability. And his eyes disturbed me. They looked, somehow, familiar.

Plautus spoke. "I was wrong. About the bothering. Stupid of me. It didn't connect." He put his goblet down very deliberately on the table top. "I will have some more, after all."

I was now experiencing the strangest feeling of being caught up in one of those Greek tragedies, as though we were all fated to perform some inexorable dance here, powerless to change the course of things. As I began to pour, the stranger started to reach for the jug, but Plautus's next words forestalled him.

"Look, stranger," he said, his voice unruffled but pitched low for our ears alone, "if you really want me to, I'll break your arm right off and jam it up your rectum, but I'd rather not." For the first time, he turned and looked at the young man standing above him. "Now, I can see that you've put yourself in a situation where your friends expect to see you make something happen, so here's a suggestion. Walk away from us, right now, back to your friends, and leave us to enjoy our wine in peace. You do that, and I'll take your horses and see that they're looked after. Then I'll come back, we'll finish our wine, and we'll leave. That way, you will look good to your friends and nobody will get hurt. Agreed?"

The young man said nothing. He just stood there,

looking down at Plautus with a strange, wild-eyed look that I still felt was strangely known to me. It spoke to me of insanity and yet familiarity. Then, without a word, he turned on his heel and walked away, straight-backed in his rich, white Grecian tunic. I heard his footsteps pause at the rear of the chariot, and then continue.

"Beautiful, isn't he?" Plautus's voice was heavy with irony.

"I think he's insane."

"He is. Crazed as Caligula." He moved to get up. "As soon as I move these horses, it's a certainty they'll bring the other chariot over. Let them. Don't move. Don't say a word, don't get involved. Just sit where you are."

I stared at him. "Then what?"

"Then I'll come back and move the other one."

"Are you serious? Why bother? Let's just face them down and get it over with. If you move both chariots they're not going to stop there. That whoreson's looking for a fight."

"Let him look. He won't get one from me. And don't you antagonize him. It's me he wants."

"Why, Plautus? Does he know you?"

"No, but that doesn't matter."

"Then sodomize him! Let's just take them now and have done with it." I started to gather myself to rise, but he pressed me back on to my stool.

"Forget it! It's not worth it. Anyway, he's the sodomite. Take a close look at the two pretty ones with him. Slap tits on them and I'd bed them myself. Just stay there, and don't get excited." He gathered up the reins and led the horses away.

As the chariot cleared my line of sight, my eyes were

on the group on the other side of the yard. They stood in a line, watching Plautus. None of them looked at me. Apart from a single dismissive glance from the big one, they had all behaved until this time as though I were not even present. I began to simmer resentfully.

The leader stood there, a pair of sword belts dangling from one hand. As soon as Plautus was out of sight around the corner, he threw one of the belts to a companion and slung the other across his own chest. Two more sword belts appeared from the bottom of the other chariot. Now four of the six were armed, and I was worried. My earlier eagerness to tackle them had vanished. Plautus and I were unarmed. Our weapons were with our horses. Lulled by the lushness of the summer afternoon, we had had no thought of violence here in this quiet *mansio*. The only item I had brought to the table with me was Alaric's cross, because it was too valuable to let out of my sight. It lay now on the table in front of me, wrapped in a square of cloth.

I watched them huddle together, talking among themselves, giggling and hatching some new mischief. One of them gave out a great hoot of laughter and threw his arm in a headlock around one of the others, and they wrestled together, ignored by the rest of the group who still listened to the big fellow. They might have been any group of normal young men having fun, except for the malevolent bearing of their leader.

Plautus returned eventually, taking his time, and sat down. His cup was still full, and he looked into it as he picked it up. "These boys are armed."

"Aye," I said. "And we are not. How long have we been soldiers?"

"Long enough to know better than to get caught like this. But we might still get away with it."

"I doubt it." I glanced towards the silent *mansio* behind us. The door was closed. "Have you noticed that no one has come out to greet these people?"

"Aye, I've noticed. Did they bother you while I was gone?"

"No. They've been ignoring me."

"Good, let's hope it stays that way. Just keep your temper in check." As he said this, my eyes were drawn across the yard to where the big, blond young man was climbing into the other chariot.

"Here comes the other one," I said.

"That's all right. I expected it." He didn't look over. Instead he said, "Didn't you recognize him? Claudius Caesarius Seneca. Does it mean anything to you, apart from the fact that you know his brothers?"

I stared at him in amazement. "You mean that's the youngest brother, the wastrel?"

"That's the one. A real beauty. The pride of the family. How far is it from here to Londinium? Should we make it by tomorrow night?"

I almost began to wonder if he was losing his mind, but then I realized that our tormentor was close enough to hear what we were saying. I nodded. "If we can make good time from here we should be able to do it easily." I fell silent as we waited for the repeat performance. The reins landed between us again. The young lout stood looking down at us silently, his hand resting prominently on his sword hilt, and then he turned and left. When he was gone I continued. "Of course. Quinctilius Nesca was the brother-in-law that Primus tried to have appointed

Quartermaster. The Commander put a stop to his plans. But the landlord said these were Nesca's nephews.''

"Two of them may be, but that young whoreson is a Seneca, not a Nesca. And he's the worst of the lot. Mad as a drunk Egyptian priest and ungovernable, even to his brothers.'' Plautus's lower lip was pushed up over his upper one, a sign I knew well as an indicator of deep and rapid thought. "Believe me, Publius, I've heard about this swine. He's worse than Nero and Caligula combined, and he's the richest son of a whore in the whole Seneca family. In the whole Empire, for that matter. The face of a god, the personality of a pit viper and a lust to be famed as the most degenerate swine in history.''

"Come on, you exaggerate. He can't be that bad. He's no more than twenty.''

"Twenty-five if he's a day, and he's worse than I say.'' He looked over at the young man. "Yes, that's the boy.'' He stood up. "I'll be back. Get ready to leave. When I come back I'll have our horses and I'll have an arrow nocked. Can you guess who I'll be aiming at? They won't take chances against a drawn bow, but don't waste time. Be ready to get up on the table and onto your horse. I've already unhitched the one chariot and scattered the horses. I'll do the same with this one. Just stay relaxed and hope they keep on ignoring you. I'll be as quick as I can.''

Once again he collected the reins and led the horses around the corner of the building as I sat staring in awe and fascination at the leader of the group across from me. Claudius Caesarius Seneca, the youngest son of the House that hated my best friend, descended of the noblest bloodlines and the wealthiest families of Rome.

I remembered Britannicus saying that he had inherited the fabulous wealth of his aged father. Under the terms of the old man's will, he was the sole heir. His brothers were already wealthy in their own right, and there had been no dispute over the terms. The Commander had gone on to say that the truly wealthy, those few people whose wealth defies credence, have their own laws and are untroubled by the laws of ordinary men.

I suddenly became aware that all six of them were now staring at me, and my stomach tightened. One of them, one of the two without a sword, came towards me, swinging his hips outrageously, parodying a woman's walk. He stopped, his hand on his hip, and leered at me. The wretch had catamite written all over him, and I stared in disgust at his carmined lips and cheeks and lustrous eyes, shaded with kohl. But I had to admit, Plautus was right. With breasts, this boy would have been irresistible.

He half turned and wiggled his fingers at his companions, and they all began walking towards me. I sat immobile, watching them approach, feeling an unusual and irrational fear writhing in my guts. And then, abruptly, I was angry again. Who were these Senecas that I should be in fear of even the youngest of them? These youths represented naked power, or one of them did, but what was that power really worth, here in the quiet heart of rural Britain? They did not know me, and had I not known their leader's name and his family's reputation, I would have faced them down alone. Four young louts and a couple of effeminate neuters!

Five of them stopped about five paces from me and stood watching with curiously apprehensive sneers as their leader approached me. He stopped right in front of me and looked me directly in the eye for the first time. I saw again the hostile, strange emptiness behind the bright blueness of the eyes, in a face that was now all too familiar.

"Move. We want this table." He reached out slowly, picked up Plautus's cup and, in a strangely formal gesture, extended his arm stiffly to one side and dropped the vessel to smash on the ground. I did not move. He reached for the jug of wine. I reached for it too.

"Don't be foolish!" The warning was a feral snarl.

I dropped my hand and let him repeat the performance with the half-full jug, and then with my cup and the empty bowl that had held our plums. I still did not move, wondering what was taking Plautus so long.

Seneca sighed. "I told you to move, old man."

He could not have chosen a worse phrase. All the resentment I had been feeling throughout the day seethed up and spilled over at the disdain in that "old man." I had the palms of my hands flat on the table and was halfway to my feet in wrath when his hand closed over the end of the cloth-wrapped cross that lay in front of me. Thinking of what the cross was meant for, fury washed over me that this animal should even think of touching it. I smashed my hand down on the cloth-covered shape, slamming it from his fingers back to the table top. Once he had felt the weight and shape of it, however, he took it for a weapon, and things began to happen very fast.

I heard the lightning slither of his sword whipping from its sheath, and the expression on his face told me I had little time. I launched myself backwards, kicking my stool away while managing to remain on my feet, and as I did so I heard the hiss of his sword point as it slashed through the air where my head had been. He came after me, around the table, and I kept going backwards, holding the cloth-wrapped cross in my right hand. Another slash, backhanded, brought his arm high for the killing stroke, and as it came slicing down I blocked it instinctively with Alaric's cross. The force of the blow almost knocked the cross from my hand, and I saw his eyes widen in shocked surprise. He had expected the clang of iron, not that solid *clunk!* And he had expected his sword to spring free! Instead, its tempered edge had struck deeply into the arm of the silver cross and lodged there. He was confused just long enough for me to realize what had happened, and to react ahead of him. Knowing what he did not, I threw myself at him, twisting around so that my right shoulder hit him solidly on the breastbone as I rammed my right arm straight out, away from him, twisting my strong smith's wrist to hold his clamped blade and jerk the sword hilt from his grasp. He went staggering as I took the hilt of his sword in my left hand and worked the blade free from its silver trap.

His friends had not had time to react, but now they came surging towards me, the three who had swords unsheathing them. Then Plautus shouted, "Hold!" and an arrow zipped in front of me and smacked into the shoulder of one of them, knocking him sideways off his feet. All eyes swung to Plautus, who sat on his horse less than six paces away, a fresh arrow already in place and the feathers of a full quiver peeking above his shoulder.

"I think we need no more bloodshed. Throw away the swords, boys. Far away. You! The pretty one! Pick up your friend's sword and throw it over there, too." He looked at me and nodded towards my horse. "Mount up. No names, no recriminations. Let's go."

I knew he was warning me, but I was too far gone in anger to pay any heed.

"No," I said, snarling. "Not yet. This dog meat called me an old man. I want to taste his tripes."

"Forget it. Let it lie. Mount up."

I ignored him, fixing my eyes on our tormentor. Let him show me his power now. I stepped sideways to the table and put down the sword and the cross side by side, and then I stepped away.

"There it is, buck," I said. "The only thing between you and your sword is an old man. Now, either pick it up and use it, or give me the belt and scabbard and I'll leave you to swim in your friends' vomit."

He glared at me and spat into my face, making me close my eyes reflexively as he leaped for me, his fingers spread like talons to rake my eyes. He really did think me an old man! I jumped a step backwards, seizing his right hand in my left, lacing our fingers and using my smith's strength again to jerk him forward and down, off balance. As he sprawled towards me, I took my full weight on my bad leg and smashed my right knee forward into his beautiful, depraved, young madman's face, and felt his nose give way. I released his hand quickly and stepped to the side, placing myself again between him and the table.

I snatched a quick glance at Plautus. He sat motionless, his eyes on the others, his bow half drawn. My antagonist was in no hurry to rise. He knelt on all fours, head down, blood and saliva drooling from his broken face.

"Finished already?" I taunted, and he raised his head slowly to stare at me with more malevolence than I had ever seen on a human face. I could have felled him again at any time as he got slowly to his feet, but I waited.

"Come on, Deus! Kill the old swine!" This, hissed by one of his friends, was the first utterance any of them had made. Deus! I thought again. Short for Claudius? If this buck is a god, he's a god from Hades.

He came at me again, more cautiously, and I felt the effect of those muscles of his. He was obviously used to fighting with *cestes*, the armoured gloves of the gladiators, for he used his bare fists like hammers. I took one solid blow on the shoulder that would have beheaded me had his aim been better. As it was, I went reeling, and he was on me like a wildcat, intent on ripping off any part of me he could lay hold of. He was well trained, but so was I, and in a far rougher school than any he had attended. I set out then, methodically, to thrash him badly enough to mar his beauty forever, and I succeeded. I cannot recall another occasion when my anger exceeded the rage I felt that day. At one point, when he stood swaying and helpless on his feet, his tunic covered with blood and sputum, his face a broken, bloody mess, I knew that I was overdoing it, but I was in the grip of some elemental fury. I heard Plautus shout to me to leave him, that he had had enough, but again I ignored him and measured out one last, sledgehammer blow. All my resentment, my anger, my fears and my disgust went into that blow, and the man went down as though I had used a real iron maul — and I was still angry. I took his sword from the table and flicked the edge with my thumb. It was very sharp. I used it to cut away his tunic from neck to hem, and then the fine woollen shorts he wore beneath it, so that he sprawled naked, and then, God forgive me, I carved a great "V" on his hairless chest.

"You'll remember meeting me, you whore's spawn," I muttered. "Be thankful I didn't cut off your dick and stick it in your mouth." I rounded on the others, who were all white-faced. "Well? Will you remember me? And leave old men in peace in future?" They flinched away from me, and suddenly I felt sick. I spat at their feet and left them, taking the still-wrapped cross and mounting my horse to follow Plautus away from the place. The doors of the *mansio* remained shut. Nobody sought to hinder our departure.

We rode in silence for more than half an hour, and for most of that time I shook as though palsied. And then the reaction set in, and I dismounted and was violently sick. When I had finished retching I still felt miserable, but with a different kind of sickness. I felt unclean, soiled inside.

Plautus waited, still mounted, until I was done. I led my horse to a convenient stump and got back onto its back, nodding to him to lead on. Again we rode in silence, and when he kicked his mount to a gallop, I followed without asking why.

A long time later we came to a stream, and Plautus dismounted and drank from it. I sat and watched him without really seeing what he was doing until I became aware of the foul taste in my own mouth. I slid to the ground and bent my head to the running water, rinsing my mouth and gargling and spitting until my mouth tasted clean again. I felt that, inside, I would never again be clean. I straightened up and stared out into the stream, which was quite wide. The sun still felt warm on my shoulders, but the strength was gone from its heat. I walked slowly out into the water until it rose to my knees and then I sank down into it, letting its coldness chill me.

As I rose to come out again, I saw that Plautus was sitting watching me, his back against a tree. His eyes never left mine as I walked to the bank and stood looking down at him.

"Feel like talking about it?"

I shook my head. He shrugged. "I think we should camp here tonight. Anyone looking for us isn't likely to come this way."

I looked around. "Where are we?"

"You're asking me? We're lost, that's where we are. Couldn't keep going south. That's where the uncle's villa is, remember? Anyway, he heard us saying we were headed south. So I turned east as soon as we were out of sight of the place. We headed east for over an hour and then I turned north. That's where we are now. Anybody looking for us would have to know where we were going. Since we don't know, they can't either. There should be fish in that big pool down there. I'll see if they're willing to eat hooks."

He got up and left, and I lay down, enjoying the cold clamminess of my soaked clothing. Minutes later, it seemed, I awoke, chilled to the bone, and stripped and rubbed myself down with my cloak. Plautus was still fishing. By the time he returned, carrying four fair-sized fish, I had a fire going and we spitted the fish and cooked them. I was hungrier than I had any right to be, and the fish were good. We ate in silence. Finally, lying comfortably in a hollow in the bank, I felt I could talk about it.

"How did you know who he was?"

"I didn't, at first." Plautus's answer was immediate, as though we had been talking about it all along. "It only came to me when somebody called him Deus. Unusual name for a living man. I'd only heard it once before, when somebody was talking about him. Then I remembered that the same person had said that he was related to Quinctilius Nesca. I remember thinking at the time that was appropriate. Have you ever met Nesca?"

"No, I've never even seen the man."

"Well, that's your good fortune. He's a nasty package. Lives in Constantinople at the Court most of the time, but he has estates outside Rome, one estate here, obviously, and an island in the Aegean where he's supposed to have nothing but pederasts and catamites. No women anywhere. The word is that he likes to eat human flesh. Babies, broiled whole and flavoured with spice and cinnamon."

"Ach!" I shuddered. "That's obscene! How can you even give ear to such rubbish?"

He shrugged his shoulders. "Wouldn't surprise me if it's absolutely true, every word of it. Wouldn't surprise me at all. I told you, he's a nasty man."

"How do you know him?"

"I don't. My brother did. He worked for him before he died."

"And this Deus is his nephew?"

"No, not a nephew, but related in some way. Perhaps a cousin."

"But the man at the *mansio* said that two of that gang were Nesca's nephews."

"So? Must have been two of the others. That probably explains why the whoreson's here in Britain. Visiting the family."

"Family?" I shuddered again. "A family suggests home and hearth to me. Values. Worthiness."

"Oh, they have values. They're just different to other people's. One of their ancestors, I forget his name, was actually removed from the governorship of a province for cruelty. Not unprecedented, I suppose, except that it was Caligula who recalled him. Caligula! Can you believe that? How bad must he have been?"

"Do you think they'll search for us?"

"The Senecas? You tell me. You carved your initial on one of them, the family favourite, with his own sword! Of course they'll be looking for us. But they won't know where to start. He can have no idea who we are, since no names were mentioned. Were they? Did you give them your name while I was away?"

I shook my head.

"Well, then. How can he find us? He'd never think of looking for me in a centurions' mess, and I doubt if he visits too many smithies. He knows you by your hair and beard. Shave them off for a month or two. Go bald and barefaced. You'll probably look years younger if you do. Remember, he thinks you're an old man."

"What about you, Plautus? What made him take after you?"

Plautus spat into the fire. "Who knows? I told you, he's mad. It's one of his well-known attributes. He just likes to kill people. Let's get some sleep and be on our way before dawn. We're still a long way from Verulamium."

"Verulamium!" I felt uncomfortable. "Do you think we should still go there?"

"Why not? That's where we're headed for."

"Only to deliver the cross, and it's ruined. I think we should head home to Colchester."

He looked at me speculatively. "Are you sure?"

I thought about it. "Yes. I'm sure. I think you're right. He and his people will be looking for us, and if he's as wealthy as you say he is, he can afford to hire a lot of people. I want to shave off my hair and beard."

Plautus smiled and shook his head. "You look bad enough normally to frighten a child, but you're going to be appalling when you're bald."

I grimaced. "Sorry I ruined your furlough."

"You didn't. That other whoreson did. What was it you called him? A whore's spawn?" He laughed. "You got your sexes mixed up, but not as badly as him."

I blinked, wondered, and said nothing.

X I V

I had been partially correct in my assessment of the reaction of the Senecas, but they did not hire just any group of soldiers to search for us; they hired the Roman army. For a week after our unexpected early return to Colchester nothing happened, and we said nothing to anyone except Equus. Then, leaving my house early one morning to go to the smithy, I was abducted. I remember a cloth of some description being thrown over my head and arms pinioning me, and then nothing.

When I opened my eyes again, I was lying on a couch in the private living quarters of Antonius Cicero, commander of the military district. I did not know where I was at first, but Cicero himself was standing over me in full uniform. I blinked at him, surprised.

"Cicero?"

He nodded in acknowledgement. "Varrus. How do you feel?"

How did I feel? Confused. I moved to sit up and my head informed me immediately that it, at least, felt far from well. Wincing and groaning, I managed to struggle up.

"What happened to me? Where am I? What's going on?"

"Here, drink this." He handed me a cup of something hot and steaming. "You are in my quarters. You are in custody."

I took the brew, making no attempt to drink it. "In custody? For what? Are you serious? In custody for what offence? On whose authority?"

"Deadly serious. I authorized it. You are here under arrest."

Wonderful! My head was pounding. I reached up tentatively and found a very painful area at the base of my skull.

"Did they have to hit me so hard? What is this? Am I considered too dangerous to simply approach and take into custody? What am I supposed to have done?"

He turned and walked away from me, picking up another steaming mug from a table and seating himself in a chair opposite me. From there, he looked at me in silence for a while as he sipped from his cup. I waited. Finally he spoke.

"What would you say if I told you a story about a brutal and unprovoked attack on an important visitor to Britain? A young man who had come here to visit his family — his very powerful family — and who was engaged in the personal business of the Emperor at the time of this attack? What if I were to add that this young man is not only a senator and a friend of the Emperor but one of the wealthiest and most influential people in the entire Empire, and that his immediate family, his brothers in particular, rank among the most senior officers of the army in Britain? What would you say if I were to tell you that this man was savagely attacked and mutilated, here in my jurisdiction, less than fifty miles away in a common *mansio*, in broad daylight, while on a visit to some equally wealthy and august, although slightly more distant, relatives? Tell me, Varrus, how would you respond?"

I was gingerly touching the bump on the base of my skull, but my mind was racing. Unconvincingly, I tried prevarication.

"What kind of response do you want? What are you talking about, apart from far too much power and influence?"

"Don't be facetious, Varrus, you know what I'm talking about. I want an answer."

"To what? My skull is coming apart. I didn't hear the half of what you were saying. Tell me again."

I drank the warm beverage — a spiced wine — while he repeated himself. I grimaced.

"I would say you might be in trouble indirectly, because this happened within your military district, but I cannot see how you can be held accountable for every madman in the country. Unprovoked assault and mutilation of a senator? Whoever would do such a thing would have to be insane. What does this have to do with me?"

"Drink up, Publius, and I'll tell you." He sipped again at his own spiced wine before continuing. "This entire town is being turned upside down at this moment in a search for a grey-haired, grey-bearded man with a pronounced limp. A very strong man. The search is being conducted from house to house by a cohort of the Emperor's own Household Troops from Londinium. They arrived here yesterday, late in the afternoon, and their Commander was here in this room last night, informing me of his mission and formally requesting my permission for his men to search the town. His orders are to find this man, no matter how long it takes or how far his search may take him."

"Oh. I see. Do they have a name for this man?"

"No. No more than a description."

"Who was the man he attacked?"

"Caesarius Claudius Seneca."

"Oh."

"Is that all you have to say?"

"What else is there? You arrested me because of the description."

"That, and the fact that I knew you were in that area when the attack occurred, accompanied by my own *primus pilus*, who just happens to fit the description of the second man perfectly."

"Plautus." I went cold with dread. "Where is he now?"

"He is where he should be. Out on the streets of the town with the Household Troops, co-ordinating the search."

I took a deep swallow of the spiced wine to cover my confusion. "I don't understand."

"Why not? It's very simple." He stood up and walked to the door of the room, opening it casually and looking out into the passageway in both directions before closing it firmly behind him and returning to his seat. "Plautus told me the entire story this morning. I could not think of a safer place for him than co-ordinating the search in his official capacity, in full uniform. You were the one I had the problem with." He shook his head. "Good God, Varrus. It's one thing to get angry at a man, but did you have to carve your initials on his chest? Knowing he was a Seneca? How would it look for Caius Britannicus if you were charged with this crime? It would put him on a par with Primus Seneca — someone who hires assassins to do what he dares not do himself. Caius would not thank you for that."

I was abashed. His assessment was absolutely accurate and, until that point, it had not occurred to me that I had endangered the Commander's reputation. I took refuge in truculence.

"He's not a man," I muttered, "he's a sick animal. And it was just one letter, 'V.' It stands for *Vae Victis*. Don't you think that appropriate? That he should carry that warning — Woe to the conquered?"

There was silence for a few moments, until I continued. "But you are right. It was unforgivably stupid of me. I acted without thinking."

"Hmmm. Anyway, you are safe for now. They will not look for you here."

"No? I'm not so sure, Tonius. If they search and ask questions, they'll find out about me — where I work, where I live."

He stood up abruptly. "That has been taken care of. They will find you and they will dismiss you. You were brought here unconscious in a covered cart under escort. The escort were all men trusted by Plautus. They will keep quiet. Nobody else saw you. Your partner at the smithy has been forewarned to send the searchers to your house. There they will find Publius Varrus. They will question him, and they will leave him alone."

"What? How?"

He smiled for the first time. "Have you ever met Leo, my major-domo?" I shook my head, mystified. He smiled. "You will. He has been with me since I was born. Before that, he served my father all his life. He is an old man — grey-haired, grey-bearded and crippled in his left leg, just like you. But he is too old now, and too feeble, to be capable of the crime you are being sought for. Today he is being Publius Varrus, in your house."

I was amazed. "Why?" It was the only question I could frame, and it covered a hundred things.

He smiled again. "As you said, a man would have to be insane to do what you are accused of doing, without provocation. I know you. And I know Plautus. I do not know young Seneca, but from all I have heard of him, he is insane, and he is an animal."

"Let's not malign animals. That man's a monster."

"Exactly. So, he will not find you, nor will he find Plautus, and he will soon have to take his monstrous anger and his power back, all unsatisfied, whence he came. He *is* on a mission for the Emperor, apparently, and that means he has little time for seeking personal vengeance. In the meantime, you will have to stay here for a week or so."

"A week?"

"At least. Until this nonsense is over and forgotten. I'm sorry about your head, but I had little choice. No way of knowing who else is in the streets out there, spying for Seneca. He has offered gold for your capture. There was no time to tell you anything, or to argue with you. I wanted to get you here unseen. That seemed to be the quickest and safest way."

I shook my head carefully. "So be it. I'm grateful, and deeply in your debt, Antonius Cicero. What now?"

He grinned at me this time. "Now you will meet a woman I know. She does magical things for women, and she is going to do the same for you."

I squinted at him warily. "What kind of things?"

"She will transform you. She will change the colour of your hair and your beard to blond, then shave off

most of your beard, leaving you with long Celtic
moustaches. She will also darken your skin. By the time
she has finished with you, not even Equus will recognize you."

I rose to my feet and began to move around the room,
my aching head forgotten in the urgency of the situation.
"No," I said. "No, Tonius, it won't work. The younger
Seneca may not know me, but his eldest brother does, and
he is the fox of the family. I have to leave Colchester. I
have to get away from here."

"Why? That is ludicrous. My friend will transform
you, believe me, Varrus. You will be safe. No one will
discover you. She will turn your hair blond, shave off
your beard, darken your skin, and we'll bandage your leg.
You'll be a veteran officer, a German mercenary,
wounded in the northern campaign."

My response was low-pitched as I thought aloud.
"Yes, and the trick will be successful for a while. Until
they can't find me. And until Primus Seneca remembers
that one man who fits the description perfectly is a close
comrade of Caius Britannicus, and that he last saw him
here in Colchester, with Britannicus, on the occasion
when Britannicus accused Seneca publicly of using
hirelings to do his killing for him." I felt bitterness
welling up in me as I realized the futility of my situation.
"No, Tonius," I continued, "your initial evaluation was
correct. I have endangered Caius, and my only hope of
salvaging anything from this morass is to remove myself.
The Household Troops may be duped by your man Leo,
but the ruse will hang together only if I am gone. If
Primus Seneca comes back here and finds me, then everything is finished."

He was staring at me in concern. "Then where will you go, Varrus? Where could you go to be safe from the spies of the Senecas?"

I grinned at him, for I had just answered the same question in my mind. "To the west. Britannicus has been forever nagging me to move to his part of the world, to help him start up his Colony when he retires. He has been almost five years in Africa. He should be home soon. When he arrives I shall be there, installed and waiting. In the meantime, no one would suspect that I'd go there in his absence."

Cicero raised his eyebrows and dipped his head to the side in a gesture of acknowledgement. "Well, I suppose you could be right. It seems reasonable. But what about your business? Your smithy?"

"Equus can run it without me. He does that now, most of the time. But you have a point. How long does a man have to be missing to be declared legally dead?"

He was frowning. "That is a strange question. Why do you ask?"

"I think I should die," I said. "How can we arrange that?"

His face went blank as he understood what I was saying, and he remained silent, deep in thought for a long time. "It can be done," he said at last. "Corpses are found from time to time, and some of them are unrecognizable. I assume that is what you mean?"

I nodded. "If I were to leave you, as a friend, in possession of my will, you would be bound to produce the document upon my death, would you not?" He nodded slowly. "Good. Then I shall write my testament, bequeathing all that I own to Equus as my only heir and my partner. The smithy will then become his in all legality and may not be taken from him. I could also leave you something recognizably mine that could be placed in the possession of a suitable corpse."

He cleared his throat. "Like what?"

"Who knows?" I shrugged. "I haven't even thought about it yet, but we'll find something."

"Varrus, this is highly irregular . . ."

"Yes, Tonius, and so are the Senecas. This will work. I will disappear, presumed dead. You will find a suitably decomposed body from somewhere and declare my death to be official. It might take months, but that won't matter. Equus, in the meantime, will look after our mutual concerns and join me if he wishes to at a later date when it is safe to do so. In any event, Caius Britannicus will be safe from the calumnies of the Senecas, at least on my account."

"You trust him that much? Equus?"

I smiled. "Implicitly. Until today there were only three men in whom I would ever have dreamed of placing complete trust: Equus, Plautus and Caius Britannicus. Now you have made it four."

"Hmmm. You place me in fine company. Thank you. When will you go?"

"Soon, but not too soon. The hunt is at its height right now. I'll wait for it to die down. Perhaps two weeks, no more. Much less, if Primus Seneca comes here. If he does, I'll leave immediately."

He made a coughing sound deep in his throat. "Very well, then, you shall stay here in the fort until the Household Troops leave Colchester. That should be by tomorrow or the following day, since they will hunt for you in vain. Stay here in my personal quarters. I'll have Plautus fix up a campaign cot for you in the other room. But you'll have to stay out of sight until I give you the word to emerge, and Leo will remain at your house until then, too."

I bent my head to him in agreement and acknowledgement of his generosity.

I spent only one night in his quarters, for the Emperor's Household Troops left the following morning. Tonius informed me that they had visited my house and had accepted Leo as me, and as too old and feeble to be their man. They had also dismissed Equus as a potential culprit because he was too big and fair-haired to fit the description of the second man they sought.

I spent the next two weeks making preparations for my journey to the west, and left a small bar of silver with my name on it in Cicero's possession so that he could use it to substantiate my death if and when his men ever found a suitable corpse. My last will and testament was brief and to the point, and this, too, I left in his possession. It read:

Since the occasion of the night attack on Caius Britannicus, when I could have lost my life without preparation or warning, I have thought much about dying. I am aware that, in the event of my death, my friend and partner, who is known to the world as Equus, would have no way of demonstrating that the smithy we operate together is rightfully and legally his property, since I would have no further use for it and am without heirs. If and when I die, if Equus remains alive, the smithy and all it contains belong to him, to deal with as he sees fit.

I leave this document for safekeeping in the hands of my noble friend Antonius Cicero, Military Governor of this District.

Gaius Publius Varrus

Three days before I was due to leave, I went into my weapons room and took down my grandfather's great African bow from the wall. It measured five and a half feet from tip to tip unstrung.

I had made several strings of gut for it, and a sheaf of arrows from the straight stems of young spruce trees. These I had shaved and then dried in the forge, tying them first tightly together in bundles so that they would not warp in the process of drying. Equus had been surprisingly knowledgeable about the art of flighting arrows, and had spent hours working on them, lovingly splitting the ends of the shafts and gluing lengths of eagle pinions into place. The finished arrows were just about a full arm's length long and were tipped with the finest iron barbs, made in my own forge.

The bow itself was a composite of three layers of wood, horn and sinew, with the wood in the middle and the sinew on the outer curve. At first, in spite of my smith's arms, I had been unable to pull it, but Equus had shown me the trick of how it was done, and my arms had soon adapted to the unusual muscular tensions required. Once I had mastered the knack of controlling it, I found that the weapon could throw an arrow hard enough to pierce a tree at almost two hundred paces.

In the two weeks since the Seneca incident I had not drawn the bow, but I decided to take it with me on the road — the bow, my skystone dagger and a serviceable sword made by my own hand.

I bought three fine horses from the garrison, two for riding and the third for packing my gear. The sale was strictly illegal, of course, but my friends in the fort, Cicero and Plautus, agreed that, as a former *primus pilus* and a valued supplier, I was entitled to arrange a long-term "rental."

Finally, on a beautiful day in late autumn, I was ready to set out on my journey. A squadron of light cavalry would escort me for the first third of the way, from Colchester to Verulamium, where they were to relieve a detachment who had been on extended duty in that town. Equus bade me farewell at the smithy, and Plautus met me there and rode back with me to the fort to pick up my escort. As he wished me Godspeed he grinned, more to himself than to me, and I was intrigued.

"What are you grinning about?"

Plautus's grin grew wider. "Oh, mere passing thoughts," he said. "Give my love to Phoebe."

"Phoebe? What is that supposed to mean?"

"You'll be going through Verulamium, won't you? Give her a stab for me."

I did not know whether to laugh or be angry. "Plautus," I said, "you're a pig. I've told you that before."

"Aye." He laughed that dirty laugh of his. "And Phoebe is a pigeon, plump and waiting to be savoured, and your journey to the west will be a long one. A soft pillow on the road will be a pleasure, at least for one night."

I frowned. "I'll stay with Alaric in Verulamium."

"Of course you will, and I will respect your chastity forever. But if you should see Phoebe, remember my request."

I smiled and embraced him and then left, riding at the head of the column with the young Commander.

The first stage of the journey passed quickly and pleasantly, although we camped each night in fields and clearings by the side of the road. I could never get used to sleeping in a military camp that was not surrounded by a wall and a ditch. It bothered me deeply, although no one else appeared to give it a thought. Britannicus and his ideas might have made me over-critical, I was prepared to admit, but there was logic behind my misgivings, too. The walled, ditch-surrounded marching camp had been the saving strength of Roman soldiers on the move for almost 1,200 years. Only within the past century had the practice been abandoned, especially here in Britain, where peace had existed for over three hundred years. The relaxation in regulations had its roots in the general, poisonous relaxation of discipline: it was deemed, nowadays, to be demeaning to the rights of the modern soldier that he should be expected to dig a ditch and erect fortifications around an overnight camp in time of peace! My mind swept me back to the high moor, on the first day of the Invasion. The fortifications around our camp had saved a thousand lives, right there. Thank God for Caius Britannicus and his stubborn refusal to accept anything less than the highest standards in anything he did! I looked around me, at the open country in which we were lying, and decided to keep my mouth shut and make no comment.

Light cavalry squadrons were no more than mounted archers, so my great African bow was a sensational success among the men. Each night after the evening meal, in the hour or so that remained before darkness fell, we set up targets by the roadside and held archery contests. I am happy to be able to say in all modesty that my bow was to theirs what a *ballista* is to a boy's slingshot.

Phoebe was happy to see me. She left me in no doubt of the fact when I turned up without warning at her place of employment. She was busy at the time, I was told, manicuring the hands of the wife of one of the town magistrates, but she left her charge when they told her I was there. She came running to greet me, throwing herself into my arms and kissing me in a way that threatened to draw the soul right out of me. I told her that I was in the city for one night only and that I had come to visit Bishop Alaric, and I arranged to meet her later in the day, when she was free.

In fact, I knew that Alaric was not in Verulamium. I had gone to his home on arriving, only to find that he was out about his Master's business. The news had not surprised me, for Alaric spent but little time in Verulamium. What did surprise me was my reaction — a mixture of relief and release. I had left my respects with Alaric's housekeeper and gone directly in search of Phoebe.

I did not know why I had lied to Phoebe, but I had the whole afternoon to myself to think about it. I bought some fresh bread, cheese and a small jug of wine from a merchant and rode out of town to be alone and think. I found a comfortable bank beneath a tree and turned my horse loose to graze, and as I ate I allowed myself to deliberate upon my feelings for and about Phoebe. My lust for her was as strong as ever; I saw little point in trying to deceive myself about that. When she had thrown herself into my arms earlier that day the arousal I had experienced was urgent and demanding. More than that, however, Phoebe was a friend. More than that? I had to smile even as I thought it. There is nothing more demanding than an upstanding phallus, and in the arms of a willing woman few other considerations can coexist with the need to achieve and prolong copulation. Phoebe was my friend, that was true — a tried and loyal, loving friend. Too loving. There was my dilemma. I was a fugitive and, if I were caught, I would be a dead man. Knowing that, Phoebe, being the woman she was, would wish to share my odyssey, my roadside bed and my danger. That I could not allow in conscience, because, for at least two reasons — her station in life, and her marriage to Cuno — I could not think of Phoebe as a wife and therefore I could not expose her to risk for mere gratification of my fleshly urges.

All of this was highly philosophical, of course, and I enjoyed the debate thoroughly, but by the time I rose to leave, I had decided firmly that I would say nothing to her of the reasons for my journey, or of my destination.

When I met her again at the appointed time and place, Phoebe was almost dancing up and down with excitement. There was a drama at the amphitheatre that evening, she told me, and she had never seen a performance. Naturally, we attended it together.

The amphitheatre, which had been built just a few decades before on the outskirts of the town, was enormous. I cannot recall the name of the play we saw, for I spent most of my time enjoying Phoebe's pleasure in the spectacle, but I remember being impressed by the number of people the place would hold, and by the ease with which I heard the voices from the stage, even though we were seated far up on the raked terraces.

Someone told me that the place held upwards of seven thousand seated spectators.

At the end of the performance, as we were leaving, a loud argument broke out close by me and I heard the word "Thief!" being shouted. I glanced to my right and saw the thief, a cutpurse, his bare blade still in his hand, coming towards me. He saw me notice him and dived backwards into the crowd before I could think to lay hands on him. The crowd was too dense for me to chase him, anyway, so I let him go. I turned my attention instead to Phoebe's prattling and thought no more about him.

There was a profusion of public shops close to the amphitheatre, catering to the appetites of the crowds who thronged to the performances, and Phoebe and I managed to find one where the food, according to others, was very good. There, during the course of our meal and after her chatter about the performance was exhausted, I told her I was leaving on an extended journey and that we would probably never meet again. I begged her not to question me about my reasons, and then I relented and told her what had happened. I told her everything except my destination, and I told her, in answer to her entreaties, that I would not, could not, take her with me.

She was subdued for a while after that, and I fell silent, leaving her with her thoughts; for once in my life I had the acuity to do the correct thing. I sat and sipped my wine, trying not to be obvious in watching the expression on her face. Was there pain there? Disappointment? Resentment? I could not tell. Her face gave away absolutely nothing of what was going on in her mind. Only her silence told me that she was thinking deeply.

As we strolled the short distance to her home, she held my hand in hers and made no further reference to my journey. Instead, she talked again about the evening's performance and about the pleasure she had had. Had I not suspected differently, I would have sworn she was the same merry, wild-eyed sylph who had thrown herself into my arms that morning.

We stopped outside the building in which she had her rooms and she looked at me calmly. Then she reached up gently and took hold of my beard, pulling my face down to where she could kiss me, gently and chastely.

"Good night, my Publius. Go quickly and go surely and come back soon to me. And in between, think of me kindly, from time to time."

I turned to leave, and she grinned and held me by the beard.

At one point, somewhere in the middle of the night, she rolled over and mounted me, riding me slowly, raising herself so high in withdrawing, and so slowly, that I found myself waiting constantly for her to lose her grip on me. But each time, when I was held in her by nothing but the merest clinging edges of sensation, she paused successfully and took me back, infinitely slowly, into the yielding, lubricated grip of her. It was an experience never to be forgotten. So sure was she of my reactions that she could stop exactly, anticipating my release by half a heartbeat, remaining motionless until the storm had receded and she could resume again. After one such lovely interruption, she sank down on me completely, bringing her knees up beneath her shoulders so that she squatted above me, her buttocks pressing into my groin. I was so deeply lodged in her that I could feel the end of my phallus jammed against the deepest recess of her living flesh, and then she began to rotate herself so that I moved around her like a stirring stick, churning the softness and the heated depths of her so thoroughly that I was afraid I must be hurting her. I said so, and she paused, grinding herself down onto me.

"Publius, sweet man, this is the kind of hurt I would gladly suffer all the minutes of my life. Are you enjoying it?"

I moved my pelvis upwards. "Do you even have to ask?"

"No. Believe this, magical man. The pleasure that you feel could not begin to match the pleasure I am taking in this. If I could cut you off and keep you here inside me like this for the rest of my life, I would die a happy woman and be buried with a smile on my face." She stopped and rose up again, letting me pull out almost completely before sinking back onto me and leaning forward to mouth a fierce, hot-breathed, tension-filled whisper into my ear. "This may be the last time I ever have you here in my body, Publius Varrus. I want to remember it, and I want you never to be able to forget it. You may have many other women after this, but you will never have one who enjoys you more, so I am being selfish. This night is mine. Your body is mine tonight. The milk of your balls is mine tonight. And this beautiful, lust-filled dagger of yours is mine to pierce myself with tonight, to die on, if I can suck it deep enough into me. So stab, Varrus! Impale me, you beautiful, rutting, rampant man!"

It was too much for me. I groaned and convulsed, throwing my arms around her, clutching her close as I lost control and poured myself violently up into the depths of her.

In the morning, before the sun came up, she bathed me and fed me, and then she spread herself for me on the table before I left, so that I took the road again with the moistness of her in my groin and the scent of her juices clinging to my face and filling my nostrils.

BOOK THREE

Westering

X V

I was two days out of Verulamium, making my way easily along the road towards the town the British call
Alchester, when I ran into trouble. I was still feeling
euphoric about my marathon encounter with Phoebe,
and I was day-dreaming. In fact, I was lost in my imag-
inings to such an extent that it was almost too late for
me to react when I finally noticed the group of five men
drawn up in a line across the road about seventy-five
paces ahead of me. I knew immediately that I was in
trouble. They had that air of menace about them that
stamped them immediately as malevolent.

I reined in my horse and looked around me. There was
open heath on both sides and nowhere to run to that
offered any hope of safety. I glanced behind me then and
was unsurprised to see three more men, slightly farther
away than those ahead of me. Once aware of the danger,
my mind automatically clicked back into legion days.
Without even pausing to think, I slung my leg over my
horse and dropped to the ground, unhitching my strung
bow from around my shoulders with one hand and reaching for an arrow with the other. I wasted no time cursing
myself for my carelessness. I merely nocked the arrow,
drew, sighted and let go in one motion. Considering the
speed with which I did it, I was lucky. The arrow took the

central man of the five ahead full in the forehead and hurled him backwards, heels over head.

The speed of their companion's death threw the others into confusion. Two of them held bows, however, and I knew they would begin making life very uncomfortable for me as soon as they recovered from the first fright. Afraid that they might hit my horses, I ran limping to the side of the road, and almost ran into their first arrow in the process. It zipped past, about a foot in front of me. I remember thinking that if they shot that badly, I should just stand still and let them waste their arrows!

I snapped a shot backwards at the three behind me, and again I was lucky; one of them fell with a howl of pain. Now, they decided to treat me with respect. One of their two bowmen knelt to steady his aim. I drew a steady pull on him, bringing the string all the way back to my ear and holding it there before loosing it. The muscles of an iron-smith, I had discovered, are frequently worth more than gold. My arrow skewered him before he had even loosed his own, and in spite of his kneeling position he, too, went flying, testifying to the power of the mighty weapon I was holding.

I swung around again to check on the two remaining men behind me. They had split apart, one to each side of the road, and were running towards me as fast as their feet would carry them. One of them was no more than twenty flying paces from me as my bow came up again. I dropped him in his tracks and reached automatically for another arrow, but his companion screamed, turned and ran like a hare back the way he had come. I let him go and turned back to the others, only to discover that they, too, had taken to flight. I breathed a shivering sigh of relief and went back to lean against my horses, which still stood where I had left them. Sure enough, I saw my grandmother's sad face and I started to shake, and then I threw up.

Four men dead in less than four minutes! I spat to clear the sick taste of bile from my mouth and went to collect my valuable arrows. Three I cleaned with a handful of grass, but I had to leave the fourth lodged firmly in the forehead of the first man I had shot. It was a highly unpleasant task, recovering those arrows, and one on which I don't want to dwell, but I could not afford to leave them there.

The country ahead of me was heavily wooded and made up of rolling hills and valleys dense with growth. Thank God for Roman roads! I continued my journey for another two hours without seeing a living soul, although I was now looking very carefully and no longer day-dreaming.

At dusk, I was looking seriously for a suitable bivouac spot when I saw a body of men coming towards me. Light gleamed on metal and I recognized them for what they were — a maniple of infantry. When they rode closer, I saw the standard of the Twentieth Legion, my own regiment, and I drew myself to attention and waited for them. The mounted centurion at their head came trotting towards me and halted several yards away. I gave him the clenched fist salute of the legions. He sat there, staring at me.

"Centurion? Commander Varrus?"

I nudged my horse towards him. "Aye, I'm Varrus. Who are you?"

"Strato, Strato Pompey, Commander. I was with the Hammers in '67."

"Strato! By all the Caesars, lad, you've grown up!"

He laughed, and we rode towards each other and embraced. He had indeed grown up. He had been the youngest man in the Hammers, a mere lad of seventeen when they were formed, but already a decurion.

"Where have you been since then?" He drew back and looked at me, and I could see genuine admiration and liking in his gaze.

"Still with the Twentieth, sir. They reformed it after the Invasion. I'm ranking centurion now, *primus pilus*, as you can see. And I've been hoping you'd stop saying 'By all the Caesars!' to every Pompey that you meet. I always thought it would get you into trouble some day. We Pompeys are a wild crew, and we mislike the name of Caesar, even today." He smiled shyly, conscious of the boldness of such a speech to his old commander. But he himself was *primus pilus* now. The young Strato was long since forgotten. "We were just about to camp for the night. There's an open stretch of high ground about a mile ahead. Will you join us?"

"Happily, my friend. I passed the place a little while ago. I would have stopped there myself, but I had some trouble with a few of the locals earlier and I was hoping to find an easier place for one man to defend. I take your point about the Caesars, however. Some of them are highly unpleasant people."

He was frowning. "What kind of trouble have you had, sir? Where?"

I nodded backwards. "Back there. About eight to ten miles. Some fellows wanted to relieve me of my horses — and my life."

"Are you all right?"

"Oh, I'm fine, but I left four of them lying in the road. You'll find them in the morning, I suppose, if their friends haven't come back for them."

His eyes grew wide. "Four of them?"

"Four." I grinned. "But not hand-to-hand. I shot them from a distance. With this." I held up the bow.

He looked at it, and his lips pursed in a silent whistle. "That's impressive shooting, nevertheless. Four of them!"

As we were talking, his maniple had marched on and were now a good hundred paces down the road.

"Come, Commander. We'd better catch them or they'll march right past the campsite."

I swung my horse into place beside him. "Where are you headed, Strato?"

"Nowhere in particular, sir. Just a routine patrol. We've been having trouble with bandits in this district. Don't know who they are, but they're making a nuisance of themselves and we have to patrol the whole area regularly. What about you?"

"Ah . . ." I had been on the point of telling him where I was going, and my hesitation seemed to me to be very obvious. "Just travelling, Strato, looking at the countryside and taking my time. Getting away from life for a few days."

He grinned with delight and was still grinning when we caught up to his maniple, who were already beginning to deploy on the campsite. Again, I saw no signs of any preparations to fortify the camp, but this time I felt free to comment upon it.

"An unfortified camp, Strato? I thought we taught you better than that."

His face creased into a frown. "You did, sir, and I never feel right about it. But that's the way it has to be in the Twentieth these days. Everywhere else, too. The legate commanding the legion doesn't want trouble with the men, and he would have it if they had to dig a ditch and build a wall every night."

"Even in hostile territory?"

He nodded. "I'm afraid so, Commander. It's not like the old days."

"Obviously." I looked around me. The camp was being set up in the orderly fashion that I knew so well. There just weren't any fortifications. "You ever get caught with your britches down?"

He shrugged his shoulders. "Not yet, thank God. We use more sentries than we used to."

"You mean the men would really rather do extra guard duty than build a safe camp?"

"That's the way it is."

It was my turn to shrug. "Well, Strato, I hope you are never in the situation of having to wish you'd insisted on what you know to be right."

"So do I, Commander."

"Where can I set up? Officers' area?"

"Why, right here, sir, in the tribune's spot. I'll detail a man to put up a tent for you."

"No, Strato, that you won't. I'll put up my own. That way I know it won't fall down in the middle of the night. You'd better see to your duties. I'll get myself settled and wait here for you. Come back when you're able to relax."

He snapped me a salute and went off to supervise the evening's arrangements.

At dinner that night, he introduced me to his fellow centurions and junior warrant officers, and the evening passed very pleasantly, with many reminiscences of the fighting retreat from the Wall in '67 and '68. I rolled into bed around ten and slept like a log until the bugle sounded.

I set out early the next morning on the last leg of my journey into Alchester. I found it to be a pleasant place, little more than a permanent camp with a marketplace, but it did boast a *mansio*, where I managed to get a hot bath and a steam as well as a surprisingly excellent meal. Then, refreshed and revitalized, I visited the market, where I found some remarkably fine pottery work done by a local craftsman. There was one beautiful vase finished in a blue glaze on jet black that for some reason suggested Britannicus so strongly to my eyes that I had to buy it for him, knowing it would please him. It had a long, slender neck and a delicately fashioned bowl, but it was heavy and very solidly made.

By that time, it was late in the afternoon, so I went over to Alchester's main camp and introduced myself to the commanding officer. He was a stranger to me, but he knew who I was, thanks again to Antonius Cicero, and he invited me to dine with him and his officers that evening. I accepted gladly and spent a very pleasant evening with them, managing to evade their casual curiosity about my destination and leaving them with the firm impression that I would be heading south-west to Portus Adurni, or Portchester as men were calling it, where I would take a ship to Gaul to search for exotic weaponry and indulge myself in indolent pursuits, as wealthy men do the world over. By the time I left the dining table to return to the *mansio*, it was dark.

The main entrance to the *mansio* was in a narrow thoroughfare that was more of an alley than a street, but it was well lit with flaming torches, which surprised me. I was about forty paces or so from the entrance to the *mansio* when I saw two men approaching me, weaving drunkenly, their arms about each other. I started to draw aside to let them pass just as the light from one of the torches fell on them, and a series of things happened all at once. I recognized the face of the knife-wielding cutpurse from the theatre at Verulamium. I also recognized his companion as one of the men who had attacked me on the road, the one who had fled screaming when I dropped his companion less than twenty paces from me. And I knew without even turning around that there were two others behind me, because four had been left alive.

I was still clutching the long-necked vase I had bought earlier in the marketplace. Now, without stopping to think, for I knew that I was absolutely right and was about to die if I didn't do something immediately, I leaped towards the two "drunkards," swinging the vase like a club. It took the cutpurse high on the side of the head and sent him smashing senseless into the wall on the other side of the alley. His friend was taken completely aback and froze, slack-jawed, for just the length of time it took me to shift my weight and kick him full in the balls with my good leg. As he bent double, I brought the still-unbroken vase down on the back of his head and heard his vertebrae crunch. I kept the impetus of the swing going and spun to face behind me, where the other two would-be assassins hung paralysed in surprise. I swung my pottery club high over my head and charged them with a roar. They turned and ran, and I chased them, knowing I had no hope of catching them. I knew I was a cripple, but they had apparently forgotten.

Shaking with rage, I finally stopped and returned to the two I had downed. The second one I had hit lay full in the middle of the narrow street, stone dead, the base of his skull crushed. I crossed to the other one, the cutpurse, as I had thought him. He was unconscious, but he was still alive and his pulse was strong. I looked up and down the street. There wasn't a soul in sight. Who were these people? It was obviously no accident that I had encountered them three times in three days, over a distance of some fifty miles.

I bent over the unconscious one and hauled him to a sitting position. Then I began to slap his face, trying to bring him back to consciousness. I had no worries about being discovered there; no one would question a guest at the officers' barracks. The man did not respond to my slapping. I drew out my skystone dagger and knelt beside him on the ground, picking up his hand and pressing the point of the dagger into the half-moon of his thumb-nail. He responded to that, quickly. As soon as I saw that he was regaining consciousness, I left him to open his eyes naturally. When he did, and saw my face bending over him, his eyes flared with fear.

"You know me, don't you?" I took a handful of his hair and inserted the point of the dagger into his nostril. "Well, I don't know you. But I do know that you have been trying to kill me, and I don't like that. I can think of better ways to die than at the hands of a dung pile like you."

My voice was calm and level, showing none of the anger, horror and revulsion that were rioting through me now that the danger was over. I twisted my hand tighter in his greasy hair, pulling him up so that his face strained in discomfort as he tried to pull his head back and away from the point of my dagger in his nostril.

"You're an ugly son of a whore, but you're not going to look any better if I have to lay your nose open on both sides. And I will, friend, if you don't tell me what I want to know. And if you are really strong and can stand the pain and still not tell me, then I'm going to cut your ears off, one at a time. And then I'll carve you a new mouth. One without lips." I pushed and sliced, and the dagger blade passed cleanly through the sensitive flesh of his nostril, bringing a gush of blood and a scream of pain. I inserted the point in his other nostril. "I learned this trick from the tribesmen in Africa. It works well — don't you think so?"

His eyes were starting from their sockets and he was gagging on his own tongue in his terror. I took the knife point away and shook his head by the hair, brutally, and then jammed the point back again.

"Now! Why are you trying to kill me? Why me?"

His mouth worked frantically, but nothing came out. I released his hair and grasped him by the front of his tunic, pulling him up to me and smelling the rancid foulness of his breath.

"I'm going to count to three, and then your nose is gone and we start on your ears. One."

It was as far as I needed to go. He was babbling, "Hired! Hired! We were hired to kill you! Ten gold *auri!*"

"Hired by whom? How did you know me?"

"We didn't we didn't we didn't! We were looking for a grey-haired man with a limp! A strong man! We saw you in Verulamium."

"You saw me?" I returned my grip to his filthy hair, twisting it violently. "Are you telling me that I might not be the man you were hired to kill?"

He was terrified, nodding his head and grinning as though an admission of mistaken identity would get him out of this situation. I felt disgust swelling in my gorge. I twisted harder.

"How long have you been looking for this man?"

"A week! More!"

"A week? You must be mad, as well as murderous." I let him go, abruptly. "A week, you say? Who wants this man dead badly enough to set a price as high as that on his head?" I asked, though I already knew. "You say you have no name for him? The victim?"

He shook his head, relieved to be released. "No. No name. Just a description. As I said. Grey hair, grey beard, lame leg. Like you."

"Like me. Do you know how many men there are like me in Britain, you imbecile? There must be hundreds! All veterans. All capable of eating your kind alive and spewing you into the gutter." I thumbed the edge of the dagger. "I want to kill you, you animal, and I haven't felt that way in years. I'd be doing the world a favour, too." I brought the point against his throat, watching his eyes narrow with fear. "You have one chance of living. Who offered the price?"

I knew he was going to lie even before he spoke. I saw it in those eyes of his.

"I don't know."

I transferred my grip again, quickly, seizing his ear and slicing half of it off, holding the severed piece up in front of him. He stared in disbelief.

"You want to keep the other half? You expect me to believe that you would not know where to go to collect your blood money? Who made the offer?"

He swallowed, hard, and whispered a name. I didn't catch it. As I reached for his other ear, he shrieked it.

"Quinctilius Nesca!"

"Quinctilius Nesca." The blood surged in my ears. I felt the tension draining from me, to be replaced by a cold anger. "You could have saved yourself an ear by spitting that out sooner." I released him and then hauled him to his feet, pushing him back against the wall. He was bleeding copiously from both nose and ear, but he made no move to staunch the flow. He never took his eyes from mine.

"You're not going to kill me?"

I looked him up and down. "Why should I kill you now? I'm going to hand you over to the army. They'll hang you." I pulled him away from the wall and spun him around, then prodded him in front of me at dagger point to the *mansio*, where I sent the owner's son to fetch a patrol from the camp.

Afterwards, when all the official inquiries were over, I was stopped on my way to bed by a young soldier.

"Commander Varrus?"

I looked down at him wearily. He looked very young.

"Yes, what is it?"

"Pardon me, sir, but is this yours? We found it on the street outside."

My vase was still intact, a testament to the workmanship that had gone into the making of it. I thought about taking it back in the morning and exchanging it for another — one with no blood on it. I changed my mind immediately, however. It had served me well, and without it Britannicus would have lost a friend and his reputation.

I went to my bed that night depressed and despondent at the virulence of the Seneca family's hatred and the personal power that each of them enjoyed. A man who could reach out, through his family, to kill anywhere in Britain was a man to be wary of.

I spent ten more days on the road after that episode, taking care now to appear as nothing more than a humble traveller. I unstrung my bow and wrapped the shaft and my quiver of arrows in a cover of cloth and carried them thereafter strapped along the side of one of my pack horses so that they looked like part of my bedroll or an extra tent. I travelled quickly for the first four days, covering a lot of miles, and then, when I estimated that I had removed myself from the ken of those who might recognize me, I permitted myself to relax and enjoy the road.

As I approached the country Britannicus lived in, the scenery changed. The massive, dense woodlands changed their character. The trees lost their height and girth and the forest grew more bushy. To my left, to the south, the rolling hills dropped gradually towards the coastal lands, while on my right they grew from uplands to high hills, hills which I came to know as the Mendips. And to the south and west of the Mendip Hills, the farmlands became more abundant and more prosperous as I drew closer to my destination.

By the time I had reached the town of Aquae Sulis itself, I was ready to enjoy the famous waters the town was named for. I arrived on a quiet day early in the week and found the place thronged. Everyone in the west, it seemed, came to Aquae Sulis for the baths, and for the marketplaces that teemed with the produce of the countryside around. When I remarked on the quality of his goods to a stallholder, he boasted that there was no farming country in the world to equal this, and I soon came to realize that this was true.

I took a private chamber in one of the local hostelries and spent much of each afternoon of my first three days in the town merely walking around the markets, sampling the foodstuffs offered for sale. Now that I was here, having travelled across Britain, I suddenly found myself unsure of my welcome. Caius was not in Britain, and I knew neither his sister, Luceiia, nor his brother-in-law, Varo. My thoughts went, time and again, to the unwelcome reception shown by my own family when I'd arrived, unannounced, in Colchester to claim my inheritance.

I was thinking exactly about that when I returned to my lodgings on the afternoon of my third day in town. I had bathed earlier in the day and eaten well in the marketplace at various stalls, and I had bought myself a new and rather fine tunic, some leather breeches and a new pair of sandals. On the previous day I had bought a rich cloak lined with the soft fur of a large number of rabbits and trimmed with ermine pelts. Wearing it that evening, even for just a few moments, I had seen just how shabby the rest of my clothes had become. Now, in an attempt to rid myself of the depression that haunted me, I changed into my new finery and went into the common tavern of the *mansio* for a pot of ale.

The place was noisy and crowded, but as I entered the room a momentary stillness settled over everyone, and I felt a hundred pairs of eyes taking in every detail of my appearance. I hesitated for a heartbeat, feeling the silence palpably, and then, as I made my way to the counter at the back of the room, the conversation began again and I was ignored. A crew of three men were kept busy pouring ale for the thronging drinkers. I bought myself a large flagon of brew and turned back to the room, sipping at it as I looked from face to face. Only one man was paying any attention to me, staring at me with a frown on his face. As I caught his gaze he shook his head slightly, as though startled, and his frown deepened. Then he stood up, unnoticed by the others at the table, and moved directly towards me, obviously intent on speaking to me.

I watched him come closer, my mind trying frantically to place his face, knowing him a total stranger and wondering what his business could be with me. Had he mistaken me for someone else? It hardly seemed likely. The only other possible alternative was that he was a Seneca spy and had been looking for me. But then why would he approach me so openly? I held myself ready for anything.

As he drew closer, I saw that he was of medium height, well dressed, stout and red-faced with a bald head and a fringe of iron-grey hair that was short and trimmed in the Roman fashion. I saw that he wore a tunic of good, heavy wool beneath a sleeveless leather coat, the sides of which overlapped in front and were fastened by a broad leather belt with a finely crafted, heavy silver buckle.

Finally we were face to face, staring each other in the eye in silence for what seemed like a long time. Then he tilted his head slightly to one side and spoke in a deep, gruff voice. "Your pardon, but is your name Publius Varrus?"

I blinked, trying to conceal my astonishment. "It is. How do you know me? Who are you?"

"By all the old gods, I knew it! Recognized you the minute you stepped into the room." The frown was gone, replaced by a wide smile as he reached for my hand and grasped it in a strong grip. "Varo. Quintus Varo. Cay's my brother-in-law. He told me all about you. Talks about you all the time. Told me you might be coming out this way some day and made me swear to treat you well. Welcome! Welcome to Aquae Sulis. Have you come to stay? Luceiia's going to be angry at me for meeting you first. Strong-minded woman, Luceiia. Have you eaten yet? By the gods, you look exactly as Cay described you. Amazing. When did you get in? What are you drinking? Ale? I prefer wine, myself. Come and join me. I have an excellent red from central Gaul that will amaze you, and the house here serves the finest beef. Damn me to Hades while I live, you look exactly as Cay said you did. Come, come, join me. I have a table."

Through this flood of words I stood gaping at him, open-mouthed, absorbing all of his questions and able to answer none of them, so quickly did they crowd together. Without waiting for me to speak, he grasped me firmly by the forearm and began pulling me behind him in the direction of the table at which I had first noticed him. I followed willingly enough, clutching my pot of ale and wondering just what it was about me that Britannicus had been able to describe so graphically and, obviously, so accurately. When we reached the table, he introduced me to the men already there as his brother-in-law's best friend, and they all nodded and spoke to me, making me welcome and making room for me to join them. Afterwards, they returned to their own conversations, courteously leaving the two of us to become acquainted. All of them were farmers, come to town for the annual cattle sale.

And indeed, by the end of an hour I felt as though I had known and liked Quintus Varo for most of my life. He and Luceiia Britannicus had married a brother and sister. The brother had died some years earlier, leaving Luceiia a widow. Varo's wife's name was Veronica, and, as I already knew, his estates bordered those of Caius and Luceiia. When I commented, questioningly, on Luceiia's ability to manage the estate in Caius's absence, Quintus quickly left me in no doubt as to her qualifications. Although he spoke of her with a genuine and unmistakable fondness, according to him, Luceiia Britannicus was not hampered by, with or from womanly weaknesses. She was a fine-looking woman, he said, but in fairness she should have been born a man, for there was little that was feminine about her. She ran the estate with a barbed, iron tongue and she knew her business. In fact, he opined, she knew more about all kinds of business than any female had the right to know.

I marked Luceiia Britannicus mentally as a woman to be courteous to and to avoid, and our talk moved on to other things, among which was the shocking information that Caius had lost his wife, Heraclita, and his three youngest children to a pestilence during their first year in Africa. I had never met the Commander's family, but I knew of his love for all of them, and in particular for his wife Heraclita, and I mourned for his grief, years old as it was by now. I recalled clearly and in detail the loving way he had spoken, while we lay immobilized together, of his family, and of his belief in every man's need for the love of a good woman. I wondered how he had coped with his loss.

We drank deeply and at length that night, between mourning for Caius and his loss and celebrating our own meeting. Varo was staying in the same lodgings as I, and I have no idea what time we staggered off to sleep, but we arranged to breakfast together the following morning and then to travel together to Quintus's home, and thence to Caius's villa.

XVI

The villa that Quintus Varo called home was enormous, far bigger than anything I had ever seen around Colchester. In fact, when I first saw it from the top of a small hill as we approached from the east, I almost took it for a small, walled village. I was to discover in a very short time, however, that the Villa Varo was, in all honesty, a modest establishment for this part of the country.

Later, when I had had time to gain some kind of understanding of the values that applied in this region, I realized that the villa suited its owner. Quintus Varo was an honest, open man of simple tastes and unsophisticated ideas. He was a farmer who had been a soldier for a time, and the fact that he was a noble and titled citizen of Rome was a matter that bothered him but little and only very occasionally, when self-important visitors demanded to be entertained and courted. His villa was a family place, dedicated to cultivating the land and raising children in a loving atmosphere. It was a compliment to me that he did not treat me as a mere visitor, but chose instead to honour me by accepting me as a fellow soldier and an honest, unpretentious guest in his home.

We had ridden south and east from Aquae Sulis on a misty, beautiful morning that soothed the ravages of the previous evening's drinking. By the time the sun had risen high enough to burn away the mists, I was feeling euphoric. Accompanied by the singing of a hundred different kinds of birds, we made excellent time on the arrow-straight road and penetrated deeper by the mile into the lushest farmland I had ever seen. The healthy fullness of fast-ripening crops of barley and oats was evident everywhere, and besides these I saw other crops that were totally alien to my eyes. Fat, healthy-looking oxen browsed knee-deep in rich grazing, and huge haystacks baked and browned in the warm, autumn sunlight. Throughout the entire day, Quintus Varo was never silent, and not once did I wish he would be. He talked endlessly and fascinatingly of the countryside, his family, his estates, his crops and his brother-in-law. And when he was not talking, he sang in a deep, strong, pleasant voice.

We left the paved road eventually, around mid afternoon, and struck out across the fields along a rutted wagon track that eventually led us to the summit of the green hill from which I saw Varo's villa for the first time.

As I have said, it was enormous, and it was laid out as a great rectangle of connected buildings, with the villa proper set in an L-shape in the north-west corner and smaller buildings — lesser dwellings, workshops, storage buildings and cattle sheds — stretching out from each wing of the house to the southern and eastern corners and turning at right angles to meet in the south-east. The central stockyard must have measured three hundred paces diagonally, corner to corner, and there was only one entrance to the massive enclosure thus formed, as far as I could see. At first glance, it seemed to me that all of the buildings were made of stone and thatched with straw, although I later discovered that the walls were of mud and timber, thickly coated with some kind of dried plaster and artfully finished to look like stone. The central area, much like a forum, was filled with animals and people.

At my soft whistle of amazement, Varo threw me a questioning look, to which I felt obliged to respond.

"It's massive, Quintus. Much bigger than I expected. It's very . . . ," I groped for a word, ". . . fine!"

He grunted, half laugh, half scoff. "It's a farm, Varrus, just a farm. Wait till you see Cay's place. That's fine! My wife and I have neither his wealth nor his taste. But it's home, and it's as near impregnable as I can make it."

"Impregnable?" The word surprised me. "Why does it need to be impregnable? Surely you can't be afraid of attack. Not here."

He reined in and I brought my horse to a stop beside him. Together we sat for a space, staring at the scene below us. He pointed at a thick column of smoke rising away to our right, its source out of sight to the north-east.

"Clearing more land over there. Not because we need the arable space, either. The woodland is just too damn close to the buildings." He sniffed loudly, hawked up some phlegm and spat it out. "Not worried about an attack today. Nor tomorrow, either. But if you believe at all in what Cay says, then it's best to be prepared against some future tomorrow. I'd rather be laughed at and ready for anything than be caught unprepared. Anyway, it's land that we'll be able to use. Can always find a use for good farmland."

Having delivered himself of that, he kicked his horse to a canter and I followed him down into the valley, where we turned onto a wide, deeply rutted track that led to the main entrance to the villa. On the way we passed several wagons, some two-wheeled and some four-wheeled, all drawn by teams of oxen. All of the drivers and all of the pedestrians we met greeted Quintus Varo courteously and cheerfully, and I noticed that they all addressed him as *Domine* or Master. He knew each of them by name and spoke to all of them in a tone that made me aware, although I had never doubted it, that the Villa Varo was a friendly, happy and well-run place.

Our arrival and my unexpected visit threw the entire Varo household into a turmoil, but in the upheaval I had unwittingly created I had time to admire Varo's wife Veronica and the control she had over both her large family and her staff of servants. A seemingly vast brood of children, ranging in age from a boy of about fifteen to a tiny, toddling sweetmeat of some eighteen months, were made known to me individually and then bustled away out of sight. Veronica lost no time in instructing her kitchen and household staff to prepare a welcoming meal and to ready the guest quarters for me. That done, she turned her attention to my immediate comfort and needs, which I tried without success to assure her was unnecessary.

Veronica was not a beautiful woman, but she was clear-skinned, healthy and attractive, and the evidence of abundant fertility and frequent childbearing was there in her matronly body. She was still young in face and in mind, and she had a sweet and cheerful disposition that made me feel comfortable and welcome immediately. Like her husband, she was fully aware of who I was and of much that I had done, including the story of my first meeting with her brother-in-law in Africa and our campaigns together thereafter. I found her attentions both flattering and gratifying, even though I was a bit flustered, being unused to having a maternal, organizing female force focused upon me personally.

Varo and I enjoyed a long and delightful session in his opulent bath house under the care and attention of a magnificent masseur named Nemo, who steamed and oiled and pummelled the hundreds of miles of road dust out of my pores and my muscles. When we emerged, a servant was waiting to tell us that dinner would be served in an hour, and Varo clapped me on the shoulder.

"That gives us time to appreciate some excellent wine . . . an exploratory sip or two. I don't suppose you'd have any objections to that?"

I grinned and bowed to him. "None worth mentioning," I said, "and I speak as a new man — clean, pampered and perfumed. A draught of good wine would be the final touch."

He laughed and led me through two massive, magnificent doors of polished oak into the *triclinium*, the formal dining room of the villa, where two stone jugs of wine from Gaul — the one a deep, purple red from the south and the other a pale, golden yellow nectar from the central lands — awaited our attention. The red had been slightly cooled and the yellow deeply chilled. I chose the latter and it was wondrous — smooth and very slightly sweet. Veronica joined us within minutes and drank some wine with us, sharing our enjoyment of the late afternoon sunlight. The household servants were evidently working smoothly, since there was neither sound nor sight of the children.

The declining sun threw long beams of golden light from the open shutters across the spacious room to spill in rectangles on the polished wooden floor and the solid, comfortable-looking furnishings, and I was conscious of a deep-seated feeling of well-being. I saw, without thinking about it, that four places had been set at the large, high table, and as I accepted a second cup of the delightful wine from Veronica, I ran my hands absently but admiringly over the carved, lustrous surface of one of the high-backed, cushioned chairs that flanked the table.

Quintus noticed my gesture and smiled. "You like those?" There was no mistaking the inflection of pride in his voice.

I nodded in response, looking more closely at the carving of the chair's frame. "Yes," I said. "They're magnificent. The man who carved these was a genius."

Veronica's laugh was like the sound of a harp. "No," she cried, "the man who carved those is a man of his time, who could never have endured lying supine to eat his meals as people did in the old days. He is a man who likes to sit up when he eats, believing it aids digestion when he keeps his back straight and his head erect. And you have made a lifelong friend of him with that remark. My husband made those and carved them himself."

I was astonished and made no attempt to hide it. "Really? You made these, Quintus?"

He nodded, his grin widening. "I did. I love working with wood. It's my favourite way of passing time. Most of my friends think I'm strange."

I toasted him with my upraised cup. "Here's one who doesn't. I know exactly what you mean, because my mind works the same way. My passion's for metal. Mainly iron, but over the past few years I've started to work with silver, too. It demands a whole different set of skills, but it rewards one's efforts in a way iron seldom does. Silver has a beauty that is unique."

We spent the next several minutes discussing crafts-manship. I learned that Quintus had literally made the entire room, from floors to doors, with his own hands. The doors were spectacular, each made from two massive, tongued and grooved planks of solid oak. On this side, facing into the room, they had been meticulously carved into panels, six to a door, depicting the labours of Hercules. The other side was plain, polished oak, ornamented only by handles. I had no need to pretend to be awed by the workmanship here as I pushed the doors open and closed, delighting in the ease with which the mighty weight of them was hinged.

I declined a third cup of wine before dinner and excused myself in order to go to my room and change. It had been a long time since I had met anyone with whom I felt so much at ease as these two, and I found myself whistling as I changed into my best clothes. I checked my chin for stubble, ran my fingertips through my short-cropped hair to make sure that it was dry and behaving as it should, and then, still whistling under my breath, made my way back directly to rejoin my host and hostess.

I had barely begun to make my way down the stairway from the bedchambers on the second floor when I became aware of what I can only describe now as a *blueness*. There are moments in everyone's life, usually spontaneous, seldom planned, that are seminal. In a brief flash of time, events occur that change the status quo, immediately and drastically, forever. One of those moments had overtaken me and overwhelmed me before I had time even to realize that anything untoward was happening.

I have tried for years to remember the exact sequence of events, actions and reactions that happened to me in the few moments that followed there on that stairway, but I have never been able to reconstruct my own thoughts clearly, or my reactions to what I thought I saw.

I remember sensing a blueness; it seemed to me that the entire wall below me and ahead of me had taken on a bluish tinge, almost as though a blue light were flickering nearby. I believe I had even turned my head slightly, looking for the source of the effect, before I became aware of the woman who was walking along the hallway below. Her back was towards me and she was within three or four steps of the open doors to the *triclinium*. I had an instantaneous and overpowering impression of eerie, almost frightening familiarity. I saw long, straight black hair, a tall, graceful form in a blue robe and a gliding style of walk that seemed to owe nothing to feet or legs.

I heard a roaring sound in my head, and I know I clutched at the handrail of the stairs for support as her name resounded first in my mind and then in the stillness of the hallway.

"Cassie?"

She stopped immediately, tilting her head forward slightly, as though listening, before turning back to face me, looking up to where I stood transfixed at the top of the stairs.

"Cassie?" I said again, my voice emerging this time as a croak. She did not speak, made no move. With a conscious effort of will, I began to move down the stairs towards her.

I remember thinking she looked far younger than she ought to, and not at all matronly. And then, as I approached her, I realized that she was not Cassie. She was a complete stranger with only a slight resemblance to the girl I had known so many years before. She had the same black hair and large blue eyes, and she wore the same colour that Cassie had worn. But this woman was not Cassie. I stopped at the foot of the stairs and looked at her, and I knew that Cassie had always stayed a young girl in my mind and in my heart. This entrancing creature who faced me in silence was a woman in every sense of the word, and her beauty brought my heart up into my throat. I shook my head, whether to dismiss the last, lingering thoughts of poor Cassie or to begin an apology for having mistaken her, I do not know, but as I did so she began to walk towards me.

As she moved, I was aware again of multiple, simultaneous impressions of height, dignity, effortless motion, breath-taking beauty and blueness. I saw her as a vision, tall and slim, self-possessed and lovely. She walked with her head high and erect, her back held straight so that the fullness and thrust of her breasts were apparent even beneath the dark blue *stola* she wore over the long, paler-blue draperies of her gown. Her clothes brought out the brilliant blue of her eyes, even in the shadowed gloom of the passageway, so that they seemed to blaze at me above the swellings of wide, high cheekbones. Long, dark hair, innocent of curl or artificial trickery, fell in straight cascades to frame her face and then swept back over her shoulders to hang behind her.

I had no idea who she was, but I knew that she was the woman I wanted above all others. My thoughts raced so that by the time she had moved two paces closer to me I had decided that she must be one of

Veronica's personal servants, although I had never seen or heard of a serving woman so beautiful. It didn't matter, anyway. Mistress or servant, she was magnificent. Her beauty, mobility and dignity deserved my homage. I clenched my hand involuntarily over my breast in a military salute and bowed to her, moving backwards and away from her, my eyes cast down as she approached me. I saw the tips of her sandalled feet come up and then stop directly in front of me. In an agonized silence that seemed to stretch forever, I decided that I had to straighten up and look her in the eyes.

When I did so, I found her to be far more lovely than I had thought from a distance. The blue of her eyes was painfully deep and the kindness and welcoming warmth of her smile dried up my mouth. She spoke my name, and I marvelled, not at her knowledge of my name but at the texture and the timbre of her voice, warm and soft and mellow and deeper than I would have expected. She reached out and took both of my wrists in her hands, and the only things in my world were her face and the warmth and softness of her hands.

"Luceiia, you're here! What took you so long?" Veronica's voice seemed to come from a great distance, and her words completed my confusion. I could see her standing in the open doorway of the dining room, and she was obviously speaking to the woman who was holding my wrists. But she had called her Luceiia! Could this be Luceiia Britannicus? The woman Quintus Varo had described as unwomanly? Unfeminine?

She ignored Veronica's comment and kept her eyes and her smile directed full upon me. "Welcome," she said. "We thought you might never come to our western land.

I was debating with myself as to whether or not I should have you abducted and brought here, just to have you nearby when Caius comes home."

I swallowed hard and worked my tongue to moisten my mouth. I know I said something banal and stupid, but I have no memory of the words. They must have been appropriate, however, because she released my wrists and walked with me into the dining room, where she embraced Veronica and Quintus. In the ensuing babble of conversation, I had time to collect myself and recover from the astonishing impact she had had on me. Nevertheless, although the memory of that first sight of her is an undying but hectic one, the passage of the next hour or so is a blank in my memory, a blue-tinctured haze of warmth and pleasure.

I know now, from subsequent conversations with both Quintus and Veronica, that my condition was obvious and afforded them great hilarity during dinner, which they graciously concealed. Quintus admitted afterwards that he had been warned by Veronica not to talk of Luceiia's beauty. They had wanted to observe the effect she would have on me if I encountered her with no advance warning.

After dinner, the major-domo of the Varo household broke the spell I was under with an announcement that the fire had been lit in the outer courtyard, and that if we would care to be seated, the entertainment was about to commence.

Quintus thanked him and led the way to a built-in courtyard at the rear of the house. A huge fire was blazing in a pit there, throwing leaping shadows on the walls all around, and about a dozen people, whom I took to be

the servants of the household, were sitting quietly in a
loose group on one side of the fire-pit, listening to a
young man seated on a log in the corner of the courtyard
who was tuning some kind of a lyre. We made ourselves
comfortable by the fireside and he sang to us for more
than an hour, accompanying himself on his instrument.
His voice was strong and clean and his songs were all of
the beauty of this country we lived in. He could not have
chosen a better theme, and he could never have had a
more appreciative audience. Quintus Varo surprised me
by remaining rapt from start to finish and offering lavish
applause and encouragement at the end of every song.

As the lad's voice rose and fell, weaving a spell of
beauty around us all, I sat and drank in the flame-washed
beauty of the woman who sat across the fire from me. The
emotion that was writhing in my breast here was a mar-
vel beyond my experience. No woman, not the Cassie of
my youth, not even Phoebe in my hour of greatest need,
had ever affected me like this. I had never seen anything
to compare with the sweep of those cheekbones, or the
perfection of that mouth, or with the mysticism of that
face, dappled as it was with firelight.

Eventually, the young man exhausted his fund of songs
and was permitted to leave, rewarded with a coin from
Quintus and another from me. His departure was the signal for all the other servants to leave, and soon there were
only the four of us — Quintus, Veronica, Luceiia and
myself — left in the courtyard.

For a few minutes after they had all gone, there was a
warm silence broken only by the guttering of the fire. I
raised my eyes to look again at Luceiia, only to find her
looking at me. Abashed, I returned my gaze immediately

to the fire. When I dared look up again, her eyes were still on me, and she smiled a small, secret smile.

Quintus cleared his throat. "Publius, I cannot remember having spent such an enjoyable evening in many years, but now I am tired and must sleep. You will be leaving in the morning, and before that I want to have my day's work allocated and well in hand. Good night, my friend. Come, Veronica."

I started to rise, but he waved me back to my seat. "No, no! There's no need for you to leave. Stay here and enjoy the fire with Luceiia. Luceiia, you know well enough by this time where your room is. Good night to both of you. Sleep well. We'll see you in the morning, before you leave."

After they had gone, I sat tongue-tied, not daring to look across at Luceiia. It was she who broke the silence.

"Poor Quintus is not very subtle, is he?"

I looked at her then, drinking enough beauty in one look to sustain me until I dared look again. "Subtle? What do you mean?"

"What do I *mean*?" Her laughter was like the sound of the boy's lyre. "I mean he's being outrageous in his matchmaking."

"Matchmaking?" I heard stridency in my voice and dropped it to a whisper instantly, so that I sounded merely foolish. "Oh. Is he?"

"Well, isn't he? I cannot imagine him leaving me alone with any other man at night under any circumstances."

I swallowed, feeling highly uncomfortable. "I see. Would you rather go to sleep now? I mean, rather than stay here? With me, I mean?" I cursed myself for being a fool, providing her with opportunities to flee.

"No, thank you. I am quite comfortable. This has been a lovely evening. I have no wish to end it yet."

That made me feel better, but the silence fell again, leaden and unbreakable by any effort of mine.

"My name is Luceiia."

I blinked in surprise. "I know." She was smiling strangely. I felt I had missed something. "Why would you say that?"

"What? That my name is Luceiia? Because it is, and I like it, and you have not said it once since we met. Although it seems to me that you called me at first by another name. What was it?"

I cleared my throat nervously. "Cassie," I croaked, then I cleared my throat again. The name sounded strange on my tongue, like one from an ancient tale. Cassie might have been a figure from some dream, a ghostly presage of the woman I saw before me now. "When I first saw you, there in the atrium with your back to me, you reminded me of her. She was someone I knew a very long time ago, when I was just a boy."

"She must have been important to you."

"Yes, and no. I only met her once, one afternoon."

"But you remember her still."

I was growing more confident, coming to terms with the long-held memories of a boy, and gauging them beside the current evaluations of a man. I shook my head, dismissing Luceiia's comment.

"Not really. I recall the feelings she stirred in me, the mood she created. But in my mind she is still fifteen. She's a memory, no more. She had your kind of beauty, dark hair like yours, and she wore blue."

"Were you sorry when you saw I was not she?" This

time her eyes were not lifted to meet mine, and I smiled at the top of her head.

"No. Not at all. How could I be? Cassie was a child, and so was I."

There was silence for the space of a few heartbeats, then she said, "It's an unusual name. Cassie."

"Short for Cassiopeiia. I don't even know if that was her real name."

"Cassiopeiia. . . . It's a beautiful name."

"No more than Luceiia. *That* is a beautiful name."

She looked up and smiled. "Say it again."

"Luceiia."

She was grinning now. "That's much better. Twice better. Now I feel as if we have been properly introduced." I found myself grinning back at her. "You are a fascinating man, Publius Varrus," she continued. "I feel as if I have known you all my life, and now that we have really met, the feeling has not changed. The only thing I did not know was what you really look like."

"And?"

"And what?"

"Do I look anything like the person you had imagined?"

She smiled, and there was a teasing mischief there. "Well, now. How should I answer that?" I waited. "I could tell you that I had imagined you to be so handsome that the reality was bound to fall short of my expectations. . . ."

I was not used to playing games of words with women, and my face must have shown some of the insecurity I was feeling, because suddenly the mockery was gone from her smile and her expression was one of total sincerity as she continued.

"Caius talked incessantly of you. It was 'Varrus this' and 'Varrus that' and 'Varrus would have . . .' from morning to night, and my brother talks that way of no one else. It is not his way. Naturally, being curious about this paragon of military virtue and solid, straight-thinking values, I used to ask him things about you that might give me some idea of what you looked like. The picture I finally formed of you was almost perfect. I knew that you were tall, broad-shouldered and immensely strong in the arms and body. I knew that your hair was dark brown and cut short in the army style, and that you wore a short beard and moustache. I knew that there was enough grey in your beard and on your head to give you a silvery look from a distance. I knew that you had all of your teeth and that you laughed easily and often. And I knew that you had received a terrible wound in my brother's service that left you crippled, or at least with a permanent limp."

I felt a head-splitting rush of mortification at her casual reference to my crippled state, and then it was replaced by a growing wonder that she was not embarrassed in any way to mention it. She did not even find it worthy of further comment. She accepted it as being part of me and kept right on talking.

"The only thing I did not know, could not know, was the balance of your features, the shape of them, the expressions you would have. So your face was always a blank to me. Until today. Until now."

I got up and placed another log on the dwindling fire, not wishing to lose the sight of her face to the gathering darkness that was crowding in on the dying flames. I had not felt so foolishly juvenile since I had stopped being foolishly juvenile, and I did not want her to stop talking. Her voice was low and pleasantly husky in a way that I had never heard before in a woman. A fountain of sparks jetted up from the fire-pit and I felt several burning pinpricks on my hand. I sat down again across from her, waiting for her to resume speaking, but she was waiting for me. I wanted very badly to ask her if she was pleased with the filled-in blanks, but I would have sat there all night before the courage came to me to voice the words.

She laughed that lovely laugh again. "And now you sit there wondering if I like what I see, but too unsure of yourself to ask me. Am I correct?" She raised one eyebrow exactly the way her brother would have done, and I had to smile and nod my head. "Well, sir, you may wonder and wonder. There are some things a Roman lady does not do, and one of them is to flatter strange men."

I had to chew on that one for a few seconds before I was able to see that it was a compliment.

"There now!" she said. "Having dealt with you, I think we should talk about me next. Don't you think that would be a delightful topic?"

I had to laugh, feeling better and more relaxed by the minute with this marvellous woman. "Completely," I said. "What do you think I should know about you, since I have not had the benefit of your brother's constant descriptions to prepare me for you?"

Her eyebrows went up. "You mean Caius failed to warn you of my beauty? My wit? My brilliance?"

"I was aware of nothing more than your name." I grinned, now feeling almost miraculously at ease. She pretended to be upset, pouting her full lower lip slightly and frowning. "But I'm grateful to him," I went on.

"Had I known the truth, I would never have been able to endure waiting to meet you. He did, however, tell me that you are his *favourite* sister."

"Well, at least that's something, I suppose. Never mind that I am his *only* sister."

"Seriously," I said, smiling in sheer pleasure. "What should I know about you?"

"I wonder," she said, and paused, frowning in mock concentration. "What should you know about me?" She pursed her lips, giving me lots of time to admire the contours and the softness of them. "First of all, you should know that I am really delighted that you are here. I really have wanted to meet you for years. I think, too, you should know that I am regarded as something of an oddity because I refuse to behave like a woman, in that I am unwilling to do nothing except have babies. I have a mind, and I enjoy learning. I can hardly wait to have you tell me about your skystone." She paused, thinking her next words over, and then went on. "You should also know that I am extremely unlucky when it comes to husbands. I have lost two so far, which explains why I am here, a twenty-five-year-old widow in the home of my brother, when I should be happy in a home of my own rearing large numbers of small Britannici."

Startled by this information, I stood up, then moved to sit on the bench by her side. "Two?"

She nodded. "Two."

"But how?"

"I don't know. Carelessness? No, forgive me. That was flippant. Perhaps I was guilty of hubris, punishable pride. I do not know."

"Two! I knew of one."

"How? Did Quintus tell you? Silly question, of course he did. Veronica is Julius's sister." She was quiet for a few seconds, staring into the fire. Her *stola* had started to slip from her shoulders and I reached out and pulled it closer around her, marvelling at my sudden bravery. She was very close. I wanted to draw her closer. A tiny smile touched her face in acknowledgement of my attempt to preserve her from the cold.

"I hardly knew my first husband. He was a boy of seventeen when he was killed by a wild boar during a hunting party. I was fifteen at the time. It seems like centuries ago, and I remember him as I would a beloved brother. His family and mine had been close for generations, although we lived here in Britain and they had moved to Constantinople with the imperial court. We were married less than three months." I said nothing, knowing she was not finished. "And then there was Julius, Veronica's brother. A very fine, upstanding man. Again, my father arranged the match. We lived quite happily together for one year, discovering ourselves, and then unhappily for three years, having discovered each other too well. He died four years ago and I mourned him only slightly, although he was far from being a wicked man. But I love his sister more than I ever loved Julius." She glanced up at me, a look of inquiry on her face. "Do you find it shocking that I should say these things to you?"

I shook my head in a negative and she went on.

"I feel very strongly about things like that, and I suppose that is unfitting for a Roman woman. But I have done my duty as a faithful daughter. My father is dead now, and from now on, I arrange my own life. I am no longer a little girl. I am a woman, and a wealthy one. A wealthy *young* woman! Twenty-five is not so old, and I flatter myself that I could still attract a husband of my own choice, if the idea appealed to me." She paused. "I really have shocked you, haven't I?" She had, but I shook my head again in a lie.

She chose to believe me. "Good," she said, approvingly. "I had an aunt, Aunt Liga. A remarkable woman. She was firmly convinced that men rule in this world simply by default, because women are content not to challenge their supremacy. She went into commerce. She bought real estate and amassed a fortune. She was quite scandalous in her youth, even in Rome, which was a scandal in itself, but by the time she died she had achieved a kind of respectability through sheer notoriety and ridiculous wealth. She left all of it, her money and her lands and buildings, to me." She stopped, looking me straight in the eye again over the two feet or so that separated us.

"I am a very wealthy woman, Publius. I own a very large amount of the city of Rome itself, and a fair-sized portion of Constantinople, in the form of land and buildings." She paused again and looked at me seriously before going on. "I love my brother dearly, but now that I have my own wealth, I find I also have the courage to indulge myself in my own ideas. I suppose what I really mean is I have come to agree with my Aunt Liga's ideas about life and the way one lives it. When I marry again, *I* shall choose my husband, much as it may distress Caius. I will not be treated like disposable property simply because I happen to have been born in a female body. I have a good mind. I read, I write, I think, and I conduct my own enterprises through my own lawyers."

By this time I was truly confused about her motives in telling me all of this. "Have you said any of this to Caius?" In her company, strangely enough, I could no longer think of him as "the General."

"No. I haven't had the opportunity." She laughed. "I'm practising on you. Caius can be formidable when his sensibilities are outraged. He's so traditional. I know he disapproved of Aunt Liga very strongly. He will have an apoplectic fit when he finds out she has left all of her ill-acquired fortune to me. She died just a year after he left for Africa, and it was about a year after that I found out she had named me as her heir. Since then, I have been learning to run my affairs with the help of my lawyers — two here and five in Rome. I have been to Rome and met all of them, and I have spent much time since then studying my circumstances. I know they are all robbing me outrageously, but one of these fine days I shall deal with that. They're all going to get a nasty surprise. In the meantime, I have not had a chance to tell Caius anything about it."

She looked away again, back into the heart of the fire, and again a silence fell. This time, however, there was no discomfort, for we were both thinking about what she had told me. A pocket of resin in one of the logs snapped loudly and the entire body of the fire settled inward; a million fireflies seemed to swarm on the burning logs signalling that they were starting to change from fuel to embers. I was wondering idly whether to add some more fuel when she decided for me.

"Put some more wood on and tell me about your sky-stone."

This time it was easy to smile at her. "What would you like to know about it?"

"Everything. It fascinates me. Before he left for Africa, Caius told me about the sword of Theodosius, about how it was made originally by your grandfather for your father from the metal of a stone he believed to have fallen from the heavens. Now I would like to hear the story from you. You believe the stone did fall from the sky, do you not?"

I stood upright. "Yes, I do," I said, "but the sword of Theodosius is nothing. Look at this." I reached behind my back and unsheathed the dagger from where it nestled in its familiar place at the base of my spine. "Be careful," I said as I handed it to her. "It is far sharper than any other blade you have ever known."

When I had finished adding more logs to the fire, I turned back to find her engrossed in looking at the blade.

"What makes the blade so silvery?" She held up the knife so that its blade reflected the flames of the fire.

I sat beside her and held out my hand and she reversed the dagger, slapping its heavy hilt into my open palm. Extending my arm towards the fire, I could plainly see the tiny print of her thumb on the shining blade. I moved the point from side to side, watching the reflection of the light as it ran up and down the blade.

"I don't know, Luceiia, but I think there's another metal in there besides iron."

"Mmm, Caius told me. But tell me about iron. He also told me you said it was a new study."

"That's correct," I said, my surprise showing in my voice. "But I said it is comparatively new. Why would you want to know about iron?"

"I told you, I have a mind. I want to know all I can about everything that interests me, and I know nothing about iron. Not a thing."

"Very well," I said, "I accept that. Where would you like me to begin?"

"At the beginning. But please talk to me as you would to Caius. Try not to think of me as a woman."

I resisted the temptation to look at her breasts or at the way the material of her gown clung to the sweep of her thigh. I tried desperately not to see her hair or the arc of her cheekbone. I fought to ignore the fullness of her lips. I attempted, deliberately and positively, to ignore everything about her that was unignorable and to consider what I would have said to a man in response to the same request.

"Well," I mumbled, "let me think about it for a minute. I've tried to explain this before — to Caius — and it isn't easy. I don't want to confuse you, and I don't want to bore you." I collected my thoughts into an approximation of logical sequence. "For a start, I don't know much more than you do about the subject . . . nobody does. You know the story of the skystone, but do you know that my grandfather almost gave up on trying to melt it down?"

She nodded. "I do. It seemed strange to me at the time that anyone should try to melt a stone, but I didn't want to parade my total ignorance to Caius, so I let it pass. What about it?"

"Well," I went on, "almost all metal comes originally from stone, but not all stone contains metal. The stones that do contain it are called ore-bearing stones, the ore being, if you like, the raw metal."

"You mean raw, as in uncooked?"

I nodded. "Exactly. Iron ore is red. Have you ever seen hillsides in your travels that looked as though they were rust-stained?" She dipped her head in acknowledgement.

"Well, that's exactly what they were. The rock that produces that red-stained effect is iron ore. We take that stone and we crush it and wash it thoroughly, and then we dry it over heat. The washing gets rid of the ordinary soil and other soluble material. What's left we burn at great heat in a tall kiln, or oven furnace, for a long time. In the course of the burning, or smelting as we call it, the metal melts from the ore and drips down into a crucible in the bottom of the kiln. We finish up, when the kiln has cooled, with what is essentially a lump of pure iron mixed with slag, the residue from the furnace. Then we go to work with our hammers, and by simply beating this mass — which is like a big, dirty sponge — we hammer out as much of the slag as we possibly can. It just falls out, and we are left at the end of the process with a lump of iron. We call it wrought iron, because it has literally been wrought out of stone by the sweat of our bodies and the pounding of our hammers. You follow me so far?"

She nodded again, wide-eyed and obviously interested.

"Good. Now, here's where it gets complicated. This wrought iron is solid iron, and good for all kinds of purposes. It's easy to shape and it's easy to work with. But it's too soft to hold an edge. A mediocre hammered-bronze edge is much keener and longer lasting than a wrought-iron edge. Of course, iron is almost impossible to work with when it is cold. You have to heat it to a red-hot state to be able to shape it." She nodded, acknowledging this well-known fact.

"Right," I continued. "Next step. Somebody, somehow, long ago, nobody knows when, made a momentous discovery. Everyone who worked with iron had known for centuries that to keep an edge on an iron blade you had to hammer the edge and then allow it to cool slowly. If you cooled it too quickly, the edge wouldn't hold. But somebody, one day, must have decided to re-edge a blade, and by accident must have left the blade in a charcoal fire for longer than was necessary at the time. He might even have hammered the edge into the blade and then reheated it. When he realized what he had done, he may have thought he had wasted his work, and then plunged the blade into water to cool it quickly, so that he could start all over again. Nobody knows how the discovery occurred. It was an accident. But the fact remains that iron, reheated in a charcoal fire and then plunged into water to cool quickly, takes on an edge that is unbelievably hard, whereas the same iron, heated without the charcoal and then plunged into the same water, will not hold its edge."

"That sounds impossible."

"I know it does. But it's true."

"Is there some kind of magic in the charcoal?"

"There must be." I shook my head, as I had done so many times over the same puzzle. "It must be magic, of some kind. But I don't believe in magic. And I refuse to believe that, with all the things in the world that are supposed to be magic but are not, there is only one thing, charred wood, that is not supposed to be magic and is. No, Luceiia, it isn't magic. It's just something that we don't understand yet."

She smiled at me, a marvel-laden smile of warmth and admiration, and I almost stretched in the joy of it like a cat.

"No wonder, Publius Varrus, that you spend all your time over a furnace! That is absolutely fascinating. It can't be the water that softens the edge, so it has to be the charcoal."

"No, quite the opposite. It's the lack of charcoal that makes iron soft."

"Yes, the lack of it . . . that's what I meant. So the charcoal holds the secret of the hard edge. And nobody knows why. That is fascinating."

"Isn't it?" I hurried on, revelling in her approval. "Of course, you understand that nobody caught on to this quickly. The hardening was a hit-or-miss process for ages. But gradually, a method for making hardened iron came into general use, and as smiths learned how to increase the heat of their fires, the quality of the iron increased from black to the pale grey colour of our iron of today."

"Wait a minute. What do you mean, they increased the heat of their fires? What can be hotter than fire?"

"Hotter fire." I laughed at the expression on her face. "That's why we force air into our coals with bellows. The air blast increases the heat of the coals. No one knows how or why. And some fuels burn hotter than others. Some burn more slowly. That's why we use charcoal. It burns hotter and more slowly than ordinary wood. It can build up to fierce temperatures. My grandfather almost gave up on smelting the skystone, as I have said. He had tried a number of fuels, different kinds of charcoal, and increased the flow of air to his furnace to an extent that he'd never tried before, but none of it had worked. And then, finally, when the furnace cooled after what he'd sworn to himself would be his last attempt to smelt the stone, he noticed that, although he had achieved no melt, the surface of the stone did look different somehow, almost as though it had started to change. So he resolved to try one more time, and to find some way of really increasing the heat in his furnace. By this time he had spent seven months fooling around with the thing, but it was his hobby, and he considered the time well spent."

Again I noted the rapt expression on her face. She was far from being bored, I felt, but then I thought that perhaps she was merely pretending interest. I allowed my voice to lapse into silence, giving her the chance to change the subject if she so wished.

"Well? Then what? I know he was successful, but how did he do it?" The eagerness in her voice was genuine. I smiled and continued.

"He mentions in his notes that an associate of his — a merchant of fuel and oils — had found a deposit of coal that he couldn't use. Apparently, this coal he had found was too brittle. It broke up into tiny little pieces and it wouldn't flame. My grandfather remembered this. The man had not said that it would not burn, you understand? Merely that it would not flame. My grandfather knew that charcoal wouldn't flame, either, and yet it burned hotter than the wood it was made from. He became curious. He asked his friend to sell him some of the coal. The fellow snorted in disgust and told Grandfather where he could find it for himself, and wished him luck.

"Grandfather Varrus collected some of the coal and mixed it with some of his highest-grade charcoal to see if it would burn hotter. It did. It burned hard and clean, and by the time he had experimented with the proportion of coal to charcoal, he had evolved a furnace fire hot enough to smelt the skystone. The rest you know. He had enough metal to make the sword for my father, and this dagger for me."

"But he mixed the sword blade with ordinary iron?"

"No," I said. "It wasn't ordinary. It was his best. But Theodosius's sword is nowhere near as brilliant as the skystone dagger."

Luceiia had a strange and thoughtful expression on her face. I waited to hear what she would say. When she did speak, however, she asked a question that surprised me.

"How long ago was this, Publius?"

"No idea. It must have been just after I was born. My father left for the last time shortly after that. Thirty-three years ago? Thirty-four? Something like that. I suppose I could pinpoint it exactly from the old man's notes."

"He was that meticulous a note-keeper, was he?"

"He was. He wrote notes on everything available, from waxed tablets to papyrus and scraps of parchment."

She smiled again, a quiet, mystical smile. "He was a wise man, your grandfather. Could you find out exactly when all of this happened? Would that be possible?"

"I suppose so. Why? Is it important? For what reason?"

She shrugged my questions off. "Oh, I don't know. But there has been something niggling at me, something I heard about quite recently. I don't want to say anything until I have checked it out, but it might be very interesting. It was something I heard, or I think I heard, last time I was in Aquae Sulis. You know the people there believe in dragons?"

I gave her my version of the Britannican eyebrow. "Dragons, Luceiia?"

She nodded.

I grinned at her. "I see. I have travelled across Britain to find people who believe in dragons."

Her grin matched my own. "Scoff not, friend. Accept them as they are. I think they are your dragons."

I could tell from the expression on her face that she had something she was not telling me, but I had no idea what it could be. I did not want to feed her a line to tease me with. My mind raced as I tried to guess just what she was referring to, and why these dragons should be mine, but it was hopeless.

"Very well, you have me beaten," I said, holding up my hands in surrender. "I don't know what you are talking about. How and why are these my dragons?"

"Because you will adopt them as soon as you hear about them, and you will hear all about them tomorrow. The fire is almost out, and I find I am tired, quite suddenly."

The fire was indeed almost dead; I had not noticed it dwindle. I rose to my feet reluctantly, unwilling to let her go, even to sleep for a few hours.

"Pardon me," I said. "I had no knowledge of the time passing."

"I know. No more did I, and I enjoyed every minute of it."

She rose as she spoke, and again I noticed how tall she was. She was standing close enough for me to be aware of the warmth and the scent of her. I could have hooked my arm about her waist without even leaning forward. But of course I did not. She looked me straight in the eye for a long moment and my mind screamed to me how soft and delicious those lips would feel against my own. Then she smiled again, softly and somehow knowingly, and adjusted her *stola* more warmly around her shoulders. She started to turn away from me and then caught herself, as though with an afterthought.

"What is it?" I asked her. "Is there something I can do for you?"

Again the same smile. She reached out her right hand and touched me, very gently, with the backs of two of her fingers on my right cheekbone. I barely felt the pressure, but it burned. "Good night, Publius," she whispered. "Thank you." And then she turned to go.

I stopped her with a touch of my hand on her elbow. She turned back, her chin cocked as she looked half over her shoulder, and I was abruptly tongue-tied again.

"Yes, Publius?"

I had to say something. "Tomorrow," I stammered. "I *will* see you? Before you leave?"

"Before I leave?" There was a question in her laugh. "Aye, and after. You are coming with me. Don't you remember? We discussed it at dinner. The Villa Britannicus is your home from now on." I had no recollection of the dinner-table conversation at all. She laughed again, obviously at the expression on my face. "Don't worry, Varrus." There was delicious mockery in her voice. "It's big enough for both of us."

It was almost completely dark now in the enclosed courtyard, but I watched the glorious sway of her hips as she moved until the blackness swallowed her up. She could not have heard my whispered, "Good night, my love."

I stared into the dying fire for a while, my thoughts in a turmoil, and then I went to my own bed in a daze.

XVII

I slept little that night, tortured by fantasies and lust and guilt. This woman was the sister of my best friend, my mentor and my commander. My family ranked as Equestrians, but hers was Patrician of ancient blood, having won their nobility before the time of the Caesars, descended directly from the founding families of Rome itself. She was wealthy in her own right, and she was wealthier still through her family's riches. I owned one small smithy. She was a noblewoman of high mind and values, while I was an artisan, a smith with dirt beneath my nails and the smell of smoke and soot in my clothes, my grandfather's hoard of gold coins notwithstanding. It was true that she deigned to speak sincerely with me and to show an interest in my welfare, but I knew in my heart of hearts that she did so out of gratitude to the man who had saved the life of her beloved brother. It was true, too, that she had showed keen interest in my iron lore, but only because Caius had been fascinated by it, and his retelling of it had sparked her unusual mind and its thirst for knowledge.

But I knew that I was damned to love her forever, and I was afoot before the larks began to sing, waiting impatiently for my first glimpse of her that day.

I had long to wait. Luceiia slept late, and then, after only a smile and a greeting to me, she disappeared into the depths of the house with Veronica and some of the children. I broke fast with Quintus before dawn and talked with him about what he had to do that day, and then he, too, disappeared about his business, leaving me to my own affairs.

I explored the buildings of the farm as daylight grew and the place began to come to life. There I found the smith who looked after the farm equipment, and I introduced myself. He was a taciturn man, friendly enough but too busy to be distracted from his tasks. I hung around the forge long enough to satisfy myself that he knew what he was doing, and then I checked my belongings and my horses, making sure I would be ready to leave when Luceiia decided to do so.

After that, still at loose ends, I took my African bow and some arrows and walked away from the buildings, looking for a place to practise my marksmanship. To my great surprise, I found not only a place but a well-used target. In a trampled area behind one of the stone-walled sheds that formed the outer wall of the courtyard, I found a man-sized, roughly human-shaped figure of straw bound with twine and wrapped in an old tunic that was pierced with circular holes. After looking around and seeing no one, I accepted the gift of the unknown archer and strung my bow.

My first shot showed me that there was a log hidden beneath the straw that formed the trunk of the target. My arrow lodged in it solidly and I had a hard time removing it. From then on, I used only practice arrows without metal points.

After a while, I grew used to the substance of the target and found that I had no need to draw my bow with anything like the strength I was accustomed to using. I was concentrating so hard, eventually, on piercing the target accurately with a minimal draw that I did not notice the approach of the man whose voice startled me.

"There's a big bow for a little target! Looks to me like a lot of wasted time and effort!"

I turned in surprise to find myself looking at a small man with enormously broad shoulders and a humped back. The hump pushed his head forward and to one side, so that his whole body looked twisted, though only one side, the left, was actually deformed. He looked hugely strong, in spite of his deformity, and there was no mistaking the scornful disdain on his dark-browed face as he looked at my great bow. I smiled at him, noting the smaller bow he held, already strung, in his right hand.

"A waste?" I asked. "How can there be waste if the arrow finds the mark every time?"

"Pshhaw!" The sound was loaded with scorn. "Hit the mark, is it? If a mark is big enough, a boyo could hit it with a rock, he could. That mark you are shooting at is my boy's plaything. Come here, then. I'll show you a mark."

Without waiting for any sign from me, he turned on his heel and strode away with a curious, bobbing gait that I recognized ruefully as being not too different from my own. I followed him for about a hundred paces until he stopped and gestured forward with a wave of his free hand.

"There's a mark."

I looked. About a hundred and twenty-five paces from where we stood, a large conifer had been blown down by a high wind, and the flat base of its root-pad formed a huge, brown, circular patch against the trees behind it. Just in front of it, I could discern a white, upright staff.

"The white stake? What is it?"

As I spoke, he hoisted his bow and loosed an arrow. The shot grazed the white upright and angled off to the right; I saw the bright scarlet of its feathers lodge in the earth of the root-pad that served as a backstop.

"It's a shovel. Lodged in the earth. Let's see you hit it, then, with that great thing you have there."

My first arrow missed, although not by much, and so did my second. The little man said nothing, contenting himself with the silence he knew must irritate me. I stifled my anger at myself and thought about what I was doing wrong. And the answer came immediately: I was still shortening my pull, concentrating on delicacy rather than strength. Bearing that in mind, I made some mental adjustments and drew again. My arrow nicked the edge of the white upright and, deflected, landed close to his first shot. I said nothing.

"There's better," he said, hoisting his bow again and letting loose without seeming to aim. This time his shot hit square on target and we both saw the white stake split. He grunted. I was amazed. It was either an incredible shot or an equally incredible piece of luck.

I forced myself to sound non-committal. "Not bad," I said. "Could you do it again?"

He did, immediately, and I was left without a word to say as his previous arrow, which had been held in the cleft of the split shaft of the shovel, spun through the air and fell to the ground. The target was destroyed. To have attempted to hit it would have been foolish, and I said so.

"Try it anyway," he grunted.

I sighted carefully and loosed. My shot was close, but we had no way of judging how close.

He turned to me with another of his grunts. "Delicacy, boyo, that's what you lack. That great thing of yours takes too much pull. You can't be accurate with a great thing like that. Delicacy's what you want, there's all! Who are you, anyway?"

I smiled and leaned on my bow. "Varrus is my name. Publius Varrus. I am a guest of Caius Britannicus."

He drew in his breath with a hiss. "Guest, is it? Roman you are." He pronounced the word as another would pronounce "toad" or "serpent."

I laughed. "Aye, I'm Roman. What did you think I was? And who are you?"

"Cymric. I took you for one of us, there's blind of me!"

His way of talking was unlike any I had ever heard. I decided that he must be one of the local Celts. "Are you from around here, then?"

"No." His eyes were on my face, weighing me against some kind of private measure in his head. Finally he resumed speaking. "No. I live here. Around here. But I am from the hills. The mountain land. Over yonder." He indicated the far horizon to the north-west, where I could see no mountains, and then he narrowed his eyes and I looked to see a man approaching us from the house.

"Master Varrus," he said as he drew close, "the Lady Luceiia is preparing to leave."

"Thank you," I said. "Please tell the lady I shall be there presently." As he walked away I spoke again to Cymric. "Wait here."

I paced out the distance from where he stood to the shattered shaft of the shovel stuck in the ground in front of the root-pad of the great fallen tree. I had gauged it correctly. It was a hundred and twenty-six paces to the shovel, which I pulled from the ground, noting that the blade was still quite bright where it had been dug in, and another twelve paces to the surface of the root-pad. It towered above me as I stood at its base and wedged the shovel, its blade upturned, securely against the sandy clay of its surface. That done, I returned to where Cymric stood watching.

"Now, friend Cymric," I said with a smile, "I have added twelve more steps to the distance, but the mark is wider, and far shorter. Let's see you hit it now. Six arrows."

He looked at me with a pitying scowl and began to shoot. Four of his arrows sent back loud noises to announce their arrival on the shovel blade, but I had wedged it well and it stayed in place. I stood behind him as he shot, lining up six of my best arrows with their points in the ground. As his last arrow, his fourth hit, clanged its arrival on the mark, he turned back to me and saw what I had done. I could not read the expression on his face as I waved him aside. He moved without speaking, fastening his eyes on the gleam of the distant shovel blade.

"Well done, Cymric," I said. "Four out of six is fine shooting. Delicate shooting, as you say. Now, watch this, and note the lack of delicacy."

I went into my smooth, practised manoeuvre, pulling all the way back to my ear and loosing all six arrows so fast that there was always one in flight as I released the next. We heard five sounds, one a clang similar to the sound his arrows had made and the other four quite different.

"Five," I grunted. "Come."

I heard him walking behind me as I led the way to the mark, knowing what I would find and positioning myself so as to hide the mark from his eyes with my back. I stopped about two paces short of the mark.

"Well, Cymric?"

I had my revenge for his scoffing and scorn when he walked past me and then stopped, silent, his eyes on the mark. His six arrows and two of mine were sunk well into the sandy base of the root-pad, around the head of the shovel. The shovel's surface showed four scratches where his points had hit and been deflected, and one deep gouge where one of mine had done the same. Four of my arrows, however, had pierced clean through the metal of the shovel and pinned it against the clay.

I spoke to his stiff back. "Not delicate, Cymric, but effective."

He turned to me, and his eyes were wide as he looked from me to the bow I held. He nodded once, and I accepted that as his recognition of a superior weapon. I stepped forward and began to collect my arrows, working them backwards through the holes they had made in the iron.

"I will be at the Villa Britannicus. If you care to visit me there, I'll be glad to see you." I packed the arrows into my quiver. "Until then, farewell." I offered him my hand and he shook it, still without saying a word. I was conscious of his eyes on my back all the way back to the villa.

As I entered the courtyard, I saw Luceiia, Veronica and Quintus standing outside the main door of the house beside a brightly decorated, four-wheeled cart harnessed to a matched team of grey horses. There were no servants that I could see, not even a wagon driver, and I found this surprising, although I wasted no time thinking about it. They all smiled as I walked towards them.

"You must pardon me if I have kept you waiting," I called out as I approached them, "but I was involved in a matching of wits and arrows with one of your people, Quintus."

"You have not kept us," Luceiia answered. "There is no rush. Who was your opponent?"

I reached them and shook Quintus's proffered hand. "Cymric," I said. "What does he do?"

Quintus laughed. "Cymric does nothing he does not want to do. Cymric simply is Cymric. He comes from Cambria, from the mountains, and does whatever needs to be done around here until he grows tired of it, and then he moves on."

"I see." I looked at Luceiia, trying not to appear too besotted with her. "I asked him to visit me at your villa. I hope that was not foolish of me?"

She laughed. "Not at all. He may even come, if he likes you. He likes few Romans."

"I got that impression. At least he respects me, that I know."

"La! And so he should." She was mocking me, I thought.

I looked around me. "You are ready to leave. My horses and my gear are in the stables. I'll go and get them."

"No, they are already gone. I sent Jacobus on ahead with them, hoping you would prefer to ride with me."

I felt my face flush with pleasure and sought to hide my confusion by thanking Veronica and Quintus for their kindness and their hospitality.

Eventually, amid smiles and waves, we left the Villa Varo and set out for the Villa Britannicus, which, I had been told, lay six short miles to the south and west. Our route lay along a well-used, rutted path that skirted the outer quadrangle of the Varo farm and swung past the great uprooted tree that had seen my triumph over Cymric. Sure enough, he was still there, watching us as we passed. I shouted and waved to him and he responded with what seemed a grudging wave in return.

Luceiia had the reins and she drove well. The cart was built for passenger comfort and obviously not for work. It had seats for six people in the bed of the wagon and a canopy of soft leather that could be unrolled in rainy weather to close in the sides. The driver's bench was cushioned and as comfortable as a wagon bench could be, and for the time being I was more content than I could ever remember being. We drove without talking for about a mile, Luceiia concentrating on the rutted path, and I on her, willing myself not to stare too hungrily at the perfection of her profile. The day was beautiful and birds sang everywhere and I was as happy and as full of bliss as any man could ever be.

Soon, however, sensing my scrutiny of her, she turned her face to me with a tiny smile. "You are very quiet this morning, Master Varrus. Is everything well?"

I sucked in a deep breath. "Perfectly well, thank you, *Domina*," I replied. "As a matter of fact, I was just congratulating myself on being alive on a day like this."

Her smile widened and she asked, "You feel no urge to talk?"

"None at all."

"Good, then we will share the silence and the day."

We travelled on in silence, and she allowed me the perfect pleasure of simply looking at her. We both knew that I was staring ill-manneredly, but she was gracious enough to take no ill of it, and confident enough to be unflustered by it.

Her hands were long and delicate, yet brown and strong, and there was a fine, fine down of the most delicate goldness on her forearms, which were not quite covered by the sleeves of the long, white gown she wore. Her mode of dress was the classic dress of Rome: long, clean, straight lines of soft, draped cloth, tied at the waist, the upper garment scooped across her bosom and gathered at the shoulder by a jewelled pin. She was gloriously lovely, and I felt a growing urge in me to say so, but I lacked the courage. I fell into a day-dream, however, imagining that I did say so, and that she smiled and laid her hand in mine that I could kiss it. And kiss it I did, in my dream, rubbing the golden skin gently against my lips and tasting the sweetness of it with the tip of my tongue. Her voice brought me back to my senses.

"This is the border of the two estates. Beyond the stream is your new home." She turned to me with that raised-eyebrow look of her brother's. "That is, if you care to stay?"

I smiled and said nothing, but my heart was saying, "I care to stay, I care to stay!"

The stream was a shallow one, no more than a brook, and our path ran straight across it and then branched into three, one going straight ahead and one along the bank of the stream in either direction. I expected her to continue along the main path, but she swung the team to the right and we followed the stream until we came to a widening pool surrounded by willow trees. She brought the horses to a halt just beneath them.

"Now, sir, if you will take the basket from behind us and help me down, we will eat here before going on to the house, and I will talk to you of dragons."

Delighted, I sprang down from the seat, forgetting all about my bad leg but fortunately landing well. Then I helped her down from the bench, feeling the wondrous softness of her waist beneath my hands for the first time.

The basket contained a variety of food and a flagon of wine, and cups and knives and even a cloth to spread on the grass, and we ate together in perfect contentment by the side of the gurgling stream.

There came a time when I could eat no more, and I made myself more comfortable, leaning against the bole of the tree.

She smiled at me. "Now, are you comfortable? Is there anything else I can do for you?"

"Only one more thing," I said, with a smile that was sheer euphoria. "Tell me about your dragons, and why I will adopt them."

Her face grew serious. She plucked a blade of grass, frowning at it in concentration as she split it carefully lengthwise with the nail of her right thumb. "What do you know of the Druids, Publius?"

I thought for a moment before answering. "Not a lot. Mainly what Bishop Alaric has told me about them. You know Alaric?" She nodded. "He says they're the priests of the Celts. They are of the old religion that held power here before we came. They used to conduct human sacrifices, and were supposed to have magical powers. They worship trees, particularly the oak tree, and the parasite, mistletoe, is held by them to be a sacred plant. Their views today are moderate and not at all at odds with the basic tenets of Christianity, in that all things were created by a benign God for a specific purpose. That's about all. Why do you ask?"

She was staring at me, an unintelligible expression on her beautiful face, her right eyebrow quirked slightly higher than the left. In answering my question she dipped her head slightly as though in acknowledgement of something.

"I was simply curious to find out how much you know about them. Do you believe that they have magic powers?"

"No. I told you, I don't even believe that charcoal has magic powers."

Her eyebrow went up higher, in that sardonic way her brother had. "Well, Publius," she drawled, "you are wrong. Magic they possess. Real magic, but purely natural. The magic of trained memory."

I dismissed that with a grunt. "There's nothing magical about trained memory, Luceiia. It's the first function taught in the legions. When a man's illiterate, you'd better make sure that you train his memory if you ever want him to remember anything, from drill to a crucial message."

She accepted my response without demur. "True, but the Druids have this on a different scale. They have carried it beyond the realms of what Romans would consider possible. They carry their entire history around in their heads and in their hearts, Publius. They are a truly wonderful people. I have several friends among them whom I value above many 'worthy' Romans."

I dismissed these sentiments too, classifying them mentally as womanly, and my next words betrayed that.

"I presume it was these people who introduced you to the dragons?"

"Don't be nasty, Publius Varrus, it doesn't suit you. As it happens, however, you are correct. They did."

"I see. Well, what have these dragons to do with me?"

"Nothing yet, and yet perhaps everything. As I told you, you will adopt them as your own."

I sighed. I had eaten well and was more than content with her company, but I was not in the mood for circumlocution. Nevertheless, I was at pains to keep any trace of impatience out of my voice, and there was a part of me, a very large part of me, that would have been content to dally in that place all day with Luceiia, even had she been babbling gibberish.

"Could you be talked into explaining that?" I asked her.

"Happily. The Celts who live here in the west call themselves the people of the dragon. The Pendragon, to be exact. I respect and admire them very much. And, as I've said, I have made friends of some of their Druids. The Christians have, as you remarked, been making some inroads into the old religion in the last few years, but the Druids are a long way from losing their place of honour in the land. One of them told me the story of the Pendragon and how they were named. It was all very mystical and I listened mainly out of politeness, understanding little of it. But then you yourself alerted me with something you said to Caius, in talking of your grandfather. He repeated it to me and I have been thinking about it ever since."

I waited. She was obviously struggling with unruly thoughts.

"You asked me if I had seen rust-stained hillsides, and of course I have, without knowing what they signified. I have seen many of them in the hills to the north-east of here, the Mendips. The Pendragon, you see, used to be best known for their crafting of metal. They worked with tin, silver, lead and iron. Their greatest tribal secrets were the secrets of metal."

She had my full attention. "Go on."

"Well, understandably enough, they wanted to preserve their secret lore from unfriendly eyes. So they used to do their smelting, as you call it, in great secrecy, in caves in the hills, mainly at night. The glow of their furnaces, the noises and the smoke gave rise to a legend, actively fostered by the people themselves, that the hills were the homes of fire-breathing dragons — monsters whose roaring and clanging could be heard in the night by anyone foolish enough to approach their lairs. And their subterfuge worked. It was the perfect deterrent to spies and raiders, and their secrets were safe for centuries."

"Until the Romans came."

"Exactly, Publius. Until the Romans came. The Romans, with their ravenous appetite for raw materials and their hard-headed refusal to believe in dragons or in anything else that couldn't be countered by sword, shield and spear. Then the furnaces were abandoned in the caves, and they have remained that way for more than four hundred years."

"So," I said, "all your dragons are dead?" She nodded. "Then how could I adopt them? And why would I want to?"

She smiled, sweetly and knowingly. "There is a legend among the Pendragon people that the dragons will return to the hills some day, when the Romans leave."

"So?"

The smile left her face to be replaced by a tiny tic of annoyance. "What do you mean, 'So?' Think about what I said."

I moved my back against the tree, seeking a more comfortable angle. "Luceiia, I have no wish to offend you, or to seem cynical, as you put it, but since I joined the legions I must have heard a thousand similar stories and legends. What's so different about this one?"

"Evidence. This one is quite specific, Publius. The dragons will return to the hills of the Pendragon when the Romans leave Britain. Caius thinks that might not be far in the future."

"You mean his theory about the Romans having to go home to defend the Motherland?"

"Yes."

I nodded. "Very well, I'm thinking. That is why your brother wants me to live here in Aquae Sulis, isn't it? To be prepared?"

She nodded, and her next words were unequivocal. "Yes, and to help us build ourselves a new life while we wait for the dragons to come back."

I grinned. "Well, why not?"

"Why not, indeed? They've already started to, it seems."

"What d'you mean?"

Now she was grinning widely, enjoying the effect of her next words in advance of their delivery. "They've started to come back. To the hills. The dragons. They have been seen. Witnessed."

"When? By whom? Your Druids?"

Instead of answering directly, she took another tack. "Last night you told me that your grandfather found and smelted his skystone thirty-some years ago?" I nodded, and she went on. "Well, according to my Druid friends, there was a visitation of dragons to the local hills one night about thirty-six years ago. It terrified the local people, genuinely. There is absolutely no doubt of that. The dragons came at night, in fire and thunder and smoke, flying through the darkness at great speed and landing with a huge commotion and concussion among the hills to the east. The Mendip Hills. The Dragon Hills."

She paused to let that sink in for a few moments before continuing.

"I had no knowledge of the event. It happened eleven years before I was born, and my family were still living in Rome or in Constantinople. In any case, your grandfather's story makes me think there might be some connection between the two events. Perhaps the 'dragons' were a rain of your skystones? The times seem to fit, if your recollection of the date is accurate. Wouldn't you agree? Or does that sound insane? The speculations of a foolish woman?"

By this time, without being aware of it, I was on my feet, almost hopping with excitement. It was more than sane — it was remotely probable. It might well be that that was exactly what had terrified the people. A rain of skystones! I visualized them falling, red-hot and roaring from the skies!

"Good God, Luceiia," I said, through a throat that had suddenly gone tight. "Of course they're connected! It's obvious! You're exactly right, I know it! A rain of skystones."

Now that she had won my conversion, however, she seemed immediately to lose her own certainty. "Publius," she said, almost in a whisper, "you really believe that theory?" She sounded dazed. "You think it might be what happened?"

"Might be! Of course it might be! I'm convinced of it, absolutely convinced."

"Oh dear. I was convinced of it, too, at one time, right when the idea occurred to me. But Caius made me feel silly, and I gave in to his logic."

I fixed her with a glare, her mention of Caius's logic chilling me like a dash of cold water. "What logic?"

She flushed and looked down at the ground. "Oh, Publius, I feel quite guilty about this. Here you are now, all excited, and Caius has me confused so that I cannot really bring myself to believe, with the best will in the world, that stones can fall from the sky. Not, at least, unless someone has thrown them up there with a catapult."

I threw myself down to the ground beside her, not quite daring to reach out and lay my hand on her. "Luceiia, that's not important. Your brother is a Roman general, his objective officer's mind simply will not allow him to believe what his senses tell him to be impossible. I know you're right in your deductions. I don't know how I know, but I do. My guts are telling me that you are right. They were skystones."

"So what do you intend to do about it?"

"That depends on you and your Druids. Do you or they know exactly where these things landed?"

"They do. Apparently there was a small herd of cattle grazing right at the spot. The cattle were all dead the next day. Some of them had been burned, others apparently devoured."

I was seething with excitement. "Luceiia, can you find out exactly where this place is? And can you find someone to take me to the exact spot? By all the gods in the universe, Luceiia, do you know how excited I am?"

Her face was radiant. "I think so. I can see you."

"Just think, Luceiia! To find another skystone!" I slapped my hands together in excitement. "I'll bring the dragons back to those damn hills, all right, if there are skystones there!"

"You see, Publius? Didn't I tell you you would adopt them?"

I looked at her and knew that, even had I not loved her already, I would have fallen afresh in love with her then.

XVIII

The Villa Britannicus humbled me. I found myself facing a statement of wealth so sublime that I felt like a pauper again in spite of my hoard of gold and my successful weapons manufactory in Colchester. I had always known that the Britannicus family was a rich one, but the evidence that now confronted me in the size and the condition of the villa and its surroundings shouted of a wealth beyond human comprehension.

On my first day there, after I had been shown to my quarters and had unpacked my few belongings, Luceiia took me in to the room she called her *cubiculum*, although she admitted it really belonged to her brother, and showed me a plan of the place, pointing out the various sections to me and explaining their several purposes. In plan, the house itself was an enormous "H" built on an east-west axis. The main family living quarters closed off the westernmost end of the "H" to form a quadrangle. All of the four buildings facing the enclosed courtyard of the quadrangle were domestic buildings, housing the villa's servants and domestic facilities such as baths, laundry, bakery, kitchens and the like. The main crossbar of the "H" was built with a portico that gave on to a second, outer courtyard at the east end. This was sheltered on three sides — by the "crossbar" itself, and by the north and south wings. These buildings housed stables, granaries, livestock barns, a spacious smithy with several forges, a carpentry shop with a barrelmaker's shop attached, a pottery and a tannery.

Luceiia took me on a tour of inspection. The entire villa was two-storeyed, and the walls surrounding the inner courtyard were of solid stone — huge granite pebbles, all smooth and rounded, bonded together by strong concrete. The extended wings flanking the outer courtyard were of timber framing and plaster mixed with broken flint.

The Britannicus family were justifiably proud of their villa. It had two completely separate sets of baths, one for the family itself and the other, a larger facility, for the servants and the tenants who farmed the surrounding land. Luceiia pointed out to me that all of the buildings flanking the inner courtyard were entered from the courtyard. This did not surprise me, and indeed seemed not worth mentioning, until she also pointed out that all the buildings flanking the outer yard opened into the fields surrounding the villa. Only four small doors permitted pedestrian access from these buildings to the outer courtyard. That did surprise me.

She saw my surprise and smiled and told me to blame the anomaly of the outer courtyard on herself. When Caius had left for Africa, she had decided to beautify the place. She had transformed the courtyard, blocking up the entrances to all the buildings around it and opening new ones on the other side. Now the threshing floor, the entries to the cattle sheds, sheep pens and swine sties were hidden from the casual visitor. Having masked the front of the building, she had then proceeded with the construction of a great, sweeping arc of an entrance road leading to the main portico. She had seeded the entire yard with new grass and lavished attention on it, and when it had grown rich, she had planted formal gardens of flowers — roses, violets, pansies and poppies. The only remnants of the days before her changes were the twelve mighty trees that had always stood there: four oaks, three elms and five great copper beeches.

"Come, Publius," she said after I had admired the scene. "You have some idea now of the layout of the place. Now we can look more closely."

That was when the humbling process began. I may have thought, as I listened to her talk about the plan of the villa, that I was getting some idea of what it was like, but I was wrong. The reality beggared description. The ground floor of the family quarters, for example, was palatial, and every room was differently floored. The floors in the main rooms were mosaic, in a multitude of colours, showing scenes of Greek myth and legend: I saw depictions of Europa and the Bull, Leda and the Swan, and Theseus and the Minotaur. The lesser rooms on that floor were merely tessellated, laid out in geometric shapes and patterns that dazzled the eyes with their brightness and colours.

The *triclinium*, the great dining room, held an open-sided arrangement of matched oaken dining tables that would seat upwards of sixty guests in comfort, and the walls were panelled in sheets of lustrous green and yellow marble so highly polished that I could see myself reflected in them. Against the walls, ranked side by side, were deep-shelved cabinets — some open-fronted, some with doors — that held the family's wealth of plate and dinnerware: platters and bowls and serving dishes and knives and utensils of gold and silver and copper and tin and bronze; exquisite Samian pottery, richly glazed and decorated; cups and beakers and vases of polished glass; and two enormous drinking cups of aurochs horn, polished and worn, glossy with age and ornamented with mounts of finely crafted gold.

The family slept on the upper floor, which was reached by a double flight of spacious, marble steps. Up there, I found real cause for astonishment. The floors were all of wood, for one thing, but such wood as I had never seen before. I asked Luceiia about them and she told me they were of pine, imported to Britain by her great-grandfather years before, and planed and then polished to a deep, reflective glaze by more than a hundred years of care and cleaning.

The most amazing thing of all, however, was that each of the ten sleeping-chambers on that upper floor had a window, and was therefore filled with light. The windows were small, and covered with wooden shutters fitted with louvered slats that could be closed completely, or angled to permit light and air to enter. I had heard of such things, and had even seen a few, but I had never seen them used so lavishly before. Normal Roman sleeping chambers were precisely that: tiny, lightless cubicles containing a bed, and perhaps a table. Because of the profusion of light, however, each of the ten chambers was decorated in a different colour, the walls and draped windows and the carpets on the floors blending their hues to give each room a character quite different from any other. My own room, which was separated from Caius's by a short, lateral corridor with a window at the eastern end and a chamber door on each side, was decorated in pale gold, while his was a spacious chamber of cool greens. Luceiia's own chamber was white and silver, with pale blue carpets and window drapes, and a bed covering of blue and silver silk the value of which must have been incalculable, made as it was in the distant lands far beyond Constantinople to the east.

The temperature throughout the entire house was uniform, thanks to the heated air carried to the various rooms by the hypocausts, hot-air ducts fed by the furnace that burned constantly beneath the bath house and was refuelled twice each day by the household servants. Luceiia led me from the upper floor to the family bath house by means of a stairway that descended to the inner courtyard from the passageway that ran along the outside of the upper floor.

Once again I was impressed beyond my expectations. The family bath house lacked none of the facilities one would expect to find in a major public bathing house. There was a spacious undressing room, divided by rod-hung curtains for privacy, and lined with niches for holding clothing. Directly outside this room were three pool rooms laid out in sequence — cold, tepid, and hot — and beyond those, closed off by heavy, waterproofed curtains, was the *sudarium*, or steam room, which held a number of stone plinths and was looked after by an attendant skilled in massage and depilation.

We did not linger in the bath house, but I asked her about the glazed tiles that lined the walls and the pools, and she told me that they, too, had been imported from beyond the seas.

It was a relief to emerge again into the scented coolness of the inner courtyard where, even this late in the year, the air was redolent of green and growing things. This inner courtyard was split into four quarters by intersecting pathways. The two plots closest to the living quarters were ornamental, lined with privet hedge and planted with a profusion of red poppies, some of which still bloomed. The far plots were given completely to vegetables and fruits. I could tell from the pride with which she described the plants that this garden was Luceiia's special concern. She pointed out two plum trees, a cherry tree and two apple trees, all pruned severely and healthy-looking.

At the intersection of the two pathways, she turned right and led me to the kitchens and the bakery, pointing out that most of the household servants lived above these places. Both facilities were enormous, spotlessly clean and well enough equipped to serve two hundred people on the shortest notice.

At the far end of this side of the courtyard, furthest from the furnaces that heated the house, Caius had placed the room in which he kept his wines. I felt my eyes grow large as Luceiia began to show me the treasures this room contained. It was filled from floor to ceiling with shelves, separated by walkways just wide enough to permit the installation and removal of the very largest of the amphorae, barrels, casks and jars of all shapes and sizes that lined the shelves. Each separate container was clearly labelled and numbered, and their contents ranged from the thick, rich, sweetened wines of Greece to the dark, red, tangy wine made from the grapes grown on the slopes of Mount Vesuvius. There were amphorae of the succulent wine of Aminea and a wide selection of the various wines of Gaul, including the light, sweet wine of the south that is neither red nor white but a mixture of both.

There was one whole section of shelves that held different wines, all in small jugs that a man could hoist easily to his mouth on a bent elbow, and one of these Luceiia broke open and passed to me. It was ambrosia! Cool and nectar-sweet, imported, she told me, from the lands of the Germanic tribes I had fought against myself, years before. Had I known they could produce wines as superb as this, I would have stayed there longer, non-combatant.

We crossed the courtyard again to the northern wall, me still carrying my open jug, and she showed me the laundries and the dry storage rooms that occupied that wing, as well as the cool room, again furthest from the furnaces. This was the only other room in the whole building that, like the wine room, had no hypocausts. It was separated from the rooms on either side of it by thick stone walls, plastered on the inside with thickly strawed mud and painted white. The floor, I noticed, was of concrete and was channelled for drainage. During the summer months, this room was packed with ice and salt and straw to keep it cool, and carcasses of oxen, sheep, pigs, deer and other game hung on iron hooks suspended from beams in the ceiling. There were no cobwebs in the corners, and no speck of dirt on the walls or on the floor.

By the time we had completed our tour of the entire villa, the day was almost gone, and I was speechless. We ended our tour in a large and spacious smithy, having been over every square foot of the Villa Britannicus, and I was looking around me at the empty forges and braziers and at the tools that hung ranged in neat rows everywhere I looked.

"Well?" Luceiia asked. It was the first word either of us had spoken in a long time. "What do you think?"

I scuffed my foot on the concrete floor. No grit. No ashes. I looked again at the brazier closest to me, and at the tongs and hammers that flanked it.

"Everything looks new."

Luceiia's eyebrow went up and she laughed. "Everything in here *is* new, Publius. This is your personal place, Publius Varrus's smithy, planned by Caius and furnished and equipped by both of us in what seemed the vain hope that you might someday come here. We both agreed that we would hate you to be bored or purposeless under our roof."

I had already guessed as much. I turned towards her, positioning myself so that I could see her face clearly in the late-afternoon light.

"You really expected me to come? Why?"

She gave me the full benefit of her dazzling, dizzying smile. "Why not? You are the closest friend my brother has. And he has hoped for a long time, ever since you left the army, that you would come to the west to share his dream with him some day. We both did, even though I did not know you. We hoped at least that if you did come, even to visit, this smithy would encourage you either to stay or to return often." She held up her hand as I made to speak and I waited for her to finish what she had to say. Her expression became serious. "Publius," she said, "I know you have made a life for yourself and built an enterprise in Camulodunum."

"Colchester." I grinned.

She returned my grin. "If you must. Colchester. But Caius will be home soon and he will no longer be a soldier. His whole life will be different, and he has been planning it for years. It would make him very happy if he were to find you waiting here to greet him. God knows there's room enough here for all of us, but Caius has a special place for you in his plans, which you already know something of. Before too many days have passed, you will know more of them."

I perched myself, smiling, on the edge of the brazier nearest me; she saw the look in my eyes and hurried on.

"In any event, whether you choose to stay or no, you will be going up into the hills to look for skystones. Am I not correct?" I nodded. "Well, then," she continued, with an eagerness in her voice that surprised and touched me, "if you find any such stones, you will probably want to start smelting them immediately. And now you can. Here." She looked around her, and suddenly she resembled a very young girl far more than a beautiful, ripe woman. "You may find that not everything you need is here. If we've overlooked anything important, we can acquire it easily in Aquae Sulis."

I sighed and smiled again, shaking my head, and then moved to where a pile of rust-covered ingots had been stacked in a corner. Beside the stack was a large, lidded bin. I raised the lid and looked inside. The bin was full of charcoal. I tested a piece between my finger and thumb. It was high-quality charcoal. I looked at her again.

"Where did you and Caius find all this?"

She looked perplexed. "I had the smith from Quintus Varo's villa buy everything he could think of that you might need. Why? Has he done badly?"

I laughed in disbelief. "No, Luceiia, he has done superlatively well. This place is better designed and better equipped than my own smithy at home. I am just amazed, that's all. Amazed and grateful. This is a gesture worthy of an emperor — and an empress."

"No, Publius." Her smile and her head shake were deprecatory. "But worthy of a friend, I hope. I am glad you like it."

"Like it? I love it." I bent and picked up a heavy iron ingot. "And if there *is* anything lacking, which I doubt, I have everything here that I would need to make it myself." I dropped the ingot with a loud clank.

"Good," she said. "Excellent. Now we should return to the house. We have guests to prepare for."

"Guests? Who's coming?"

"Friends and neighbours, all anxious to meet the redoubtable Varrus."

She took my arm and led me out into the daylight again, into the lane that ran along the outer walls at the back of the villa. Away to our right, to the north-east, a line of hills loomed in the evening sky, their flanks shadowed by gathering dusk, their upper slopes still catching the rays of the sinking sun. I nodded towards them.

"Are those your dragon hills, the Mendips?"

"Aye. That's where your skystones are."

I stared at their darkening shapes, feeling excitement stirring in my gut, and my feet stopped moving of their own accord.

"I know you have said so, but do you really know someone who can take me there, to the exact place?"

Her hand still lay on my arm, which I held bent to support it, and now she squeezed the muscle of my forearm comfortingly, although the pressure almost stopped my heartbeat.

"It is all arranged. Meric, one of the local Druids, knows where to take you and what to show you. You will meet him tonight."

"You invite Druids to dinner?"

She laughed. "Of course! They are people, just like us. They even eat the same food, so it is quite simple to entertain them, except that, most of the time, they entertain me. You will enjoy the Druids, Publius Varrus, I promise you."

We started to walk along the lane, and the liquid song of a thrush suddenly reminded me of the confrontation I had had on the road with Nesca's assassins. Luceiia must have been watching me closely, for she noticed my abrupt change of mood and asked me what was wrong.

"Nothing," I answered. "The bird's song reminded me of some trouble I had on the road, that's all. It's nothing for you to be concerned about."

"It is if it concerns you." Her voice was low and serious, and I turned to be able to see the expression on her face. And seeing it I decided, on an impulse, to confide in her.

"Well," I admitted, "I will confess to a slight concern. It has to do with my reason for coming here."

She frowned. "That sounds ominous. Tell me truly — what was your reason for coming? You have not mentioned one. Not that it would make any difference," she hurried on. "I am only glad you came, but I sense a trouble in you now that has not been there since we met."

I thought for a few seconds, then I asked her, "Do you know a man called Quinctilius Nesca?"

She glanced towards me, taking her eyes from the road ahead of her. When she answered me her tone was quiet and non-committal.

"Yes, but not well. I have met him once or twice. Why do you ask?"

"What kind of a man is he?"

She threw back her head, hard enough to toss her long, dark hair, and this time her tone was definitive. "He is completely odious. Fat and repulsive and disgusting. A banker. A money-lender. But that's not what you mean, is it?" She pursed her lips delicately, and we walked on in silence for a few paces before she said, "Quinctilius Nesca is not a man whose company Caius would tolerate for long, nor would he ever seek him out. Where do you know him from?"

"I don't." I took a deep breath, wondering as I did so that I should be so open with this woman who, twenty-four hours ago, had been an unmet stranger. Then I began at the beginning and told her the whole story of Caesarius Claudius Seneca and our confrontation, together with its aftermath on the road from Colchester. She listened without interruption, and by the time I had finished we were back at the main entrance to the family quarters. She led me directly in to her *cubiculum* and nodded me to a seat, where I waited while she poured us both a cup of wine. I drank in silence while she mulled over what I had told her. Finally she spoke.

"All of this has happened since Caius left the country?"

"Yes. All within the past few months."

"And you only ever saw this Seneca that one time?"

"That particular specimen of Seneca, yes. Once was enough."

"Yes. I agree. But he shares his peculiar gifts for winning popularity with all his breed." A pause. "How long ago, exactly?"

"Two months ago . . . three at the most."

"And they are still looking for you?" She shook her head. "A pity about your limp."

"Aye. And my grey hair."

Another short pause, then, "You are still angry at Seneca, aren't you?"

I took a sip of my wine. "Yes, I am."

"Why?"

"Why not?"

"I can answer that," she said. I was amazed at how she reminded me of her brother. He would have said exactly the same things to me, in the same tone of voice. "You won the fight. He was the loser. You did not suffer at his hands. Only at his tongue, and that you should have forgotten by this time. At least, you should have put it out of the forefront of your mind."

"Luceiia," I said, knowing she was correct, "you may be right." I scratched at a sudden itch under my arm. "I probably should have. I just don't seem to be capable of forgiving or forgetting either the man or the occasion."

Her voice was insistent. "I ask you again. Why?"

"I don't know why, Luceiia!" I heard a note of irritation coming into my own voice. "Pardon me, but that is the way he affects me. I have been asking questions about him. The man is notorious — infamous. And it seems the more I hear about him, the more I detest him. He offends everything I hold in esteem. I sometimes think . . ."

"Go on. Finish it." Again her brother's tones. "You sometimes think what?"

I shook my head. "I don't know, it suddenly sounded foolish even to me. I was going to say that I sometimes think he's the personification of everything that is rotten in the Empire, but that would be giving him too much importance. He's simply an evil little man with too much power and too much money."

Luceiia got up and crossed to the side table on which the wines rested. She picked up the jug again and replenished my cup.

"The Seneca family is immensely wealthy, Publius, and wealth is power. We Britannici have learned that about the Senecas to our cost over several generations. But an evil little man? You told me he was a great, hulking brute of a fellow!"

"He is. He's big and strong, well muscled and in good shape. That's not what I meant by 'little.' I meant it more in the sense of mean and petty."

She sat down again. "Never make that mistake, Publius. This man is not petty. No Seneca is petty. Mean, malicious, malevolent and cruel, yes, but not petty. And your thought was far from foolish. He and his whole clan *are* the personification of all that is sick in Rome. It has been bred into him. Unfortunately, as a family, they are far from unique. I have heard Caius say many times it is those very attributes you describe that have brought down our country and the Empire. All the corruption, all the vices, all the faults and all the weaknesses of Rome are centred in its so-called nobility, and the Seneca family is typical of its worst excesses. You have made a bad enemy there, I am afraid. You say he returned to Constantinople?" I nodded. "Good," she said, emphatically. "Let us all hope he stays well away from Britain in the future. In any event, you are not likely to come face to face with Quinctilius Nesca around here."

As she finished speaking, the major-domo came into the room and announced that we had only half an hour to be prepared to welcome our guests. Luceiia excused herself and left immediately, leaving me to make my way back to my quarters.

I walked slowly, thinking about the amazing depths I had discovered in this remarkable woman in so short a space of time, and as I walked I caught sight of my own reflection in the marble walls of the room I was passing through. I stopped and looked at myself, trying to raise my right eyebrow the way she and her brother raised theirs.

"That, my friend," I said to my reflection, "is the woman you are going to have to learn to live without for the rest of your life. Forever. Unless you can find some miraculous way to win her." But guilt squirmed in my belly with my lust and in my heart with my swelling love, and I refused to allow myself to contemplate what Caius's reaction would be if he were ever to discover my presumptuousness in daring to dream about his baby sister.

Dinner that night was both a delight and a trial. I was "on parade" — under inspection as surely and as thoroughly as I had ever been under Caius's command in the army. I fought my natural aversion to meeting strangers and tried with all my heart to be friendly and affable. To my surprise, I seemed to be successful, and I found myself enjoying the attention being lavished on me and responding to it in a way that I had never been capable of before.

Of course, it goes without saying that I had Luceiia to thank for my new-found ease. She glowed that night with enthusiasm for everything I had ever done, it seemed. She led the dinner conversation with an infallible knack for making me and my opinions the centre of the evening and the standard against which all other opinions and experiences must be judged. And all through the long, formal meal I was aware of her presence, her shimmering beauty there at the opposite end of the table.

There were sixteen people seated there, and I have long since forgotten who they were, although I came to know all of them well in the years that followed. Only three people stand out in my memory, because they all stayed at the villa that night: Meric the Druid, who was far less outlandish and barbaric than I would have guessed; Domitius Titens, a local landowner and former tribune with whom I later became fast friends, and Cylla, his beautiful and waspish wife, who sought then and forever after until her death to take me to her bed.

That she failed to do so is no great source of pride, for it was not my steadfastness that kept me from her willing body — only circumstance at first, and loyalty later.

She began her assault on me at first meeting when, in that way that women have, she let me know in no uncertain terms, yet only with her eyes, that she would rut with me at my whim. Her husband was oblivious. Not so Luceiia, however, and I was later witness to a series of smiling, verbal thrusts that would have disembowelled a mere man. I missed the start of this exchange of savage wit and feminine venom and could only assume later, in the light of things Luceiia said, that Cylla had made a lewd comment about the convenience of the arrangement Luceiia and I shared, alone together in the villa. Luceiia made little of the comment at first, dismissing it as unworthy of response. Cylla, however, was persistent, going on about it with envious tenacity until Luceiia decided she had had enough, and told her so. It was at that point that I approached them, unwarily, and heard their exchange of pleasantries before they noticed me. I pretended to have heard nothing, and they abandoned their dispute when, shortly afterwards, we were called to dine.

By the end of dinner, I was again enmeshed in Luceiia's beauty and had lost all awareness of Cylla's charms. I thought no more about her until she came to my bed in the small hours, awakening me and throwing me into a panic.

I had been dreaming of Luceiia, feeling her there beside me in the bed, warm and strong and silken, and then suddenly I was no longer dreaming. The breast I was fondling was warm and real, and the body pressed against my swollen penis was alive and urgent. I awoke very quickly, and must have called Luceiia by name, for a laughing, whispering voice said, close to my ear, "No, not Luceiia. Luceiia isn't here."

And as I struggled to raise myself on one elbow, blustering in sleepy panic, I heard Luceiia's voice say, "Ah, but she is, my dear, and you, I think, are in the wrong bed."

By the time I had sat up and shaken myself completely awake, Cylla was gone, and Luceiia spoke from the doorway of my room.

"Go back to sleep, Publius, and sleep well."

I saw her shape, outlined in the moonlight as she turned to leave.

"Wait! Wait, Luceiia!" She turned back to me as I rubbed the last of the sleep out of my eyes. "What's happening?" I asked her, though I knew, finally. "What was that all about?"

Her voice was low-pitched. "I sent Cylla away. She is a foolish woman and a dangerous one. Her husband is not as stupid as she thinks he is. Had he awakened and found her gone, he would have come right here. There are only two beds she could visit, apart from his, and Meric is too old and too holy to appeal to her."

"Uh," I grunted, at a loss for words. Then I found my tongue. "Thank you for that. I was asleep and thought it was a dream."

"I know." I could have sworn I heard a smile in her voice. "I heard you."

"But . . . how did you come to be here? What hour of night is it?"

"It is late, Publius, but I have known Cylla all my life. I knew she would come to you. So I waited for her. Would you rather I had not?"

"No! No. I thank you for your thoughtfulness. You may have saved my life. You were right. That was both foolish and dangerous. And unsought."

"Then your broken dream was not of Cylla?" Again there was that smiling sound in her tone.

"I cannot remember," I lied. "No, no, I was not dreaming of Cylla."

"Good. Then go to sleep again. She will not be back tonight, and we have to be afoot early tomorrow. Meric is not a patient guide. Good night, Publius."

She closed the door gently as she left, and I had a hard time regaining my lost slumber.

XIX

I know that there are people who love hills and mountains. I hate them. They stink of blood and death and ambush. They hide enemies. I have lost too many good friends among hills ever to be impressed with their beauty. Hills are a hazard to the lives of travellers, and of soldiers. Place me on the top of a high hill with an unobstructed view of the countryside in every direction and I might be tempted to relax for a while, but I could never lie down and sleep on a hillside, nor can I ever be cheerful and talkative on a journey that wends through valleys. As I said, I hate hills.

The Mendip Hills are no different to any of the other hill ranges in south Britain. They look exactly the same. But the Mendip Hills held the promise of skystones, and because all of my experiences since landing in this part of the country had been happy ones, I was prepared to treat the Mendips as friendly territory for the time being; for the first time in my life, I did not feel threatened or claustrophobic. I only realized that, however, when we pulled our horses to a halt at the crest of a high hill and looked down into the valley on the other side, a valley that had been visited by dragons.

"Well, what do you think?"

The voice belonged to Meric. I did not answer him immediately; I was too busy scanning the floor of the valley.

Even from the top of the hill I could see that the grass was thick and rank, mottled already with the browns and yellows of wintertime. Everything I saw had that wet, chilled, unwelcoming look that meant December, and I felt no promise in the prospect in front of me, even though I could count about thirty large boulders scattered across the floor of the valley. The surface of the lake at the far end looked cold and hostile, opaque with wind ripples, and the excitement of the trip turned suddenly to disappointment and depression. I glanced sideways at my two companions. Both of them sat huddled on their horses, swathed in cloaks against the bitter, gusting wind.

"I don't know what to think, Meric," I answered. "Are you sure this is the place?"

He started to snap a response but restrained himself and turned his eyes away from me, down into the valley. It was obvious that he had decided not to lower himself to the level of my ill-mannered tone of voice.

"Yes, Varrus, I am sure this is the place. I have been here several times and it has not changed." He nodded towards the valley floor. "Are those boulders the stones you think fell from the sky?"

"They might be. I doubt it. I think they're too big. You realize I've never seen a skystone either? I have no idea what they look like." There was a roughness in my voice that I tried, too late, to conceal. It wasn't Meric's fault that this place was different from my expectations. To tell the truth, I hadn't known what to expect. "Tell me again what happened that night, Meric," I said more gently.

He shivered and drew his cloak more closely around his shoulders, and when he spoke his voice held no indication that he might be irritated by my request.

"Very well, but remember, please, I am only reporting what was told to me. The event took place during my boyhood, before I joined the Brotherhood. Apparently, the night it happened was a wild one — cloudy and windy, with great gaps in the clouds through which the stars were plainly visible. At about the second hour before midnight, many lights were seen in the sky. Each of these lights was separate from the others at first, but as they approached, at great speed, they became blindingly bright and were accompanied by a great roaring noise. They crashed to earth among the hills in fire and flames that lit up all the undersides of the clouds, turning them red as the fire itself, and the smoke of their coming blotted out the stars. This was all seen by hundreds of people who live in and around the hills here, and it was obvious to every one of them that the dragons of the legend had returned.

"On the following day, some of the more adventurous among the people came into the hills to see what had to be seen. Among them was Athyr, the old man who became my teacher. He was the one who told me what he saw with his own eyes. He brought me here to this very spot and tried to describe for me the devastation that had been wrought."

He paused, and for the space of many moments there was no sound on the hilltop except for the bluster of a gust of wind and the clump of hooves as Luceiia's horse sidled away from us slightly. Meric cleared his throat and took up his tale.

"There had been a small herd of cattle grazing in the valley that night — the riches of the village. The whole herd was dead, and the villagers left with nothing. Some of the cattle had been torn to pieces and the pieces scattered far apart. Some had completely disappeared. Vanished without trace. Others had been roasted alive. The entire valley had been drowned in mud, feet deep in places. Athyr said the mud reached the tops of the surrounding hills." He pointed to a cliff face to the west. "The entire side of that hill over there was blasted to rubble. You can still see the rocks at the foot of the cliff, although they're almost overgrown now." I looked and, sure enough, the bottom of the cliff over by the distant lakeside which I had taken, from this distance, to be sloping hillside, was in fact a tumbled confusion of ruin overgrown by rank, tufted weeds and scraggly shrubs.

"Everything was covered in mud, and yet Athyr said the cattle were roasted alive. I still don't understand how that could have happened, how it could have been true." He shrugged his shoulders. "I can do no more than accept it on faith. Athyr would never lie about anything. I have never known a more truthful man. He told me that is what he saw, therefore that is what he saw. He believed what he told me, and I believed him. By the time he brought me here, more than ten years had gone by and the grass had begun to cover everything again, although not so thickly as it has now."

I interrupted him. "What about the lake?"

He looked at me in surprise. "What about it?"

"I don't know what about it. That's why I'm asking. Did Athyr say anything about the lake?"

He frowned, remembering that day. "No. No, Athyr said nothing about the lake. Why do you ask?"

"I don't know." I was examining the valley more closely now. "That whole valley is shut in. How did the cattle get there?"

He looked mystified. "I don't know. They must have crossed the hills."

I kept my voice free of impatience. "Why would they do that? There's no shortage of grazing on the other side of the hills. Why would the villagers go to all the trouble of bringing their cattle all the way up and over the hills to let them graze in a shut-in valley?"

"For protection, perhaps?"

"From whom? Did you have trouble with raiders back then?"

"Not that I know of."

"And you're sure he said nothing about the lake?"

"Nothing. I am convinced of that."

"Has the lake always been here?"

"What kind of a question is that? Of course it has."

"Then where did all the mud come from?"

"I don't know, boyo."

"What else did he tell you? Think hard, Meric. It's important. Was there *anything* else he said to you about this place that might have slipped from your memory? Something that you might not have thought important at the time? Anything at all?"

His face became thoughtful as he turned back to the valley below us. I watched him closely, not taking my eyes off his face for a second. His gaze swept across the valley from right to left, and then I saw it — a momentary tic between his brows. I held my breath as it became obvious that he was searching his memories of his first visit to this place and recalling something, something vague that had lain disregarded and forgotten, for years.

"There was something. Something he said about that hillside." Then it was as though a light suddenly shone in his eyes. "I remember now. He said the Sun God's face was there in the mud of the hillside."

"What? What in Hades does that mean?"

He grinned a quick grin and looked at me. "I wondered the same thing and asked him to explain. He said that the mud on the hillside over there had a circular gap in it, where there was no mud at all. He said it was as if one of those dragons had scooped out a perfect picture of the Sun God from the mud all around. A perfect circle of silver-grey rock, he said, in the middle of a sea of mud."

I was silent for a while. There was something tugging at a loose end in my mind. I felt that irritating anticipation you feel when something is just about to pop into prominence in your mind and then will not. I blinked my eyes hard and shook my head to clear my thoughts.

"Where?" I demanded. "Where was it?"

He pointed. "Over there, on the flank of the hill."

I stared hard in the direction he was pointing. Nothing. I could see nothing.

"How big was this circle?"

"I don't know. Athyr did not say, and I did not think to ask him."

I mumbled a curse, scouring the hillside with my eyes, willing the Sun God's portrait to be there. But there was nothing. And then my stomach churned as I remembered what had caused the tugging at the loose end in my mind: a hot, dusty summer day in Germany, twenty-odd years earlier. We had been marching all day and had stopped for a ten-minute rest. I hadn't even had the energy to unload my gear; I sat hunched on a milestone by the side of the road, staring blindly at the dust that covered the cobbled road surface.

There had been thunder growling around for most of the afternoon, but the rain had held off. As I sat there, a scattering of big, fat, heavy raindrops fell sullenly around me. It was literally just a scatter of drops, each one of which left its own singular mark in the dust: a perfect circle, a blob of water in the middle of a perfect circle of dust thrown up around it like a wall. If I had not been so tired I would never have seen it. As it happened, the first one that I did see just happened to land right in the centre of the very cobblestone I was staring at. I was mildly surprised by the perfection of the shape it had caused, and I looked at the next one closest to it for the sake of idle comparison. And they were all the same! All the same size and all the same perfect shape, not only on the stones in the road, but in the dust by the roadside. I was sitting in a field of tiny, perfect circles. And then the centurion started yelling and I forgot all about it in the renewed agony of the long march.

I had remembered it again a couple of days later, however, when we arrived at the end of our march and were installed in camp. The dust was thick everywhere, and our centurion had detailed a couple of men, of whom I was one, to wet down the area surrounding the tribune's tent. I tried then to reproduce the effect of those raindrops, scattering drops high into the air and watching how they fell. Sometimes it worked and sometimes it didn't. It seemed to depend on the size of the drops of water. Big drops just splattered everywhere. It wasn't important to me, just a matter of curiosity, and when the other fellows around noticed what I was doing and started to mock me, I felt foolish and quit.

For months after, however, I became very conscious of the effects of falling rain. I saw how it landed on water, creating circular ripples. Eventually I lost interest in the phenomenon and forgot all about it, until one day about five years later when we got caught on the extreme edge of a freak summer hailstorm, and I saw the same circle effect in the dust of the field we were crossing.

I hadn't thought about it in years, and yet it had been there at the bottom of my consciousness, waiting to be remembered. Now I had recalled it, and it excited me. I remembered that my father had found the skystone at the bottom of a hole — a hole punched by the fury of its descent from the sky. And old Athyr had seen a circle in the mud on the hillside, a circle big enough to attract his attention.

My reverie was interrupted by Luceiia, who had been silent for a long time. "Shouldn't we go down and take a look at the boulders, Publius?"

I smiled at her delicacy in not pointing out that she was freezing to death sitting up there on an exposed hilltop.

"We can go down and look, of course, but I doubt if we'll find or see any skystones today."

Her face fell. "How do you know that?"

"I don't. I don't know it at all. But I just have a feeling that those boulders are not skystones. Anyway, let's go and see. I could be wrong."

We started to move down the hill, and I could see from the expression on her face that she was having doubts about something.

"You look concerned, Luceiia. What's the matter?"

She jerked her head in a negative. "Nothing, really. I was just wondering how you would know whether a stone, any stone, is a skystone or not?"

I grinned at the seriousness of her expression. "I seem to be saying this a lot today, but I don't know that either. I have no idea how I'll know, or even if I will know. Unless we find one that is pure metal. I won't know until I try to pick one up, I suppose."

"Publius Varrus! Are you telling us you really don't know what a skystone looks like?"

I shook my head. "Haven't got an earthly idea. I've only heard about them. I've never seen one."

"You said you won't know until you try to pick one up. Were you joking? Those boulders in the valley are huge. Nobody could pick one of those up."

"I'll grant you that, Luceiia, but a man with half a brain in his head should be able to break a piece off one of them, eh? Don't you think so?"

She flushed, thinking I was teasing her.

"No, I'm serious, Luceiia. I'll have to break each stone to see what's inside it. Metallic ore is easy to see inside a newly broken stone. The outside's usually weathered and discoloured and the veins of ore are often hard to see at a glance. You'll see, I'll show you when we get down there." I turned to Meric, who was making his way down directly behind me. "Seen any dragons yet, Meric?" He only grunted, not even lifting his eyes from the ground where the horse was placing its dainty feet. I relaxed and left my own horse to find its way down, remembering the day of the Invasion, many years before, when Britannicus and I had both trusted our lives to the sure-footedness of our horses.

As we descended, the clouds parted and allowed the pale December sun to shine through, with beams too weak to counteract the chill of the wind. The bottom of the valley was exactly the kind of spot that gave me the professional soldier's indigestion; it was completely surrounded by hills. The ground sloped down gradually, westward to our right, and the extreme western end of the valley was blocked by the waters of the lake. It was easy to imagine a whole legion getting trapped there with their backs to the lake and being slaughtered from the hills above.

"Does the lake have a name, Meric?"

"Not that I know of. It's just a lake. There's another in the valley below it, to the west. Much smaller. But no name, just another lake."

We spent the next half hour examining the closest of the boulders we had seen from the hilltop. I chipped a piece off each of them and showed Luceiia the striations in the material, but there was nothing there that indicated metal to me. It was Luceiia herself who pointed out that the inside of the rock was not much different from the outside, and she was correct. These boulders were brand new, no more than thirty or forty years old. They were great lumps of rock that had been blasted away from the glowering cliff face to the north, on the night of the dragons.

The footing was very uneven for our horses, with long, rank grass growing in tufts and hummocks as high as their knees. I was satisfied long before half an hour had gone by that all of the boulders in this valley were the same. They were only rocks, as the lake was just a lake. Luceiia, however, with the exuberance of the amateur, wanted to check every one of them, just in case there was one that was different from the others. She had no idea what she was looking for, but she crossed the valley from spot to spot enthusiastically, examining the surfaces of all the boulders in the hope of a revelation of some kind. Meric and I finally drew our horses together and watched her as she ambled about, leaning from her horse to peer closely at each new stone and growing a little more dejected with each one that turned out to be the same as all the others.

I was enjoying looking at her without being obvious. She had astonished me that morning by appearing in the leather breeches of a legionary beneath a long, knee-length tunic. The tunic was what took my breath away, for it was slit from knee to hip-bone on each side of her body. It was eminently sensible for a woman who wanted to ride like a man, but the degree to which it showed the curves of her legs and thighs was devastating. I had managed to betray nothing of my thoughts, although only with great difficulty, and had been at pains to keep my eyes away from her legs all day. Now that she was at a safe distance, I was able to feast my eyes on her.

The shadow of a cloud scudding across the hillside in front of her caught my eye, and I was watching it idly, trying to gauge the speed of its progress, when Meric spoke.

"That's strange."

I looked at him. He had turned his horse around and was staring up into the hills behind me. A cloud swept over the sun and a sharp gust of wind made my horse skitter nervously.

"What is?" I asked.

He shook his head, his expression one of slight perplexity. "I thought for a minute, there, that I could see a circle on the hillside."

"What?" I swung around, wrenching my horse with me so that it grunted in protest. "Where?"

He pointed up the hill. "Up there, just where Athyr said he saw it. But there's nothing there. I must have imagined it."

He was right. There was nothing to be seen on the bare hillside. I quartered the entire flank of the hill with eyes that wanted to see a circle shape, but it was useless. There was nothing. I swung my horse back around again in disgust.

"Your eyes are playing tricks on you, my friend. We'd better be getting back. It's growing late." I cupped my hands and yelled to Luceiia, signalling her to come back.

"Look, Varrus! There! Look!"

I swung my horse around again, and as I did I caught the merest, fleeting suggestion of a ring shape in the corner of my eye. It vanished even as I saw it, but not before I had identified it for what it was. My heart leaped into my mouth.

"It's a shadow, Meric. A shadow! Look, the sun's gone again. When it breaks through the clouds it throws the edges of the ring into shadow." I gazed up at the great cloud that was obscuring the sun. "It'll be back in a few minutes." I was seething with excitement. "As soon as it breaks through, mark the exact position of the ring on the hillside. I'll go up to it and you stay here and direct me in case I can't find it."

It seemed to take years for the sun to find its way from behind that cloud again, but when it did, there, stamped on the side of the hill, faint yet clearly defined, was the shape of the ring. I kicked my horse into motion and tackled the side of the hill at a gallop. The sun continued to shine, but I had not gone fifty paces before I lost sight of the shape. I had marked its position by an outcrop of rock, however, and I kept going.

It took me about five minutes to climb up to where I thought the shape had been, and eventually I reined in and looked back down at Meric, who by this time had been joined by Luceiia. The sun was still shining, but I could see no trace of the ring shape. Meric's voice came floating up to me from below, accompanied by wide-armed gestures.

"Right! To your right!"

I moved slowly to my right for what seemed to be a long way, until he yelled to stop.

"Now this way! To me!"

I moved forward, down the hill again.

"Stop! Stay there."

I sat there and waited as they made their way up to me. Meric arrived slightly ahead of Luceiia, whose eyes were roaming the whole hillside constantly as she climbed. Meric was panting slightly.

"Well," he gasped, "whatever it is, you're right in the middle of it."

"How far am I from the edge?"

"I tried to gauge that from down below. As far as I could tell, judging by your size in the middle of the ring and the length of your shadow, the outer edge should be about four or five paces on either side of you." I looked where he indicated. My shadow was long on the grass of the hillside.

"I lost sight of the ring as soon as I started to climb the hill," I said. "Did you?"

"I saw it plainly as you climbed the hill, and that's why I was able to guide you into it. But I lost it, too, as soon as I began to climb. There may be something magical about this place."

"There is." I slid from my horse's back to the ground, heading directly to my right, my eyes fixed firmly on the ground ahead of me, and within five paces, there it was: the rim of the ring. Unless a man had been looking for it in exactly that spot, he would never have noticed it. It was no more than a ridge of slightly raised earth, about ten or twelve inches high at its highest point, but once detected, the entire perimeter was easily traceable. I too was breathing hard now, barely able to contain myself as I realized where I was standing. I stepped over the raised outline and walked another twenty paces across the hillside before turning to look back. Sure enough, there was a slight but definite bowl-shaped depression within the ring. I walked back to the middle of the circle with triumph swelling in my chest.

"What does it mean, Varrus?" Meric was completely bewildered. "Is this important?"

I laughed aloud, my excitement making the laugh sound false even to me. "Important?" I looked at Luceiia, who was still mounted and was looking at me as if I had suddenly become possessed. "Luceiia, do you think this is important?" Her eyes were wide and baffled. "I want you to go over there, both of you, to where I was a few minutes ago, then tell me what you see. Please."

They exchanged looks of polite mystification and moved off obediently. As they went, I led my horse out of the circle and returned to stand in its centre.

"Now, what can you see?"

They looked at each other, and then back at me, and Luceiia said, "Nothing, Publius."

"The ground, Luceiia! Look at the ground. Meric, I'm standing in the middle of the ring. Do you notice anything about it? Anything different? Anything at all?" Meric's brow furrowed in concentration, and then I saw astonishment spread as he saw what I wanted him to see.

"It's bowl-shaped! As though it has been dug, hollowed out. There's a dip."

"Yes, Meric. Luceiia? Can you see it now?" She nodded wordlessly. "Good! Now you can come back."

They rejoined me on foot, leaving their horses outside the circle. Both of them still looked distinctly puzzled.

"Don't you know where you are yet?" I asked them.

Meric frowned. "We Druids have a circular temple to the sun on the great plain, but this is too small for such a place."

"Hah!" I shouted. "Temple to the sun? Nothing so tame, Meric! It's a dragon's nest! We're standing in a dragon's nest!"

It was an unkind thing to say to them, and I almost choked with laughter when the colour drained abruptly from their faces and they immediately and instinctively looked around as if expecting to be seized and devoured. I could see instant, total belief in their eyes, and still laughing, I drew my sword and stuck it into the ground at my feet, probing for bedrock. There was practically no soil, except at the centre of the depression, where my blade sank almost to the hilt. I straightened up and sheathed the sword again.

"Come," I said. "It's late. Next time we come back, we'll bring shovels and dig out the dragon's egg."

There was still fear on their faces and wild laughter in my belly as I gathered some stones to build a cairn in the middle of the ring. After that, I helped Luceiia to mount before vaulting onto my own horse, and we headed for the crest of the hill with the sun now far down on our left. I had marked the site well. The cairn thrust upward, a finger for tomorrow, marking the location of the skystone that every instinct in my body told me lay buried beneath it.

"We'll be travelling a long way in the dark tonight," I said, feeling again, for the first time in over an hour, the keen bite of the wind.

"Publius! Look!" It was Luceiia, and I heard awe in her voice as I reined in and turned. The sun was almost gone now, and, shadowed by its dying light, the outlines of five more circles were clearly visible on the hillsides and on the floor of the valley itself. I stared in astonishment and spoke into an almost religious silence.

"Dragons, my friends." I said. "The place is a colony of dragons."

XX

I had quizzed Luceiia about the distance facing us on our trip to the Mendips, long before the time came to set out. Her response had been that, according to Meric, the round trip was easily achievable in the space of a day.

It occurred to neither of us that Meric, being a Druid, looked on things like weather, time and distance from a perspective different to most people's. He would walk all night and all day and all night again, to get where he was going, and still not count it a two-day journey if he arrived before the sun rose again.

We had been on the road out for several hours, borne up on the excitement of the journey, before I began to have misgivings about the distance involved, and the length of time it might require. My doubts were fired by Meric's optimistically imprecise answers to such questions as, "How much further do you think we have to go now?"

It became clear to me eventually that the distance — despite the old Druid's protestations — was simply too great to permit an easy return journey in one day. By the time I realized it fully, however, we had been too far from the villa to return for extra supplies. It became a matter of returning home and starting again the next day, or suffering the inconvenience of a long, one-day, two-way trip on this single occasion. Luceiia's had been the final decision. At that time, it had still been a beautiful morning, with not a cloud in sight in the December sky. That changed within the next two hours. The weather grew gloomy and overcast, and on top of that we began to realize that we had underestimated the hardships of the excursion. For myself, I would have minded little, but Luceiia could hardly have been described as a hardened veteran of overland journeys. Meric, of course, was oblivious to all of this.

Even so, knowing what we knew, we had still allowed ourselves to overstay our time in the valley, caught up in the hunt. Darkness began to fall quickly as we turned for home, and the rain that had been threatening all afternoon began to fall in earnest, adding to the chill of the biting wind. Meric's sense of direction failed him at one point and we spent almost an hour floundering around on the hillside, leading our horses and in grave danger of falling down inclines that were far steeper than any we had faced on the way up.

By the time we finally made it down from the flank of the last hill, it had been pitch-dark for hours and we were all three soaked to the skin and chilled, it seemed, to the marrow. The rain had become a steady downpour and the wind howled in gusts so violent that our world was reduced to nothing but Stygian blackness and dementing noise. There could not have been three more miserable people on the face of Britain that night, and we were still at least twelve miles from the Villa Britannicus.

Luceiia grasped me by the arm and leaned close to me to shout something into my ear, but so strong and loud was the wind that her words flew off into the darkness without reaching me. I waved and shook my head to indicate that I had not heard her and leaned even closer, angling my plodding horse so close to hers that our legs were pressed together. This time her lips almost touched my ear and I felt her warm breath on my skin, stirring that entire side of my body to goose-flesh, in spite of my chill.

"Shelter," she shouted. "We have to find shelter quickly! We're hours away from home."

"I know," I yelled back. "But where? Do you know where we are?"

I could tell from her headshake that she did not, and we must have ridden for another three miles, sodden and sore and half frozen, before Meric suddenly appeared right beside me, waving wildly to indicate a change of direction. The suddenness with which I became aware of his closeness told me that I had been dozing, and the knowledge flared in my mind like a signal-fire warning of danger. I shook my head hard, trying to clear my thoughts, and began paying more attention to what was going on around me.

I had never been out on a more hostile night in all my years with the legions. The blackness was absolute, unrelieved by any gleam of light or any break in the solid cloud above us, and the lancing rain was still being driven relentlessly by a buffeting, icy wind that howled like a pack of hungry wolves. I thought about how long we had been travelling like this and felt a leaden fear grow in me with the realization that any or all of us could die of exposure on a night such as this, in the middle of nowhere without warmth or shelter of any kind. And suddenly, just as that thought occurred to me, the wind died away for the first time in hours, and I could hear again.

"What is it, Meric?" I screamed too loud into the sudden stillness.

"I think I know where we are, but I cannot see enough to be sure. If I am right, there should be a hut close by that will shelter us from the wind, at least. It has no roof."

"Where? How far?" My heart leaped at the realization that I could see the outline of his shape and the motion of a quick headshake.

"I don't really know. Can't really be sure. If I could see the hills I'd be able to be more certain." The outline of his shape was growing plainer. I turned and looked at where Luceiia should be and, sure enough, there she was, faint and indistinct but visible. As I saw her outline, the rain began steadily to lessen. I lifted my eyes to the sky and saw the shapes of cloud masses roiling above me.

"Look," I said. "It's breaking up."

As I spoke, a gap was torn in the clouds directly above Meric's head, and I saw the moon for a second before it was obscured again. The rain had stopped, and as all three of us sat there immobile, staring up at the clouds, I became aware of a strange noise in the stillness that now surrounded us. My ears quickened immediately, straining to identify the sound until, with a rush of pity and sympathy, I realized that I was hearing the chattering of Luceiia's teeth. I knew how bad I was feeling, and I had spent years on the open countryside campaigning in all weathers: I could only guess at the extent of Luceiia's misery.

A great rent appeared among the clouds now and moonlight spilled through, brilliantly bright after the long hours of pitch-blackness. Meric swung his head all around, looking in all directions for recognizable landmarks.

"I have it!" I heard relief and decisiveness in his voice. "I know exactly where we are."

"Good," I responded. "Are we close to the hut?"

"No." His gaze was directed away from me. "That's miles from here. But there is a hamlet of four families close by, down in that little fold in the land over there. Less than half a mile. Come."

Our horses were exhausted, and I could tell from the way mine moved beneath me that he was close to collapse. I slid down and began to walk after Meric, leading my own horse with one hand and Luceiia's with the other and willing my bad leg back to life.

The tiny hamlet we came to seemed to us more luxurious than the Villa Britannicus. All four households were awakened by the noise of our arrival, and Meric's presence was enough to win us the utmost of their hospitality. Banked fires were stirred back to life, and Luceiia was taken by two women into one of the houses to struggle out of her soaked clothing and dry off in the warmth of a welcoming hearth. Meric and I led our three horses to the shelter of a lean-to against one of the houses and towelled them down with dry rags before heading into the warmth ourselves, leaving the animals to eat with four cows.

The inside of the small, stone house was warm and filled with dancing shadows from the flames of the fire. Luceiia sat huddled close to the heat dressed in a long, dark robe of some kind, clutching a bowl of something that steamed. I went directly to her and laid my hand on her shoulder, asking her if she was well; I was acutely aware that this was the first time I had laid a hand upon her. She looked up at me and nodded slowly, but she did not speak. She did, however, reward me with a tiny, not-quite-certain, surprisingly childlike smile. Relieved, I stepped into the shadows at the back of the room, away from the firelight, and began to strip off my own sodden clothing, believing quite firmly that I would never feel warm again.

Twenty minutes later, however, sitting on a three-legged stool close to the flames and nursing my own bowl of warm rabbit stew, I was feeling wondrously well, staring contentedly into the fire and revelling in the comfortable weight of Luceiia's body as she sat on the floor at my feet, leaning against my leg. I had no robe to cover my nakedness; instead, I was wrapped in an enormous bearskin taken from the pile of skins that served the household as a bed.

Luceiia's head began to droop, and she jerked suddenly erect. I smiled at the top of her head. She was deathly tired. I put down my bowl of broth and looked around me. We were alone. The family had moved in with neighbours, as had Meric, leaving the tiny hut to us. Something in the fire cracked loudly and she twitched erect again. My smile felt fixed on my face forever as I examined the nape of her neck, where her long, straight hair split into two torrents cascading down in front of her to dry in the heat of the fire. I felt love and protectiveness such as I had never known filling my throat.

I stood up and bent over her, drawing her gently to her feet and ignoring her sleepy, incoherent objections. I led her to the pile of warm skins and laid her down on them, and then I covered her with one of the largest. She smiled with her eyes closed and snuggled down into the warmth and softness and was instantly sound asleep. I waited for a few seconds and then eased myself down onto my elbows beside her, gazing closely at the perfection of her beauty in the gentle, dancing light of the fire. For five minutes, I told myself, I would feast my eyes on her, and then I would go and sleep by the fire.

Sometime in the night I awoke, chilled again because the fire had died down and my bearskin had slipped off me. As I pulled its warmth back across my body, I felt her stir and realized with a thrill of fear that I had fallen asleep beside her. Instantly tense and wide awake, I began to ease myself away from her, afraid that she might waken and find me almost in bed with her. But as I moved away, her arm came out of the blackness and wrapped itself around my waist beneath the bearskin, the palm of her hand scalding me as it caressed the skin of my side and then cupped itself in the small of my back, pulling me closer to her. Tensed as I was, I did not move, so she did, and I held my breath as she wriggled close to me, snuggling her head into the hollow of my shoulder and wrapping one long, smooth, warm bare leg over my own. The smell of her hair filled my nostrils and I felt the warm fullness of her left breast pillowed against my small ribs. I tried to breathe without moving, waiting for her to relax so that I could move away again, although not one iota of me wanted to move away. This time when I moved she was fierce in her denial. She hung on tightly and refused to release me, and then she began to wriggle and tug and burrow, making delightful little sleep noises in her throat, until my left arm lay beneath her head and my fingertips rested lightly and timidly against her back.

I lay staring at the dark roof space, feeling every inch of her length through the stuff of the robe she wore and knowing that it was rucked up, somehow, to her waist. I could not relax. Delicious and awestruck lust beat in my veins and alternate waves of joy and guilt riddled me. Then I felt her become very still.

"Publius Varrus," she said, "you don't really believe I'm asleep, do you?"

I froze in shock, unable to respond, and for a few moments there was nothing, until I felt the soft wetness of her mouth kissing my breast and she continued.

"Because I am awake, and I would far rather be kissing your mouth . . ."

Although I have no wish to describe the wondrous intimacies we shared that night, or any of the others that have passed in the years since then, I will admit that we had little to say to each other in the first few hours of exploration and discovery. There came a time, however, when, in spite of the willingness of the spirit, the weakness of the flesh demanded recognition, and we lay together close-wrapped and sharing the joy of what we had found, each in the other. And it was then that we began to talk. She began it, and the sound of her voice, quiet as a whisper in my ear, seemed almost dreamlike in my euphoria.

"Publius? Will you say my name?"

"Mmm? What d'you mean?" I was half asleep.

"My name. What is it?"

"Luceiia."

"That's right. Say it again."

"Luceiia. Luceiia Britannicus. Why do you want me to tell you your name? Don't you know what it is?"

"Mm'hmm." I could almost hear a purr in her voice. "But I love the way you say it. When you say it like that it sounds like an exotic stranger's name, the name of a famous heroine from some great, tragic tale."

"Well," I smiled, "some day you will be famous. You are the sister of Caius Britannicus, after all, and if he has his way, everyone will know him, down through the ages, as the father of the Bagaudae of Britain."

"Ah, I would enjoy being famed, I think, Publius. But I have no wish to be tragic."

I kissed her forehead. "There is no tragedy in your future, Lady. I know. I asked your Druid friends and they assured me you are blessed of God."

She stirred lazily, moving against me. "Publius Varrus, that is blasphemy. Say my name again." I did so, and she sighed. "And to think that only days ago you had never said those words."

"True." I drew her closer to me. "That is true, I had not. I had heard your name, but had never thought to dream of it. But I will never stop thinking of it now."

"Why?"

"Why? Because now I know you, and my world has changed forever."

"Will you enjoy the change?"

"I will."

"Good, I think I will, too." She moved luxuriously against me, stretching her thigh along mine. "You are a fascinating man, Publius Varrus. Have I told you that before? Well, you are, far more so than I had imagined, and I have imagined much of you. Even before you came here I felt I had known you all my life, and now that I really know you in person, the feeling has not changed, except that now that I know you with my body, I feel that everything has changed. Am I making sense to you?"

"I think so," I said. "But be gentle with me, I am not used to such unstinting praise. I shall grow vain."

Her fingers suddenly dug gently at the muscles of my belly. "And what of women? Are you accustomed to having many of them around?"

"No more than ten at a time."

"Aha, the soldier is an arbiter of women!"

"Not quite," I said. "I think we should talk seriously about that, one of these days."

"Seriously?" She turned on her side and snuggled towards me.

"Seriously," I said, slipping an arm across her, feeling again the fullness of her breasts and caressing the smoothness of her with the tips of my fingers. "I know little of women, Luceiia, even the kind that soldiers tend to know. Of grand ladies, I know nothing. And of you, I know only that I am here, and you are here, and I still cannot believe we are together. What did I do to deserve such fortune?"

"You mean good fortune, I hope? Is that not strange? Here was I, thinking I had been the fortunate one. Tell me more about your women, Soldier."

"You know already all there is to know. I was a smith, living a dull existence with only little excitement, and then you entered my life, and I began to know how little I know of life, or of women. Now tell me about you, about Luceiia Britannicus. We spoke a little of you when I first arrived, but not enough. Nowhere near enough. I am a parched man, craving to drink your life after a life of thirst. So tell me, please, what should I know about you?"

"Ah! The wondrous me! What about me? Let me see, now." She paused, and then turned to face me in the darkness. "What should you know about me?" She held her silence as my hand palmed her left buttock, giving me plenty of time to admire the heft of it, its smooth contours and soft strength.

"First of all, you should know that Caius thinks I would make you a good wife, and that you would be a fine husband to me. Then you should know that I think the same. I arrived at that conclusion over dinner with Varo, before Cylla tried to seduce you."

I was stunned for an instant, overcome by the suddenness and the meaning of what she had said. Finally I managed to find my tongue again. "You mean . . . you mean the Commander . . . your brother . . . Caius would approve?"

"Absolutely, of course he would! But that is neither here nor there and has absolutely no bearing on the matter. My brother is unimportant and powerless in this, Publius Varrus."

I moved to sit upright, but she hooked her hand behind my head and pulled me down to her, and just before our lips met again she whispered, "I am the one who must approve my marital arrangements."

I could not hold the kiss, delightful though it was. I broke away and tried to speak again, but her fingers closed my lips and she interrupted me before I could say any more than her name.

"You are concerned about my brother's feelings, I know, but that is only because you are a man, with all a man's loyalty and nobility and stupidity. Did you not hear what I said? My brother's approval would not influence my decision to have you or to refuse you."

There was an edge in her voice that I managed to recognize just before I rambled on again. I decided to hold my peace and think for a moment, and she moved her hand, unbelievably smooth and soft and warm, down my neck to my breast and spoke now, still whispering, without a trace of raillery.

"Caius, my darling brother, is an idealist. Of course he approves of a marriage between us! He thinks of you as some kind of paragon, and so he decided years ago that I could not do better for myself than to become your wife. The fact that I might choose to have a say in the matter did not occur to him. I love him very much, but he believes that he can apply his undoubted tactical brilliance everywhere as effectively as he can on the battlefield. He just does not know that there are circumstances and conditions under which it simply does not work. I would not have allowed him to arrange your life any more than I will allow him to arrange my own. Before we met, a few short days ago, you had no idea that I was alive. You have lived, how long? Thirty-seven years? Thirty-seven years without me. You could have lived another thirty-seven the same way, and just as happily.

"I have had two marriages arranged for me, concerning which I was not consulted. It was no one's fault that neither of them was happy, but enough is enough. I have told you before, when we first met, that I have done my duty as a faithful daughter. Two of my husbands have died. Do I need another? I had asked myself that and decided that the answer was no. I needed no man, I swore, to help me to exist and be myself." She paused. "But then I met you and discovered that the idea of being a wife again appeals to me very greatly. And I saw, being a woman, the effect I had on you when you met me. I know

I will make you a good wife, and I know I will make you happy, because you, Publius Varrus, are the man the Fates, the gods and the gentle Jesus have decreed to be my lord and master. Does that shock you?"

It did, but I lied. "No. But it surprises me. You talk a lot."

"Only when I have something to say. Now kiss me again."

It was some time before we began to talk again. Eventually, unwilling to quit her arms but in need of cool air, I sat up and rested my elbows on my knees. The darkness in the room was complete.

"We let the fire go out," I said. "Now they'll have to light it again."

"That's nothing," she whispered from beside me. "They'll bring a brand from another fire. Publius?"

"Yes?"

"Have I shamed myself? Do you think me brazen and too forward?"

I reached out and laid my hand on her breast. "That would not be possible, Luceiia."

"Then why are you so quiet? Have you no wish to marry? Because if you have not —"

"Hush, Luceiia, and let me talk for a while. You've given me much to think about, and you have made me slightly mad with joy, but now you must give me time to say what is in my mind, and before I do that I must order my thoughts. Will you allow me time to do that?"

"Yes, Publius."

For a time, there was a silence, during which I found myself listening for her breathing. Finally, I lay back against the rolled skin we were using as a pillow and gathered her to me so that she lay again with her head on my breast, her face in the hollow of my shoulder. As I spoke, my fingers combed her long, black hair.

"Luceiia," I said, "I can only think what my mind moves me to think. I have never been in love. I don't know what love is. I have never had the time or the urge to try to discover what it is. I have known few women carnally, and most of those were paid. And I have never met anyone like you before. Your beauty frightened me when I first saw you, because I thought that you must see me as no more than a cripple. I know now that was unworthy. But your mind, Luceiia! Your independence, the way you express yourself, the way you smile and laugh and move, the colour of your eyes, the shape of your mouth — these are all new to me, and they excite me. You are in my mind constantly, every waking moment, and also while I sleep, it seems . . .

"I had no thought of sleeping beside you tonight. It happened by accident because I was so tired. God knows I never hoped to possess your body. But now I have, and it is the most wondrous thing that I have ever known. I feel like a virgin boy again. No other woman has ever known what I have given you of myself this night. You have had my soul, and you possess it still, and that possession will never cease to be. I am yours, body and soul, from this time forward, no matter what may befall us.

"Now, if this is love — and I think it might be — then I have discovered it at last. I can look at you here, in this darkness, and see every feature of your face and every nuance of your smile, and I can say I love you and know that it is true. And if, as you have said, you would be glad to be my wife, to share my life and bear my children and make a home for me to call my own and yours, then no man could be happier and still be alive. For it seems to me that such happiness is only found in the Heaven that the priests speak of."

I stopped and drew a deep breath, weighing my next words carefully before committing them to speech.

"There is but one thing I fear. Your brother, Caius. He has meant more to me than any other man since the death of my grandfather. I would never have dared to hope that he would bless a marriage between me and his sister. Tonight you tell me that he hoped for it, and I believe you in spite of myself, and I am glad. But, my love, I tell you truly after tonight I will forfeit his friendship willingly — not happily, but willingly — should he refuse to allow us to wed. I will forsake my friend to keep you. I love you. I can say no more than that."

I was feeling more than a little surprised and pleased by my own eloquence, and the warmth of her treatment of me during the next few long and glorious minutes convinced me that I had managed to say exactly the right things.

Some time later, I opened my eyes to see the brightness of dawn at the window. Luceiia was already astir, and I was alone in the small room we had shared. I leaped from the bed and pulled on my clothes, my thoughts racing as I tried to separate dreams from reality. I was lacing up my sandals when she came back into the room. I immediately stopped what I was doing and stood up, my eyes straining to read the expression on her face in the dim half-light.

She came straight to where I stood and placed herself in front of me, her hands on her hips. She was tall enough to look me straight in the eye, and I was relieved to see that she had a smile on her face.

"Well, Publius Varrus, now that the day is here, do I still have the right to think of you as husband?"

I reached and pulled her to me. "Aye, my love, my beloved," I said. "As long as I have the breath and the life to call you wife."

Our kiss was brief, however. She disengaged herself and smoothed her gown over her hips.

"So be it. You will not regret this, my love. But there are things to arrange. We must return to the villa, and I shall begin to prepare for our wedding. You, in the meantime, will serve us both best if you spend your time digging for your skystone. That way, neither of us will distract the other from what has to be done. I will write to Caius today and send the missive by military courier tomorrow." She stopped abruptly, as though in mid thought, and then came back to me, taking my hands in hers and raising her mouth to mine.

"I almost forget to tell you," she whispered. "Last night was heaven on earth, and I love you. And there are no fleas in my bed at home, you'll see."

BOOK FOUR

The Dragon's Nest

XXI

In the month that followed, Luceiia busied herself with preparations for our nuptials. For my part, I kept my word and stayed out of her way by digging for skystones. Greatly to my disappointment, I unearthed seven stones — I presumed them to be skystones — the largest of which was little bigger than the skull of a new-born babe. My knowledge of smelting, scant though it was, nevertheless made me certain that, even were I to succeed in smelting these, I would get little metal for my trouble.

The truly disheartening aspect of all of this was that I had been at pains to excavate the largest "nests" first. If these finds were the biggest skystones in the valley, then all my dreams and effort had been for nought. And yet, I thought, there was something I was missing. My grandfather's skystone had made enough noise in falling to awaken only one man. I had never seen the stone itself, but I knew that it had been big enough to yield several pounds, at least, of raw metal. None of the stones I had unearthed would run to as much as one pound of metal. The mystifying thing was that *their* descent had been witnessed — both seen and heard — by hundreds of people, over a range of many miles. Something, therefore, was missing from my calculations. There had to be more and bigger skystones buried here somewhere; I must be looking in the wrong place, perhaps even in the wrong valley.

Discouraged and frustrated, I decided to leave my digging for a while and make a try at smelting the stones I had found. I would have to build a smelting furnace — a kiln — somewhere on the grounds of the villa, so I broke camp and headed for what I now thought of as my home. Luceiia would be expecting me today, anyway. I had been away for five days and was beginning to run low on provisions. In spite of my pleasurable anticipation of seeing her, however, my frame of mind was not a happy one as I set out on my return journey.

It was now the middle of January, and although the winter had been reasonably mild, there was now a real threat of snow in the wind. I reined my horse in at the very crest of the hill and turned around for one last look back into my valley of dragons. It was barren and hostile, cold and inhospitable. The signs of my puny excavations were invisible from this height, and the surface of the lake at the far end of the valley looked like a bed of rough slate beneath the angry sky. I pulled my cloak tighter about me and determined not to return for at least three months. By that time, I hoped, spring might have made the place look more welcoming.

By the time I reached the villa I was in a foul frame of mind. The threatened snow was falling as sleet and it had caught me on the road, eight miles from home. I was chilled and I was hungry, but I had enough sense to go directly to the bath house before seeking out Luceiia. Hot water and hotter steam would improve my disposition.

I had not finished bathing when I was interrupted by Luceiia's personal retainer, a Greek called Diomede, carrying fresh clothing for me. He welcomed me home and informed me that the Lady Luceiia was entertaining guests, and that dinner would be served in half an hour. In the meantime, would I please go, as soon as I was ready, to the anteroom, where the guests were having a cup of wine? I thanked him and, cutting short my wallowing in the pool, dressed quickly in what I saw to be some of the best of the fine clothes that Luceiia's tailors had been making for me over the past month. In a short time, scrubbed and cool and quite resplendent in my new and stylish clothes, I hurried through the colonnades from the bath house to the main building, curious about who these guests might be. There were three of them, all young, all handsome and all soldiers. They were dressed in what had become fashionable as "undress uniform," decorative tunics cunningly fashioned to resemble armour. I felt an irrational wave of jealous resentment that they should be here, with Luceiia, when I might be still away in the hills but for a bout of frustration. I swallowed the feeling, however, recognizing it as petty, and schooled my features into a smile as I went first to greet and kiss Luceiia, favouring them only with a pleasant, impersonal nod in passing.

Luceiia was radiant in the light of what seemed to be a thousand of the household's finest beeswax tapers. I had never seen her so lovely, and I told her so, but her eyes were sparkling with a joy that I could see was not due solely to my presence. She squeezed my arm strongly with an inexplicable excitement as she introduced me to her guests, all of whom were from the garrison to the south at Portus Adurni, now called Portchester. I greeted each of them personally, welcoming them to the Villa

Britannicus, and then accepted a cup of wine from Diomede before turning back to face them, Luceiia still close by my side.

"So, gentlemen, your health! May I ask what brings you here?"

"I do, Publius." The voice, from directly behind me, made me turn so quickly that I spilled my wine, and there was Caius Britannicus, arms spread wide to embrace me, striding in from the doorway, his face split into a giant grin. He threw his arms around me and lifted me completely off my feet, swinging me around in a complete circle before releasing me and stepping back to look at me.

"By the gods, Varrus, you look good. And clean! No sign of Vulcan in this fellow! My sister tells me there has been no ousting you since you heard about our local skystones."

Still speechless and floundering for words, I looked from him to Luceiia, whose grin was as great as her brother's. She stepped forward and took us both into her embrace.

"Forgive me, my dear," she said through her smiles. "Caius arrived yesterday, escorted by these three officers. He wanted to ride in search of you and your valley as soon as he heard you were here, but I refused to allow him. I knew you would be home today or tomorrow, and I wanted to surprise you and to see the look on your face when you met. So I swore everyone to secrecy until I could bring you face to face. Was that cruel of me?"

Finally I found my voice. "No, it was not cruel. But I suppose it was feminine, and therefore obscure. Anyway, it was successful. I am . . . surprised . . . astounded, in fact." I smiled at Caius. "Welcome home, Proconsul. How was Africa?"

"Hot, smelly, fly-ridden and pestilential. Little changed since you and I last knew it. But I left the Proconsulship there in the hands of my successor. I am now plain Caius Britannicus, farmer and man of few pursuits."

"Aye." I grinned. "And Proconsul of Numidia, Senator of Rome, General of the Legions and Magistrate. None of those titles can be relinquished."

"No, my friend, but they are only titles, and I have had enough of them for one lifetime. Plain Caius Britannicus will do from now on." He put his arm around my shoulder and turned to the others. "Gentlemen, we will go in to dinner now, but first a toast. To Publius Varrus, my finest friend, to whom I owe my life several times over, and to the marriage that is soon to be celebrated between him and my beloved sister."

Luceiia took my hand as the others drank to our future, and when they had done, Diomede stepped forward to usher everyone into the *triclinium*. Caius, however, held us both back, a hand on each of our arms, until the others had passed into the dining room. Then he swung me around gently and spoke in a soft voice, looking me straight in the eye.

"Luceiia tells me you doubt my approval of this marriage?" He sighed and shook his head in mock-regret. "Publius Varrus, you amaze me, but I wish there were more like you. Once and for all, hear me on this. I could think of no better match for either of you. You are both of pure Roman blood and you are my two favourite people in the whole world. I love both of you equally. Together, as a pair, you will be formidable and provide me with a tribe of remarkable nieces and nephews whom it will be my duty and pleasure to spoil outrageously. You have my full and unqualified blessing and I give it gladly, knowing that this will make us brothers in fact as well as in spirit."

My throat choked up completely and I embraced him in silence, as a brother, for the first time.

As we approached the dining table, I noticed, that there were seven places set for only six diners. I made no comment, but Caius noticed it, too.

"Where is Picus?" he asked, just as a tall, handsome boy of about sixteen walked into the room. "Ah, there you are. You're late."

The boy nodded, coming forward. "I know. Forgive me, Father, Aunt Luceiia, gentlemen." His eyes met mine and held them as he came straight towards me and bowed.

"Publius," his father said, "this is my son Picus. Picus, my friend Publius Varrus. You have heard me talking about him for years, and finally it's time to meet him. He is soon to be your uncle."

"I know." The lad's smile was open and confident with a quiet, pleasing self-assurance. I offered him my arm as an equal and as he gripped it he asked, "May I call you Uncle Varrus?"

"Uncle Varrus." I nodded, keeping my eyes on his. "It sounds well. So be it."

Dinner was a celebration of many things; the conversation was prolific and frequently hilarious. I noticed, however, that Caius refused to talk about his time in Africa. He spoke freely of his visits to Rome and to the Imperial Court in Constantinople, and his caustic wit had

us all laughing many times. But not a word of his residence in Numidia.

The meal passed quickly, and in the course of it I
learned that the three young officers were to return to
their garrison immediately; they would be leaving at
first light. Picus would be travelling with them as far as
they were going, and from there he would journey on to
Londinium, where he was to begin his military service,
as his father had and I had, in the ranks. Starting as a
common soldier, he would be expected to win the rank
of centurion on his own merits. After that, he would
begin officer's training.

As soon as I heard this, I excused myself from the table
and sent Diomede to my rooms to fetch a package. He
brought it to me casually, as I had instructed him to, and
I left it lying by my feet until the correct moment.

When that moment came, I cleared my throat, wanting
to say what I had to say simply and exactly, the way my
friend Alaric would have said it.

"Picus," I began, "I have some words for you, as my
newest nephew." That drew a general laugh and relieved
me of the little embarrassment I felt. Picus was looking
at me expectantly from across the table. "You join the
legions soon. Tomorrow, in fact, if leaving home for the
purpose qualifies as entry. I have a gift for you, and you
will honour me if you accept it."

The boy's eyes widened as he wondered what could be
coming. I reached beneath the table and produced the
package Diomede had brought me, unwrapping it as I
continued speaking.

"Before your father left for Africa, he asked me to
make this sword for him. It wasn't ready by the time he

left, for I had no idea that he was going until it was too late. And now he swears he will soldier no more. Anyway, I made this for General Britannicus, and it is a fine weapon, I think. The hilt is made in one piece, by a new technique I've been experimenting with. Now that the General has no further need of a sword, I can think of no more appropriate place for it than hanging by the side of his son." I drew it from its bronze-covered sheath. "The designs on the scabbard and hilt are Celtic — the art of the people of Britain — as appropriate to a Britannicus as his name. The iron of the blade was mined, smelted and wrought here in Britain. Believe me, Picus, you may wear it and use it with confidence. It will serve you equally well in battle and in dress uniform." I sheathed the weapon and handed it to him.

None of us spoke as he took the sword from my hands and gazed at it with reverence, his eyes tracing the whorls and scrollwork of the Celtic designs that covered it. The scabbard was of sheepskin, lined by the natural wool of the animal; I had scraped and shaved it to a point approaching baldness to protect the blade against rusting and to polish the iron each time it was sheathed or drawn. The outer surface was covered by a skin of bronze, thin as the finest parchment, beaten and decorated by my own hand. I had had no wish to do less than the best I was capable of for my friend in the making of it.

Picus drew the blade from its sheath respectfully, testing its weight in his hand and cutting tentatively at the air.

"Uncle Varrus," he said, "I have never owned, or held, or even seen anything as beautiful as this. I thank you for the honour you did my father by crafting this for him, and for the honour you do me by considering me worthy of receiving it." He turned to his father. "Father, I swear to you that I will try to bear this sword with all of the honour you would have bestowed upon it."

A pretty speech indeed for a mere lad. I could see that Britannicus was moved. He stood and approached his son and embraced him without speaking. I felt Luceiia's eyes on me, and when I looked, they were awash with tears. Britannicus turned again to me and I saw approval in his eyes. He cleared his throat, and I wondered what he was going to say.

"Another cup of wine, Publius, my friend, to wet the head of the Empire's newest recruit."

While Picus reverently showed his prize to the three officers, we toasted him, and we toasted the old Twentieth Legion, and then we toasted Varrus the sword-maker. When we had emptied our cups, Britannicus looked at his son again, his eyebrow high and imperious.

"Now, young man, you may retire. You are still a civilian and not yet of a legal age to bear arms. We bid you good night."

When the boy had gone we sat down again.

"He's a fine-looking young man, Caius," I said. "Looks like a Greek god."

"Looks like a damned Hun, is what he looks like! His mother's family all look like that. They maintain they're of pure Roman stock, but one of their ancestral grandmothers became overfond of a northern slave, if you ask me."

Picus's departure seemed to be the unspoken signal for the break-up of the dinner party. Shortly after he had gone, the three young officers also excused themselves. They had to be astir before dawn and had a long journey ahead of them. Luceiia left Caius alone for a short while and went to confer with Diomede and the kitchen staff about arrangements for an early breakfast and rations for the travellers, and when she came back she bade us both good night and warned us not to stay up too long talking.

Caius picked up the wine jug, which still held a good amount, and the two of us went into his *cubiculum*, where one of Diomede's people had a roaring brazier prepared for our comfort.

We sat together in companionable silence for a while, each of us busy with his own thoughts. Caius broke it by thanking me again for the gesture of the sword, and I shrugged it off, saying I could think of no better purpose for the weapon.

"Nevertheless," he insisted, "it was a gesture worthy of a noble friend."

"Good," I said with a small smile. "I was a little worried — not much, but a little — that you might object to my giving it without consulting you. I did it on impulse, but the sword was made for you in the first place."

He shook his head. "No, Varrus. How could I possibly have any objections? It is a magnificent sword and one which I would have been proud to carry. But I no longer need a sword, and Picus will love it. There will be no other like it in his legion. And, by the way, I know I've asked you something like this before, but how did you get the iron of the blade so light in colour? Is it skystone metal?"

I grinned, shaking my head. "No, no skystones, no magic — merely one of my grandfather's tricks, Commander. We mix charcoal into the iron during smelting and tempering. It toughens and hardens the blade and somehow enables it to hold a much harder, finer edge. As a side effect, it seems to lighten the colour, too."

"Ah, yes, your melting and smelting. You started to tell me about that once before, last time we met. Tomorrow I want to talk to you about it at more length. And what about the Celtic scrollwork on the sheath? It's the same as the work on the one your grandfather made, isn't it? The one Theodosius has now."

"Yes, more or less. It was your friend Bishop Alaric who got me interested in that . . . among other things."

He smiled. "Alaric is a catalyst. No one who meets him is ever unchanged. But Luceiia tells me you are a wealthy man now — a legacy from your grandfather, I understand? It sounds like a fascinating tale. I'd like to hear it, if you have the time."

"There's not much to tell, Commander." I sat silent for a few minutes, gathering my thoughts. Then, in as few words as possible, I told him the story of finding the golden hoard in grandfather's pikes.

He listened carefully, as always, and then began asking questions that led from the gold all the way to everything else I had been doing over the past five years. I answered them all briefly, hoping to get them out of the way and then get him talking about his adventures, but try as I would, there was no way I could sidestep his questions and work in some of my own.

I ended up by telling him the whole story of my run-in with Seneca, my flight from Colchester, and my troubles on the road to Aquae Sulis.

"So," he said, finally, "it is to the Senecas that we owe the pleasure of your company. You have been here how long, now? A month? Two? And your initial

encounter with the Seneca brat was a month before that,
more or less?"

"Less," I said. "About two weeks, perhaps three."

"Does Quinctilius Nesca know you by sight?"

"No, not at all. None of them really knows who I am.
The scum I met on the road were looking only for a grey-
haired man with a bad limp. That's all they have to go on.
They'll never find me here."

"Hmmm, unless Primus Seneca remembers that I had a
friend with grey hair and a bad limp when he last saw me,
which is not too unlikely! Never underestimate these
Seneca creatures, Publius. They are not like other men.
They have a capacity for evil that is almost supernatural."

"In that case, Commander," I said, troubled by the
ominous tone of his voice and his immediate
identification of a point that had occurred to me months
before, "I had better move on. I see no point in attracting
trouble here to your home."

"Don't be naive, Publius, that will solve nothing.
If they come here, they come; your absence will not
deter them. You and I should get some sleep. It is late,
and we have to be astir early tomorrow. We will talk
more about this in daylight. But there's no need to
worry, my friend. I have resources of my own. The first
thing we shall do is check on the status of their spleen
— ask a few questions and find out how active the hunt
is today. It is more than possible that Primus never made
the connection between you and me, with only a sparse
description to go on. I have been away for a long time,
out of sight and, we can hope, out of mind. Either way,
we will know within fifteen days. Now we had better
get to bed."

"Commander." I struggled with my thoughts. "Before we do, Commander, I have a question."

His chin sank onto his chest, and I had the distinct impression that he was not listening to me.

"Commander?"

"Commander! That's three damned Commanders in one breath!"

I blinked at this unexpected explosion, and he sighed in exasperation before turning to face me and continuing.

"Varrus, you and I have known each other, as men and as comrades, for over eleven years. I cannot think of one other man I admire more or esteem more highly. I am privileged, I believe, to call you friend. I know there is a part of you that has never stopped thinking of yourself as a centurion and of me as a senior officer, but I made you my *primus pilus*, Varrus, and I have never regretted it for a moment. I didn't do it out of friendship, either. You earned that promotion. Your talents and your natural abilities demanded that you achieve that rank. In many ways, you, my friend, are the embodiment of all that I hold worthy of honour in the term 'Roman.' I know career officers by the hundred, and politicians, senators and emperors who cannot begin to be worthy of comparison with you. Don't look like that! I know you find it embarrassing to hear such things, but hear me, and heed me. My name is Britannicus to all of my colleagues and associates. My friends call me Caius. Nobody calls me Commander any longer, except you. My name is Caius. Now let me hear you say it."

"Caius."

"That's right. And I shall call you Publius. Except when we both forget in the heat of the moment, we shall address each other as friends and brothers. Agreed?"

I nodded. "Agreed."

"Good man! And I know you'll look after my sister. She's a fine girl, Publius. Make you a grand wife and fill this house up with babies. Sons, Publius, sons! that's what a man needs. You can't have too many children. Look at what happened to me. I lost three of them in a month, and now my oldest is going into the army. If he gets himself killed, my name will die with me."

He lapsed into silence, and I covered the pause by pouring more wine, after which we sat quietly for a few minutes before he spoke again.

"Well? What was your question?"

"It was about your family." I hesitated and then plunged on. "I have not expressed my regrets since you came home, and you have made no mention of what happened. What did happen in Africa, Caius?"

His hand shook as he stared into the bottom of his cup, leaving my question unanswered for so long that I started to excuse myself for asking, but he waved me to silence.

"It was bad, Varrus. Very, very bad." His voice was low-pitched and lifeless, but I had no trouble hearing him. "I had known that it would not be pleasant in the first place, and I wanted to leave my family here in Britain, where they would be safe, but Heraclita would have none of that. She was adamant that Britain was not safe, with the way the damned Saxons were stepping up their raids, and I have to admit that, at the time, I tended to agree with her.

"Anyway, she insisted that this time we would go as a family. I had always soldiered alone, as you know, leaving her with the children, and she had never complained. I told you about it in the letter I wrote to you before I left, you may remember." I nodded. "Well, against my own better judgment, I gave in to her arguments. Numidia had been settled for centuries and there would be no danger there, she said. Like a fool I agreed, because it would be pleasant, for once, to have my family close by. It was pure selfishness. I rationalized every objection that came into my own mind and I shut my eyes to the thousand and one possibilities that could work against us.

"On the way over, as you know, we stopped in Rome, and then again in Constantinople. She hated Rome. So did I. It is a very depressing place nowadays. Since the court moved away it's been almost deserted. There is still a court there, nominally at least, maintained by the so-called Emperor of the West, but it's a joke. Everyone who is anyone lives in Constantinople now. There's really only the Mob left in Rome, and the civil service people who keep them as happy as they can. It is quite dreadful. Constantinople, on the other hand, is altogether different. Alien and orientally mysterious. We would have enjoyed being able to stay there longer." His voice trailed away, his thoughts obviously on the enjoyment they had known there, and then he snapped himself back to his narrative.

"Well, we arrived in Numidia eventually, and at first it was . . . sufferable. My work load was considerable and I had very little time to spend with my family, even though they were within easy reach. And then, within six months of our arrival, I fell sick of this pestilence. Our best physicians were helpless against it, and it spread like ripples on water. Nothing could stop it. You know what our army physicians are like. The first thing they did was to ban the drinking of water, but it made no difference. Our men were falling like leaves in autumn. Hundreds died, hundreds. And those who did not die did not get better — they just seemed to hang on, getting sicker again the moment they seemed to begin making progress. I was one of these. There were times when I thought I was going to die, and there were times when I was afraid I might not die. It was indescribable. It weakened me close to death, but it did not take me.

"And yet it took my wife, my daughter Meleiia and my two youngest sons, Marcus and Paulus. All of them within one month. That was the month when I was at my worst, and they decided not to tell me about my family, for fear the news would kill me. The medics expected me to die every day, but God had decreed, for reasons of His own, that I should live, and I did. The rest of my time passed as a penance, with neither military nor civil distinction but without further disaster, either. And here I am."

"I am sorry, my friend," I said. "I knew nothing of this until I came here a few weeks ago. Then I was appalled."

"Aye, well!" He sniffed loudly. "It was years ago and I have grown used to it, almost. Except for the sometime memories that spring out of hiding to assail me when I least expect them."

"What about Picus, General? Was he not affected?"

"No. The sickness never touched him, and thank God he had the strength of boyhood to block his grief and memories."

There was nothing more I could say that would not have sounded foolish, so I said nothing further. He changed the subject abruptly.

"I wish you had been here when we arrived yesterday. I'd have been interested in your reaction to the table conversation at dinner last night. Fascinating discussion of a terrifying topic. Wish you could have heard it."

"What was the topic? Tell me."

"We were talking of morale."

"Morale? That's a terrifying topic?"

"Yes, it is." The seriousness of his tone did not even dent my tolerant smile at first, but as he continued to speak it faded quickly.

"I tell you, Publius, the morale of the legions has never been so low, not even during the Invasion, although that only affected Britain. It's a sickness that affects the whole Empire. The rot is everywhere. Mutiny is widespread — no discipline, no order, no structure left with any meaning. More barbarian mercenaries in the army today than there have ever been before, although every one of them now calls himself a Roman citizen. You know how I feel about that. But it's the structure that's lacking, Varrus. The foundation. There are no standards left. No symbols of worthiness for the young people of the Roman world to align themselves with. No values that can be accepted on faith and relied upon. The whole world's falling into chaos." He fell silent for a space, then, "Do you know, Publius," he went on, "that if I had made just a bit of an effort in Africa before the pestilence struck us, I could have had myself elected Emperor of Rome by my own legions? Do you realize what that means?"

I stared at him, wide-eyed, wondering what was to come next. I had never seen him so despondent.

"I, Caius Britannicus, now sitting here in front of this fire, could have been appointed, or elected, Emperor of Rome by my own soldiers. And I had fifty thousand of them under my direct command in Africa, with many thousands more who would have marched to join my standard."

It never occurred to me that he might be exaggerating. I knew that he was telling me the absolute and literal truth. I waited for him to go on.

"The soldiers of Rome have no loyalty to Rome, Publius. The State has deprived them of too much, and has betrayed their interests and their trust too often. There's no focus for the soldier's loyalty, so that when he does find someone in authority with whom he can identify, he will adhere to that man's cause with total, suicidal devotion. I was approached very quietly by some of my officers. No specifically treasonous statements were made, but I was given to understand that the armies were ready to install someone in power who would look after their needs and see to the refurbishing of the frontiers. I could have done it, Publius, had I not fallen ill."

"You mean, you considered it?"

He was gazing into his own mind. "Considered it? I suppose I did. Of course I did. I thought about it."

"And would you have done it?"

"Would I have accepted the Empire?" His eyes drifted from me to the fire. "I don't know. Perhaps I might have. I was tempted, at first, but I saw the temptation for what it was, and I resisted it until I fell ill. I had been in Rome, you remember, and in Constantinople, and I had seen nothing there that inspired any loyalty in me to anyone. And when I looked at my men and saw the way they were being treated by the same government, I felt guilty and disloyal to them." He paused again. "Rome is nothing without her legions, Varrus. And yet she has consistently treated them like dirt for two hundred years and more, now. The few fine emperors we have had have all been soldiers — apart from Claudius, whom I believe, nevertheless, to have been the finest of the lot. Soldiers understand the needs of Empire. They appreciate the need for discipline. They understand logistics and the laws of supply and demand. And they understand the need for strong communications over long distances, and the necessity of leaving command decisions to the discretion of the commander on the scene in times of emergency. Perhaps I would have made a good emperor."

My response was emphatic. "There's no perhaps in my mind, Caius. Your resistance to the temptation is what I would have wagered on. But that's not what's at issue here, is it? What do you expect to happen?"

He shook his head. "I don't know. But nothing good has happened for a long time. If my soldiers were willing to make me emperor, then it stands to reason that other soldiers will elect other emperors from among their officers. God knows there's no lack of precedent."

"But . . ." I stopped.

"But what?"

"Well, even if that happens, I can't see any danger to the Roman State itself. I know armies have elected emperors before. It was the Praetorians who put Claudius on the throne, although they did it as a mockery — they had no idea that they were doing a great thing for the Empire. There have been mutinies and even civil wars, but the Empire has always survived. And I don't see how a civil war in Rome could have much effect on us here in Britain."

"It probably wouldn't," Caius responded. "Not a civil war. But my fear is of invasion, not civil war. The point

I was trying to make before I digressed is that there is no spirit left in the legions. The soldiers no longer care about Rome. There are barbarian peoples everywhere who are bitterly hungry for survival, Publius. For escape from their barren homelands to some place where life will be easier. Where they won't freeze in their thousands every winter. Where their children won't starve. And they all see the Empire as their Promised Land. Mark my words, Publius, one day, and probably soon, the hordes are going to penetrate the heartlands of the Empire, and when that happens, it will be too late to save Rome. But the first effect of the invasions will be panic. And the armies, every legion, will be called back from the frontiers to defend the city and the Campana."

I stood up and walked over to the glowing brazier, holding my hands out to its heat. When I heard Britannicus put his misgivings into words so clearly, it upset me. I didn't really want to continue this conversation, and yet I felt I had to.

"You think this is going to happen soon?"

"Too soon, Publius. Yes, I do. There is already talk among the rank and file in Britain that the legions want to elect an emperor here."

"Here in Britain?" The thought came as a complete and unpleasant surprise to me. "Do you think they will?"

"Who knows? They might. There are some men serving here in Britain right now who are ambitious enough to make the attempt."

"You think so? Who, for instance?"

"Oh, I've heard a few names. Magnus Maximus, for one."

"Who is he?"

He looked at me in amazement. "Who is . . . ? My God, Publius, you really are out of touch! He is the blue-eyed wonder of all the legions. His men think he can walk on water. I'd put my money on him, if anyone's going to be in the running."

"You'd give him your support?"

He smiled tightly at the dismay in my tone. "I didn't say that. I said that if anyone is likely to try for the Empire here in Britain, I'd wager it would be him."

"So you wouldn't support him?"

"Never. The man's a politician. He is totally ruthless and completely self-centred. He makes a business of being beloved of his troops because he needs their support, but if they ever put him in power they had better look to their futures."

"Could he win the Empire if he were elected?"

Britannicus shook his head dubiously. "It's one thing to be emperor in Britain, but to go to Rome, get rid of the western emperor and then take over the eastern Empire too? That would be a major undertaking. He would be setting himself against every vested interest in the Empire except his own troops. He'd be opposed by every other military commander in every other part of the Empire who dreams the same dreams of grandeur."

I was becoming depressed. "God, Caius! You make everything sound hopeless. When do you expect the legions to be withdrawn to guard against this threat of invasion?"

"Next month. Next year. Ten years from now. Twenty. I really have no idea. But I do believe that it's bound to happen sooner or later."

"And what do we do then?"

"Nothing, Publius. We do nothing." His smile was genuine. "We remain here in Britain, right here on this villa, and enjoy our old age, watching our children grow up around us, minding our own business and living our own lives here in this beautiful land."

I couldn't help grinning in return. "Undisturbed?"

"Why not? If we make our preparations in advance."

"You mean by isolating the villa and fortifying it."

"Yes, more or less. We will need the capacity to defend ourselves."

I shook my head. "You frighten me, Caius, even though I'm smiling. Why do we always seem to get into these discussions late at night? I had intended taking you over to the smithy tomorrow. I have some things to show you. But it's almost tomorrow already."

Caius stretched and yawned as though I had reminded him. "You're right, my friend," he muttered. "It's too late to be solving the problems of Empire. Far too late, in every way. Let's get to bed."

We rose and took a lamp each, and I blew out the one remaining.

I undressed slowly, savouring the remembered sensations of Luceiia's kisses. I knew I could go to her now, but the mere fact of Caius's presence in the house deterred me. That would be disloyalty to him, although perhaps in my mind only. Still, that was reason enough.

Thank all the ancient gods that Luceiia could read me like a book. She scurried into my bed before I was undressed.

XXII

Caius had been home for a full two weeks before I came to realize that he was a fraud. In truth, he was a harmless fraud, deluding himself more than anyone else, but an undoubted fraud he was, and I loved him the more for it. I realized long afterwards that I had been aware of his false pretences for years, but they were so much a part of the man that I had accepted them without question and almost without recognition.

His falseness lay in that he called himself a Roman and he liked to think of himself as embodying all of the virtues of Rome in the days of its true greatness. To tell the truth, he did embody those virtues, but Caius Britannicus was also a Briton, both by birth and by conviction. He was born in Britain as the culmination of a chain of events that began with the first of his ancestors to be named Britannicus, and he was the first-born of the third generation of his family to be born and bred here. In all his wanderings as a soldier of the Empire, he liked to say, he had seen no place, no country, that could be compared to this land for beauty or pleasantness of climate, or for the stability, strength and simplicity of its people.

It was growing dark outside on the night I made my discovery, and Diomede's people had lit the lamps and piled the braziers high against the winter chill, even though the day had been unseasonably beautiful. Caius was in a restless mood that evening, and he was prowling around, looking for something to distract him. He found it in the shape of a *codex* that lay on one of my tables. It was a simple enough book, roughly bound, but it was something new. I watched him as he picked it up and examined it closely. The front surface bore an intricate rendering of complex Celtic scrollwork, and I watched him open the book at random and find more of the same. No words at all, just a collection of drawings, all obviously done by the same hand.

"Well, what do you think?" I asked him.

"This is marvellous!" he said, examining the way the individual sheets were fastened together. "Did the priest do this? Andros?"

"Yes," I told him. "He did. Told me he got tired of carrying awkward bundles of parchment all over the place. He saw you carrying a *codex* one day, asked me to show him some more, and then he began to make his own. Not bad, eh? He cut all his parchments to the same size, and now he says his life is ten times more simple."

Andros was a wandering priest who had turned up on Caius's doorstep one day and never left. He was a very simple man, true to his name, "the man," and he had the most amazing gift I had ever seen for rendering likenesses of things with a stick of charcoal. His drawings were magnificent, and yet he could neither read nor write.

"But this is marvellous! Look!" Caius was shaking his head in admiration. "Who else in this country today would have thought of using a strip of wood, front and back like this, and tying the whole thing together with thongs? This thing is easy to add to, one page at a time, in any order one pleases! And the wood gives it rigidity and makes it easy to carry. This really is astonishing, Varrus." His admiration was immense and sincere. "And this parchment is superlative. Where did Andros find it?"

"He made it."

He blinked at me. "He makes parchment? Andros? Himself?"

"Himself." I shrugged. "Himself and his two brothers, to be accurate. But I find it more exciting that they know how to make excellent papyrus."

"Where in God's name did they learn to do that?"

"Their father taught them. He learned in Rome — or in Constantinople. Maybe both places. He was a craftsman there for years. Came back here with his master before the sons were born. Taught them his trade as they grew up. He was North African, I think, from Egypt. They lived on one of the big villas out by Aquae Sulis. Andros tells me they used to supply this stuff to clerks all over the country."

"Why did they stop?"

I shrugged. "Who knows? Anyway, Andros became a priest, but he never did learn to read or write. He only wanted to draw. Have you ever seen such skill?"

"No. These drawings are not exactly classical, but they are superb."

"Classical?" I was astounded. "Not classical? General, you amaze me!" He looked at me oddly, and I went on. "If you look closely, and I mean really look, you'll see that those drawings *are* classical in every sense but the Roman. They're perfect — exact transcriptions of pure Celtic design. Ancient. Not the worthless rubbish that the pedlars are hawking all over the Empire. That is the history of your beloved Britain you're looking at. I thought you would be ecstatic about them, once you saw what they are."

He looked more carefully then, and I saw him realize that the *codex* that he had at first glance categorized as simple and crude was anything but that.

"You are right, of course, Varrus. I should be admiring them. They are magnificent."

"Caius, you and I have both seen murals and mosaics in some of the finest houses in the Empire, created by celebrated artists who have no grasp of what this man does without thinking. I swear he can draw a perfect circle with one sweep of his hand."

Caius was musing, obviously thinking about something that this *codex* had suggested to him. "You are right, my friend. You are absolutely correct. Ask him to visit me, next time you see him, will you?"

"Why?" I asked him, immediately defensive. "You wouldn't be thinking of depriving me of his services, would you? I find his drawings very helpful in my work."

He smiled at me. "No, Varrus, I would not, so you may relax. I need his parchment and his papyrus, not his pen. I have a feeling that time might lie heavily on my hands now that I am no longer on active duty, and I have often thought of writing down my own theories on military tactics. It has been a dream of mine for years, but no more than a dream, due mainly to the fact that the materials for writing in bulk are not readily at hand, and I have never had either the patience or the time one needs to assemble spindle books. But this talent Andros has could give me access to a source of parchment and to a simple means of binding sheets together to protect them against loss and damage."

I demurred, I believe, for the first time ever in my personal dealings with him.

"Why, Caius? I mean, why write military memoirs? To emulate Caesar? To leave Rome the benefit of your experience? Why would you not write of your villa, here, and of your life in Britain?"

He threw me a glance of pure surprise, thinking I was belittling him. His answer was slow and measured.

"I would write a history of my military service to the Empire because I am a soldier. It is what I know best. It has been my life. Do you find that surprising or distasteful?"

I shook my head. "No. Not at all. But it seems to me it could be a waste of time, if what you have been hinting at is true and the Empire is about to fall."

His frown was impatient. "Come, Publius! Time spent constructively cannot be wasted. I would be writing for the benefit of those who follow me. Someone is sure to, no matter how bad things are."

"Oh," I said. "Well, that makes a difference."

"But?"

"What do you mean, 'But?'" I asked innocently.

"You have a reservation." His tone was cool. "I can hear it in your voice."

I held up a disclaiming hand. "No, Caius, you are mistaken. I think you should write. But you should write for Britain. For your son Picus, and for my sons, too. You will be their uncle. It would be good for them to know their antecedents were more than just names."

He smiled, mollified. "That is an amusing but worthwhile thought, Publius. Very well then, I shall write for future citizens of Britain. You are a facile persuader."

I grinned at him. "You needed no persuasion. Would you not like to return home to Rome again, now that you have the time?"

His face underwent a transformation from humour to disgust. "No, I would not. The place is a cesspool!"

I was enjoying myself, for I had finally made the realization I have spoken of.

"A cesspool?" I said. "Rome?"

He looked at me warily, sensing that he was being teased. "Publius, you are baiting me. Why? You have never been this way before."

I laughed. "No, Caius, I have not. I've been in awe of you, I suppose. But now that we are to be brothers, I feel less reluctant to discuss things openly with you."

"What kind of things?"

"Things like this — your self-delusion."

"My what?" His voice was bristling with affront.

"Your self-delusion. You talk of your Romanism, but you are really no more Roman than Meric. Your loyalty is to this place, this land, these people you call the Pendragon. This is your home, Caius. The very thought of going to Rome is repugnant to you. You've just admitted it."

"Perhaps I have." His brow was creased now in perplexity. "Perhaps I have. But that in no way alters my obligations to the Empire."

I threw down the book I had been holding. "What obligations, Caius? You have fulfilled them all and done it honestly and openly and with good will, in spite of all your reservations. But you pay only lip-service to what you have done. You haven't yet accepted that your debts are all paid in full."

His face cleared. "That's true, isn't it? I have. That is the truth, Publius. I have fulfilled each and every one of my obligations to the Empire."

"Yes, Caius," I said emphatically. "You have. Now take the time to consider your obligations to yourself. Write down your life's story, by all means, but write for your own people, your family, not for the sybarites in Rome."

He snapped his fingers. "That reminds me! I have a letter I meant to tell you about. It arrived earlier today, by courier. It seems your friend in Rome has fallen foul of Theodosius."

I frowned. "What friend in Rome? I have none."

"Quite. I was being facetious. I meant young Seneca."

"Seneca?" He nodded. "I thought he was in Constantinople. When did he move to Rome, and how has he offended Theodosius? And how did you find out?"

He shook his head, smiling. "I have my sources. You forget, I made some inquiries. This one has been answered already through a fortunate combination of military emissaries to and from Rome. Its source is an old friend whom I have known for years. He has little good to say of Caesarius Claudius Seneca. Apparently the man's excesses are become so bad, even for a Seneca, that they offend the nostrils of Theodosius. Our Emperor is abstemious and really quite a devout Christian, for all that his ambition led him to the throne."

I dismissed that as irrelevant. "So did Constantine's. What happened between Seneca and Theodosius?"

Caius shook his head. "No one really knows, it seems, but Seneca was close to Valentinian, and that would not endear him to Theodosius in any way." He was interrupted by the clamour of a flurry of crows that came swooping down over the rooftop, haggling viciously over some morsel of carrion that one of them clutched in its beak. We watched them until they swirled away, neither of us making any effort to compete with their raucous uproar.

"In any event," he continued eventually, "the Emperor handed down an ultimatum that I find interesting. He made it known that Seneca, and several others like him, were doing little for the common good. How did he phrase it? 'They are depriving the Empire of the benefits of their station, experience and breeding.' That was it. The upshot of it was that Seneca should undertake a period of public service, under implicit threat of forfeiture of all his worldly goods. I thought it quite ingenious."

"How? What do you mean, 'ingenious'?"

His eyebrow went up. "Think about it. Seneca could refuse an imperial edict only under penalty of forfeiture of all his wealth. The alternative — acceptance — also puts his wealth at the Emperor's disposal for all intents and purposes. You may be sure Theodosius will find a post for Seneca that will make optimum use of his financial capabilities, and that Seneca will bestir himself to enlarge his wealth while in the imperial service. But no matter what Seneca does — short of absolute, treasonous theft on a vast scale — Theodosius will benefit by it and from it. Rest assured that the Empire will be keeping a very close and meticulous watch on its richest citizen and servant."

"And Seneca accepted that?"

"How could he do otherwise? He has not the heart to

live as a pauper, and were he to attempt it, my friend in Rome swears he would not survive the first day."

I whistled in wonder as the implications of what I had been told began to hit home to me. "Then he will be at the Emperor's bidding for a while. I wonder how he will come out of it?"

Caius cleared his throat in disgust. "Probably very well. He is still a Seneca. But he will be under some restraint. Theodosius will watch him closely, as I said, but I have no doubt that Caesarius Claudius Seneca will contrive somehow to continue to enlarge his fortune."

He was to be proven prophetic within the month.

Shortly after our conversation, Caius invited Andros's two brothers to come live at the villa in return for their parchment-making services. They accepted his invitation and began making parchment specially for us, and Caius began to write. He did not find it easy at first. He had the discipline to marshal his time but not, as he soon discovered, his thoughts. There were too many things that he wanted to write about, and he quickly found that the greatest danger lay in writing too much about too little. Eventually, however, he fell into a way of writing about whatever caught his interest at that particular time. And eventually, too, it became a habit to discuss his ideas with me.

He wrote down his thoughts and theories on life in general, and on the life and past times of Britain. We talked of the kings of Rome, and of how Rome had foresworn such men. We talked of the Republic that was born, and had lived in glory until the advent of the Caesars — Julius and his cousin Octavius, who became Caesar Augustus.

From that moment on, for all intents and purposes, the kings had returned. They called themselves emperors, but they were kings, with all the powers of despots. And they had killed Rome.

We talked also, at great length, of Britain and her future, for Caius honestly believed in God's great plans for this green land. On most of these occasions, Luceiia was with us, and her contributions to our discussions were insightful and refreshing. During those long winter nights I learned fully to appreciate the keen intellect that underlay her beauty.

She astonished me most particularly one night by proposing the thought that Rome had starved to death, and she went on to support her thesis. The mother country, she pointed out, is largely infertile. It could never produce enough food for its citizens, so they turned to conquer fertile lands. And, of course, the fertile lands they conquered were never rich enough to feed their own people and Rome, too, and so it went on, to embrace the whole world.

Britain, my love believes, will never starve. The soil is rich and fruitful. As the people grow, she says, they will clear the forests and till the soil. I believe she is correct in this, for the people here are strong. The local Celts are a noble people — industrious for the most part, proud, certainly quick to anger but equally quick to forgive — and great lovers of music and the arts. The quality she finds most admirable among them, however, and I agree with her in this, is their mutual respect. The Celtic wife and mother is no chattel. She fights as well as her man, making the Celtic family a unit to be dealt with respectfully. No domestic decisions are made without her advice and concurrence. She has dignity and pride of place, as did the Republican women of Rome, and she is skilled, like the Roman matrons of old, in the arts of weaving, pottery and the rearing of children to respect all that a child should respect. When Luceiia talked of all of this the first time, I earned myself a savage clout on the head by remarking with a smile that four hundred years of Roman occupation had bred much Romanism into these Celts.

Those were idyllic days, but they were soon to be marred by a development that seemed at first to contain no hint or threat of disruption.

Caius received a missive from Antonius Cicero, welcoming him back to Britain and advising him of three things, the first of which was my own official death. I had been found in a ditch far to the south of Verulamium, my identity established only by a lozenge of silver with my name on it that was found in my scrip. The second piece of news was that my house had reverted to the State and would be occupied by the new Procurator, Claudius Seneca, who had been appointed to fill the post left vacant by the retirement of the incumbent. He was expected to arrive in Colchester at any time, contingent upon weather conditions in the seas between Britain and Gaul!

That was an ironic twist that had its effect on all of us! But it was followed by another even stranger, at least to me. Equus, as my beneficiary, had taken all of my belongings into his own possession, and, apparently disheartened by my disappearance and death, he had closed down the smithy, loaded everthing onto a couple of wagons and left Colchester to establish himself in some other town. I was mystified by this. Where would he have gone? He knew I was not dead. Could he be coming here? To return my belongings? If so, why wouldn't Tonius have said so?

Caius put my mind at rest on that one, chiding me for being too literal in my interpretations. Of course, he said, Equus would be headed this way. But the letter from Tonius was quasi-official, carried by a military courier and therefore subject to censorship. How could Tonius make any reference, no matter how oblique, to my continued survival if there was the slightest consideration of the letter being exposed to scrutiny? Tonius, he insisted, was intelligent enough and experienced enough to know that Caius would put his own interpretation on the letter and draw his own conclusions. In the meantime, he had apprised us that I was now considered dead and therefore no longer pursuable. Furthermore, he had informed us, in plainest and yet unimpeachable terms, that my enemy was back in Britain in a position of power, and my friend was on his way to join us with my worldly goods.

Reassured, and suddenly relieved of a great mental weight, I realized just how great my debt was to Antonius Cicero. Caius agreed with me.

"What was the name he gave you after he abducted you to save your worthless skin?" The expression on his face was inscrutable.

I had to think for a few seconds before the name came back to me. "Gratens. Publius Gratens. Why do you ask?"

"Oh, it just occurred to me that Tonius might want to take some time off — a furlough — to attend the nuptials of his old friend Publius Gratens, since he knows the bride, and he and I have been friends for a long time."

Luceiia leaped to her feet and kissed him. "Caius, my beloved brother, I know you are a great soldier but there are times when you show streaks of absolute brilliance. I would love to see Tonius again, wouldn't you, Publius?"

I was as enthusiastic as she was. "Aye, I would." I grinned. "I still owe him a bad headache. It would be appropriate to cause it with bridal wine." I had another idea. "Particularly if he had the abominably poor taste to bring Plautus with him as part of his escort."

But Caius was quick to throw water on that notion.

"No! If he comes, he has to come alone. No escort. No one here will be calling you Publius Gratens, remember, and Publius Varrus is dead. No one who is not a good friend can even be allowed to suspect otherwise. Too dangerous. And Tonius will know that. I shall write to him tonight and send a man into Aquae Sulis to the garrison commander tomorrow, with a request to have it forwarded immediately."

Of course he was correct, as usual, but I felt a keen sense of disappointment that Plautus would not be able to celebrate my reconstituted virility and my good taste in choosing a wife.

Tonius's response took exactly ten days to arrive, causing Caius to wonder what the reason was for the obviously intensified stream of communications between garrisons. Messages sent through normal military channels would go from Aquae Sulis to Londinium and thence to the outlying garrisons. The speed of this return had to mean that priority messages were being sent directly between military district headquarters. Even before he opened the letter, he had decided to go himself to visit the garrison at Aquae Sulis, to find out personally what was in the wind.

The letter from Tonius was longer and less formal than the previous one and anticipated, at least in part, our concerns. He would be delighted to visit us in May, partly to renew his delightful acquaintance with the bride-to-be, partly to see his two old friends, Caius Britannicus and Publius Gratens, but chiefly to share in the joining of two such fine and noble families, the progeny of which union could only be a benefit to the Empire. He was long overdue for an extended furlough, he pointed out, since, being himself without family, he seldom had reason or desire to absent himself from his posting and his charges. This, however, would be a joyous celebration, and he would be happy to request a whole month of leave to be able to participate in it properly.

He had taken the liberty to inform Caius's good friend Bishop Alaric of Verulamium of the wedding, since Alaric had been in Colchester when Caius's letter arrived, and Alaric had immediately decided to attend the wedding on his own invitation. The two hoped to be able to travel west together, but this would be entirely dependent on Tonius's ability to find a suitable replacement for his *primus pilus*, one Pontius Aulus Plautus, who had been appointed, to the pride and despair of Tonius himself, *primus pilus* to the Household Troop officers' training school in Londinium. A great honour for Plautus but a great inconvenience for Antonius Cicero. Plautus had already left Colchester to use up his accumulated furlough time of three months before taking up his new posting, and in the meantime, no one had been seconded to Colchester to replace him in what was a crucial and highly responsible position.

In closing, Cicero mentioned that the new Procurator had arrived and was installed in poor Varrus's erstwhile home. Tonius had met him officially, but had had no particular dealings with him prior to the time of writing. Tonius looked forward to seeing all of us again, and hoped that we would be able to find some time to talk together at length amid the press of the many dear friends who were bound to be descending on the Villa Britannicus for the nuptials.

Less than two weeks later, on the Ides of March, while I was working in my smithy and having no success with my design for a smelting furnace, a long and bedraggled procession of wagons arrived at our door. They'd travelled through the foulest spell of weather in what had already been a particularly nasty winter. There were three large draft wagons and three slightly smaller ones, each pulled by a pair of horses, and the sight of their occupants delighted me and touched me.

Equus was driving the lead wagon, and he had brought his whole family with him. Plautus held the reins of the second wagon, and at first I did not recognize him, out of uniform, muffled in a cloak and heavily bearded as he was. The third wagon was driven by the son of my own major-domo from Colchester, and his father and mother were in one of the other wagons. I was amazed and flattered and quite touched at this display of loyalty, even though they were, all of them, very quick to point out that they had come only for the wedding festivities and would be moving on afterwards. To where? None of them could say.

It took only moments, when we finally got around to talking about their future plans, to convince them that all

of them had a place and a future here on the Villa Britannicus, since Luceiia and I would be setting up a household of our own after we were married and would have
need of servants. Also, I was sadly in need of Equus's
professional help in designing a smelting furnace for my
skystones. They were not difficult to convince, and I
knew that all of them had been hoping that we would be
able to invite them to stay. When they were assured of
this, the reunion became a celebration.

That night, after dinner, the others left Equus, Plautus
and me alone to reminisce together. Equus was obviously
bursting to tell me about his decision to close up shop and
bring everything out to the west. For a time after my
departure from Colchester, he had hoped that all the
furore would die down and that I would return to run the
smithy with him, but the report by Cicero of my "death"
a month or so later had ended that hope, and then the
announcement of Seneca's appointment as Procurator
had put *finis* to everything.

Equus had then begun amassing all of the equipment
and material that he suspected I could want or require,
including my grandfather's collection of treasures,
which he had dismantled and packed. He had disposed
of the smithy by trading it to a wagon-maker for the
three big wagons, and he then bought the three smaller
wagons and all the livestock with some of the gold I had
given him. He had used Tonius Cicero and Plautus as
intermediaries in this instance, not wishing to advertise
the fact that he possessed gold. By the time he had
loaded all of our belongings, including the amphora
containing my grandfather's gold, onto the wagons, he
had also recruited his other companions on the journey.

Plautus had left town separately and joined them on the road.

I could only embrace Equus and thank him warmly for his foresight and his loyalty. He gripped my arm tightly in silence, tears gleaming in his eyes.

I blinked my own tears away and turned to Plautus.

"And you, my friend. Tonius Cicero informs us you are to be congratulated."

"On what? My posting?" He grunted. "Cicero pulled some strings. I'm to be the new *primus pilus* at the military officers' training school there. An honorary position."

"I know," I said with a smile. "Tonius told us. A signal honour for a worthy fellow. Felicitations, my friend."

He glowered. "For what? I'm a soldier, Varrus, not a courtier — not a wet-nurse to puking young officer whelps. Keep your congratulations for yourself, once you're married."

I was taken aback. "You're unhappy about it?"

His look withered me. "Unhappy? Publius, you were always ugly but never stupid. Of course I'm unhappy. It's an abomination of a posting!"

"But . . ." I was at a loss for words. "But then why did you accept it? Tonius Cicero seemed proud that you had obtained the posting."

"Oh, he is, and I'm grateful to him." His tone suggested otherwise. "I wouldn't have got it if Tonius hadn't pulled some strings. But I'd rather stay where I've been for the past ten years."

"Oh." Belatedly, I realized the cause of his anger. "Seneca."

"Aye, Seneca, the son of a spavined whore! The new Procurator. Who or what else could make me give up the best billet I ever had?"

"You really think he would still recognize you?" I could hear incredulity in the tone of my own voice. "I was the one who fought with him, remember — the one who marked him. I'm the man he's looking for. You were merely a spectator. You had little to do with the affair. And anyway, he would never dream of seeing a bandit when he looks at a *primus pilus*."

Plautus grunted. "If you throw your mind back, my friend, you might recall it was me the swine took objection to in the first place. I have the kind of face he hates. As soon as Cicero heard of the appointment, who the Procurator was to be, he sent for me and told me. We decided that I would be better off in Londinium. I have leave due me. Enough to let me stay here to attend your wedding and then head straight to Londinium to my new posting."

"I see." There was little I could add to that, but I felt I had to try. "Plautus, I'm really sorry. I know regrets can't cure a thing, but I feel our friendship has cost you dearly."

He looked at me as though I had started talking to him in some strange tongue. "What in Hades is that supposed to mean?"

"The truth. I've cost you your soft billet. If I hadn't overreacted that day none of this would be happening."

"Horse turds! It was fated. If you hadn't crossed the son of a whore, he'd have found some way to get me to spill his tripes. And I would have done it. I was close to it, as it was. I'd have killed him. Then we'd both have been in shit. They wouldn't have let us get away so easily with a corpse on their hands. You left him alive, and that saved us. His friends were too busy looking after him to chase us, so let's not have any more guilt from you. Understand?"

I nodded. "I suppose so. Well, let's have another cup of wine to your new posting, unwished though it might be, and to Seneca's early recall to the Imperial Court."

"I'll drink to the animal's early and painful death, and may he fester in Hades until his bones melt into jelly." He emptied his cup at one draught and belched loudly. "I think that was one cup too many, my friends. I am tired and my head will ring like a brazen gong come morning. Varrus, have your servants avoid my door until noon. After that, I may rise to face the day." His voice dropped a little and he stared into his cup. "You might not be far wrong, just the same. I had dinner with him, you know."

"With whom?"

"What?"

He blinked at me, and I realized that he really was quite drunk. I glanced at Equus, who was grinning at me, nodding affirmation. I rephrased my question.

"You said you had dinner with him. Who are you talking about? Tonius?"

"Damnation, no. Seneca!"

"You had dinner with Seneca?" I was incredulous. "When? How?"

He nodded ponderously. "Night before I left Colchester. Official dinner. Legate Cicero commanded me to be there, so I went. I went and watched the animal Seneca as he defecated on the decency of our military table. 'N he didn't recognize me . . ." His voice drifted downward to the point where I was straining to hear him. "Mind you, you wouldn't expect him to, as you said. I was in full regimentals, all burnished bronze and brass and polished leather. He looked at me and saw *what* I was, not *who* I was. But I couldn't be in uniform all the time, and he would have known me sooner or later, and then I'd have been dead."

I reached out and shook him by the shoulder. He tossed his head and strained his eyes open, trying to shake off the wine.

"Plautus," I said urgently. "Sober up! I want to hear about this."

He blew a fricative, sounding like a horse, but his eyes cleared and his voice became normal.

"Then, Publius my friend, you must point me towards some cold night air. If I am to talk longer, I'll have to clear my head. The heat from the brazier there is breaking me down."

I led him into the atrium, which, in the classical style, was open to the sky. It was cold, and I began to shiver immediately. Plautus, however, seemed impervious to the chill and merely stood breathing deeply, drawing the chill night air into his lungs and holding each breath for a long time before exhaling it in a plume of smoky vapour. Finally, just as I was thinking of retiring to the brazier and leaving him alone out there, he barked a short, stifled laugh, half-grunt and half-curse.

"By the Christ, Varrus, I have seldom been so frightened. If he had recognized me I would have been dead meat, *primus pilus* or not. Let's go back inside, before you die. Luceiia would kill me more painfully than Seneca could if you were to expire of cold before the wedding."

When we were seated again by the glowing brazier, he continued.

"It was the night before I left. I had been out inspecting the guard on the south wall for the last time that afternoon, and when I got back to the fort I found the courtyard filled with strange soldiers. Seneca had arrived! I've been scared badly several times over the years, Publius, but never as badly as I was when I saw those soldiers of his. I thought — I was convinced — they were going to arrest me and haul me in front of the swine right then and there, and I'd be tried, condemned and executed before the sun set.

"I scuttled for my quarters, keeping my head down, but no sooner had I got there than a soldier came to my door with a note from the Legate, Cicero. It was an invitation — a command — to dine with him in his quarters that night, to meet his other guests. There wasn't a thing I could do but accept.

"I dressed carefully for that dinner, you can be sure. Seneca had seen me only once, dressed in rough, peasant clothing and wearing three days of beard. Tonight I would be in formal, full-dress uniform. Even dandified, every inch the fighting Roman, I still wasn't sure, and before leaving for the Legate's quarters I went by the baths and looked at myself in the big, bronze mirror on the wall there. That made me feel a little better. To have recognized me as the man from the *mansio* yard, even Seneca would have needed magic powers. I've heard a lot of stories about the whoreson, but none of them said he was a sorcerer. I sucked in my gut and went to dinner.

"Everybody else was already there by the time I arrived, and Tonius made a great ceremony of introducing me as the pride of the garrison, his *primus pilus*, who had been honoured with a transfer to Londinium, to the training school for officers there. Seneca had his back to me at first, I remember, but just as we reached him he turned and looked me up and down with an expression on his face that made me feel like a pile of dung. I was gritting my teeth, trying to look like nothing and nobody, trying not to think of what would happen if he recognized me. He nodded and held out his hand and I shook with him, and as our skins touched, he smiled. I swear, Publius, for the space of a heartbeat, that smile of his had me wondering if this was the wrong man. But it was only for a second. His teeth had escaped permanent damage in our fight, but his nose was a mess — flat and crunched and scarred. Then he said something pleasant — can't remember what, but it didn't mean anything — and I mumbled something back. And then he was being introduced to someone else."

Equus and I were both fascinated, and Plautus looked from one to the other of us, knowing he had a rapt audience. There was no sign of drunkenness now as he continued his tale.

"I tried to keep my eyes off him all through dinner, but I couldn't. Twice he caught me staring at him, and each time I had to pretend to be looking off over his head. But I wasn't afraid of him any longer, because I knew who he thought I was. When he looked at me, you see, he saw only the uniform, the *primus pilus*. I began to relax, even though I'd never sat at table with Tonius Cicero and his Staff officers before. I knew he was watching me, Cicero I mean, watching to see how I was doing. He must have noticed I had begun to relax, because after a while, he didn't look at me nearly as much.

"And then he started baiting Seneca. Of course, nobody knew what he was doing except him and me. But he went right for the throat. 'You know, Procurator,' says he, 'I have been curious about the outcome of your misadventure here in Britain a few months back. We had the pleasure of being hosts to some Household Troops who were here in town about your business, or at least on business connected with you. They were searching for the ruffians who attacked you while you were on embassy for the Emperor. That would be, what? Three months ago? Four?'

"I swear to you, Seneca went rigid in his chair." Plautus's voice was exultant. "Course, Tonius pretends not to notice, and keeps right on going. 'Anyway,' he says, 'you will forgive my curiosity, I hope, Procurator, but I never did hear the end of that affair. What happened? Did you find the men? I find it unbelievable' says he, 'that such a thing could happen to an envoy of the Emperor. Especially in my district. Of course, the fact that you used the Household Troops to search for the criminals cut off any possibility of our following the matter up from here, even though it was a local affair.'

"I tell you, Varrus, Seneca was blue in the face! I was watching him so hard that it took me a while to realize that all talk around the table had come to a halt. Nobody was speaking. Everybody was staring at Seneca. While I'd been watching him, his face had gone from blue to white as a death-mask. He was gripping the edge of the table so hard I expected him to break a piece of it off. His knuckles were as white as his face.

"Anyway, Tonius lets it stretch out as far as he can without being too obvious and then he starts up again, being the plain, blunt soldier. His eyebrows go up and he starts looking from face to face as though wondering what on earth he could have said to cause such a reaction. But as he starts in to apologize or something, Seneca cuts him off in mid word.

"'No! He was not apprehended,' Seneca says, in a voice that sounds as though he's talking through a mouthful of sand. 'But he will be. Believe me, the whoreson will answer to me some day for his sins.'

"Tonius is still playing the innocent. '*He* will be? You mean there was only one? And you still expect to find him? After all this time?'

"If a look could kill a man, I swear Tonius would have dropped dead there and then. 'There were two of them,' Seneca snarls, 'but one of them, at least, will die some day at my pleasure. He will be found, Legate. Trust me in that.'

"'Ah! There were two of them,' says Tonius. 'I thought there were. Which of them are you searching for?'

"'The old one.' I could hardly hear him. His voice was a whisper, but as though he was being strangled. 'There were two of them,' he says. 'But one of them marked me! Look!' He screams like a madman and leaps to his feet, ripping his tunic open to show the scar you carved in him. 'He branded me!' He was still screaming, and everybody at the table's squirming by this time, except for me and Tonius."

Here Plautus paused, and both Equus and I hung on that pause until we could bear it no longer.

"And then? What happened then, Plautus?"

"Oh. He changed. As suddenly as he had lost control of himself, he got it back again. It was almost as though a light had been put out behind his eyes. He stopped moving, holding his tunic open, and looked around the table at each of us. And then he laughed, pulled his torn tunic together again and sat down, picking up his goblet as if nothing had happened. 'Your wine is excellent, Antonius Cicero,' he says, in a perfectly ordinary voice. 'And so is your kitchen. Gentlemen, I propose a toast to our host.' I swear, Varrus, he's crazed. That was it."

Equus and I sat silent, absorbing this strange tale, and I, for one, did not want it to end like that.

"Is that all?" I asked Plautus. "Was there no more to it?"

He shook his head, pursing his lips. "That was it. I got out of there as quickly as I could, though. I was ready for a good night's sleep and I had to be on the road next morning. Oh, there was one other thing. Gave me a smile, anyway." He turned and grinned at me, the shadows from the dying brazier making black hollows in his face. "One of the fellows there had a bad limp. Nobody noticed it until the poor whoreson had to get up to go and relieve himself. He had almost got to the door when Seneca noticed him. 'You there!' he yells.

"'Procurator?' The poor fellow didn't even know if he was the one being yelled at.

"'Where did you get that limp?'

"Tonius spoke up. 'Tribune Scala was wounded in action, Procurator. During the great Invasion, years ago.'

"Seneca wasn't impressed. And he wasn't charming. He was drunk and he was hostile and he was scowling. 'I don't like people who limp,' he snarls. 'They offend me. Where are you going?'

"'To relieve myself, Procurator.' I could hardly hear Scala's answer. He didn't know how he'd offended the whoreson but he knew that he had.

"Seneca sneered and I wanted to throw my knife at him. 'Relieve your limp, too, you dung pile!' he says. 'Either get rid of it, or don't come back!'

"He definitely doesn't like cripples, Varrus. I'd drink to cripples, but I've had too much already and I'm tired. Where do I sleep?"

By this point, Equus was obviously far gone, too, unable to smother his yawns, and I decided to allow them both to get some rest.

"By the way," I asked Equus as we got to our feet, "did you visit Phoebe in Verulamium on your way out?"

Equus was scratching his head and beard. "No," he said. "We went looking for her, but she changed lodgings, and the old crone didn't know where she had gone to. I left a letter for her with Bishop Alaric. If she goes back there, she'll know how to find me."

After they had gone to bed, I sat alone by the brazier for a time, thinking about my life and the changes that had taken place in it, and anticipating the pleasant changes that were to occur in the future — the assembly of all the guests for our wedding, and the life of companionship with Luceiia that stretched ahead. The day was close at hand now; less than three weeks remained until the date of our nuptials. I was pleasantly relaxed and ready for sleep by the time I found my bed.

XXIII

The arrival of Equus and Plautus and their group seemed to be the signal for our wedding guests to begin arriving daily in ever greater numbers. The majority of them were strangers to me, old friends of Caius and Luceiia, although I did find a few familiar and welcome faces scattered among them. All of them, however, wanted to meet me, to evaluate the man who had won Luceiia Britannicus.

I was with Luceiia constantly for the whole three-week period leading up to the wedding, but such was the press of people and duties that I can remember spending no time alone with her. Equus and Plautus I neglected completely. In all of the mounting excitement and the constant round of meeting new people, I was unable to take them out to my skystone valley. I knew Plautus was indifferent to that, but I felt occasional pangs of guilt over Equus's disappointment, even though he gave no sign of it.

Tonius Cicero and Bishop Alaric arrived fifteen days after the original Colchester party, seven days in advance of the marriage ceremonies, and they were immediately absorbed into the throng of guests who had by then spilled out of the villa and were encamped by the score throughout the grounds. I missed their arrival completely. They came in late in the day while I was away hunting deer in the open woodlands to the south-west, Luceiia having

439

belatedly begun to fear that we might not, after all, have laid in sufficient provisions for the crowd that was still arriving. The sight of the two of them with Equus and Plautus was a welcome surprise when I got back the following day with half a wagonload of freshly butchered venison, but we had no opportunity to exchange much more than casual pleasantries. Only late in the evening, in response to a direct request from Alaric, did I lead them away from the revelry around a crowded campfire and conduct them to Caius's day-room, which was brightly lit with a profusion of oil lamps and a blazing brazier. Once there, with the doors closed against intruders, I threw myself down onto a couch in mock exhaustion.

"Now then," I asked with a grin, "what is so important that you must make me run the risk of my love's anger for abandoning our guests before they all pass out? Or is it simply that the two of you have missed me so greatly that you are jealous of the throng and must have me to yourselves alone?"

They glanced at each other with looks of such unmistakable apprehension that my own good humour disappeared at once, to be replaced by a clammy chill of fear that seemed to suck away even the heat from the brazier. I sat upright, bracing myself for evil tidings, even though I had no idea where they might come from. Tonius had seated himself across from me. Alaric remained standing close by the fire-basket.

"In God's name, Alaric," I asked him, "what is wrong?"

"Varrus." It was Tonius who answered, and my eyes swung to his frowning face. "We have bad news for you. News that has no place at a wedding feast."

"Then damn your news," I flashed back at him. "I will not hear it." My mind had immediately thrown up the spectre of Seneca, but I could visualize no possibility of threat from him now. Tonius made to say something more, but I cut him off with an upraised hand.

"No, Tonius, my friend. Hear what I have to say. My mind is clear. All of my friends are here — every person in the world who is dear to me. There is no threat to any of them, and so I am content. Therefore any evil tidings you bring from beyond this district can have no effect on me between now and my wedding feast. Surely you can see that? That's why I'll have none of your news. Not, at least, until I am wed."

Tonius grimaced with discomfort at this and looked to Alaric for support. So did I, but I found none.

"Publius," the Bishop said, "Tonius and I think, no, we *believe* that Phoebe has been killed. Murdered. We believe she was abducted and killed in an attempt to find you."

For a moment my mind was unable to grasp what he had said, so unexpected was his suggestion. Phoebe? Dead? Murdered for me? The idea was preposterous. I knew it to be preposterous because no one could connect Phoebe with me! Not even Equus, her brother. The only other person who knew of our brief association was Plautus, and he would never breathe a word of it. I finally found my tongue.

"That is impossible," I said, hearing the strangeness in my own voice. "You must be mistaken. Phoebe could not be affected by me, she does not even know where I am. You are mistaken. You must be."

"I pray to Our Saviour that we are, Publius, but I

cannot find it in my soul to believe that she lives." Alaric's voice was low and troubled. "There is too much evidence to the contrary, and it has been collected by two unimpeachable sources — myself and Tonius."

"What . . ." I had to clear my throat before I could go on. "What is this . . . evidence? Tell me."

Alaric told me without embellishment. Equus had left a letter with him for delivery to Phoebe on her return to Verulamium. The following day, one of Alaric's own congregation had made a confession that troubled the Bishop. The penitent admitted having accepted money from some strangers in return for information about a young woman. He had thought himself lucky at the time, because the woman was widely known to be no saint and the men would have found her anyway, red-haired and pretty as she was.

Then, weeks later, he had heard that the woman had been found dead, stabbed and mutilated, the day after he had sold the information. His conscience had troubled him ever since, and now he sought absolution. Alaric had absolved him, even though there was no sin on the man's part, but the Bishop knew that Phoebe was red-haired and pleasant to look at, and began to worry. He questioned the man closely and learned to his relief that the woman in question was not Phoebe. Nevertheless, he decided to visit Phoebe's old haunts and speak to anyone who had known her.

At the bath house where she worked, they told him they had not seen her in more than a month. Not since the evening of the Calends, the first day, of February. The toothless crone who owned the building where she had stayed told him only that Phoebe had disappeared

— run off without paying her rent. The rooms she had occupied now housed someone else. Dissatisfied, and growing more alarmed, Alaric paid the old woman her delinquent rent. He assumed that Phoebe was too intelligent and responsible to have intentionally disappeared so casually, leaving no word of her whereabouts for her brother or her friends. He told himself he was being too suspicious, but he set his own people to find out what had happened in the case of the woman "sold" by his penitent.

What he discovered was far from pleasant. Two women had been found dead on the morning in question, and both had been red-haired and good-looking. Both had disappeared the previous night, on the Calends of February, the same night that Phoebe, who answered the same description, had vanished. Immediate inquiries with the Roman military police had established that the second woman was not Phoebe, either. But apart from being able to tell him that the two — and now, with Phoebe's disappearance three — women had been abducted for reasons unknown, they had been able to tell him nothing more. That had been just over two weeks before he left Verulamium to come to the west.

At this point he stopped, appeared to hesitate, and then said that Tonius would continue the chronicle. I did not speak; I merely waited for Tonius. He was deep in thought, and I suspected that he was looking for a suitable starting point for his contribution. At last, he started with a question.

"Did Plautus tell you about the dinner he attended with Seneca?" I nodded and he continued. "Did he mention Seneca's outburst about you?"

"Yes. He also told me that Seneca turned the rough edge of his tongue on another of your guests, one who walked with a limp."

"Scala. Yes, he did. Poor Scala started him off again. Seneca must have ranted and raved for more than an hour after the unfortunate man had departed in disgrace, unaware of what he had done to give offence. It was typical Claudius Seneca behaviour — drunken madness and nonsense. He insulted everybody, myself included, and sent his own cronies off in humiliation. And that left me. And him." His face twisted. "A great honour I could have done without."

"Well," I said, "I presume you were well insulated. You must have been very drunk by that time."

Tonius shook his head. "He was. I was not. I drank enough, but I think my fear of the man's potential for causing grief and chaos kept me sober."

I wondered what he was moving towards. "So?"

He twisted his face again, registering distaste and disgust. "Malice," he said. "That is the only word I seem able to think of when that man crosses my mind. Malice. Aye, but worse than that, Publius. Malevolence. The man's malevolence is boundless. He is still actively hunting you. At least, he is hunting the man he perceives you to be. His wretched relative Nesca has had his bullies on the watch for crippled grey-beards ever since this happened."

I jerked my head in a nod. "I know."

"From what I have heard, for you know I never laid eyes on him before you did, he was physically quite remarkable before you destroyed his beauty." I nodded an unnecessary assent, and he went on. "Well, he isn't any longer. He will never forgive you for that. The fact that he doesn't know who did it only makes it worse."

I grunted. "He wasn't beautiful. Not really. He was warped even then, long before I met him. He may have *thought* he was beautiful, but he was far from it."

"Very well, I'll accept that. He thought he was beautiful. But that's all that's necessary. For a man of his . . . tastes, physical beauty is all-important. You marred him, Varrus, permanently and incontrovertibly. If he ever finds you, he'll kill you. Unpleasantly."

"I know." It was getting late, and I stirred, feeling that I should be moving. "What has this to do with Phoebe?"

He shook his head in a way that conveyed extreme impatience. "I don't know. Perhaps I am just being a pessimist. But our noble Procurator let slip a reference in his cups that night to at least one woman who died under interrogation in the matter of a limping, grey-haired man."

"Phoebe?"

He shook his head. "I don't know. As I said, he let the reference slip out and then covered it. It wasn't mentioned again. I knew nothing of Phoebe at that time, and I did not want to bring the matter up again openly. Nor did I want to arouse either his anger or his suspicion by attempting to question him subtly. I let the matter rest, but it worried me. As Military Governor, my job is difficult enough. I have no desire to become involved in the actions of our inestimable Procurator. Had I obtained any more information, I would have been forced to initiate inquiries, without knowing where to start or what to look for."

Outraged, I glanced at Alaric. He was listening attentively, his face devoid of any emotion. My own emotions were more volatile.

"Damnation, Tonius, that's abominable! What did he say?"

"I didn't catch all of it. I had been drinking heavily myself, remember. I heard him muttering something about almost having had the whoreson. Had had his whore, but the bitch was stubborn. Died without saying a word. It was the mumbling of a drunken man I heard, Publius. By the time I had begun to hear what I was hearing, if you know what I mean, it was almost over. I thought about it for a few seconds and decided I didn't want to hear any more. But it stayed with me. I could not get it out of my head."

"I'm not surprised. Murder is against the Roman law, Legate."

"Perhaps. But was he really talking of murder? I don't know that, Varrus. And even if I had known for certain, there was nothing much I could have done about it. My only informant would hardly have been likely to repeat his self-condemnation when sober, would he?"

I was seething with impatience. "Well? Was that all he said?" Tonius nodded. I made no effort to keep the anger out of my voice. "So what makes you think this has anything to do with Phoebe, in God's name? A drunken man's hint about some woman who died, and may have been deliberately killed, in a hunt for a crippled man. That doesn't say 'Phoebe' to me!"

Tonius stood erect. "It does to me, Publius. Be serious. The crippled man we're talking about is you! And the woman was from Verulamium. That much I heard. I didn't think about Phoebe because I didn't know of her existence. It was only when Alaric told me of his own concerns for her that I made the connection."

Though I was angry, it was not at Tonius, but at this situation. I knew it had to be coincidence. In my frustration, I rose to my feet and held my open palms towards the fire.

"Damn it, Tonius, nobody in Verulamium except Alaric knows who I am, let alone that I knew Phoebe! What you two are suggesting just isn't possible! There is no way, absolutely no . . ." but I stopped in mid sentence, and my flesh crawled with cold bumps as I saw a face in my mind — the face of the cutpurse in the crowd leaving the amphitheatre in Verulamium, the face of the man I had handed over to the army for execution in Alchester. He had been holding a bare blade in his hand, coming towards me. Someone had been robbed and had shouted, and I had looked and seen the man I supposed to be the thief. *That* had been coincidence. But there all coincidence ended. He had already singled me out. He had been watching me. And that meant he had seen Phoebe with me. He had died in Alchester, but he had been travelling with seven companions on the road, two of whom were still alive. One, or both of them, might have been with him in that crowd. Or he might have spoken to them about recognizing me for the first time that evening, when I was at the theatre with a woman. And he would have described the woman.

My stomach heaved with sickness. That would have been all that was necessary. A recollection by one of the two surviving assassins that I had been seen in the company of a pretty woman with red hair. Verulamium was not a big town, and I had made no effort to be secretive while I was there with Phoebe. A hundred people could have remembered seeing us together, and any number of them might have recognized Phoebe. All of this flashed through my mind in an instant, and I knew beyond any doubt that Tonius and Alaric were right, and she was dead, and the burden of guilt crashed down and physically buckled my knees.

Alaric caught me before I fell against the brazier, and he and Tonius almost carried me between them back to my couch, where I sat like a man in a swoon for many minutes before they could get any response out of me.

I have no recollection of any of that. I can remember only the realization that I had killed Phoebe with my lust. Had I not gone to see her on my way through Verulamium that day, she would still be alive. After that, I have only blankness in my memory until I became aware of Alaric sitting across from me, leaning forward and staring intently into my eyes, his face drawn with lines of worry.

Later, much later, I accepted the fact that my guilt was futile and unjustifiable, but that made the pain no easier to bear. I also accepted the fact that Claudius Caesarius Seneca and I were fated to the death. One of us would kill the other, and I was determined that I would survive the outcome.

That same night, I told Luceiia what had happened, and she mourned with me for the unfortunate young woman who had died simply because I had befriended her. In the endless time of a sleepless night, I decided to conceal my grief from the wedding guests and swore to mourn Phoebe later, when there would be time for mourning. I swore to avenge her death, and I fantasized about what I would do to Seneca when next I faced him.

XXIV

The wedding celebrations went on for two more weeks. Civic dignitaries and provincial administrators mingled with military officers and soldiers of all ranks and descriptions, including young Picus. There were bishops and Druids and priests, merchants, landowners, farmers, stonemasons, smiths, clothmakers, shoemakers, weavers, soothsayers and musicians. There were Romans of Roman descent, Romans of British descent, Greeks, North Africans, Britons of all descriptions, Gauls from across the sea and Celts from the mountain country at our back. It was a holiday celebration to rival the Saturnalia of bygone days, and it was enjoyed to the full by everyone.

On the day of the wedding itself, the sun shone bright and warm, and I was even more expansive than a bridegroom has the right to be. I had spent the previous night in the arms of my love, and the last seeds of doubt over Phoebe had been purged with the gouting of my own seed and the love and understanding of the woman I was to marry the following day. Spring had finally arrived; everything was green and bedecked with flowers. There was no wind, and the air was rich with the perfumes of springtime and alive with bird-song. My bride looked brilliantly beautiful in her wedding gown of African cloth, and I knew in all modesty that I looked magnificent in the suit of supple leather clothes Luceiia had made for me with her own hands. As we exchanged our vows, binding each to the other, even the birds seemed to stop singing so that all might hear the sound of our voices — Luceiia's clear and sweet, and my own surprisingly timid. Our contract was sealed with a kiss, and the celebrations were under way in earnest.

Each glorious spring day was filled with games, athletic competitions of all kinds, hunting contests and the like. There was food in abundance and everyone had his fill of it whenever hunger irked him. The evenings were filled with song, dance and dalliance, and I fancy I was not the only man who consummated a relationship in the course of that time.

I know that Caius enjoyed himself thoroughly during those two weeks, although his motivations were hardly connubial, for he saw in this gathering of all his most trusted friends a unique opportunity to sound them out on their views of the Empire's affairs, and to promote his own beliefs.

During those two weeks, I was to witness and be midwife to a miraculous birthing; I would remain forever after a nursemaid to the entity that was born then. There may be some who are inclined to scoff at those words and dismiss them as fanciful, but I am prepared to stand by the truth of them. My wedding feast was the occasion of the spiritual birth of what we came to call our Colony, and I recall clearly the circumstances that triggered the chain of events that was to reshape the destiny of all of us.

Caius had been talking for years about his ideas on the Empire and his fears about its future, not only to me but to each and every one of his friends and acquaintances.

Some agreed with his opinions; others disputed them; still others suffered them good-naturedly, humouring him and casting long-suffering glances heavenward whenever he launched into one of his diatribes. All would admit, however, under pressure, that he was partially correct; all was not right with the Roman world. Nevertheless, few could really bring themselves to believe that things were quite as black as Caius liked to paint them, and I counted myself among the doubters.

Terra and Firma Atribatus changed all of that in the course of one evening.

The brothers were identical twins whose real names were Terrix Polonius and Arpius Fermax Atribatus. They had grown fabulously wealthy as joint owners of the richest fleet of seagoing trading ships in Britain, and it was inevitable that their nautical activities should result in their becoming known to their friends as Terra and Firma. I did not know them personally, but they had been close friends of the Britannicus family since boyhood. Their names were high on the list of invited guests, so when they had failed to arrive by the end of the first week of the festivities, their absence had been generally noticed. They did arrive, however, after dark on the evening of the tenth day, and their welcome was the more tumultuous since, by then, they were no longer expected.

I met them very briefly and welcomed them with Caius, and then I returned to the open-air fire, leaving Caius to see to settling them in their quarters.

I had enjoyed these evening gatherings more than anything else except my new wife, for it was then that Caius and his friends were at their best, assembled by a blazing fire with a cup of wine or Celtic mead or a jug of locally brewed ale. Then it was that conversation and debate emerged and was enjoyed for itself. The talk from evening to evening might be of politics or philosophy, of religion or of poetry, or of agriculture and the weather patterns of past years, but always it was enjoyable. On this particular evening, before the arrival of the newcomers, we had been talking about the great Republic and the Roman way of life — the old days and old ways. Caius had been in his element, and even Plautus had thrown himself into the spirit of the debate, forgetting his normal reticence in the casual company of Tonius, his Commander. Without the catalytic presence of Caius, however, the conversation had become desultory. I was thinking lazily of seeking my new wife and hauling her to bed when Quintus Varo commented that it was taking Caius a damnably long time to bring the newcomers back to the fire. I stood up and stretched, yawning loudly, which earned me a round of laughter and lascivious comments. Gaius Gallus, another close friend of Britannicus, leaned elegantly forward and threw a small stick onto the flames.

"Tired again, Publius? So soon? Did no one ever tell you that beds are for sleeping in, too?"

I grinned, feeling peculiarly shy, and denied myself.

"Who's tired, Gaius? I'm bored, that's all. I'm going to go and find Caius and our new guests. We need some fresh wit to leaven the conversation around here." I walked away from a chorus of jibes and pleasantries and went to look for Caius.

I found him in his private day-room, deep in conversation with the twins. Seeing their general demeanour and the intensity of their talk, I stopped in the open doorway, reluctant to interrupt them. I was turning to leave when Caius, who had seen me from the corner of his eye, stopped me with a peremptory wave of his hand. As I hesitated there, he half-turned his face towards me, keeping his eyes fixed on the twin who was talking. As soon as the man's voice reached a natural pause, another gesture of that upraised hand held him to silence momentarily.

"Pardon me, Terra." He turned towards me. "Publius, you must pardon me, too. I had no thought of being ill-mannered, but I didn't want you to leave. Terra, Firma, this is my new brother-in-law, Publius Varrus. You met him earlier, but your arrival was rather hectic. Publius, these are two of my oldest and dearest friends, and you have heard me talk of them many times. This one here is Terra — notice the blue tunic. This one is Firma — white tunic. Tomorrow they may change clothes and confound us both."

We all nodded to one another, smiling, and then I shook my head to Caius.

"I'm sorry, Caius, I had nothing important to say to you and I didn't mean to interrupt you. I was on my way to bed, and the others were wondering what had become of you. I said I would look in on you on my way and send you out, but you are obviously talking about important matters and so I'll leave you to it and tell them not to wait for you." I moved to leave again.

"No, I want you to hear this, Publius." He paused. "But then again, I think the others should hear it too. How many of the crowd are still there?"

I ran my eyes around the mental vision of the group I had left by the fire. "Gaius, Varo, Tonius, Plautus, a few others, about five. That's all. The rest left before I did."

"Good. Those are the ones I want." He turned back to the twins. "I think we should finish our discussion here and then tell Varrus and the others what you have told me. Do you agree?"

The twins shrugged identical gestures of acquiescence and Caius turned back to me.

"My respects to the others and please ask them to wait for us. We will join them shortly."

I smiled. "Does that include me? I believe my wife is waiting for me somewhere."

He did not respond to my smile. "Yes, I'd like you to stay, too. We have a lot to discuss."

I shrugged my shoulders, my curiosity aroused. "As you wish," I said. "I'll ask them to wait."

I rejoined the others, and we spent several minutes in speculation about what could be so important that it must keep a new bridegroom from his duties.

Caius and the new guests came to the fire a short time later, to the severe detriment of a filthy story being told by Quintus Varo. Their three faces were sombre enough to put a mantle of seriousness on the greetings that were exchanged across the fire, and as soon as they had seated themselves Gaius Gallus asked the question we were all thinking.

"What's going on, Caius?"

Caius looked from face to face around the group before answering. "Terra and Firma want to buy a villa in the area. Do any of you know of one for sale? Or two?"

There was a short silence, then Varo asked, "Two? Are you serious?" He looked at Terra and Firma, his face showing tolerant disbelief. "You two are looking for a retirement home? Here? Among the peasants? What about your villa outside Londinium? And your place in Aquae Sulis? And your island in the Aegean? Your palace in Constantinople? If I had your money and your youth, lads, I'd be basking in the sunshine, not trying to gull people into believing that I'd be interested in living in a quiet backwater like this."

Firma grimaced. "They're all gone, Quintus."

"Gone?" This was Gaius Gallus. "What do you mean, gone?"

"Just what I said. We no longer have those places."

"You mean you had to *sell* them?"

"No." The word was said with a rising inflection that demanded attention to the words that followed it. "We had to forfeit them."

"Forfeit!" Gaius Gallus's shocked tone reflected the astonishment of everyone there. "You mean you're bankrupt? Cleaned out?"

It was Terra who responded. "No, far from it. But we are out of business." He cleared his throat and then continued. "We've been losing a lot of shipping to pirates, recently. Too much."

"How much?" This was Varo again.

"Seven ships in the last two months."

"*Seven?*"

"Seven. One ship, one crew and one cargo every eight days, and it grows worse all the time. One of those ships was a quadrireme. The others were four triremes and two biremes — big ships, big cargoes, big losses."

"By the Christ!" Varo was outraged. "Nobody can sustain losses like that! Where was the navy?"

"Where it always is — at sea." The sigh that followed this was short and frustrated. "It's not the navy's fault, Quintus. They can't do a damn thing. They're powerless. Too few ships, too much sea and too many pirates." He paused and looked at each of us individually. "Tell them, Firma."

His brother stood up and moved closer to the fire, holding his hands out to the heat and speaking down into the heart of the fire.

"It's no exaggeration. There is not a single safe route for shipping left anywhere in the world. Not one. It's not general knowledge, of course, because the ports are still full of vessels loading and unloading. Hundreds of ships are getting through safely. But there are hundreds more being taken, and every one of them is owned by merchants like us who can no longer afford the risks. The money-lenders and the bankers have closed their coffers and are concentrating only on collecting bad debts. Even the Seneca family have closed down their maritime operations, and they were our bankers, world-wide."

I felt the hair on my neck prickle at the mention of the Seneca name and glanced at Caius, but he had other things on his mind.

"So," Terra continued, "we are out of the marine mercantile business, as are most of our major competitors." He sat down again and his brother took up his point, almost without pause.

"In other words, my friends, the Empire is out of the trading business, and you know what that means."

Plautus, who had sat still during all of this, was blinking in perplexity, a worried frown bisecting his forehead. "I don't know," he said. "What does that mean?"

Firma looked him straight in the eye. "It means dis-solution, my friend — gradual, at first, but definite, progressive disintegration. Break-up. The end."

Poor Plautus was baffled. "The end of what, in the name of God?"

Firma snorted with disgust. "Of everything! The end of the chain of supply that keeps the Roman Mob fed and clothed. The end of the web of commerce that keeps the Empire from collapsing. The end of the status quo. The end of Rome's dominion. Shall I go on? Caius, here, has been prophesying it for years, and we have all been laughing at him and calling him an alarmist."

"But what about the government?" This voice belonged to Quintus Varo. "Can't they do anything to help you?"

Terra's raised, sardonic eyebrow was eloquent. "Ah, yes, of course. The government. They have a lot to say about helping us. For one thing, they are graciously allowing us to remain operative — fully operational and fully liable — in spite of the fact that we choose to opt out. The government has ordered us to continue trading, to continue losing all our investments, and threatens us with seizure and confiscation of all our property if we refuse to obey." Shocked silence greeted this remark.

"About a week before we left to come here," he continued, "we received advance notice from a trusted friend that a military detachment was on its way to visit us, 'to help us protect our interests.' We tidied up our affairs as well as we could in a week, collected our collectable assets — again, as many as we could assemble — cleaned out our vaults, signed a voluntary legal transfer of our fleet to the imperial government and left town before the military arrived." He eyed us all again. "Everything we could not realize and carry with us has been forfeited as penalty for our crime of non-performance. We are out-laws now — proscribed fugitives. Does that answer your question, Quintus?"

"By God's wounds, this is infernal!" Varo was on his feet, glowering around him, his eye finally settling on Tonius, the only military officer present. "Is this true, Cicero?"

"Don't breathe fire at Tonius, Varo," Terra said. "We are not even from his district."

Tonius got up and went to pick out a new log to throw on the fire before he answered Varo's question.

"Let's say it doesn't surprise me, Quintus. I suppose it had to come to this, or something like it, although I hadn't seen it before now." He looked around at all of us. "They feel they have to blame somebody, so they're blaming the merchants for the breakdown, on the sea, at least. But it's not only the sea routes that are closed. Land caravans are almost an extinct phenomenon. Time was when we could dispatch a maniple to escort a major caravan and protect it. Now it takes an army. And even then there are no guarantees."

Gaius Gallus spoke up. "It's true. It's affecting every-one. I have three warehouses filled to the roofs with tiles. They've been waiting for shipment for almost six months. To Gaul. Straight across the narrows. There are no ships available, or willing, to take them. Tiles! Clay roofing tiles."

Poor Varo was almost spluttering in his hopeless efforts to comprehend what was being said here. "But . . . but . . .

what does it all mean? You mean . . . you mean the government's impotent? That it's victimizing innocent merchants, making scapegoats out of them, and there's nothing anyone can do? What about the army?'' He was looking in bewilderment from me to Tonius and back to me. "Why doesn't the army do something? They've done it before. Elect a new Emperor and form a new government! Why not?''

Gaius Gallus shook his head. "It's no good, Varo. That won't work. It's too late. No new government could undo the damage done already. Even the idea that an army can elect an emperor is an admission of the futility of the whole thing." He pointed a thumb towards Caius. "Ask Britannicus."

All eyes switched to Caius, who sighed deeply as though suddenly feeling the weight of his age. "What do you want me to tell you, Quintus?" he asked. "That they are wrong? That all is right with the Empire and the world? You want me to change my opinion after all the years you've known me?" He shook his head. "No, my friend. They are right. They are right. The signs are all around us, everywhere, world-wide. I had no idea until now that they were so bad, so strong, so final. But I've seen it coming — we all have, from time to time, if we will but admit it. Rome has finally starved the whole world into rebellion. And it is happening today."

"But not here in Britain," said Plautus.

"No, Plautus. Not here in Britain. But Britain stands alone in that."

"Britain will always stand alone!" This was Tonius Cicero, and Caius took him up on his comment.

"How so, Tonius?"

"Because Britain is an island — surrounded by water — defensible."

"Against whom?"

"Against all comers!" There was anger in Cicero's voice.

"Even Romans?" Caius was gently mocking.

"Even Romans!" Angry still, but now he looked uncomfortable.

"That's treasonous talk, my friend. It could get you killed."

Cicero's face was flushed. "This whole conversation is treasonous, Caius. According to those maggots in Rome and in Londinium, Terra and Firma commit treason by refusing to bankrupt themselves throwing good money after bad. By refusing to destroy themselves to provide an illusion of normality for faceless thieves who live in terror of the Mob, the Mob that wants everything for nothing. Why do you people think the Emperor and his Court live in Constantinople? *They* decided long ago that they wanted nothing to do with Rome and her sweaty, evil-tempered, vile-smelling citizenry. Think about that!" He glowered at the faces that watched him, as if defying any of us to disagree with him. "According to the maggots, none of us around this fire has any right to life. We exist for their benefit. And at their pleasure. Faugh! It makes me want to spew to think that SPQR, the symbol of the Senate and the People of Rome, was once the greatest symbol of freedom and the rights of free men in history! The people *in* Rome are a herd of murderous, carnivorous cattle, and the Senate is a eunuch! If it be treason to refuse to sacrifice everything we hold noble to the gluttonous maw of the Roman Mob, then I am a traitor!"

At the end of this outburst there was another period of silence. Tonius had risen to his feet, and now he subsided into his seat, his face flushed, angry and defiant.

"Well said, Tonius." Caius spoke softly into the silence. "You will find no dissenters from your viewpoint here, I think. But I have to remind you that you are a general of the armies of Britain and bound by holy oath to maintain that status. That opinion of yours places you squarely in conflict of interest."

"Not so!" Cicero sat forward, the intensity of his feelings obvious in every line of him. "Not so, Caius. Not at all. I am a general of Britain, true. Commander of a military district. For how long, God alone knows, since imperial favour is as fickle as it ever was. I may have been replaced since I came here, but, by God Himself, as long as I hold the rank and the privilege, I will direct all of my energies to the care of my responsibilities, which are all things military and civil within my jurisdiction. I will discharge my duties fairly and to the best of my abilities according to the ancient laws of Rome, which are the only laws I believe in. And my duty is to maintain the *Pax Romana* in my district and in this land. Nowhere else!" He stared around at each of us.

"You all heard Varo speak of the army appointing a new emperor. It would not be the first time, but this time it may be the last. I have heard talk that the army in Spain has done just that. One of their generals. I forget his name. If it's true, he'll have to fight for his title, and he'll be up against many another with ambitions the same as his. That is what makes the Empire's case so hopeless. It has become a matter of the conquest of the strongest, for the good of himself!" He had everyone's attention as he went on.

"You have all heard me clearly, I think. This island of ours is still an island of peace. But I know that there are some here in Britain who would like to see an emperor of Rome who lived right here. And, to an extent, I can agree with that. But only to a clearly defined extent. Where any man tries to set himself up as emperor of Rome from Britain, he will find himself in conflict with me. For that *is* treason. Rome *has* an emperor — three of the swine, in fact, all appointed and anointed by due process.

"But if, on the other hand, I should hear news of upstart emperors appearing as if by magic from the ranks of the armies in other lands, usurpers who would claw like vultures for the carcass of the world, then, on that day, I would rule in favour of establishing a just government on Roman, Republican lines to govern Britain. But Britain alone! Not the world. A government in Britain, for Britain, with a Senate for the governance of law, according to the Republican standards of our ancestors."

"Bravo, Antonius Cicero! If such a day comes in our lifetime, you will have my support in your rebellion." Caius leaned towards him. "But what will you do about the other possibility?"

"What other possibility?"

"The possibility that the emperor might go unchallenged? And that there will come a day when all the armies of all the far-flung outposts are recalled to Rome, on orders of the emperor himself, to defend the Motherland?" Caius continued to speak into the silence he had inspired. "It has to happen, my friends. We have starved the whole world to feed the maw of the Mob that Tonius spoke of. Now the world is full of angry people with no room to live, with no food to eat. And all of them can see that whatever they lack, Rome seems to hold. They want their share now. They see it as their right. Their sons have died for Rome, died by the million, down the centuries. By the million! And those that did not die went home as trained soldiers of Rome. These people *know* the Roman legions are a myth today. We all know it. We simply will not admit it."

Varo interrupted. "Caius, Caius! You exaggerate to prove your point, I think. It can't be all that bad! Listening to you, I can almost hear the screams of savages coming to burn this house! You argue for effect. Admit it."

"No!" The denial was emphatic. "Not true, Quintus. I am not exaggerating. There are only a few outposts of the Empire where the legions still retain some real strength, and they exist almost by accident. Tonius will agree with me." Cicero nodded his assent as Caius went on. "This island is one of them, because people like us — like you, like Varrus, like me — are kept away from the seat of power, from Rome and from Constantinople. Men like us are too prickly, Quintus, too unbending for Rome today. We offend their sensibilities just as surely as they offend ours. So we, and others like us, remain in the outposts and maintain our forces. And we, Quintus, and those others like us, are the last hope Rome has."

Caius turned to Cicero again. "When the crisis comes, Tonius, and it will — when the Roman homeland itself is about to be invaded — our legions *will* be recalled to the defence." He paused to let that sink in. "What will you do then?"

"I'll resign." It was a deep-throated growl, an unusual sound from his aristocratic throat.

Caius smiled. "No, Tonius, you won't be allowed to. That *would* be treason. Direct refusal to obey an imperial command. Instant death."

Cicero flared again. "Better to die that way than march my men into Hades for a cause I have no faith in, and then watch them slaughtered!" He paused and cleared his throat and spat into the fire. "Anyway," he went on, "it's not going to happen. At least not tomorrow, or the day after. I know for a fact that the Supreme Command is getting itself into an uproar. We're going to be seeing an upgrading of military values and spirit right across the world. For a while, at least. You mark my words: anybody trying to blunt the beak of the Eagle in future is going to be in for some rude surprises."

"Is that official? What's going on?" I asked him.

He looked at me and grunted. "Yes, you could say it's official. Official enough. Recruitment is on the increase all over, and the old standards are supposedly being revived and revised. Valentinian commissioned a study of the military a few years ago. It was done by some fellow called . . . I forget his name, but I've read his book. Pretty good. Nothing new in it, of course. But it praises the way things used to be done — the old ways."

"*Of Military Matters.*" Caius's voice was quiet. "Flavius Vegetius Renatus. I read it and enjoyed it. Is it going to do any good, do you think?"

"Required reading now for all officers. It's been accepted, if not as a training manual, then at least as the official text on weapons, methods and tactics."

"Good. Will it mean a return to armed camps?"

"Armed camps?" Tonius laughed scoffingly. "Hardly! You ask for miracles, Caius! Armed camps! We are far too civilized nowadays for that kind of nonsense! Our poor soldiers couldn't handle it."

"They handled it in my command."

"Ah, Caius! But you were a martinet. You were that crazed whoreson Britannicus whose men were all possessed by evil spirits, so that they behaved like machines instead of men! Nowadays our blasted officers are too afraid of mutiny to insist on discipline. Can you believe that? Roman officers afraid of their own men!"

I was inspecting the faces around the circle of firelight. They betrayed a wide range of reactions to what was being said by the two speakers, but every one of them was rapt, totally taken up by the discussion.

Now Caius sighed aloud. "Aye, I believe it, Tonius. I have seen it. So you think this grand new spirit is doomed?"

"Of course it's doomed. You said yourself, the rot is too far gone. It'll have an effect for a few years, I suppose. Perhaps ten, maybe even twenty, although I doubt it. But it cannot last. There is nothing to sustain it. All I can hope for is honourable retirement in the meantime."

He stopped talking and gazed into the embers again. The fire was almost out. I saw Caius look around him at his guests. Without exception, they wore expressions of gloom and despondency.

"My friends," he said, standing erect and stretching, "it is late and we're all tired. Tomorrow is a new day. There are games scheduled in the morning for the children. I suggest we leave them to their enjoyment and meet here again before noon."

We all eyed him curiously, wondering what was coming, and he did not leave us wondering.

"I have thought long and hard about this problem before tonight, as some of you know, and I have a few plans of my own. Tomorrow I will outline them for you. They may tie in with your plans; at least they will give you something to think about over the coming months. For now, let me say that you should not let tonight's discussions depress you too much. We have many things in our favour, believe me. Nothing is ever as bad as it seems. Good night. I'll see you all in the morning."

Gaius Gallus, however, was in no mood for going to bed, and neither was I, I found.

"Hold hard, Caius," he said. "It's not too late, unless you are too tired to continue." He looked around at the others. "What about you people? I for one would like a preview of some of these plans before I try to sleep tonight."

There was a chorus of assent from everyone, and I saw Plautus sit more erect and cross his arms over his chest, as though settling in for a long spell.

Caius looked all around the group, his eyebrow perched high on his forehead, and smiled slightly. "You all wish me to go on?" He clapped his hands together lightly. "I warn you, you might all be letting yourselves in for a late night." He looked at Terra and Firma. "Are you two hungry? You've been talking since you arrived and no one has even offered you a bite. There is plenty of food around. I could use another cup of ale before I start talking again."

Gallo, the steward, had been standing listening, and now he nodded to Caius and hurried off to organize more food.

"Everyone, a pause. We've been talking for a long time and I think it might be wise, before we go any further, to stop for a while and let things settle in our minds. Please, get up and move around a bit. Have something to eat, or something to drink. Talk among yourselves, or think things through on your own. If you have questions, think about them and get ready to bring them up.''

"I've got a question." The speaker was a man from Glevum, a friend of the family whose name escaped me.

Caius looked at him. "Ask it."

"Well, I know there's a latrine out here, somewhere close by, but I can't remember where and my bladder's about to burst. Where is it?"

The gathering broke up amid laughter as Caius answered him.

X X V

I stood up, rubbing my buttocks, and caught Plautus's eye as he crossed diagonally in front of me, headed for the courtyard of the main house where there was another, smaller latrine. He jerked his head at me, indicating that I should follow, and I fell into step beside him.

"Well, what d'you think of that?" he asked me.

"What, the whole thing?"

"Yes, the whole thing, the end of the Empire. A bit extreme, isn't it? I couldn't believe what I was hearing at first. I tell you, if I'd heard that from anyone other than Britannicus, at any time or place other than here and now, I'd have been out summoning the watch and getting ready to lay charges of sedition." He shook his head in disbelief and stepped aside to let me lead the way to the latrine in the far corner of the courtyard. "I've never heard the like," he continued, talking now to the back of my head. "Have you? Didn't that shake you up?"

"No." I glanced back at him. "Not really. I've heard it before. Caius and Luceiia and I have talked about it often." I stopped walking and turned to face him. "But you hadn't encountered this before. Tell me, did you believe what they were saying? What you were hearing?"

Plautus's face was troubled. He looked away from me, towards the lighted buildings on our right, his lips pulled

468

down in a grimace. I waited, saying nothing, until he turned back to me.

"Yes, damnation, I did," he said, his voice sounding tight and strained. "And it scared me."

I nodded, and we started walking again, coming finally to the walled latrine, where we did our business quickly, wasting no time in distancing ourselves from its odorous dankness.

Back in the cool night air, I paused again. "Listen," I said, "I'm going to go and say good night to my wife. I haven't seen much of her today, and I'd hate to have her thinking I prefer your company to hers. I'll join you back at the fire. But before I go I want to say this, just between you and me. You say you're scared. I think you've got good reason to be. We all have.

"I believe Caius, Plautus. I believe he's absolutely right. The Empire is finished. Everything's breaking down. I know it seems inconceivable. It did to me, too, for years, but there's just too much evidence that can't be ignored. What Terra and Firma told us is true, and they were among the biggest marine traders in the world. Now they're finished, not because they were incompetent, but simply because the system has collapsed. And their business is only one aspect of the mess. The rest of the world's in the same condition."

Somewhere in the darkness, quite close to where we stood, a woman laughed aloud, her voice subsiding into giggles and whispers. I took Plautus by the elbow and began to walk with him again, heading towards the flaming torches by the main doors to the house. He walked in silence, his head down, obviously grappling mentally with this concept of coming chaos.

"Hey!" I said, pulling him to a sudden stop so that he looked me in the eye. "I don't want you to be suicidal, soldier. It's not all bleak. Believe me, Caius has a plan to survive the chaos. I don't know exactly what it involves, but I'm sure it's a solid proposal. And no matter how outlandish it might seem tonight, it will work, believe me. Have I ever lied to you? Plautus? Have I?"

He looked at me and heaved a great, gusty sigh, grinning sheepishly at his own fears. "No, comrade, you never have. Not about anything important."

"Right. And I don't intend to start now. The world as we know it won't end tomorrow, or even next year. It might take decades. Go and listen to Caius, what he has to say. I'll join you in a few minutes. Listen well. And count yourself into whatever he suggests."

I watched him walk away to rejoin the circle around the fire and wondered about the unseen but terrifying dimensions of any information that could have this kind of profound effect on a man as basic and straightforward as Plautus. I had known him ever since my first military posting. Plautus was a bull: nothing daunted him and he feared no man. When he had gone, I went to my wife to tell her I would be late.

I was already late. She was soundly asleep and lusciously warm beneath the covers, and I was sorely tempted to join her there, but I kissed her gently without waking her and contented myself with lying on the bed beside her for a few moments. When I was sure she would not awaken I slipped one cautious, caressing hand beneath the covers and snuggled my face carefully into the hollow of her shoulder, revelling in the warm, perfumed scent of her. The few moments stretched into an appreciable time span, and I almost fell asleep, so that I had to force myself to get up again. I went on my way then, reluctantly, with the memory of the warmth of her breast caressing my palm.

By the time I got back to the fire, Gallo had produced what seemed like a wagonload of fresh food and drink, and everyone was clustered around it. The meeting had already resumed by mutual consent, even before the food's arrival, and things had moved on so far that Plautus had to bring me up to date while everyone was eating.

"You were right. Your friend Caius there has the whole thing sewn up like a mummy's gut."

"How? What's his plan?"

He grunted, wrestling the thigh bone of a large fowl from its joint. It came free with a voluptuous ripping sound that started my own saliva flowing. He slapped it onto a wooden platter and picked up half a loaf of bread, wiping his greasy fingers on it before taking a bite and speaking through a full mouth.

"Bagaudae. He ever talk to you about them?"

I laughed and looked across at Caius, who was standing alone, pouring himself some mead. "Yes, frequently. Caius admires them. He thinks their way of life is a good one."

"Hmmph," Plautus mumbled, swallowing the food in his mouth. "Good? He makes them sound like they own the universe."

"You think he plans to set up a Bagaudae community here?"

"Sounds like it. Sounds like it might work, too, until some son of a whore decides to come along and upset the whole cart. That's the only drawback I can see, but it's a big one. I wonder if he's thought about that? About the impossibility of defending the place?"

I smiled at him. "Plautus, if he hasn't thought about it, it will be the first time I have ever known him to miss anything important. Caius is a meticulous animal when it comes to details."

He quaffed half a cup of wine and ripped off a mouthful of succulent cold fowl, speaking around his mouthful again. "Well, we'll see. It's the first thing I'm going to ask him about. Right now."

The others were all moving back to their seats by the fire and I loaded a platter hastily, ripping off the other thigh of the fowl that had looked so good and sprinkling it liberally with salt. By the time I had poured a flagon of ale and turned back, they were into the discussion again, and Plautus was talking to Caius.

"Don't misunderstand me," he was saying as I sat down. "I think your concept is a good one. I like the idea of everyone pulling his weight and contributing. No parasites. That's good. But — and I think this is a big but — where will you find the right people to make it work? And how would you define your priorities in setting up this community?"

Surprised at the unusual fluency shown by the normally taciturn Plautus, I glanced around the faces of the group and saw that they were all endorsing his questions.

"All right, Caius," I thought, "I've been wondering about that, too."

Caius was smiling. "Valid questions, Plautus, and I'll try to answer them as clearly as I can." He looked around the group again. "But let's be clear in our understanding of the context, all of us. Bear in mind that we are doing more than merely talking about survival here. We are now planning for it! This is real. We are talking about the end of the world we know. We believe, each of us, that, like it or not, that end is going to come, and when it does happen, when the Empire falls, nothing that we know today will ever be the same again. *Nothing*! The legions will be gone — gone completely. That means there will be no law. Think of that! The law will be gone! That means no judicial system backed by the force of arms or government. No civic law, because the towns and cities will have no garrisons and no system of enforcement. On the bright side, there will be no taxes to pay, and no bureaucrats to demand them.

"No more roads will be built, and those that exist now will fall quickly into disrepair. There will be no troops in the forts of the Saxon Shore to defend against seaborne raiders." He paused again and looked at every man. "And there will be no food available to those who do not grow their own. Think about that one fact alone, my friends. No food, unless you grow your own! The cities are going to starve. You heard Terra and Firma. It is happening already."

His next words fell on us with the force of hammer blows, bludgeoning our disbelief.

"The entire world is going to go down into chaos when Rome falls, and the biggest danger facing anyone today is the temptation to believe that it cannot, or that it will not happen. Believe me, my friends, the only people who will survive that fall will be those people who have prepared for it by preparing themselves. By preparing their own defences. By preparing their own food supplies. By planning for their own continued, structured existence in advance of the time of chaos."

He took a coin from a pocket in his robe and flipped it into the air, catching it as it fell. "You may think I am being over-dramatic, but here's another thought." He held up the coin. "There will be no more of this made. No more. Even today, it is next to useless. The price of gold has risen beyond belief! So, what will we do without money? Those who have it will hoard it, but with no new supply, the hoarders will soon face the day when it has lost all value, for men will have stopped using it. They will have gone back to the barter system. Among ourselves, in our community, we have to stop using it immediately." His pause held us as much as his words and his automatic assumption that we were going to go along with his suggestions. "I say 'immediately' because I want you to be aware that we, the people gathered here, with all our families, our friends, our servants and our neighbours, are going to survive. All of us. We have the will, the intellect, the necessary skills, the ability, the tenacity and the advantage of foreknowledge. We *will* survive. And we will prosper. And we will preserve an island of real Roman virtues, Roman values, Roman worth and Roman standards of freedom and dignity here in this island of Britain."

It was a stirring piece of rhetoric. When he had finished, he sat there looking from one to the other of us, and nobody moved or spoke. The silence stretched and grew, and eventually he started speaking again, taking up where he had stopped.

"Of course, as you have heard Tonius say, the end is not going to come tomorrow or the day after. But you have also heard Terra and Firma, and you know they are correct. It may take ten years, it may take twenty, or even more, but it is going to come, my friends."

Another silence, then Gaius Gallus asked, "So, when do we start organizing this community you speak of? And how? You still haven't answered Plautus's questions."

Caius pursed his lips. "I will now, and yours, too. We have started. It has begun, tonight. You asked about priorities, Plautus. Well, let's start with defences. Tonius? Am I wrong to place this aspect first?"

Plautus and Tonius both smiled, Plautus looking at me, and Tonius said, "No, Caius. I would doubt your sanity if you placed it anywhere else."

"Well, then. How do you see our case?"

Tonius, now in the role of Legate Cicero, General of the armies, shrugged. "I have no idea. How big a territory do you want to hold?"

"This valley."

"All of it?" There was surprise in his voice.

"Why not? It is a Roman enclave."

"But it must be twelve miles square, Caius!"

"Fourteen long by about eleven wide, I estimate."

"That is a lot of land to defend."

"Nowhere near as big as the Empire, Tonius. The entire plain is four times that large. Eventually, I hope to cover all of it."

"That's all very well, Caius." This was Plautus again. He seemed to have completely forgotten his awe of officers. "But where will you find the men?"

"We will find them, Plautus, have no fear of that. Given the time, we'll breed them! Grow them ourselves!" This brought a welcome gust of laughter. "In the meantime, every able-bodied citizen of the new Colony will bear arms, as our ancestors did in the beginning.

Soldiering will be a part of farming. It will be a feature of our community life. As our numbers grow, our armed strength will grow. Tonius, where would you base our forces, when we have enough?"

There was a pause as Cicero mulled this over. "Up on the hills. There are some old Celtic forts on the high hills of this region, without getting into the mountains. I would refurbish them. They are well placed."

"Aye." Caius nodded. "They overlook all of the plains below. I had already decided the same thing myself. Hearing you back my judgment settles it. There is one less than a mile from where we sit right now. When it was in use it must have been prodigious. I have examined it, and I believe it could be adapted to our needs with very little effort. Comparatively speaking, of course."

Plautus smiled a wicked smile. "General Britannicus, how firm are you on the old disciplines?"

"Completely."

"Then I'm with you." He smiled that wicked smile again. "So! There's your first priority: defence. How many forts do you think we'll need?"

Caius's tone was confident. "One will suffice for now. The others can come later. As we grow stronger."

Plautus nodded, accepting this. "Then you think we will grow stronger?"

"I know it."

"Good. What next?"

"After defences?" Caius looked around his listeners, catching each man's eye before continuing. "People. We have to start planning for our future needs. We will need builders, stonemasons, bakers, weavers, thatchers, barrelmakers and a hundred other tradesmen."

Tonius Cicero interrupted. "What about control? In the sense of law, I mean. Government. Have you thought about that?"

"I have. I would like to see a Council established, exactly like the ancient Senate."

There was a murmur of approval. Our start had been well made. The rest of the night was given over to planning in more detail. The more we talked, the greater grew the problems we foresaw, and yet, in spite of that, our vision grew apace with them, and our thinking became the more ambitious.

Plans were made to buy up surrounding villas and to link them all defensively as soon as possible. We knew we had time to measure in years, but we could not bank on even one decade.

Lists were compiled of all the skilled people we would need to make us self-supporting, and each man there was alert from that time on to finding men of the calibre we sought. Before the discussion ended, everyone present was sworn to secrecy in the knowledge that, until the day came when the legions left, our entire scheme was treasonous. Talking carelessly of it could mean death for everyone concerned.

By the time the wedding feast came to an end four days later, others had been recruited, and each man who knew our plans took home with him a dream of hope for the future. Each knew that the safety and well-being of his entire family lay in his own hands. And each had already begun to plan how he would transport his worldly goods to Caius's Colony when the time came. There were heartfelt smiles and handclasps at the time of parting.

XXVI

On the morning after the last of our guests left, I was up with the larks and away into the Mendip Hills alone, not even wishing to share this visit with Equus. I left my wife abed, smiling with smug satisfaction, while my own mind concentrated singularly on the search for my skystones.

Now that all the festivities were over, I was frustrated and impatient. The stones I had found were all too small. They were far from tiny, but none of them was large enough to offer me any great hope of being able to smelt heavenly metals from them. I felt strongly that there was something in the Valley of the Dragons, as we had come to call it, that I was missing — something that lay just beyond my vision, or just beyond my comprehension. More than three months had gone by since my last visit, and I was hoping that the time lag would enable me to see the valley with new eyes.

My hope was fulfilled that day in a way that I could not have dreamed of. The information my eyes relayed to my brain was so startling and so overwhelming that I did not trust myself to believe the evidence of my own senses. I rode back to the villa at breakneck speed, almost choking on my excitement.

It was dark by the time I got back. I leaped from my horse before its hooves stopped clattering on the cobblestones of the courtyard and shouted a greeting to my wife, who came running to welcome me home. We bathed together and I told her of my discoveries, and then for a long time we made little noise.

It must have been approaching the tenth hour when I entered Caius's *cubiculum* and found him reading by the light of two bright lamps. I was surprised to find him there, for I had presumed him abed long since. He was immersed in Ovid's *Art of Love* and feeling, he told me later, mildly nostalgic for the vanished pleasures of youth.

"Caius? Am I disturbing you?"

He looked up with pleased surprise. "No, not at all! It is a pleasure to see you back on your feet again."

I felt the blankness of incomprehension on my face. "What?"

"I said it's good to see you up and around again. Marriage makes more men take to their beds than illness ever will."

"Ohh!" I smiled, suddenly self-conscious. "I see what you mean."

"Come in. Sit down and pay no attention to me. I was merely tweaking your nose. Perhaps I am growing jealous of your youth."

"Are you so old, then, General? So suddenly?"

"Don't call me that. I'm old enough to know what I can do and what I'll never do again, my friend. What have you done today?"

"Caius —"

I started to blurt out what it was I had to tell him, but then I restrained myself. He watched me clench my lips and inhale deeply through my nostrils. Then I bit down on my breath and expelled the air explosively between

my lips, the way a horse does. Caius waited, patient as
always, for me to arrange my thoughts in order. Finally,
I began speaking, feeling that I had the right words.

"I wanted to come to you with this as soon as I got
back, but I was — distracted — as you have observed."

He smiled. "Where is she now, that your distraction
has faded?"

"Asleep. Caius, what had you planned to do tomorrow?"

"Nothing that cannot be changed. What do you have
in mind for me to do?"

"Could you stand the journey up into the hills with
me? There's something I would like to show you. I need
your advice."

"I can think of nothing I would enjoy more. What do
you have to show me?"

I shook my head. "I would rather not say, right now.
You might think I had lost my wits. But it's important. I
think I'm right. In fact, I know I'm right. But I haven't
got the courage yet to back up my conviction. That's why
I want you to see this for yourself, and to advise me. If
I'm wrong, and I could be, I'd feel very foolish."

The Britannican eyebrow was up. "You intrigue me,
Publius. This sounds fascinating. I can hardly wait to see
what it is. Will I recognize it?"

"I hope so, Caius. I hope so!"

"It has to do with your skystones, obviously."

"Yes, it does."

He raised his thumb and forefinger to the sides of his
mouth, pinching his lower lip outward and downward,
as though wiping away dried crumbs from a recent
meal. "I saw some of them this morning, in the smithy.

Equus told me what they were. I was hoping to talk to you about them."

"What were you doing in the smithy? You don't often go down there."

He smiled and told me what he had done that morning.

Apparently the villa had been as quiet as a tomb that day, after all the preceding weeks of hurly-burly, and Caius had been hard put to remind himself that this was normal. He had prowled the grounds like a lost soul, angry at himself for having slept later than usual and losing some precious hours. Then he found out I had been gone since dawn, up into the hills, and that increased his bad temper, for some reason. Luceiia, he said, had tried to be nice to him over breakfast but knew her brother well enough to see that he was in one of his most foul frames of mind and left him to his own devices.

He had spent two fruitless and frustrating hours trying to write, but found himself too volatile to concentrate for any length of time on what he was about, and eventually, some time after noon, he had found himself in the smithy, watching Equus pounding a glowing ingot.

Equus had looked up and seen him standing there, and had greeted him, calling him "Gen'ral!" He had picked that up from me.

They had exchanged pleasantries for a while, and then Equus had returned to his work, leaving Caius to his own devices. Caius had then walked to the back of the smithy and idly examined the bizarre-looking stones that lay there on the shelf along the wall.

"Funny-looking things, aren't they?" Equus's voice had startled him.

"What are?" he'd asked.

"Them skystones."

Only then had Caius realized what he was looking at, for I had kept them secret even from him, so keen was my disappointment in their size. Now he examined them more closely. There were seven of them, ranging in size from the smallest, about the size of a new-born baby's head, to the largest, which was the size of a half-grown boy's head. They were all the same kind of stone, a heavy, dull grey-black. And all of them were smooth: not the worn smoothness of a watered pebble, but more of a glassy texture. He had picked up one of the intermediate ones and hefted it, thinking that, if I were correct, this thing had fallen from the sky! His logical Roman mind told him that was impossible. Everything must come from somewhere, so where had it fallen *from*? Caius knew, as every child knows, that in order for something to come down from high in the air, it first has to be put up into the air. But the weight of this thing, he realized as he held it, made the thought of its being hurled upwards from the earth into the sky more than ludicrous. It was impossible. He knew how high and how far the strongest catapult could throw such a stone. He had seen his own armies hurl them, and they never were lost from sight. So how could this thing have fallen from the sky, on fire, as he knew I believed, and struck the earth with such ferocity that it could bury itself and throw up a ring of earth twelve or more feet across?

And yet, as he admitted to me that night, its surface did seem as though it had been melted at some time. And he knew I had dug it up from the middle of one of my "dragon's nests." At least, he thought he knew that.

At this point in his recital, Caius stopped and looked at me, waiting for me to say something. I did not know what he expected, so I shrugged.

"That is correct. I dug it up from a dragon's nest. What are you struggling with, Caius?"

He shook his head in bewilderment. "I don't know, Publius. All my education tells me that what you are asking me to believe is impossible. And yet you stand there facing me with all the confidence of an augurer who has just pulled a rotting heart from a healthy chicken. Until I see metal from these stones, I will never be able to accept your contention that they fell from the sky. And even then, I feel constrained to point out, any credence I give to the matter will be based strongly upon nothing more than my faith in your peculiar style of madness." He paused for a short space. "But, as I say, your positive results have me mystified. What is it that you want me to look at tomorrow?"

The following forenoon found us high on the hill overlooking the valley of my dragons. There were only three of us — Caius, Equus and me — and Caius, at least, had enjoyed the ride up into the hills.

"So, Publius, this is the valley of the famous dragon's nests. I had forgotten how magnificent it is." He nodded towards a newly dug hole in the hillside. "I presume that is one of them?"

"Yes. And there's another down there to your left. And one more to your right, across there. Seven of them in all, General."

"Seven. I can see only four. And each of them has yielded you a skystone?"

"Yes."

"So what is worrying you? Are there no more?"

"Oh, there's more. I've found ten that I haven't dug for yet. But they are all too small." I hawked and spat. "The largest of the seven I have came from the largest 'nest' I could find. The nests are really impact rings, thrown up by the force of the stones' landing. The biggest of those is twelve long paces across."

"Twelve paces?" Caius began to gnaw his lower lip. "Varrus," he said at last, "I have to be honest. I know I've said this before, and I know you're probably sick of hearing it, but even if your stone *did* fall from the sky, my mind cannot grasp the prospect of a stone that small falling hard enough to blast an impression that big."

"No more can mine, General." I tried hard to keep my voice impassive. "But the fact remains: it happened. Believe me. It fell. And it created that impact ring. Only God Himself can know where it came from. Perhaps it fell from a star. Perhaps it *was* a star!"

Caius tutted disapproval. "Stars are light, Publius. These stones of yours are black."

"They are now, Caius. But they fell as fire. Iron is black when it is cold, but heat it and it takes on a white and blinding brightness. And we are hampered by the fuel we have to heat it with! Given the fires of Heaven, who can tell how bright it might become?"

I knew there was no answer for that. Caius stared at me in perplexity.

"Anyway," I went on, "that is the biggest I am likely to find here, unless my guess today is correct. The stone my grandfather found was more than twice that size, and by the time he smelted it, he was left with just enough metal for a dagger and the best part of a sword. That's all."

He was quick to see my chagrin. "But if you smelt all seven of them together? Would not that produce enough to fit your needs? And what of the other ten?"

I shrugged. "Perhaps. Who knows? I have no way of knowing how much metal there is in such small stones. There might be none."

Caius looked down into the valley again. "What was it that you wanted me to see?"

"A dragon's nest, Caius, bigger than all the rest combined. A mighty dragon's nest."

"Where? In the valley?"

"Aye. In plain sight. But you must see it for yourself, with your own eyes. I cannot help you. If I did, I might not be convinced myself that you could truly see it. I looked at it for months, not knowing it was there. You know it is now. Find it for me, Caius. You too, Equus."

Heeding the plea in my words, they began to scan the valley, and I watched them closely as they looked. I saw them discern each of the rings I had already found and identified with a cairn of stones, but nowhere could either of them see a mighty ring, try as they would. I watched Caius in particular as his gaze ranged the entire valley, from the raw cliff at one end to the lake tucked into the folding hillside at the other. He scanned each hill from top to bottom. Nothing.

Finally he spoke again. "Are you sure what I am looking for is there, Publius?"

"Aye," I said, with more confidence than I felt. "It is there. What I am not sure of is that it is what I *think* it is."

"And I should be able to see it? Now?"

"Correct."

He tried again, sweeping from north to south, from east to west, again and again, not knowing what he was supposed to see. And then I saw him catch a shape from the corner of his eye, or an impression of a shape. He jerked to look, and it was gone. But it had been there, I knew it had been there, for I had seen the same thing the day before. I watched him move his eyes off slowly and held my breath, praying he would see it again. Then, from the quickening of his gaze, I knew he had found it again and recognized it for what it was. Now he looked straight at it and saw it clearly. Not a circle, but a segment of a circle — a clear-edged part of one. I watched his startled gaze adjusting to the size of it, and my heart began to beat faster.

"The lake, Varrus," he whispered at last in a voice full of wonder. "The lake is a dragon's nest! But huge! Enormous!"

I leaped from my horse and dragged him down from his, pinning him to my breast and swinging him around in triumph and shouting at the top of my voice.

"I knew it, Caius! I knew you would see it! The lake is it! A huge bowl full of water! Not circular, because the hillside absorbed much of the shock. And the debris and boulders blocked the flow of water down through the valleys below, and turned the impact ring into a lake!"

I set him back on his feet and together we stared down at it.

"And that explains the cattle, too," I added, suddenly realising the truth.

Caius looked at me. "What cattle? What d'you mean?"

"The dead cattle." I realized then that he had not heard that part of the story. "There was a herd of cattle, apparently, in the valley the night the skystones landed. They were all killed, naturally enough, but there was something about it that didn't make sense. It bothered me. I thought it was highly unlikely that anyone would drive those animals all the way over the hills, into the valley, when the grazing was just as good on the other side." I nodded down again towards the lake.

"But there's the answer. The valley must have been open at that end before the cataclysm, so it would have been accessible to the cattle, offering shelter from the winds. The upheaval caused by the skystone blocked off the access and threw up the rim that now contains the lake."

"But didn't Meric say there had always been a lake there?"

"Aye, and there probably was. But it would have been smaller, and shallower. That's where the mud came from that coated everything the day after. The skystone must have blasted every drop of water and mud out of the lake and punched a deeper bed for it."

I turned to Equus and he was gaping at both of us as though we had gone mad. Caius saw this too, and we both broke out in laughter.

"Equus!" I asked him, "what's the matter? Can't you see it, man?"

"Aye, I can see it. It's a massy lake! So what's all the excitement about? How will you find a skystone at the bottom of a lake? That's what I'd like to know."

"The same way he found the others, Equus!" Caius was jubilant. "He will dig for it!"

Now Equus knew that we were both quite mad. It was plain on his face. We fell about with laughter as he became completely confounded. Finally I took pity on him and pulled myself together enough to put his mind at ease.

"Equus," I said gasping, "it's a simple matter of military engineering. We'll drain the lake, letting the water run down into the other valleys. Then, when the mud at the bottom of the lake has dried out, we'll dig up the skystone."

Poor Equus! He was enormously relieved, and we soon sat down to eat the meal that we had brought with us. We had not brought much wine, but we were so light-headed that what we had was ample.

XXVII

The buck was magnificent — sleek, beautiful, graceful and not yet come to prime. He had emerged almost unnoticeably from the copse in the dawn light, solidifying magically from the low-lying mist and moving forward delicately, picking his way on tiptoe through the knee-high, dew-drenched grass of the meadow. His breath steamed visibly in the motionless air so that it seemed he was producing the mist by himself, and through the screen of young leaves that hid me from him, I could see water droplets hanging from his antlers like precious stones. Slowly, careful to make no sudden sound or motion, I drew my bowstring back towards my ear, feeling the tension of the braided sinew on my calloused fingertips and the long, lethal glide of the shaft of the iron-barbed arrow against my thumb. My drawing thumb touched my cheek and as it did so the buck froze, head up, ears forward, a perfect target. I closed one eye, sighting carefully.

"No, Publius! No!"

The cry startled me as much as it did the buck, shattering my concentration so that I flinched and jerked the bow high, straining my muscles against the instinct to release the arrow. By the time I looked again, my beautiful buck had vanished. Slowly, gritting my teeth, I released the tension on my bow. Then I turned around to where Luceiia stood watching me, the fingertips of one hand touching her lips and her eyes wide and filled with apprehension. With her other hand she clutched a blanket she had wrapped around her against the morning chill. I made no move towards her and she simply stood there, waiting for my anger to break over her for the first time.

"Why did you do that?" I asked her, calmly.

She blinked her own deer-like eyes at me. "I . . . he was too beautiful. I didn't want you to kill him."

"I divined that much already, Luceiia. But why did you find it necessary to frighten me out of a year's growth as well as tonight's dinner?"

"What? Frighten you? How did . . . ?" Her eyes changed slightly, crinkling to a smile. "Did I startle you?"

I nodded slowly, seriously, drinking in her marvellous beauty as she stood there unaware that her nakedness beneath the blanket was clearly visible.

"Half to death," I said. "What would you have done had I fallen dead? How would you have felt? Would the buck have comforted you?"

Her hand moved up to cover her mouth completely, masking the laugh that now danced in her eyes. "You are not angry?"

"I asked you how you would have felt had I died of shock, woman. Answer me."

Instead of speaking she shivered, giggled and turned to dart back towards the leather tent hidden among the saplings behind her. I chased her and caught her at the entrance flap and bore her down onto the still-warm pile of furs inside.

Hours later, riding through a golden springtime morning, she was still talking about the deer whose life she had saved, pointing out that, had I killed him, I would have had to spend time cleaning, skinning and butchering him, so that we would have lost the glory of the early day. Besides, she said, the buck was young — too young to have experienced life and the wonders of mating. Was I so jaded and indifferent to life that I could deny its pleasures to another, even to a deer?

The spring sun shone warm and strong on us, and her eyes sparkled with health and humour. The long, clean lines of her thigh filled out the soft leather breeches she wore for riding. My breath thickened in my throat as I followed her contours with my eyes, although for the moment I was content to ride alongside her, listening with pleasure to her prattling and feasting my eyes on her crystalline beauty. This was my wife! Even after almost a full month of marriage I still had to keep reminding myself of this. She was mine! I could have her and enjoy her any time I wanted to, for the remainder of our lives.

"You are not listening, Publius."

The singsong notes of her comment brought me back to attention with a start.

"I was day-dreaming. Forgive me. What were you saying?"

"I was saying, husband dear, that I feel a sorrow, a sympathy, for the poor animals."

"What animals? Deer? Why?"

"Not merely deer — all animals." She was grinning at me, mischief dancing in her eyes. "Because of the way they are tied to seasons and have no hands."

I felt myself frowning. "I don't follow you."

"I know you don't, because you haven't been listening. But you would follow me if I slipped from my horse and from my clothing here in this long, lush grass, would you not?"

"What?" I felt my stomach tighten with anticipation and glanced around me involuntarily. "You mean here? On this open hillside?"

"Open?" Her laugh was tinkling bells. "We are miles from anywhere, husband, and I want you. I want to feel your hands and your body and the cool greenness of this grass on my skin."

Somehow our horses had stopped moving, and the air between us seemed to solidify and tremble, drawing me towards her.

"You are a shameless wanton," I muttered, hoarsely.

"Completely, with you."

She laughed again and seemed to flow down from her horse's back and into the long grass, and I almost fell from my own mount in my rush to join her.

Our horses grazed contentedly nearby for more than an hour while we dallied in the rich warmth of the sun, and then she suddenly sat up and reached for her clothes.

"I am lost, husband," she said. "How far are we from the valley?"

I remained where I was, supine and spread-eagled, and pointed with my thumb over my head in the direction of the crest of the hill above us.

"Just on the other side of the summit, there," I told her. "About a half hour ride to the top, and we'll be looking down into it."

She leaned across to kiss my chest and then caught hold of my flaccid maleness, pulling it gently but firmly upwards as if it were a handle by which she could lift me.

"Well then," she said, "up off your lazy rump and let's go and look at it."

I started to rise and then lay back, staring into the sky.

"Look, up there, right above us."

Sitting as she was, she could not see anything, so I pulled her back down beside me and we lay side by side for minutes, watching two tiny crosses floating in the sky a mile and more above us.

"What are they, Publius? Dragons?" I could hear the smile in her voice.

"No," I said, "those are eagles. A mating pair."

"A mating pair? You mean they are mating now?"

"Hardly, my love. I meant that they are male and female."

"How do you know that? And how do you know they are eagles? They could be hawks."

"No, too high up. And look at the wing span, even from here." I reached out and took her hand where it lay beside me. "Those are eagles. They're probably watching us watching them."

"You mean they can see us from that height?"

"Probably better than we can see them. The eagle's eye is the keenest in the world."

She squeezed my fingers. "Do you think they are in love?"

"Probably. Eagle love. They mate for life."

She leaned up on one elbow, looking down at me. "Really? I didn't know that."

I squinted at her. "Come now, I thought you knew everything!"

"No." She lowered her head to my chest. "Not every-thing. Just the things I need to know and the things I want to know." She paused for a while, then asked, "Where do you think their nest might be?"

I lowered a hand to caress her hair. "I don't know, but it must be around here somewhere. This is the hatching season. They must have chicks. Wherever it is, it's somewhere high up. Probably on one of the hilltops, on a cliff face. They nest in the same place every year, too, you know."

"The same mate and the same nesting place for life? They sound almost human."

I still had not taken my eyes from the two solitary shapes wheeling above us. "Don't malign them, Luceiia. Some humans, very few, attain the dignity and honour, you might almost say the purity, of eagles. Very, very few."

"What do you mean, Publius?" Her voice was very quiet.

"I mean that only eagles can be eagles, my love, and eagles can only be eagles. They are unique. They never demean or disgrace themselves. Their purity is absolute because they are incapable of voluntary imperfection."

She kissed me. "Just like you, you mean?"

I returned her kiss. "No, Luceiia, not like me at all. I'm far too human."

"Then, husband, if you are too human, no man can ever hope to be an eagle."

I sat up and reached for my own clothes. "That's not true, my love," I said. "Have you ever looked closely at your brother?"

She lay still and blinked her eyes in silence.

The great birds were still circling above us when we crossed the summit of the hill and looked down into the Valley of the Dragons. I showed her where we had unearthed the skystones we had found, and then I pointed out the circle segment in the lake side. As I started to lead the way along the crest of the hill towards the lake, she spoke again.

"It seems strange to realize that those massive stones at the bottom there are broken pieces of mountain." She stared at the cliff opposite. "Could that be where the eagles have their nest?"

I turned and looked across the valley to the great rock face. "Very probably. It's sheer enough, and inaccessible."

She rode in silence as we approached the lake, and soon we reined in our horses right above it, looking down into its depths. It was a genuine lake, much larger than a normal mountain tarn. This close, all sign of the circle segment we had seen from the distance had vanished. The bright sky and the sun above gave the surface a much friendlier aspect than some I had seen, and I was pleased that she was seeing it at its most appealing.

"Well," I asked her, "what do you think? Have I wasted your time dragging you out here and making you spend the night in a leather tent?"

"No." Her voice was subdued. "It's very large, Publius. Much larger than I remember. How deep is it?"

I angled my mount closer and placed a hand on her shoulder, feeling the strength of her.

"I don't really know. No way of telling. But it's deep. My estimate would be about a hundred feet or so at its deepest, judging from the slope of the valley floor, but I could be short by half as much again or even more."

"A hundred and fifty feet? And you intend to drain it? How? Where will you drain it to? Where will it all go?"

"Come, I'll show you." I led her for another half mile around to the western rim of the lake where she could see for herself the steep fall of the land down into the neighbouring valley. "Can you see what happened here? The impact of the falling stones threw up this rim across the end of the valley, building up the natural dam that was here already and strengthening it. You can see how new the fall is here, on this side. See it?" She nodded and I went on. "The lake here is like wine in a bowl. All we have to do is crack the side of the bowl, down there, by digging a hole into it, and the wine will spill down into the valley below, there, and then down into the next one, and so on until it reaches the plain and flows into the streams and rivers."

"That will be dangerous, Publius, won't it?"

"How?"

"Digging that hole into the side of the bowl, as you call it. It will be dangerous. What if you dig too far?"

"No." I shook my head disparagingly. "It's simple engineering, Luceiia. There's nothing to it."

She was staring at me keenly. "Perhaps not, for an engineer. You are not an engineer."

"So? What of it? Engineers can be bought, my love."

"Where?"

I shrugged. "Anywhere."

"Where?" Her voice was edged with determination.

"Many places."

"*Where*?"

"Ye gods! I don't know! I haven't even started searching yet, Luceiia."

"Where will you start?"

I shrugged again, suddenly uncomfortable with this inquisition. It seemed she was determined to be difficult. I was wrong, however, as her next words showed.

"This is very important to you, Publius, so it is also very important to me, but I will not have you grubbing and digging around down there on your own, so think! If you had to find an engineer, urgently, for anything, where would you start looking?"

I gaped at her, feeling the surprise on my face. "The army."

"Exactly. The army. Surely you and Caius have enough friends and influence between you to arrange to borrow a decent engineer? What about Tonius Cicero? Could he not arrange something?"

For the space of a few seconds I was filled with elation, but then my spirits slumped again. She was watching my face closely and noticed it.

"What's wrong?"

"Nothing," I said. "And everything. It is a fine idea, but it would not work. Caius would never condone the use of imperial troops for a private operation like this, and when I think of it, I wouldn't, either."

"Why not, if it benefits the army, too? I heard Tonius myself, during the wedding feast, saying that his people are always trying to find something to do to give their men experience in different areas. It seems to me that this operation would make an exciting training project — a tactical exercise in the physical removal of large volumes of water."

I couldn't get close enough to her to kiss her, but she came to me. "My love," I told her, "you are your brother's sister!"

"No, I am the wife of Publius Varrus."

I hugged her to me with one arm and looked above to the silent birds wheeling overhead.

The eagles were still there when I returned exactly one month later and sat in the same spot with a small group of serving officers, a special team assembled from Glevum, Venta Belgarum and the great gold mines of Dolocauthi in the mountains of Cambria. Each of these men was a professional in the manipulation of water, and Verecundius Secundus, the senior among them, was directly responsible for drainage and water flow at Dolocauthi itself, where two great open-channel aqueducts, one of them seven miles long, delivered three million gallons of water a day to wash the crushed, gold-bearing ore. Secundus had the responsibility of maintaining the great wooden water wheels that drained all of the overflow of this water from the open-cast workings and the underground galleries of the mine, some of which went down more than a hundred feet.

The group sat silent for a spell, each man gazing around him, noting the fall of the land below, the steepness of the gradients and the angle of the retaining wall of the dam-like structure on which we sat.

"Well, Secundus? How does it look to you?"

"Cicero was right." He did not look at me, his eyes still busy gauging and estimating. "An interesting exercise. Straightforward enough, but a degree of difficulty that'll keep our trainees on their toes." He glanced at me, and then at Rufus Seculus, his colleague from Venta. "I like it. I think we should do it. Rufus?"

Rufus Seculus grunted. "Aye. As you say, though, there are problems. It's not going to be an overnight job. This is going to take a lot of planning. Hit that hillside the wrong way and you could wash a lot of men away when that juice squirts out. Especially since we'll be using trainees and not experienced sappers. What's your opinion, Rasmus?"

Erasmus Lecio was the third member of the group, a grey-haired veteran of many wars. He had been listening to their exchange with his lips pursed and a frown of concentration on his face. Now he spat a glob of phlegm and spoke.

"I think if we tackle this without at least a major contingent of veterans we should all face a court martial. It's a good training project — I've got no objections on that ground — but it could be nastier than a sharp-toothed whore. I'd hate to have to rely on green sappers all the way in this one. You're right, Seculus. This dam is new, from the looks of it, and it wasn't built by Romans. No telling what kind of mess is underneath us, or how unstable it is. Every shovelful that comes out of the sap down there could be the critical one that's holding the whole whoreson lake in check. I wouldn't want to be the one responsible for it if some green trainee who doesn't know his rectum from his throat makes a mistake and empties the whole sewer at the wrong time. Let's do it, by all means, but let's be sure we know what we're doing, every step of the way."

Seculus turned back to me. "What did you say you wanted this drained for?"

I grinned. "There's a stone buried in the mud at the bottom of it. I want it."

"I thought that's what you said. A stone. In the mud. Did you throw it in yourself?"

"No." I grinned. "It fell in."

"I see. And now you want to get it out. Is it a big stone?"

"I think so."

"You think so."

I could see by his face he thought I had lost my wits, but he was not going to insult me openly to my face by saying so.

"Have you any notion of how much mud there is at the bottom of a lake, Master Varrus?"

I nodded, still smiling. "Quite a lot, I should imagine."

"It doesn't dismay you?" I shook my head, and his eyes narrowed as he asked, "What are you really after?"

"I told you. A stone. A big stone in the mud at the bottom. Look, Seculus, I know you don't believe me, but it's the truth, and if I told you any more you would really think me sick in the head. I think the stone is really there, and it is valuable to me, and only to me. At least, I think it is valuable. It may not be. But I have to find it first, before I'll know." Their expressions were wondrous to behold and I laughed aloud. "I swear I'm speaking truth. Come, let's go back down to the villa. By the time we get there it'll be almost dark. Over dinner tonight, I promise you, Caius Britannicus will tell you the whole story. In the meantime, even if you do not believe it, and even if the stone is not there, your trainee engineers will have gained the experience of draining a lake and no harm will have been done, except to my dreams."

They accepted this, and later they accepted Britannicus's story of my quest for the stones from heaven, and because they were who they were, they asked intelligent questions that I tried to answer as well as I could. Thereafter, they went about their tasks of planning and organization as if it were the most natural and the most urgent thing in the world that the millions of gallons of water and mud between me and my skystone should be removed with the utmost possible haste.

The three military men returned with an army of engineers and sappers before the end of the following month, and within days of their arrival a military camp was well established in the valley and the work was under way. It proceeded with all necessary caution for, as Erasmus Lecio had pointed out on that first inspection, there was no way of determining how thick the dam was on the lakeward side, or how far the waters had penetrated the rubble of the dam itself. It was dangerous work every foot of the way, but it was not until mid July that the first seepage occurred. From then on, it was merely a matter of time — a little more cautious digging, and then the wait for the water of the lake to find its own way out.

In the small hours of a summer morning, the sappers were awakened by a roar and a rumble, and for the next week the lake poured itself down the hillside, emptying like the broken bowl it resembled.

There can be few things or places less attractive than the newly exposed bottom of a suddenly drained lake — mud and stench and noxious vapour steaming under a hot sun. There was nothing to do but leave it and hope that the sun would dry it quickly.

August came and went, and the sun blazed into September. Strong autumn winds sprang up to help, and I watched, waiting and fretting in a fever of frustration and impatience. October remained dry and clear, and finally, driven to distraction by the waiting, I decided that the time had come.

I had made careful drawings before the lake was breached and had calculated to within ten paces where my treasure had to lie. All summer long, as soon as the mud had become firm enough to bear a man, I had men digging ditches, channelling residual water away from the centre, so that by late autumn the lake bed was a maze of drainage ditches, some of them wide and deep.

I had also kept a team of men and horses busy building mountains of fuel on the lakeside — bushes, dried grass and thistle, dead wood, even whole trees. Now I began to burn it in a monstrous pyre above the spot where I hoped and believed the skystone lay. We burned for two days and then left the ashes to cool, and when we scraped them away, the clay beneath them was baked. We tackled the baked clay then with mattock, pickaxe and spade until we found moisture again. Then we repeated the whole process. It was tiring, hard and dirty work, but the day came, towards the year's end, when a workman's pickaxe struck rock, and a shout of triumph told me we had found what we were looking for. The skystone was there. My guess had been correct. The size of it, however, left me breathless. Caius, I thought, would never believe this.

XXVIII

With the perspective of time, I am tempted to say that I chose the wrong day to bring my skystone home in triumph, but that would be neither true nor accurate.

My homecoming with the skystone was a triumph for me and, in a strange way, for Caius. By vindicating myself in the finding of the stone, I had also vindicated his faith in my strange obsession. He had wanted me to find a skystone for years; it meant a lot to him. Only occasionally did his fine mind balk at the impossibility of everything involved in the quest. The day I found the stone and brought it back to the villa should have been a day for rejoicing all day long. But it was not to be. The arrival of the skystone at the villa was an event whose light was soon eclipsed by other happenings. That particular day was a day of days for all of us, although our human frailties precluded us from identifying the directions in which we were being steered.

We had had a fruitful and excellent year on the villa, which we had already started to call the Colony. Our crops had prospered, and we had more land under the plough than ever before. Quintus Varo, our neighbour to the north, had worked his fields with ours, as had Terra and Firma, who had bought two villas to the east and south of us. In all, we now held a block of nine contiguous villa farms, forming a solid rhomboid tract of arable land some twelve miles long by five miles deep at its widest, and we were confident of adding to those holdings in the coming year.

There were at least three villas that Caius knew of to the south and west, and several more in the north and east, whose owners lived outside of Britain: one on the Emperor's island of Capri, one outside Rome itself and one in southern Gaul. These we knew we could have — by default, if things progressed too quickly. They were maintained and farmed by trusted staff of the finest quality — people of the type our plans called for.

Throughout the summer and the autumn months, we had also had a steady trickle of newcomers to the villas — craftsmen and artisans, all with families, selected by various members of our newly formed Council.

The first of these to arrive was a family from Verulamium. The father and his two adult sons were tanners; the mother, daughter and the wives of the two sons were highly skilled workers in leather. Caius welcomed them with open arms. They were followed within the month by a family of coopers, sent by Tonius Cicero from Londinium. Domus, the father of the clan, was also a skilled carpenter, and his son Andronicus shared all his father's talents.

In August came a family of brewers from the hop country far to the east, and the next month brought the arrival of another family of carpenters and wagon-builders, and a man from the north who, with his wife and daughters, had taken the art of basket-weaving to new virtuosity. Within a week of their arrival, they were making baskets that would hold water! A potter arrived shortly after them, bringing his wheel with him — a huge device on which he threw amphorae and other large storage jars and pots.

Caius had begun to list all the resources we had at our disposal, and the people in our group who were best able to make use of them, and it was from this task that he was summoned by the commotion of my arrival. He was waiting with Luceiia at the gates as I turned my heavily laden wagon around the last bend in the road, and I could see his teeth gleaming in a grin from a hundred paces. The excitement being generated by my coming might have seemed, to a stranger's eyes, more suited to the arrival of an important visitor than a lump of rock, but everyone in the Colony had been aware for months of the importance I placed on the stone I had been searching for so painstakingly.

I stood upright on the wagon tongue, holding the reins, feeling my grin threatening to split my face in two. And then I was in front of them, and I stopped and leaped down to kiss Luceiia and embrace Caius.

"So! You found it!" he said. Luceiia said nothing, smilingly enjoying my obvious pleasure.

"Aye. I found it. Right where I knew it was." Elated beyond words, I squeezed him tightly to me, hooking my right elbow round his neck in an unusual display of my affection, unaware that I was endangering his dignity. He eased himself gently free from this uncharacteristic embrace and eyed the canvas-covered heap on the bed of the wagon.

"Well, then? Let's see this prodigy! Let's have a look at it!"

I leaped back up onto the wagon bed and threw off the covering. It was huge. Or rather, they were. There were four of them. Four massive stones, the smallest of them as big as a strong man's torso, the largest like the hindquarters of a draft horse.

I had known what this sight would do to Caius. I saw all his doubts come crashing back to him at the sight of them. How could these mighty things have fallen from an empty sky? He bit his lip. Everyone had fallen silent.

The rocks seemed to gleam in the sunlight. They almost looked ordinary — four big stones. But they had that polished, glassy look in parts that marked the other seven, smaller stones.

Caius cleared his throat, since he could see that I, and everyone else, was obviously waiting for him to say something.

"They . . . They're very clean."

I laughed aloud. "And so they should be! We washed them."

"You . . . washed them?"

"Yes, of course we washed them. They had been buried under tons of muck for years. I had to wash them to be sure of what they were. Their weight told me they were skystones, but I couldn't be sure from looking at them, so we stopped at the first stream we came to and cleaned them. And there they are!"

There they were, indeed.

There was still a look of dreadful doubt on Caius's face. "Did you not expect to find only one, Varrus?"

I slapped my right hand onto one of the smooth surfaces. "They *are* only one, Caius. At least I think they are. My guess is that it shattered on striking the earth. If you look closely at them you'll see that each has smooth surfaces and jagged planes. I fancy that if a man had the

time and the strength to juggle with them, he could piece
them all together like a broken nut."

"I see." The tone of his voice told me he really did not
see. "What will you do with them now?"

"Break them in smaller pieces and smelt them."

"Will that take long?"

"Who knows?" I said. "I hope not. It depends a lot
upon the kiln we build, the degree of heat we can generate and on the hardness of the stones themselves and the
quality of iron they contain. It could take a month. Perhaps much longer. I only know I'll do it, no matter how
long it takes."

I could see the doubt tugging at Caius's mind.
"Varrus," he said, "Publius . . . what if the stones contain
no metal?"

I leaped back down to the ground. "They do, Caius!
They do." I suddenly became aware that everyone
around was listening to us, and I turned to address them
with raised arms, acutely conscious of their scrutiny, their
curiosity and the scepticism that few of them were able
to conceal as well as Caius.

"My friends," I told them, speaking into their polite,
attentive silence, "these are the skystones you've all
heard me talk about." I glanced from face to face, smiling at the studied non-expressions on most of them.
"They're not much to look at, are they? But they're big,
and that's what I was hoping for."

I jumped up onto the bed of the wagon and rubbed
my hand against the smooth curvature of the biggest
piece of stone.

"Don't let their plainness mislead you. They are real,
and they were found where I expected to find them, and

their true magic remains to be discovered in the months that lie ahead." I drew my skystone dagger and held it up so that they could all see its shining, liquid-silver blade. "They contain metal," I said, raising my voice to reach everyone there. "Metal like this, and as real as this is. I don't know what kind of metal it is, but it's more than simple iron. Whatever it is, I'll get it out of them."

I saw in their faces — and in a few kindly but scepti-cally shaken heads — that they were prepared to accept and make allowance for my strangeness. They had begun to go about their interrupted affairs even before I jumped down from the cart again. I turned to Equus, who had not left my side in weeks.

"Take the wagon to the smithy and get a few men to help you unload it. And make sure you warn them these things are heavier than they look. Don't let anyone get hurt handling them."

I turned next to Luceiia. "My love, I have to bathe, and I'm as hungry as three starving men. Would you organize a bath and some food for me while I talk with Caius?"

She smiled up at me and squeezed my arm, stretching on tiptoe to kiss my cheek, dirty as it was.

"Gladly, my lord and husband," she said, smiling. "Welcome home. I'll be waiting for you." And she was gone.

I watched her walk towards the house, then turned to Caius with a contented sigh, throwing my arm around his shoulder. We began to walk together.

"Caius, have I ever thanked you for your sister?"

"Only ten thousand times. No more, I beg!"

"So be it." I laughed again, throwing my head far back. "Caius, I feel so good that I could dance a jig!

There's iron in those stones! I know there is. Do you recall the time I told you of my grandfather's struggle to smelt his stone?" He nodded that he did, and I continued. "Don't you remember, then, my telling you that at his last attempt, just when he was about to give up in despair, he noticed that there had been a change in the surface texture of the stone?"

"Yes, I remember that. But what —?"

"What he had noticed, Caius," I interrupted him, "was a glazing effect, as though the stone had started to melt just as the fire died down. The same glazing effect that is already present in these stones!"

He shook his head, mystified.

"Don't you see, Caius? When these stones fell to earth in fire, the heat of that fire must have been enough to start that melting process."

But this was stretching Caius's imagination too far. He sought refuge in ridicule.

"So? Are you saying you don't need a kiln? That if you just throw these stones up in the air, they'll melt themselves?"

I stopped him short and turned him to face me, reading his disbelief straight from his eyes. We stood together thus for quite a space, and then we resumed our walk. When I spoke again my voice was more sober.

"Caius," I said, " I wish that I could prove the truth of this to you right now. But I can't. I can't even explain the way I feel — how I know I'm right. It's just something that's in me. You think I am being foolish, and I know you well enough to know that you would suffer long before you'd take the chance of hurting me by saying so. But I also know that, of all the men I know, you are the one who wants most to believe that I am right, and to understand.

"You've seen the dagger, and you've heard the tale, and you believe what your eyes tell you is true. Everything inside you wants to believe that I am right and that I will smelt iron from these stones. Is this not so?" He nodded, and I went on, "The only false note in this scale is that your mind, rational being that you are, will not allow you to accept the truth of rocks of any size at all falling from the skies in fire. Unless they were pre-heated and shot up from catapults."

We had arrived outside the bath house, and one of the servants already waited to assist me. I indicated that I would be there and looked back at Caius, smiling.

"Well, General, I can't give you an eyewitness assurance, but I promise you this. You leave me to indulge my folly in my own good time, and one of these days I'll give you metal from those heavenly stones. I swear it. In the meantime, if you would turn your mind to assuring everyone else in the world that I am not insane, I will be greatly in your debt."

He looked me straight in the eye and blinked rapidly, and for one incredible moment I thought I saw the beginnings of tears in his eyes. Then he swallowed hard, clapped me on the upper arm, nodded and said, "Done!" Then he left me to my bath.

By the time I had bathed and eaten, Caius was once more immersed in his lists, and I did not see him again until we sat down to dine that night. No sooner had we begun our meal, however, than we were interrupted by the arrival of our old friend Bishop Alaric, accompanied by two of his priests. Caius insisted that they join us immediately, dusty and travel-weary as they were, and after our greetings were exchanged, they set about the meal with the single-minded gluttony of men who have not eaten for days. All of us noticed it, but apart from exchanging glances among ourselves, no one passed comment.

Finally, Alaric set down his knife and washed the grease from his hands.

"Caius, on behalf of my brethren here, I thank you for the meal. We have not broken fast since the day before yesterday."

"In God's name, why not?" I responded, astonished.

"In God's name we could not afford the time, Publius, and I knew we could eat here before going on."

Caius was frowning. "Going on to where? You are upset, my friend. What's happening outside there, in the world?"

Alaric returned Caius's frown with one of his own. "You have not heard? No, obviously you have not. There is bad news on every hand, Caius. Invasions in the north, across the Wall. Nothing that's organized, but heavy raiding parties range far south, destroying whole towns and marauding widely. They have kept far apart from each other, moving fast, so that the northern legions have been split to combat them."

"Has no one sent them help from further south?"

"No. The garrison at Arboricum has mutinied, stirred up by discontent, they say, over the newly commenced crackdown of discipline. It could not have come at a worse time. The garrison is confined within the city and the field forces containing them were faced with a choice of marching to the north to stem the Picts or staying there to quell the mutineers. It is chaos. They had to stay, of course. So the depredations of the raiders in the north have been massive and more or less unchecked."

He fell silent, but I could see from his expression that he had not finished.

"There is more, Alaric, isn't there?"

His eyes switched from Caius to me. "Aye, there is more. A fleet of Saxon longboats has landed in the south-east, on the Saxon Shore, and ravaged the country there. They managed somehow to outwit and ambush the forces sent to deal with them — slaughtered them all."

"How many?"

"A full cohort of the Seventeenth."

I felt the hairs on my arm stand up. "Good God!" I whispered. "Five hundred men?"

"A thousand! It was the First Cohort. The Millarian."

I leaped to my feet. "That's impossible! A band of undisciplined Saxons? Never!" My reaction was involuntary, pure shock, for I knew Alaric was no liar.

He ignored the implied insult and looked me straight in the eye. "Not impossible, Publius. Improbable, perhaps, but it happened."

"How, in the name of all that's good in Rome?"

He shrugged, shaking his head. "No one knows. All that is known is that they were taken on the march. The Saxons set fire to the grass. It has been a dry summer and the winds were strong that day. From the way the corpses were found, it was clear that they had been driven by the flames into a defile in the hills. They were trapped there and butchered."

"It still seems impossible," said Caius, his voice betraying shock similar to mine. "They must have had scouts out! Light cavalry. No Roman army, cohort or legion, marches blind!"

Alaric shrugged and had no comment to make.

"So, Alaric, where are you going now?" I asked him.

"South. To the coast. They have need of us. It seems another fleet has landed there, where no raiders have ever come before. The people were unprepared for them, and there is much suffering."

It was Caius's turn to interrupt. "A fleet? South of here? But how? They couldn't sail along the Saxon Shore without being challenged by our naval forces. What's happening?"

"It seems, Caius, they came across the sea. From Gaul."

"No!" Caius shook his head in denial. "How could that be? The Narrows — that I could understand. But a war fleet across the widest part of the sea? At the start of winter? Who would dare try it at this time of year? The Gauls have neither the courage nor the ships."

"I'm told that these were Frankish pirates."

"Franks? God! They dare much today, for petty brigands!"

Alaric was quick to contradict him. "They are no longer petty, Caius. The Franks today dare much more than you know. They have bred warrior kings. The word from mainland Gaul is that they are highly organized and are quickly becoming a force to be reckoned with. The legions are in trouble over there."

I looked across the table to where Caius and my wife sat in awe, seemingly spellbound by the chronicle of disaster Alaric was presenting. For what seemed the longest time, a silence lay over all of us, almost suffocating in its density. I was the one who eventually broke it.

"Well, Caius," I said, my voice sounding flat, hard and heavy even in my own ears, "this could be it, the start of what you've been warning us of for years."

He looked at me as though he didn't understand what I had said, a tiny frown of puzzlement appearing briefly between his brows.

"What?"

I carried on, my tone unchanged. "It looks as though your ending might have begun. To do what they have done, these Franks must be hungry. And that means they'll be humourless and hard to reason with, for hungry people seldom stop to laugh. If they really are, as Alaric contends, emerging as a coherent fighting force — damnation, if they're foolhardy enough to dare the sea between Gaul and here at this time of year — they could destroy the entire balance of the Empire. They could be the final straw that breaks the camel's back and sends the whole world toppling into ruin."

He nodded wordlessly, thinking my comments through before addressing Alaric again.

"Tell me what more you know of these Franks, my friend. Why have they suddenly become so troublesome?"

The Bishop shook his head. "I cannot answer that with any ring of truth, Caius, for I truly do not know."

"You spoke of warrior kings. Who are they?"

Alaric shook his head. "I have no names. I only know they exist, bred of the troubles of their people. The Visigoths have leaders, too, today. Leaders with great talent for warfare."

"Heathen bastards!" I interjected.

"No, Publius." Alaric shook his head again. "Not heathens. Many of them are Christians, forced into war by injustices against their people. This I know to be true. We have bishops and priests among them now, preaching the Word of God with great success, except where it concerns war. These people will not stand still any longer and be exploited like cattle at the whim of Rome. They choose to fight. As they see it, they fight for their survival as a race."

"Aye, and they're all Roman-trained!" I said.

"That may be the least troublesome thing about them." Alaric's voice was solemn. "The Franks have taken to horse. They are highly mobile now, capable of covering great distances far faster than the legions. It makes them difficult to contend with."

"The Franks now, too?" Caius's voice was rich with disgust. "Rome had enough trouble with the Ostrogoths in Asia Minor when *they* took to horse! That was, what? Five years ago? A whole consular army wiped out! Six legions, totally destroyed! Forty thousand men! I still can't believe that, after all this time."

"An imperial army, Caius." My interruption was soft spoken. "Valens himself was there, remember."

"Valens! He was no emperor! He was a popinjay pretending to rule in the West, with Valentinian sitting in Constantinople, permitting it because it was expedient. Two Emperors at one time! Faugh! And now we have three! Gratius and his catamite, Valentinian — co-emperors, if you please — and Theodosius. It disgusts me to the pit of my stomach!"

Caius was growing really angry, allowing himself to be distracted.

"But we were discussing horsemen. The Ostrogoth cavalry that day, ill-equipped rabble as they were, destroyed the myth of Rome Invincible." Caius turned again to Alaric. "Where have these Franks found horses in such numbers as you seem to be describing?"

Alaric's shrug was matter-of-fact. "They breed them. They've been doing so for years. Some of them, most of them, came from Asia. The Franks bought them or stole them in great herds. Horse-breeding has become an art among them."

"Strange we've never heard of it," Caius said.

"Nonsense, Caius Britannicus. It has been under your noses now for years. You simply chose to pay them no attention, so long as they remained peaceful. Rome has had no great and pressing need for horses, least of all the small, rough-bred horses of the Franks."

Caius expelled pent-up air through his lips with a rasping sound. "You are correct, my friend. You are correct. Rome, it seems, will not learn. If the Franks are horsed at all, they are a threat! A big one! If massed horsemen smashed six legions at a time on one ill day, rolling the cohorts up like carpets, they'll do it again, you mark my words. What has the Emperor done about this? Is Rome training horsemen?"

"Which emperor, Caius?" Alaric was smiling gently. "A moment ago, when you were ranting about three of them, I hesitated to interrupt you. Now I must tell you that you are out of date. There are four emperors now."

My heart began to pound. Caius sat stunned.

"What do you mean?" I asked.

Alaric shrugged again. "The legions here in Britain have elected Magnus Maximus their emperor by acclamation. He is, at this moment, assembling an army to cross into Gaul to pacify the land and fortify his claim.''

"God's blood! I was afraid of that man's dark ambition! Varrus, did I not name him to you?" Caius's face was sombre as he spoke to Alaric again. "What of Antonius Cicero? Where is he?"

"Tonius is dead." Alaric's voice was heavy with sorrow. "Loyal to Theodosius and dead, Caius. He marched against Magnus when he heard the news, but his own men deserted him and crossed to Maximus. Cicero was executed.''

I had to fight down nausea at this news. Noble Tonius. He had done as he said he would at our wedding feast and had died for his nobility. I was heartsick.

"When did this happen?"

"Very recently. I heard the news myself only days ago.''

"Alaric," I asked wearily, "how does it happen that you hear so much so fast?''

"The Church has many eyes and ears, Publius, and threatens no one. That word was brought to me by Father Cato, here, who had it from a priest who saw Cicero die.''

"Legate Cicero!" I corrected him.

"Legate Cicero. May God rest his soul!"

I felt a burden of depression settle on my shoulders, remembering Tonius the night he swore he would oppose a self-proclaimed emperor from Britain. Poor Cicero. He had been prophetic. How many others had, that night, I wondered?

I had a sudden thought. "What about Seneca? Where is he?"

Alaric shook his head. "I do not know, Publius, but he is no longer in Colchester. He disappeared shortly before Magnus's insurrection."

I frowned at him, alerted by something in his tone. "Disappeared? Before? What do you mean?"

"Only what I said. He disappeared."

"But you said 'before,' did you not? Before the insurrection? And there was something in the way you said it. You have some thoughts on the matter, I think."

Alaric sighed. "Publius," he said, "I bring you only facts. I do not deal in rumour, and rumour is all I have to go on in this matter. I have no interest in the man Claudius Seneca. He is not the sort of man on whom I choose to spend valuable time."

"What is the rumour, Alaric? Please, it is important."

He sighed again at my insistence. "You should put Seneca away from your mind, Publius. He is an evil man. No good will come of brooding on him or on his actions."

"I know that, Alaric. But he owes me a life."

"He owes you nothing." His voice sounded dispirited. "There is talk that it was he who financed Magnus Maximus in his bid for the imperial throne."

I slammed the table in frustration. "Damn the man to the blackest pit in Hades. Now he has killed two of my friends! Phoebe and Tonius."

"Publius!" Alaric's tone was remonstrative. "You cannot say such a thing. I have told you that this is only rumour."

"Aye, Alaric, you have. But now I am telling you that never was rumour better founded. The deed fits the man perfectly. It stinks of his plotting and his mental sickness. If Magnus Maximus succeeds in making good his claim, he will overthrow Theodosius, and that will be to no one's advantage more than Seneca's. The serpent has found a perfect stone under which to hide. Magnus's revolt will take the Emperor's eyes away from Seneca and from his thieving, scheming villainy. If Magnus wins, Seneca wins. If Magnus loses, Seneca still wins. You can be sure that there will be no living soul left to relate how Seneca helped Magnus raise the funds to win an army. And Theodosius can hardly blame his Procurator for being unable to perform his duties in a province that has been usurped by an upstart emperor. No, you mark my words. When the dust of this revolt dies down, one way or the other, Claudius Seneca will emerge unscathed and richer than ever."

I suddenly realized that I was ranting. Luceiia sat wide-eyed, watching me. Alaric was expressionless. I looked at Caius. He had sunk his forehead onto the heels of his hands. Alaric saw my look and spoke to Caius.

"I am sorry to be the bearer of so much bad news, Caius. It had not occurred to me that you might be ignorant of all of it. I tend to assume that others all have the sources that I do."

Caius was subdued. "Think not of it, Alaric. We are in a quiet backwater here, out of the way of news."

This was too much for me. "Damnation, Caius," I exploded, "is that all you're going to say? This is Claudius *Seneca* we're talking about, not some exalted nincompoop none of us has ever heard of! I would have thought you'd have more reason than I do to get excited about this."

"You think me dead, then?" Caius snapped, and the tone of his voice silenced me utterly. He drew a deep breath and pinched the bridge of his nose between his finger and thumb. When he spoke again, his voice had regained its usual dispassionate calm.

"Publius, I know better than anyone how easy it is to hate the Senecas — the entire tribe of them. But I cannot simply allow myself to be thrown into a convulsive reaction every time one of them demonstrates what I know to be the nature of the beast. . . . There are more important things at stake in our lives right now. Neither you nor I has the time to concern ourself with the personal treachery of a Seneca. Leave them to time — to history and God. We have our own priorities. What we are doing here in this Colony is far more important than anything any Seneca might do out yonder, where the world is coming apart. Our success here will mean our survival . . . and that will be all the revenge we will ever need against a family who are headed directly for extinction.

"Don't talk of scores and debts, Publius. You have no need to fret about such things. Time itself will settle such debts very soon."

There was nothing I could say in response, and there was silence at the table for some time. Luceiia excused herself and left the room. It was I who finally spoke again.

"You're right, Caius, of course. I'm sorry. I find I'm growing more emotional as I get older. Time will take care of Seneca and all his kind. . . . But if I can change the subject, I find it hard to believe that with things as bad as they are, Magnus intends to leave Britain and cross to Gaul."

"Why not?" The bitterness in Caius's voice must have burned his throat like vomit. "We are talking of ambition here, my friend, not duty! Rome's new emperor must make a name for himself beyond these shores. He is known here in Britain. Now he must make his Divine Presence known in other lands."

"But how could his generals permit this?"

"Don't be naive, Varrus! Each of them sees himself commander of the new Praetorian Guard, personal body-guard to the new emperor. They'll fight like demons not to stay behind."

"But some will stay, surely? He'll not denude the country of armed strength?"

Caius's anger gave way to disgust. "No, you can rest assured he'll leave enough strength behind to guarantee himself a bolt hole if his plans fall through the net of fate. He will keep Britain strong for now. He's no man's fool, our noble, newest Emperor!"

"Publius, is Luceiia ill?" Alaric's voice was concerned. "She was deathly pale when she left here."

"Was she?" I felt alarm flare in me. "I didn't notice. Please excuse me. I'll just check that she is quite all right." I rose quickly and left to find her.

When I re-entered the room my face must have looked strange, because Caius immediately asked me what was wrong. I crossed to the table and picked up a jug of wine.

"What day is it today?"

Alaric answered me, "The Calends was two days ago, so we are at the third day of the month."

"What year?"

"This is the eleven hundred and thirty-sixth year of Rome," he said. "It is also the three hundred, eighty-third year of our Lord. Why do you ask?"

"Because it has been momentous." I poured a cup of wine for myself and then moved around the table, filling their cups, too. "First, I brought home my skystones. Then you arrived, Alaric, an event of some importance on its own. Then we learned of invasions, treason, mutiny and war, of a new emperor and the death of a noble and worthy friend. And now, my wife tells me she is with child. This is a momentous day."

I raised my cup, and my friends drank with me. A silent toast.

XXIX

As I grow older, it becomes clear to me that life is like campaigning: long periods of quiet and boredom when nothing seems to happen, and then short, intensive spasms when everything important is compressed into chaotic action.

The year just past, 383 of the Christian calendar, was a chaotic one — at least in its final months. By comparison, the four years that followed were somnolent.

There were many things happening, of course, throughout the country and all over the Empire, but none of them affected our quiet Colony. For us, it was a time of building and consolidation, with very few traumatic incidents.

Caius's son Picus sent us word that he was marching off to war with the new emperor, Magnus Maximus, to help him claim the imperial throne, and after that we heard no more of him. It hurt Caius deeply that the boy could not see the glaring imperfections of the man, but Picus was young, only eighteen that year. He would have to do his own learning, like every other man.

Caius and I discussed that, along with several other topics, one crisp morning after he had found me actively debating the techniques of combat with three husky young trainee soldiers. At that point, we had not yet developed a regular, formalized program for training our young men as fighters; that development still lay a full year in the future. We had, nevertheless, begun a program of informal training for youths fifteen and older, accepting the need to make a start somewhere if all of our Colonists were to be expected to bear arms and comport themselves knowledgeably in their own defence.

No one knows the origins of the Roman practice sword; the name of its creator and the story of its beginnings are lost in time. The efficacy and practicality of its design, however, have never been altered and could not be improved. It is made of wood — a piece of heavy, ash dowel — and is circular in section, more like a club than a sword. It is cut to the same length as the *gladium*, the classic Roman short-sword, but it possesses twice the weight, which makes it awkward to wield and difficult to work with. The extra weight builds the strength of the user's arm so that when real violence occurs, when blades are bared in earnest, the sword's real weight seems as nothing in the hand of a well-trained soldier.

Attracted by the clattering of these practice blades, Caius came upon me working at close quarters in a small, cobbled, dung-strewn courtyard, face to face with the three strapping young recruits. They were all attacking me at once, trying to get their blades around my shield and above or beneath my guard. They couldn't, and I was enjoying myself greatly, aware of the advantage I had over them. They were young and inexperienced, rash and undisciplined. In a matter of mere months, I knew, they would learn enough to overwhelm me quickly at this game. For now, however, I was taking advantage of their youth, strength and clumsiness, encouraging them to attack me more and more strongly, and with less and less success as their frustration increased. As soon as I noticed Caius standing there watching, however, I brought matters to a close swiftly, rapping each of the three soundly with a heavy, telling blow of my blade — one on the helmet, one on the elbow and one in the ribs — before stepping back and lowering my guard to dismiss them. Crestfallen and subdued, they made their way out of the yard, convinced that they would never be able to best that old whoreson Varrus. I loosened my chinstrap and pulled off my helmet, wiping my sweaty brow with the kerchief I kept tucked into my breastplate.

Caius, watching me closely, said nothing for several moments. Then, "You looked like you were enjoying that."

I stood on tiptoe and stretched my arms above my head, drawing a deep breath and then bending from the waist to touch my toes. "I was," I answered, puffing slightly as I straightened up and began wiping the headband of my helmet. "I enjoy the activity. Keeps me in trim. Don't get much chance to work up a sweat nowadays. Besides, it's good for the youngsters. It lets them work off some energy, trying for a free whack at authority, and none of them ever see it as a lesson in foolhardiness." The leather rim of my headband was dry again, and I slapped the heavy, crested weight of the helmet back onto my head, adjusting it as I continued. "Mind you, we both know, you and I, that I wouldn't dare try that trick on them after they've learned even a *little* more than they know now, but sneaking it in on them like this gives them a healthy respect for the people in charge of them."

He smiled and turned away. "Walk with me," he said, over his shoulder.

I left my things where they were and followed him. We went out through the main gates of the villa and walked in silence for almost half a mile, until the sights and sounds of the farm and its buildings had dropped out of sight behind us, screened from our view by bushes and undergrowth.

Directly ahead of us stood the only large tree on this part of the villa lands, a solitary copper beech, massive and beautiful, that seemed to owe its survival to its mere presence. It had been standing here for a very long time and no one had ever thought to cut it down. Now no one ever would. It was part of the place. Everyone referred to it simply as "the Big Tree." Caius paced directly towards it and stopped some ten paces from the trunk, which swept straight upward for thirty or more feet to the junction of the first major bough. He gazed at the smooth, silver-grey bark and then turned to me.

"You have your dagger with you?"

I nodded. "I do. Why?"

"Balanced for throwing, isn't it?"

"Yes. Why?"

"Can you throw it from there, where you're standing, and stick it in the tree?"

I glanced at the tree, gauging the distance, visualizing the tumbling flight of the knife and then seeing the result. "Easily," I told him, "but I'd rather not."

"Why not?" From the way his eyebrow shot up, I saw I had surprised him.

I shrugged my shoulders, making light of the reason for my reluctance. "Convenience, I suppose, and cleanliness . . . or laziness. Tree sap does strange things to the skystone dagger. It stains the blade. Doesn't damage it, but it discolours it slightly, and it's very hard to clean off, unless you do it immediately." I stopped, looking at him. "Why d'you want me to throw it, anyway?"

He cleared his throat and then met my eye. "I didn't, particularly," he responded. "I was hoping you might show *me* how to throw it."

"Well, of course I will, happily!" Filled with sudden pleasure, I whipped the dagger from its sheath at the small of my back, swung it up shoulder high, aiming as I did so, and flung it hard and true at the tree. It flipped end over end once and thudded home in the centre of the bole with a deep, satisfying *thunk*. I crossed to it, worked it free of the wood and dried the sap from the tip immediately, then took it back to show the slight discoloration to Caius.

"You see what I mean?" I held the blade angled to the light. "That doesn't happen to any other blade, at least, not to any I've noticed. But, as I said, it comes off easily enough if you wipe it immediately. Leave it to dry, however, and you've got a black stain that almost can't be removed. Here."

I handed him the knife and he examined it closely, holding it loosely in his fingers the way he had seen me hold it prior to throwing it. I showed him the throwing grip and gave him a brief lesson in how to throw properly, with enough strength to flip the knife and hammer it home into the target. Eventually, I allowed him to try a throw, and he sank the point a good thumb-nail's depth into the trunk. We retrieved it and he did the same again five times in succession. Then we increased the distance to the tree and he had to make the required adjustments. He threw two misses, the knife clunking lengthwise against the bark, before he captured the correct weight again, and his shots were unerring from then on. When I estimated he had had enough, I retrieved the knife, dried the blade and slipped it into its sheath.

"So," I asked him, "what made you decide you wanted to throw knives?"

Before responding, he linked his arm through mine and pulled me into motion. We moved on as he spoke, leaving the big tree behind us.

"I didn't really want to throw knives, Publius. I merely wanted to do something different. Does that make sense?"

I made a gesture of agreement, although he had me mystified. But he paid no attention to me. My reactions were not important to him at that moment. He was talking simply for the sake of talking.

"I'm restless," he went on, "and I don't know why . . ." I could almost hear his thoughts churning. "I don't like the way I'm feeling, Publius . . . don't like feeling I haven't come to grips with my life or my own desires. Do you know what I mean? I feel I'm missing something. Do you ever feel that way?"

Conscious of the impossibility of responding intelligently to that, yet wanting to clarify what he was driving at, I said, "I don't know, Caius. Perhaps I do, from time to time, but I'm not sure if we're both talking about the same thing. What is it you're missing? Have you any idea?"

He threw me a sidelong glance and then returned his eyes to the path at his feet. "Yes, I'm missing my son, for one thing. I'm not happy with his decision to follow Magnus."

I answered him firmly on that point. "That's because you would never have decided to do that, Caius. You wouldn't have to. You're Caius Britannicus, Legate, Senator and Proconsul of Rome. But we're discussing Picus's decision. He's only a lad, and a grunt, at that, not even a centurion yet. He has to do what he's told, like any other soldier. More than likely he had no choice at all. It's pointless to fret over it, anyway, because there's nothing we can do about it."

He kicked at a clump of grass. "Damnation, Publius, I know that. But I still don't like it. I should have kept the lad here on the Colony."

"How? You mean you should have forbidden him the privilege of serving with the legions? Of following in the steps of his ancestors? How long has it been since the last Britannicus stayed at home and didn't serve the Empire?"

"It's never happened, you know that."

"Then why start it now? You know the experience will be the making of the lad."

"I know it will, of course! But what if . . .?"

"What if what? Do you mean what happens if he's killed?"

He answered, his voice a whisper, "Yes, I suppose I do."

I reached out and grasped him by the shoulder. "Then your name will die with you, my friend. But it won't happen. Picus won't die. He'll come home because he knows he'll be needed. There is a position waiting for him in our Colony, and his experience and skills will be important. The lads who stay here with us will learn their trade with us. They'll be good soldiers, but they'll be home grown.

Our Picus will bring back the training and experience to round them out and make real fighters of them, real Romans."

"I suppose so." He heaved a great, deep sigh. "I know you're right, my friend," he said. "My intellect knows you're right, but my heart — "

I cut in on his words. "What's really bothering you, General?"

He stopped short, in mid stride, and looked at me. "*That* is, Publius. What you just said."

I blinked at him. "What did I say?"

"You called me General, and that's what I'm missing. Soldiering, Publius! The excitement, the challenge, the movement, the constant stimulation and requirement to be prepared for anything. The constant need to think on one's feet and keep abreast and ahead of developments."

I had stopped walking, too, and now I was staring at him in amazement. He took my stunned silence for recognition of the problem.

"Don't you agree?"

"Agree?" I said, hearing the wonder in my own voice. "I can't even believe what I heard! General, can you recognize horse turds when you see them?"

His gaze went blank. "What d'you mean? Of course I can."

"So can I." I nodded. "Aye, and I can hear them when they hit the ground, too, fresh dropped. But I seldom hear them dropping from the horse's mouth."

The old Britannicus surfaced quickly. "Varrus, what in Hades are you talking about?"

"What *you* were talking about. Horse shit. I've never heard the like. You were the one who loved to talk for

hours about the pettiness and uselessness of the military
life — the inactivity, the boredom, the frustration, the
bureaucratic meddling, the ineptitude and the general
folly bred by the army's 'hurry up and wait' mentality.''
I stopped to draw breath, and he did not interrupt me as I
continued. ''You know, if I didn't know who I was listening to, I'd be tempted to think you were sorry for yourself. But I know that's not the case. You've a huge job to
do here in this Colony, and you're doing it well. What
you're feeling right now will pass. It's nostalgia for a way
of life that's over. You've done it all. Trying to repeat any
part of it would drive you insane. The job you have to do
today means more, and demands more, than anything
you've ever tried before.''

Now it was he who stared open-mouthed at me. ''By
the living Christ, Varrus,'' he breathed, his eyes wide in
wonder, ''you've never dared speak to me like that
before. I've never heard you talk to anyone like that!
You're really eloquent in fury . . . I must have pissed on
your cooking fire to make you that angry!''

I could see laughter dancing in his eyes, and I tried to
keep my own face stern.

''You did,'' I snarled, ''and no wonder!'' I tried to
mimic his earlier words, but the harder I tried, the louder
he giggled, and the more foolish this whole conversation
seemed. ''The activity of soldiering! Judge him not, ye
gods! The excitement! The requirement to be prepared
for anything . . . The horse turds and the dung in the
mutton stew . . . Gods! I may puke!''

I couldn't even talk after that. Caius was giggling
openly and helplessly, like a boy, and my own laughter
broke out in guffaws, so that our hilarity fed upon itself

and we staggered around, clutching at each other for support until our knees gave way as completely as our dignity, both weakened by our hysteria, and we collapsed to the grass. From that day forward, there was no more talk between us of discontent, or of nostalgia for the days that were gone. Our friendship grew richer by another layer of shared experience and we dedicated all our time and our collective energies to the development of our Colony.

Luceiia and I came to know each other better, too, during those quiet days, and our first-born arrived with summer. A girl, Victoria. An angel child who grew lovelier with each passing day, as had her mother in carrying her. Today, decades later, I can clearly recall the amazement with which I watched Luceiia grow more beautiful from day to day as her pregnancy advanced, so that by the time she came to term, she was radiant, shining with health and wholesome ripeness, flaunting her femininity and carrying her belly proudly before her as a symbol of her feminine ascendancy. The birth itself was astonishingly easy, involving little time and — according to my wife — little pain, so that motherhood in all its aspects came easily to her, and such was her pleasure in the entire process that she was with child again in less than a year. Throughout the period of both pregnancies, I struggled with my skystones, which remained obdurate in the face of all Equus and I tried to do, refusing to melt and yield their secrets.

Caius had his hands full that summer, and the one that followed, too, learning to administer our Colony. The death of Tonius Cicero, and the consequent loss of his counsel, influence and power to find and recruit new colonists, had been a blow to our plans, but we continued as before, goaded to new urgency by the suddenness of the previous year's developments.

Caius and I together began training the Colonists formally in the art of soldiering. We drilled our conscripts brutally, especially the young men, training them in the ancient way — toughening them to run and march and walk laden with heavy packs and spears and the true legionary's heavy fighting shield, the scutum. And the men responded magnificently, for they shared our dream and knew that our survival might depend at any time upon their fitness to repel attack.

In the long summer evenings, Caius set everyone to work refurbishing the ancient hill fort at our back. It had no name, because until Caius Britannicus told everyone what it was, no one had ever known it was a fort. It was just a hill, and it had always been there, completely disregarded, until a bright summer afternoon in that year between the birth of my first child and the conception of my second. That day, Caius loaded more than twenty of the most influential Colonists into a brace of wagons and led them out into the fields and over to the base of the hill, about a mile from the Villa Britannicus. There they disembarked from the wagons to be told that the kitchen staff from Caius's villa had arrived earlier in the day and had prepared a meal for them on the summit. By this time, of course, there were far more people at the scene than those who had set out with Caius. The sight of two wagons loaded with people heading out and away, obviously bound for somewhere specific, had attracted many followers, and there must have been close to a hundred people climbing the hillside that day.

At the top, Caius's people were waiting with bread and ale, nuts and roasted grain, crushed, sweet berry paste and a whole sheep roasting to perfection on a spit. When their meal was over, Caius demonstrated the reason for his efforts to get everyone up there. He had prepared a model of the hilltop and used it to aid his demonstration of the defensive genius of the early Celts, the people who had built the place, thousands of years earlier.

The entire top of the hill was laid out in concentric ramparts, separated by deep ditches, and the extreme centre, a level, roughly circular area about a hundred paces across, had evidently been intended to serve as the final refuge of the defenders. The layout was simple, and for all practical purposes impregnable. Any attacking force first had to climb the steep hillsides and then begin an arduous and bloody struggle to the centre, forced to fight their way across each ditch and then to climb each rampart before sliding down into the ditch that lay behind it. And throughout all of this, the defending forces on the ramparts always had the upper hand, retreating from crest to crest only after they had wreaked maximum damage on the advancing attackers massed below them.

When Caius had pointed all of this out to everyone, he also pointed out the inevitable corollary: any defenders prepared to commit themselves to the defence of the fort as it stood must also be prepared to die, should the attacking force be numerous enough or stubborn enough to accept the losses inflicted upon them. That, Caius suggested, needn't be inevitable. This fort was defensible, he suggested, but it would be ten to a hundred times more secure were it surrounded by a wooden wall of pallisades.

It would be a thousand times stronger were those walls of stone. Such was his eloquence that no one argued.

We dug embrasures and soon began to erect strong wooden fortifications in strategic places. And eventually, as the work progressed, we began to build a stone-walled citadel. It became the norm that, in addition to his standard duties and to the normal stone-gathering activities of the work crews, each man was required to find one stone each day and take it to the hill, and our stonemasons were set to work to build a mighty wall.

It was slow, tedious work in the first two years, and Caius worked hard to keep people's enthusiasm for the project high. He reminded them constantly of the legend of Rome's walls, finding a thousand different ways to remind them how strong those walls had been, down through the centuries, and pointing out frequently how easy it was to see how Remus had angered Romulus by jumping across the "walls" of Rome. He urged them, all the time, every day of every week of every month, to watch the progress of their own work and to watch the progress of the work as a whole. And sure enough, as day followed day and stone was laid on stone, year in, year out, the shape of our walls became more pronounced, more evident, so that now a man could see what would be there, in time.

Apart from my struggles to smelt the skystone, and to drill new soldiers, my days were filled with ironwork. I had apprentices in plenty now, and I taught them how to smelt, and how to forge new tools and weapons. I had organized some of the local Celts to find the scarce iron ore of the local hills and bring it to our smelters. In return, I made them goods and taught them Roman skills in ironwork. Some of their ironsmiths became friends, attracted, I suppose, by that mutual respect that exists among professionals of any kind, and Caius remarked with a smile one evening that my smithy had become the liveliest place in the Colony.

Cymric, the Celtic bowman whom I had met on my arrival here in the west, became a regular visitor, and because of that I still practised regularly with my great African bow of horn and sinew. The fame of that bow soon spread, for the hill people were avid archers, and the Pendragon men in particular were awed by it. One day, one of them made me a gift of several dozen arrows, beautifully made, flighted with coloured feathers and tipped with iron barbs. They had been made especially for my bow, I knew, for those the Pendragon used were half the length. I was delighted with them and reciprocated with an axe of solid bronze, after which I became friends with the fletcher, who was Cymric's brother, and allowed both of them the use of the bow. Cymric used to spend hours with the great bow on his knees, studying its design.

By the end of the third year, 386, we were strongly established. We had a private army of six hundred well-trained soldiers who could march all day and dig a fortified camp at the end of it, break it down next morning and fill the ditch before marching all day again.

And as the time went past, our numbers grew. Not a month passed without some new arrival landing in our midst: carpenters and cobblers; coopers and coppersmiths. All were made welcome and put to work at once. We soon had six shoemakers among us who spent all their time in making heavy sandals, which were shod with iron nails made in a smaller forge built beside the first one.

A silversmith from Glevum joined us with three strong, young sons in their mid teens, one of whom was an artist like his father. The other two wanted nothing more in life than to be soldiers. They were our youngest recruits. Two more stonemasons came to us from the east and were quickly put to work on our fortifications.

An armourer, who had worked in the south, was sent to us by Plautus and told us that Plautus himself was still with the holding garrison in Britain, apparently having switched allegiance to Magnus. I found that hard to believe, but I was able to come up with no other explanation for either Plautus's continued existence, or for his ongoing presence in Britain. Had he spoken up at the time of Magnus's rising, he would no doubt have shared the fate of Tonius Cicero. I was grateful that he had done neither. But I wondered how he had managed to avoid having to cross to Gaul with Magnus. By rights, a soldier of his experience should never have been allowed to remain at home in a safe billet while there was fighting to be done, but Plautus, old soldier that he was, had found a way. In the meantime, having worked his ruse, whatever it was, Plautus had found the new armourer on one of his patrols and had dispatched him to find us. I had work for him before the poor fellow had had time to eat.

In a short space of time we had to start building new homes to lodge all the newcomers, and a small town grew up outside the main gates of the villa. The houses were of stone, quarried in the hills and brought in by wagon. A family of thatchers had been early arrivals, so all of the new houses were strongly roofed with woven reeds, straw or grasses, depending on the season of the year when they were finished.

From time to time we heard rumours of increasing raids along the Saxon Shore. Magnus's departure with so many troops had not gone unnoticed, it appeared. The forces left to garrison the island were spread too thin to do a proper job, and on one of his visits, Alaric told us their morale was very low, since they were constantly faced with the problem of doing too little too late.

Like the Franks with their horses, these Saxon raiders were a new form of warrior. They came by night, landed in darkness and attacked at daybreak. They operated most of the time in single boatloads of thirty to fifty men. They could attack a hamlet, burn it, steal all that they could carry, sate their lusts for flesh and blood and be back at sea again before the word of their attack had reached the garrison troops who were supposed to stop them. The only danger they faced was the prospect of meeting a naval patrol, but the seas were big, and the patrols were few.

In the autumn of 387, a boatload of Saxons infiltrated the river estuary to the north-west of us. There they left their ship and struck far inland, being careful to avoid the towns in the area and somehow managing to escape discovery.

They struck the most northerly of our villas. Fortunately, most of our people were out in the fields at the time. A squadron of our soldiers was in the area and smelled the smoke of burning thatch carried on the wind. I was in the area myself, passing by with a small escort of men and wagons on my way to Aquae Sulis for supplies. It was Lorca, one of my wagon-drivers, who made me aware that something was wrong. His nostrils were sharp, and had he not been with us we might have ridden by without noticing anything amiss. He smelled the familiar stink of burning thatch and told me what it was. Although I doubted him at first, I sent two of our strongest runners to check on it and find out where the faint smell was coming from.

Less than two hours later, I was in hiding on a shrub-covered knoll overlooking a narrow pathway that was ditched on both sides, and hoping that my cursory reading of the land and routes available had been accurate. They had, and the enemy played right into our hands. We had surprise on our side, and the fight was brief and bitter. I had split my force and found myself fighting with the larger of my groups against the enemy's vanguard, a fearsome band of brutal fighters. The majority of the raiders fell back from our first attack and found themselves cut off by our second party. I was dismounted, fighting on foot, and one of the fleeing raiders found my horse and took it. He was the sole survivor of his party, and I hope he had thews of iron for he must have had to row their long boat homeward alone.

Murder was done much further back from where I fought, where the fleeing enemy met our second fighting force. Although the men of their vanguard fought to the death and went down fighting, each and every man, the ones who fled our first attack were made of softer stuff. When I went back to check my own rear guard, I found the path littered with enemy corpses piled one on the other like firewood. Along the path of flight, all of the enemy were very soundly dead.

What to do? This was a dilemma I had faced before. The enemy was vanquished, but justice had not been done. We should have had prisoners — wounded, at least. Some should have survived. I found myself looking at the heaped dead and recalling the words of condemnation uttered centuries earlier by a chieftain of the Picts: "They make a desert and they call it peace." He had been describing the atrocities of Julius Agricola's army when it attempted to conquer the highlands of Caledonia, and my grandmother had adopted his words as her favourite expression for the inhumanity of the military mind.

I sighed to myself and sent for the centurion who had commanded the rear guard, only to find that he was dead. So were his two decurions, which left no one in authority over the surviving soldiers of the squadron. Then I knew what had happened: fear, excitement, blood-lust and the need for vengeance had run rampant here among these young, untested soldiers.

Feeling like a hypocrite, I assembled them and excoriated them, telling them all a few blistering truths about responsibility and about murder. Certainly, they were soldiers, but they were also Christians, each of them having sworn his oath of loyalty upon the cross, and the Christian Commandment was specific: Thou shalt not kill. In the heat of battle, I told them, there was remission; then, kill or be killed took precedence over the Commandment. Afterwards, however, when the danger passed, the rule resumed its dominance. The killing of any man who was no longer fighting was murderous.

I was careful to look at no single man too closely during this harangue, and to make no specific accusations, for this particular task struck home to my own innermost problems, and I knew too well the despair I felt from time to time to want to foist anything like it onto these young men. They had done well, after all, in their first engagement. I excused them on the grounds of their lack of experience and let them off the hook with a stern warning that, in future, they would be held responsible for such atrocious slaughter. When I had finished, I assigned one of my own men to them as acting centurion and sent them back to the Colony with the news of the raid, while I continued with the remainder of my men towards Aquae Sulis.

BOOK FIVE

The Dragon's Breath

XXX

Two days later, on a dull, overcast afternoon in Aquae Sulis, I was still pondering "the soldier's dilemma," as I thought of it. When is it permissible to kill and when is it not? I had discussed the matter in the past with Caius and with Bishop Alaric, and at no time had we reached a satisfactory conclusion either way. The existence of the soldier is predicated upon a perceived need to kill, for any of a dozen reasons, and yet the Christian law is categorical and absolute: Thou shalt not kill.

I had just purchased a wagonload of hemp for rope-making and had left my retainers to load it while I made my way to the public *mansio* to eat. I was deep in thought and more or less unconscious of my surroundings when I gradually became aware of a commotion ahead of me in the crowded street. Had I been less pre-occupied, I might have noticed it sooner and gone around another way, but by the time I became aware of it, I was in the marketplace and surrounded by a densely packed crowd. I made my way with some difficulty to the edge of the roadway and hoisted myself precariously on a raised gutter-stone, bracing myself with my hands on the shoulders of the man in front of me and lifting my head above the crowd to see what was going on.

A horse-drawn coach, a wealthy man's conveyance,

took up almost the whole of the thoroughfare just ahead of where I stood, and as I looked, its grossly fat occupant was hauling himself up from the cushioned seat, preparing to climb down. An expression of distaste was stamped on his face as he scanned the crowd that thronged around him, gawking at his wealth. His retainers bustled about, forming a wedge and clearing a pathway through the crowd to the entrance of the building he was obviously headed for, less than four good paces from where I stood, perched on my small eminence. One of these retainers, a mindless-looking hulk with the face of an ape, pushed an old woman roughly from his path with a shout.

"Way! Make way for Quinctilius Nesca!"

So unexpected was the name, here in this place, that my head flew up in shock and I jerked my eyes back to the occupant of the coach. He was just on the point of stepping down into the street, and willing hands were supporting his huge arms to ease his grotesque weight. As I turned my face towards him, our eyes met. It must have been my expression of surprise and shock that alerted him, for there was nothing else to distinguish my face among the multitude. His eyes narrowing, he reached his right hand back to the framework of the open coach, holding himself there, half in and half out of the conveyance as he stared at me, and I saw suspicion dawning in his eyes. Too late, I cursed the vanity that had made me keep my grizzled beard, for in a Roman town a well-trimmed beard stands out among clean-shaven faces and wild, unkempt bushes. I hung there frozen, my eyes locked on his, incapable even of looking away from him as I saw his hand come up and point at me and his mouth frame the unheard words, "You there! Come here!"

My skin crawled with panic, for I knew I was staring death in the face and I could not move. I thought of brazening the confrontation out, but I knew that my first limping step would betray me. All he had seen until now was my grey beard, but something in the look of me had alerted him; let him once see my crippled gait and I would be dead meat. Now he was shouting, drawing the attention of his men to where I was perched, looking down on them.

"Bring that man to me!" He was yelling, pointing at me. "That one! The grey-beard there!" The simian-faced brute closest to me had turned and seen me, and now he started to move towards me through the densely packed bodies separating us, his clawed fingers stretching to take hold of me. The sight of his blackened, snarling teeth brought me to my senses. I shoved the man whose shoulders I had been leaning on right into his grasp, sending both of them reeling as I threw myself backwards into the crowd. As I disappeared from view I heard a howl go up, and I knew that I was running for my life. I used my shoulders like battering rams, ploughing through the crowd, aware of the fright and incomprehension on the faces of the people I was jostling. Then suddenly I was free of the press and diving into a narrow passageway between two buildings. It was a short alleyway leading to a common midden behind the tenements that fronted the street. I came out into this and dodged to my right, along the wall, hearing as I did so the clatter of running feet in the alley behind me. I was running hard in the style I had developed, a series of limping leaps, using my bad leg only to balance me for the next leap with my good one. It was awkward and not at all aesthetic, but it covered ground at a good rate over short distances.

An open door appeared on my right almost immediately and I swung myself inside, into near-total darkness. It was a stable of some kind, full of straw and animal smells. I saw the dim outline of a ladder ahead of me, stretching up in darkness to a second level, but it did not attract me. I had not run far enough yet to hide, and the chase was too hot behind me. I flung myself into a dark corner by the door, pressing myself back into the wall behind an untidy sprawl of forks and shovels, and drew my sword.

I listened to the running feet approach and come to a stop outside the open door, less than a step from me had the wall not been between us. There were two men, both of them breathing heavily. I held my own breath, feeling the pulse hammering in my throat, hearing the silence of their motionless pause grow and extend for an impossible length of time. As clearly as if I could see them, I knew they were standing side by side, peering into the blackness beyond the doorway where I stood. Gradually their breathing steadied and then one of them spoke.

"What d'you think? He's in there?"

The other's voice was a low growl. "Oh, he's in there, all right. No place else he can be. He didn't have time to go anywhere else. He's in there."

"I'll get help."

"No!" The command was barked, and I could imagine the expression of surprise on the first one's face. "You'll get no one. We'll handle this ourselves."

"Why? The others are around here somewhere. It won't take a minute to get them."

"We don't need help, you fool! Use your head, for once in your life. Don't you know who this whoreson is?"

"No." The voice sounded vaguely plaintive. "Who is he?"

"I don't know his name. Nobody does. But you remember a few years ago we were all told to find a grey-bearded whoreson with a twisted leg? Nesca was offering ten golden *auri*. Remember? It must be at least five years."

"Aye, I remember that. No one ever found him. You think this is the same one?"

"I don't know, but the whoreson has a grey beard and a twisted leg and he ran. You want to share ten gold *auri* with the others?"

There was a short silence, then, "What if he's not the right one?"

"If he's dead when we take him back, he's the right one. You think they're going to question a corpse? Let's go in and get him."

I took a deep, silent breath as they stepped into the doorway and stood there, so close to me that I could smell them. I could have reached out and touched them from behind the pile of fork handles between us.

"It's dark," the smaller of them breathed.

His companion took one step into the gloom and crouched there, his head moving as he scanned the darkened space in front of them. He held a sword in one hand and a dagger in the other. The smaller one moved forward, too, and noticed the ladder stretching upwards into the gloom. He touched the other's arm, nodding towards it. Neither of them so much as glanced behind in my direction. They were convinced that I would have sought safety in the darkness ahead of them.

I looked hard at them in the light that fell through the

doorway. The large one was the one with the apelike face. Neither of them wore armour of any description.

Ape Face pointed to the ladder and signalled to his companion to go up, indicating that he would remain there, on the floor, and they both moved forward cautiously, scanning the shadows ahead of them. Then, apparently satisfied that I must be up above, the big one signalled again, more urgently, for the other to go up the ladder. The smaller man started to climb, slowly, using only his right hand, his sword clutched in his left, his eyes straining up into the gloom above him where he thought the danger lay. Ape Face stayed where he was in the middle of the floor, about four paces from me.

I transferred my sword into my left hand and grasped the hilt of the skystone dagger in my right, my arm stretched across my body, not daring to unsheathe it lest the sound alarm them before I was ready. When the climber reached the eighth rung, I judged the time was right and launched myself like a lance, my left arm extended to cut down the distance between Ape Face and myself and my right whipping the skystone dagger out of its sheath. The point of my sword took the big fellow low in the back with all my weight behind it, and as he arched away from the stabbing blade I brought my right hand whipping round in an arc and plunged the dagger, point first, up into the softness beneath his chin, driving for the brain, killing him instantly. I released the sword immediately and kept on turning with the impetus of my swing, pulling the dagger free and dropping to my right knee as my right arm came back behind my head ready to throw.

The man on the ladder made a perfect target. His companion's death had come so suddenly and unexpectedly that he was caught completely by surprise. He teetered there, gaping at me, lacking the presence of mind even to shout and presenting the full breadth of his chest for me to aim at. I threw with all my strength, aiming for the centre of his chest. The skystone dagger made a silver streak and thudded into the hollow at the base of his throat, cutting his chance of screaming forever. His chin snapped downward against the hilt; his eyes flew wide and his mouth moved uselessly, making a wet, gurgling, choking sound. Then he fell slowly forward, bolt upright, crashing head-first to the floor. I was beside him almost as he hit the ground, pulling my dagger from his throat. I cleaned the blade roughly on his tunic and then scrambled to the body of his ape-faced companion, rolling him over without ceremony to retrieve my sword. My heart was hammering in my ears and I was ready for anything, fully expecting the noise of the killings to have been overheard. But the moments passed, and no one appeared in the doorway; I heard no shouts of alarm.

My eyes had grown accustomed to the dimness by this time, so that the shadows were no longer quite so black, and the sprawled corpses appeared to be lit now by bright sunlight. I looked about me more carefully. There were bundles of hay piled in one rear corner of the stable and a tall heap of straw in the other. Apart from those, the place was empty. I reviewed my options and discovered, not to my surprise, that I had virtually none. I could stay there and hide, or I could try to run. My own companions were less than two streets away from me, still loading our wagon with hemp, but it might as well have been twenty miles. I was a marked man. The whole town would be looking for a grey-bearded man with a limp, and there were people everywhere. I might be able to hide my face somehow, but I couldn't possibly walk without limping. I had to stay there and hope for the best, which meant that I had to hide the bodies of Ape Face and his friend.

It took me several minutes of strenuous pulling and hauling to drag them over to the piled bundles of hay and rearrange the stooks to cover them, and at every second I expected someone to appear in the open doorway to the midden. Finally I had them lying together and almost out of sight. I broke the binding of two bundles and scattered loose hay over their sprawling forms, and then I crossed the floor and scattered loose straw over the blood that lay puddled where they had fallen, stamping it down to soak up the moisture and scattering more fresh stuff on top of that. There was a lot of blood, and as I tried to hide it I was thinking ironically of my debate with myself on the morality of killing. Satisfied at last that I had done all I could to hide the signs of violence, and more conscious than ever of the door that gaped so widely onto the midden, I withdrew into the opposite corner from the corpses and crouched behind the pile of straw, my eyes fixed on the white rectangle of light. I did not even consider climbing up into the loft. I was trapped badly enough, there on the ground. This was one of the few occasions when I experienced no urge to vomit after violent action. That would come later, only after all danger was past. I had another sickness in my gut that told me I would have to wait a long time.

I gave not a moment's thought to the possibility that one of my own men might unwittingly betray me to Nesca's people. My own soldiers were encamped a few miles from the town, in a clearing within sight of, but well hidden from, the road. The six men who had come into town with me were all farmers and all taciturn. They did not enjoy having to travel to the town and they had no trust in, or patience with, the people who made their living there. If asked by any stranger about having seen a limping, grey-haired man, they would automatically assume I was in trouble, and they would deny any knowledge of me. At the same time, I hoped, they would start looking for me themselves.

I had almost schooled my heartbeat to a moderate pace when a new danger set it to racing again. I had completely missed seeing the door that suddenly crashed open, spilling lamplight into the darkened stable and bringing my heart bounding in terror into my throat. It was flush with the wall I was crouching against, and made from the same rough planking. It was flung open with such violence that it crashed all the way back to the wall, missing me by inches, and then rebounded to mask me from the man who stepped through the opening, muttering under his breath. He crossed the open floor in eight great strides and busied himself with closing and barring the outside door, all the while keeping up a string of curses and imprecations.

Quietly and carefully, my heart still pounding in my throat, knowing that he could turn and see me at any second, I stood up and stepped around the open door into the short passageway beyond, hoping against all hope that the place I was going to would be empty. It was — empty and almost dark. The only light came from two lamps and a few narrow cracks between the boards of the shutters that sealed the single window. The door leading to the street was solid-looking and solidly barred.

The place was a chandler's shop, cluttered with clay lamps of all shapes and sizes and amphorae and smaller jars of oil. It smelled pungently and aromatically of oils and camphor. To my left, a set of dangerous-looking steps led up to another loft, where the owner obviously lived. I crossed the room quickly and pressed my eye to one of the cracks in the shutters. There was chaos in the street outside; people were running in every direction and the scene reeked of panic. As I watched, I saw an old, grey-bearded man being hauled bodily across my line of sight by two hulking bullies. I had time to see no more, for from behind me came the roaring voice of the shop owner, arguing with someone. I looked again for somewhere to hide as I heard a slamming noise from the stable at the rear and the quick, angry sound of approaching footsteps. I moved quickly and tried to conceal myself behind the rickety steps in the corner just as the man came back into the room.

He was big — tall and broad-shouldered — so that he had to stoop coming through the doorway. As he began to straighten up, he saw my feet and froze for a heartbeat, and then he straightened up completely, eyeing me warily. He made no sound, and I saw that he carried no weapon. He looked me straight in the eye, and then his gaze dropped to my left knee. I remained motionless, my hand on the hilt of my sword. Unhurriedly, he closed the door behind him and moved two steps into the shop, coming to rest facing me with his buttocks resting against the small counter that held many of his wares. There was no fear in his eyes. The only sounds came from the street outside, where one woman screamed above the general noise, her voice ululating like a demented owl's. When he spoke, his voice was deep, and clearer than I would have expected.

"There's a lot of grief out there," he said. "I hope you're worth it."

I reached into my tunic with my left hand and pulled out a heavy purse. I tossed it onto the countertop beside him, where it landed with a solid, full sound.

"The price on my head is ten gold *auri*," I said. "There's at least that many in that bag, perhaps a few more. That presents you with an important choice. You can yell for help and die now, or you can pretend to help me and claim the reward later, hoping you'll get it. My guess is you won't smell it, once I'm taken, and you won't get what's in the bag there, either."

His face was expressionless. "There has to be a third choice, one where I keep the money. What is it?"

I told him. "There's a ropery, about two streets from here. You know it?"

He nodded. "I know it."

"Well, my men are there, loading a wagon with hemp. They don't know what's going on. Bring them here, to your back door, the one you just closed. Once I'm safe in the wagon, covered up, we'll leave, and you can keep the purse."

"Ten gold *auri*? Do you take me for a fool? You'd leave me choking in my own blood for a tenth of that. A twentieth!"

I shrugged. "I wouldn't. The money's not important. I can't expect you to believe that, but nevertheless, it's true. I carry it with me in case I ever find the opportunity to buy iron."

He was glaring at me sceptically. "Iron? You buy iron with gold?"

I nodded my head. "That's right, I do. Raw iron. Ingot

iron. At least I would, if I could. But iron ingots are becoming more hard to find than gold *auri*." I could still see doubt and disbelief in his face, and I shrugged. "Take my word for it. We're going to have to trust each other, I fear."

He was silent for a spell, looking me straight in the eye with a speculative glare, then, "Look, stranger, I don't know who you are and I don't want to know, but nobody is worth ten gold *auri*, that's too ridiculous for words."

I nodded to the pouch. "Count it."

"Oh, I believe it's there. That's a heavy little purse, and you didn't pack it with flat stones knowing you'd be meeting me. But what I'm wondering is this: what did you do to Quinctilius Nesca that makes your hide worth ten gold *auri*?"

I could have lied to him, but something in his expression prompted me to tell him the truth.

"I broke his favourite nephew's face and carved my initials in his chest."

"You what?" There was laughing disbelief on his face now.

"You heard me."

"Aye, I heard you." He shook his head. "Who was his nephew?"

"He still is — I didn't kill him. I just put my mark on him. Caesarius Claudius Seneca."

His eyes grew round. "The crazed one? Him? He's Nesca's nephew?"

I nodded. "Aye, or his cousin. They're related."

He frowned. "But isn't he the Procurator?"

"He was. He's disappeared. But he was here before, about six years ago, visiting on business for the Emperor. That's when we — met."

He shook his head again and then moved suddenly to the window. I tensed and jerked my dagger out, prepared to throw it, but he merely put his eye to a crack as I had done and made no move to open the shutters. I relaxed slightly, and after a few seconds he turned back to me.

"You haven't a hope of getting out of this town today. Not a chance. They're searching door to door, and the less luck they have the harder they'll look. Nesca's a powerful man and a bad one to cross. He won't stop looking for you until he's tossed this whole town upside-down. You're safe here, for now at least. They've already been here. That's why I shut up shop, and why I knew who you were the minute I saw you. How did you get in?"

"You passed me on your way to close the back door. I slipped in here while your back was turned."

"Just as well you did. They came there, too, while I was shutting up — the same ones who had searched the front here earlier. I sent them packing."

"They searched the stable?"

"Not thoroughly, just had a quick look. I told them there was no one there and I was still angry at them from the first time, so they believed me. Why?"

I decided to hold my peace and said nothing.

"Hmmm," he said, tapping a thumb-nail against his teeth. "You're a lucky man."

I grimaced. "Lucky? You think so? Why?"

"Got away from them, didn't you? And you finished up here."

"That makes me lucky? I suppose it does."

"It does, friend. That makes you lucky."

He was hinting at something, but I didn't know what. "How? I don't follow you."

He picked up the bag of gold and opened it, pouring a stream of coins onto the countertop. One of them he picked up and held towards me, between finger and thumb. "Because of this," he said. "And because I hate Quinctilius Nesca's lard-filled guts because of this." I said nothing, waiting for him to continue. He flipped the coin. "If I'd had ten of these, six years ago, I could have kept the business I had for five years before that gross slug came into my life. I borrowed some money from him and then lost my venture. He took everything I had. Even my wife. Not that she went to him. She just left me. Couldn't adjust to the pauper's life." His big fist closed suddenly over the gold coin and he scowled. "This Seneca, Nesca's cousin. It never occurred to me the Procurator might be the same man. What does he look like?"

"Why do you ask that? Have you seen him?"

The big man shook his head. "I don't know. I may have. You said he was here in Britain six years ago. That's when I had my trouble with Nesca, and he had a fellow with him at that time who caused a deal of trouble around here. I'd never seen him before, and neither had anyone else. But he was a really unpleasant bastard, handsome as a god and evil as a snake." He jerked his eyes away from mine and moved towards the window.

"That sounds like Seneca," I said. "He was always good to look at, providing you didn't look too deeply. Did he offend you personally?"

"Aye, you might say that." His voice was low and deep in his throat. "You might indeed." He moved back to the small counter he had been leaning against and began to smooth his thumb over its wooden surface, concentrating tightly on the grained pattern of the wood. "I had a son, a boy of five. He disappeared, and we never saw him again. Wolves, we were told, or a bear in the woods. Stupid to say the boy knew he was forbidden to go into the woods. He was gone. My wife was, too, soon after . . ." His voice choked into silence, and I saw his shoulders shake, but then he went on. "Later, months afterward, I found out that there were five young boys went missing that summer. Five of them. And it worked out that they all disappeared while Quinctilius Nesca's unpopular houseguest was in residence. And there were witnesses who saw the houseguest with two of the boys just before they were reported missing . . . Seneca. His name was Seneca . . .

"When we went looking for him, he had gone, back to the Court in Constantinople. Nesca laughed at us and threw us off his land. And the witnesses against his houseguest disappeared, the same way the boys did."

"I see." It was time to change the subject. My host's self-possession was deteriorating rapidly. "What business were you in?"

He blinked his eyes rapidly, clearing them of the tears that were gathering there, and he flipped the gold coin again.

"I was a wine importer. Not a big one, but comfortable. I learned the ins and outs of shipping the stuff while I was in the navy. Started small, once I got out, and did well. Then I saw a chance to operate on a bigger scale and borrowed the money to do it."

"And?"

"The ship sank. Or pirates got it. Either way, it makes no difference to me. Nesca took everything I had."

"How long were you in the navy?"

"Fifteen years. Got out when I was thirty."

"And after fifteen years, you risked everything on one shipload?"

He smiled, without humour. "No, on two, but the second one didn't arrive within three months of its expected date. By the time it did, it was Nesca's."

I felt a stab of sympathy. "He wouldn't wait any longer?"

"He wouldn't wait at all, the fat son of a whore. He paid the second shipmaster to take a tour. I found out afterwards. That was seven years ago, so you can keep your money, it's too late to do me any good. I'll get my satisfaction out of cheating that fat pig out of his. Are you hungry?"

Suddenly I was ravenous. I nodded.

"Good," he said. "Let's eat. There isn't much, and it isn't epicurean, but it'll fill our bellies. I'm Tertius Pella."

I gripped his outstretched arm. "Publius Varrus."

He produced bread and cheese and onions pickled in sour wine and we devoured them, and then he brought out a jar of truly wondrous wine, rich and red as blood, and I stopped with the cup halfway to my lips.

"What's the matter?"

I lowered the cup. "Guilt. You're giving me your hospitality and I've brought you more trouble than you know."

"How so?"

"There are two dead men in your stable, under the hay."

"Ayee!" He twisted his face. "That's awkward. Two of Nesca's?"

I nodded. "I'm sorry."

"So am I! They're bound to come back this way and search again. We'd better move them."

"Move them? Where to?"

"Dump them into the cellar under the floor and cover the door with straw. I'll bury them later."

"What about the blood stains? If they search, they'll see them."

"Are they bad?"

I nodded. "They bled like pigs."

"Not inappropriate. But where are they? I didn't notice them when I was out there."

"You weren't looking, otherwise you couldn't have missed them."

"Damnation! I can't claim ignorance, even though it's the truth. They'll never believe I didn't know the bodies were there when I wouldn't let them search. They'll haul me in front of Nesca, and as soon as he sees my face I'm done for. He knows I know he robbed me. This will be a perfect chance for him to silence me for good."

He stopped and looked at me strangely.

"Where will you go when you get away from here? Where do you live?"

"On a villa, about forty miles south of here."

"A villa, eh? You own it?"

I shook my head. "No, it belongs to a friend of mine. You'd like him."

"Can I come with you?"

He had surprised me again. "Come with me? You mean for good? What about your business?"

He looked around the shop. "What business? Nesca

can have it, as a shrine for the bodies in the cellar. I'm sick of it."

I laughed, quietly. "Tertius Pella," I said, "if we ever get out of here alive, you will be welcome at our villa."

"Excellent!" He lifted his cup in a toast. "Here's to new friendships, new futures and a lingering, evil death for fat thieves!"

We emptied our cups, and he rose and went again to the shutters and stood there for a time, peering out through the cracks. The noise in the street outside had died away almost completely. Finally he spoke over his shoulder.

"You said you had a wagon being loaded with hemp. Is your driver a big, red-haired fellow, wearing a blue tunic?"

I was at his side in a second, and there was my own wagon, outside in the street.

"That's it! Get him in here! Can you do that? His name's Cerdic."

"Cerdic. Give me a minute."

It took him about three minutes, and then they were both back, Cerdic as glad to see me as I was to see him. My men had recognized me from the description they were given by the searchers, although they had said nothing to any of them. They had split up then and were now combing the town looking for me. Cerdic had stayed with the wagon, unwilling to abandon it. They had planned to reassemble at our camp outside of town and spend the night there before renewing their search for me tomorrow.

Cerdic was in a fever to get me into the wagon and covered up from sight. He had just been searched, he said, at the end of the street, and if we moved quickly, he thought he could go back the same way without being searched again. It was time for a quick and dangerous decision. Tertius showed him the back entrance and I waited there for them, opening the door when I heard them returning. Cerdic backed the wagon in immediately and I dived into the evil-smelling hemp and burrowed deep. I could feel Tertius Pella rearranging the load to hide all signs of my entrance. We pulled out again immediately and within ten minutes we were back at the checkpoint where Cerdic had been searched. I heard the watchman's challenge.

"Come on, man!" Cerdic roared. "You've just searched me! You've been through the whole whoreson wagon! I went to the end of the street to pick up my friend, here, at the *mansio*. Do you want us to strip for you? Want us to empty the whole whoreson lot right here on the road? If you're going to search, get to it! I've got better things to do than waste my time squatting here while you shed your fleas all over me."

I couldn't hear the answer he received, but we sat there for long, long minutes. I felt somebody's weight moving around on the wagon bed, standing on the cargo piled above me. I imagined whoever it was to be stabbing at random among the hemp with a spear, and my mouth dried up as I waited for the point of it to find me. It was hot and uncomfortable under there, and I started to have difficulty breathing. My throat grew dry and raspy, and I began to develop an urge to cough. I worked my tongue frantically, trying to generate saliva to kill the dryness. And then the wagon lurched forward and we were moving again, for a few paces. I heard Cerdic shouting something else, but I couldn't hear what he said. After a few more minutes, we moved on. The relief was overwhelming, and I lost the urge to cough.

As the wagon rattled through the cobbled streets, I found I was protected from the jarring by the springiness of the hemp, and I was almost lulled to sleep. Strangely, I thought, we were not stopped again for a long time, and when we did stop it was only for a second. I heard Cerdic shout goodbye to someone and wondered what was happening up there. Had Tertius Pella changed his mind about leaving after all? I knew that Cerdic would call me when we were safe and not before, so I made the best of my enforced idleness by going over the list of supplies that I would not be taking back to the Colony this time.

Suddenly we stopped again. There was a commotion above me, and I felt cool air on my face.

"Publius? Are you all right?"

I spat hemp out of my mouth and sat up. "I'm well. Are we safe?"

Cerdic laughed. "Aye. We're out of it. Thank the gods you kept your mouth shut. I didn't know if that first guard had killed you with his spear, but there was nothing I could do about it until we were safely out of the town, beyond the gates."

"What happened to Tertius Pella? Why did he leave?"

He looked puzzled, standing there staring down at me. "Leave? He didn't. He's here."

"Then who got off the wagon?"

"Oh, that!" He laughed. "That was the centurion who was riding with us. He got us through all the guard posts and we dropped him at the gates. That's why I was glad you kept your mouth shut. If you had squawked, I'd have had to kill him, and we'd really have been in trouble. Let me help you out of there."

Half an hour later we were at our camp. All of the

other wagons had arrived ahead of us, and only two men were missing. They had stayed in Aquae Sulis, lodged at the *mansio* in the hope of hearing news of my escape or capture. They would rejoin the others in the morning.

I introduced Tertius Pella to his new neighbours. When I told them all the story of my misadventures that day, and how he had befriended me, they welcomed him as one of themselves.

Our two absentees joined us shortly after daybreak the next day and were astounded to see me. I laughed at the stupefaction on their faces.

"What kept you two?" I asked them. "We've been waiting here for you all night."

"All night?" Tarpo Sulla, the elder of the two, looked confused and upset. "What d'you mean, all night? When did you get here?"

I looked at Cerdic, surprised by the vehemence of Tarpo's question. "When was it, Cerdic? The eighth hour? Just shortly after dark. Why?"

"Then it wasn't you."

"What wasn't me? Tarpo, you're not making sense."

"Oh yes I am," Tarpo growled. "That whoreson Nesca was murdered last night. Strangled. Right after supper, on his way to bed. Somebody jumped him in the privy and almost cut his head off with a thin rope. They're blaming it on you."

I sat down heavily on the stump behind me. Every eye in the camp was on me, waiting for my reaction. There was no question of suspicion in anyone's mind. I had sat talking with them around the fire until almost midnight. The mere linking of my name with the murder of Quinctilius Nesca, however, was a serious matter. My name!

"They're blaming it on me, you say? Do they have my name? Are they looking for Publius Varrus?"

"No, they're looking for a grey-bearded, strong-looking man who walks with a bad limp in his left leg. They don't know your name. But there must be a lot of people in that town who do. The people we do business with, for a start. Sooner or later, one of them's going to mention your name and point the finger."

If he was right, I would be wanted for a triple murder when the bodies of the other two were discovered. I tried frantically to think of how many people there were in Aquae Sulis who could identify me, and try as I would, I could think of none. I had only been to the town once before. I had spent three days there, as a stranger, passing through on my way to Caius's villa for the first time. I turned to Cerdic.

"Cerdic, think hard. When we were at the ropery yesterday, did I tell him my name? Can you remember?"

His brow furrowed in thought. "D'you know, I don't think you did." He thought further. "No, I'm sure of it. You didn't. He was a surly bugger, and you argued the price with him, but you weren't friendly at all. You paid him cash and then spoke to me. Told me you were going to the *mansio*, and then you took off."

"You're right, Cerdic. I didn't tell him my name. Did you tell him yours? Did he know you?"

He shook his head. "No. Never seen him before. I think he's new. I wouldn't have given him the time of day, never mind my name. Why? Is it important?"

I looked around at all of them. "Aye," I answered him. "It's very important. You people are known in that town, but I'm not. That's the second time I've ever been there, and the first time I was just passing through. Nobody knows me there, and the only person who saw me with any of you this time was the roper. That means they won't find out my name, and they won't tie me to any of you. It also means I won't be going back there for a while." There was a small ripple of laughter at that as I went on. "I don't know who killed Quinctilius Nesca, but a man like that is never short of enemies. I do know, however, and you know, too, that it wasn't Publius Varrus. Now we'd better get back to the Colony as quickly as we can. The sooner we're away from here, the happier I'll be."

I stopped as a curious thought occurred to me, and I turned again to the men who had brought the news.

"You say Nesca was attacked and murdered in the night. Who found the body, and where?"

Tarpo Sulla scowled in thought. "I don't know. He was on his way to the privy, that's all I know. And whoever did it almost took his head right off. Willy heard somebody mention something about his cousin being the one that found the body, isn't that right, Willy?"

His cousin! Seneca? I immediately began to wonder if I might have located the missing Procurator, and the thought did not seem far-fetched. Nesca might well have provided his wealthy cousin with a hiding place, a safe retreat to wait out the fortunes of Magnus in his bid for the Empire. And then I made an intuitive leap. If there had been ill-feeling between them, if bad blood had developed, Seneca might have perceived a way to get rid of his fat cousin and foist the blame onto the same crippled assassin who had tried to kill him once before. It was pure supposition on my part, but it made grim sense.

We had no difficulties on the road, and we were back in the Colony two days later. Caius listened carefully to the tale I had to tell him, shook his head regretfully over the idiocy and pettiness of men and then dismissed the topic and told me about the strange embassy he had received from Ullic, the High Chief of the local Pendragon Celts. He seemed to put no credence at all in my theory concerning the killing of Nesca and the whereabouts of Claudius Seneca, discounting it as pure conjecture, irrelevant and unimportant beside his own news. I can recall being hurt and angered by his indifference to my report and my suspicions. At the same time, however, I was able to recognize the importance of the embassage from Ullic and to acknowledge that there might be good reason for the evident excitement it had caused during my absence.

Just after I had left for Aquae Sulis, Cymric and his brother, my arrow-flighting friend, had approached Caius formally on behalf of their Chief, Ullic Pendragon. Ullic, they said, wanted to meet with Caius to discuss matters of mutual interest. This was a great honour, Cymric had added, since never before had a Pendragon Chief had truck with any Roman.

Intrigued, Caius had naturally invited the Chief to be his guest in the Colony, but this was not acceptable at all. The meeting, he was told, must be a formal one held in a holy place. Caius had asked where that might be, and was told Stonehenge.

Of course, I knew where Stonehenge was. It is an open temple, sacred to the Druids, ancient as time itself, and it stands, or rather its ruins stand, on the highest ground of the great plain south of us, more than a day's march from the villa. Caius had demurred at first at having to go so far, but Luceiia, who was with him at the time, was wise enough to convince him to agree to the meeting. He had asked what kind of escort he was permitted to bring to such a formal meeting, and had been told that Ullic would be accompanied by his Druids and by a warrior escort, so it would be in order for Caius to bring an escort of his own.

Caius had been insistent on postponing the meeting until I could accompany him, and had set it two weeks away; that meant six days from the day I should have returned from Aquae Sulis. The prospect of meeting the Celtic chieftain interested me, but I was still preoccupied with the reappearance of the Seneca clan in my life. I tried again to interest Caius in my theory on Seneca and his whereabouts, but I could see it was a waste of time. He was completely engrossed in planning for the upcoming meeting, and he had so many things on his mind that he could not allow himself to be distracted by a Seneca who was not an immediate source of danger.

For me, however, the reverse was true. I could have no interest in meeting a Celtic savage when my arch-enemy might be within reach of my vengeance. Disappointed and slightly angered by Caius's lack of interest, I decided to take steps of my own to deal with the possibility that Seneca might be in Aquae Sulis. I made my arrangements and mentioned none of them to either Caius or my wife, both of whom, I knew, would have disagreed wholeheartedly with what I proposed to do. In my arrogance and anger I fear I lost sight, as I often did, of the possibility of repercussions from my own rash actions. Secure in my righteousness, I breathed new life into an old hatred and started a chain of events that would haunt me and mine years later.

XXXI

Five days later, Equus brought Tertius Pella to see me. I was at work at the place behind the villa where we had built the furnace to smelt the metal from the skystone. When they arrived, I was working with the special clay we intended to use as a liner for the fire-box, and while I washed the stuff from my hands and dried them on a rag, Equus entertained Tertius with a description of what we were hoping to achieve with the new kiln. At length, my hands clean and dry, I took off my leather apron and welcomed Tertius. It was a hot, dusty, sunny day, and Equus poured each of us a mug of cool beer from the supply he always seemed to have at hand, stored out of the way of the sun's heat. As we drank the first, deep draught, I examined Tertius Pella again, confirming my original opinion of him.

He was a tall man, well set-up, as the local Celts say, in his late thirties, with broad shoulders and a waist that was just beginning to thicken, where most men of his age were already pot-bellied with overeating. His dark, saturnine face, with its eyes surrounded by deep creases, showed his years of squinting against the sun's glare off the ocean, for Tertius Pella was a true navy man, a soldier who had lived on water for most of his years with the Eagles. I had already learned that he was strong and shrewd and solid, dependable as one of his beloved quadriremes, and the jut of his chin was reminiscent of the ramming beaks of those same vessels.

"Well," I asked him, "what did you find?"

He grinned, a vulpine grin with no humour in it. "What I went to find. He's there all right, in a townhouse rented for the year by the unlamented lard-sack, Nesca."

"You saw him?" I needed to be sure.

"Aye, once. Only for a few moments, but it was enough and more. He came to an open portal, less than fifteen paces from where I stood. No possibility of error — it was him. Caesarius Claudius Seneca, Senator of Rome and Procurator of South Britain, hiding from the sunlight in a darkened house. That's appropriate enough, come to think of it. God, I wish I'd had a bow in my hand! I could have slipped an arrow into either of his eyes so fast —"

"Did anyone see you? Anyone recognize you?"

"No, of course not. You told me to make sure I wasn't seen."

"Good, good. So!" I cut him off, excited by his confirmation of what had until that moment been nothing more than a suspicion and a hope. "He *is* there, obviously in hiding, as you say." I was talking half to him and half to myself, voicing my milling thoughts. "But why is he hiding? Who is he hiding from? From the whole world, and particularly from Theodosius and his spies and informers, because the rumours must be true. He *did* finance Magnus! He used imperial revenues to arm and equip the armies of a usurper, and now he is hiding, waiting for the outcome of his gamble!"

"Wait, I don't understand." This was Equus. "Why does he need to hide? Britain belongs to Magnus.

If Seneca is a Magnus supporter, he has nothing to be afraid of."

"Two reasons, Equus," I answered him. "The first is that Magnus is only Emperor in Britain. He might fail in his attempt for the whole Empire. If he does, then all who aided him will stand proscribed under sentence of death. And that leads to the second reason: Seneca is not stupid. Rest assured, he has a back-up plan ready should Magnus fail. He'll have done something to safeguard himself if disaster overtakes him. As Imperial Procurator of South Britain, he must be seen to be loyal to Theodosius — for his own safety he cannot appear to be otherwise. So he has 'disappeared,' presumably to conduct the Emperor's affairs from a safe place. He is unable, of course, to communicate with Rome because Britain is in rebel hands. If Magnus is successful, Seneca will be triumphant — the Maker of the Emperor. And if Magnus is defeated, Seneca will come out of hiding with his reputation unblemished. He'll make up any shortfall in funds out of his own coffers. God knows they're deep enough! That's really the only gamble he is taking. But he has to stay hidden."

Equus was still unconvinced. "How can he stay hidden in a city? Somebody is bound to recognize him. There are still people around who are loyal to Theodosius and the Empire."

"Of course there are, Equus, you're right." I turned to Pella. "What was he wearing when you saw him?"

Pella looked surprised. "Nothing special, a tunic."

"An elaborate tunic? Brightly coloured?"

"No, not elaborate. It was plain — plain white."

"Aha! Was it bright, stark white?"

"No!" He was beginning to look annoyed. "It was plain white, same as the one I'm wearing. Just an ordinary, everyday tunic."

"Good man, Tertius. You have an eye for detail. How many guards on duty at the gates?"

He looked from Equus to me and jerked his head in a negative. "None, and that surprised me at first."

"At first?"

"Aye, until I began to see what was going on."

"And what was that?" I glanced at Equus, whose brow was creased in concentration as he tried to miss nothing of this. "What *was* going on?"

Pella looked narrowly at me and then shrugged his shoulders. "Nothing, really. Nothing noticeable. Nothing that any of the neighbours could see, unless they were *really* looking. But there's at least eight men in that house with Seneca, and they all look like professional gladiators. I counted eight for sure, and there may have been a ninth. It took me two days to make the tally."

"Are you saying they are all in hiding?"

"Aye," he said, "at least, most of them stay out of sight. There's three fellows who come and go all the time, but the others keep their heads down. Except late at night. I saw four of them slip out on the second night. They were back well before dawn."

"Equus," I asked, "do you see what Tertius is telling us?" He shook his head, frowning. "Think about Seneca. He is the Imperial Procurator of South Britain, one of the most influential and most highly trusted administrators in the entire province. He is also one of the wealthiest men in the Empire. And above all, he is Caesarius Claudius Seneca, Senator of Rome, renowned for his profligacy and for his debauchery. People expect many things from Seneca, Equus. They expect outrageous, fashionable clothes and all the trappings of power and wealth — rich wagons, magnificent horses, uniformed personal retainers, absolute physical security. They do *not* expect silence, seclusion and the appearance of poverty. Now do you see?"

"Guards and soldiers!" I saw comprehension flare in Equus's eyes. "No guards! So he is in hiding, disguised as an ordinary man!"

"Exactly! Completely unremarkable, completely untraceable. Nobody will recognize him in Aquae Sulis, Equus, nobody! Because no one will think to see him! The man is such a swine that he can escape detection completely simply by ceasing to be himself." I returned my attention to Tertius, who was helping himself to more beer. "Can you take the place?"

"Aye." He nodded. "I think so."

"How many men will you need?"

"Twelve." He had thought it through already, but the number surprised me.

"That many?"

"Aye, to do it right. Four to lay hands on the whoreson to make sure he comes to no accidental harm, and eight to look after his bullies."

"And you? Where will you be?"

"I'll be in reserve," he answered, grinning that grin again. "I warn you, though, I think your plan is a waste, and dangerous. If we are going in there anyway, it would be easier to put him away there and then. Kill the whoreson and have done. Then we wouldn't have to worry about getting him out, or hiding him, or any of that nonsense. Getting him out and away is going to be the most hazardous part of the whole thing!"

I was already aware of Pella's feelings on this. He wanted Seneca dead as quickly as possible, in payment for the death of his own son. But he considered the right to kill Seneca to be his alone. I contradicted him before he could develop his theme.

"Forget that, Tertius," I said. "We've talked about it before. A quick, clean death's too good for this man. We want him to suffer. We want him to wonder why and who has done this to him. We want him to squirm, to squeal for mercy. And we want him to know, beyond any doubt, that he can't buy his life from us. He will know, before we are finished with him, that Justice has caught up with him."

"Ach!" The expletive had a disgusted note to it. Pella was not impressed. "Justice be damned! Kill him and get it done, I say, just so long as he sees my face before the blade slips in! That whoreson wouldn't recognize Justice if he watched her take off her blindfold and use it to polish her scales." He stopped and smiled. "But you may be right again, Publius. You have not been wrong on anything, so far. We'll do it your way, in the hope of a few laughs."

"Good," I said, not knowing how else to respond. "Now, I'll be leaving for the south with Caius in two days. We expect to be gone for six days, and then I will spend another two days at home with my wife before coming to find you. You are absolutely sure of the location we are using?"

"Absolutely. Went by there on the way back, this morning. It will do fine."

"Excellent. As soon as I get back from Stonehenge, Equus will deliver that message to you and you will wait for me where the path enters the forest at mid-morning of the second day after my return. Equus, do you know where to go to find Tertius?" Equus grunted an affirmative and I spoke again to Pella. "Have you picked your men?" He nodded. "They are all trustworthy and sworn to secrecy?" Another nod. "Good. When can you leave?"

"Tonight. Everything's set up."

I reviewed the entire plan in my mind, and to this day I can recall exactly how I felt and what I thought as I stood there. I was in the grip of a powerful lust, governed completely by an irresistible thirst for vengeance, and my heart was hammering heavily in my breast with the knowledge that I was close to achieving it. I had been bothered by dreams of Phoebe for several nights, and I fancied that her spirit cried out to me for justice. I had not the slightest qualm over what I intended to do. There was no pity in my breast. Seneca would die by my hand, and I would kill him as I would a snake, a scorpion, or any other hostile, dangerous creature.

I have never known a compulsion, a bloodthirsty imperative, as strong as the one I was under then. That may have been the peak of my entire life in terms of cold, implacable, condemnatory judgment. My raging anger was as spontaneous as rain. It is extremely doubtful that I could summon up such rage today, no matter what the provocation. I finished visualizing the details of my plan.

"Perfect," I said, nodding at Pella. "As far as I can see, everything is in place. Once you have him, keep him disoriented. Shackle him and keep his eyes covered at all times. Check his blindfold often, at least every hour, and make sure he can't reach it with his hands. Don't be gentle with him, but don't hurt him unnecessarily, either. Above all, don't talk to him. Not a word. Remain with him yourself and keep two more men with you. Send the others home as soon as you have him safely in your custody. Feed him regularly, but not well. He has to know, through all of his senses, that he is a prisoner in extremely hostile hands." I paused, thinking over what I had said before continuing. "Don't even let him hear you talking among yourselves. Can you manage that?"

"Of course! Simple discipline."

"Good. The more off balance we can keep him, the better it will suit our purposes. By the time I get to him I want him thoroughly cowed, confused and afraid. That reminds me, keep him naked, too. But don't let him freeze to death. You may have to throw him a blanket if the weather turns bad. If you do, make sure that it is old, coarse, scratchy and evil-smelling." My mind was racing. "Another thing. After you have him and you're safe from pursuit, if you ever are, tie his wrists and make him run behind your horse, blindfolded. He should find that an interesting introduction to his new life. But watch him carefully, Tertius. If he falls, don't drag him. Get him back up on his feet. And again, above all, don't talk to him!

"When you get to the spot we've chosen, make camp and wait for me. Shackle him to a stake beneath the big oak branch, and make sure he spends hours at a stretch with his arms drawn up above his head, fastened by the wrists. I'd like him to have about a week of that before I get there. Will you have enough time?"

Pella grunted. "More than enough. We'll leave tonight and I'll watch the place for a day or two before we go in, just to see if there are any established patterns of behaviour we can make use of. If four of them do go out regularly, that will make our job easier."

I nodded, and Equus spoke up again. "They probably do — go out regularly, I mean, after dark. Probably revolve, like regular guard duty. Otherwise they'd go insane, stuck in that house day in and day out. I mean, it's not as if they can bring women in, is it? Not without causing talk. My guess is some will go off duty every night, after the ordinary people are asleep and the town has quietened down. They probably go to the same place all the time, some crib where they can get a drink and a woman. Find out where they go, and you can take them any time. That'll make your house job easier." Pella was grinning again. He had already been where Equus was telling him to go. I slapped him on the arm and got up from the stone I had perched on.

"So be it!" I said. "The heavens may not approve of what we are planning, but I don't think we will hear thunderstorms of protest. And not too many men will judge us, either."

"Caius Britannicus wouldn't approve." Equus sounded almost condemnatory.

"No," I agreed, "he would not. Not of the means, at any rate. The end he might applaud."

"You think the end justifies the means, Varrus?"

I turned and looked Tertius straight in the eye. "I couldn't care less. I just want Seneca stopped, and I don't want Caius Britannicus to hear anything about this until it is over. Do you both understand that?"

They nodded, and Pella scratched his upper lip reflectively with the tip of one finger.

"You know," he said quietly, "I've got good reason to hate Seneca, knowing the animal killed my son, but you, Publius Varrus, you don't like the man at all, do you?"

"That's as good a way of phrasing it as any, my friend," I answered with a slight smile. "Go with God, Tertius. I'll look for good news on my return from the south."

Pella was looking over my shoulder. "Here comes Caius Britannicus. Tell me, what do you think you're going to achieve at Stonehenge? Why are you even going? And who is this Celt, that he thinks he can summon Romans with a crooked finger?"

By the time Caius reached us we were well into a genuine discussion of the Stonehenge excursion, and the conversation flowed smoothly on from there. I felt only a small twinge of guilt at hoodwinking my friend Caius, but I knew that if I were successful, he would enjoy it. And besides, my anticipation of vengeance on Seneca left little room for guilt or regret.

Four days later, I found myself remembering that meeting and the hazy summer heat of that afternoon with nostalgia. I was cold and I was wet. And I was unimpressed by the fact that the great, lichen-crusted stone column against which I rested my back had been standing in this place for thousands of years. In front of me, the rolling hills of the great plain of Sarum fell away in swooping waves until they were shrouded in the drizzle that hid the horizon in every direction and defied the eyes to tell where the sky ended and the ground began. There were times when Caius's beloved Britain left much to be desired. We had been here for hours, and so far there was no sign of Ullic and his Celts.

I suppose we had made a fine sight as we approached Stonehenge, but there'd been no one there to see us. The massive temple stood empty, outlined against the late afternoon sky. Caius and I were on horseback, leading two wagons bearing gifts for Ullic, and we were accompanied by a full maniple of men, arrayed in their finest trappings.

We had come late on purpose, but when we saw the great temple deserted, Caius was piqued and prepared to be angry. Seeing his mood, I was able to tease him out of it, pointing out that we had merely been outmanoeuvred, and so we camped for the night close by the temple itself, posting guards all around our perimeter. Caius had made a conscious decision, against all his training and better judgment, not to dig fortifications around our camp. We were, after all, on an embassy, and he felt strongly that this was a time for discretion, both in appearance and in deportment.

When Ullic Pendragon and his people arrived at last, at dawn, they made a spectacular entrance. They came in silence broken only by the hooves of their ponies and the squeaking wheels of Ullic's barbarously magnificent wagon.

He must have had five hundred warriors with him, many on foot, some mounted on shaggy little hill ponies with their feet reaching almost to the ground. All of them seemed dressed for war in a welter of garish colours.

Ullic himself was a giant of a man, a full head taller than me. The big Celtic chieftain wore a leather helmet on his head, studded with iron, with armoured flaps that came down over his shoulders. But it was the decoration of his helmet that caught my attention. The head of a golden eagle crowned the front of it, the eyes, bright and alive-looking, glaring out at the world above the savage beak. I wondered how it had been preserved to look so lifelike, and how it was attached to the helmet beneath the ruffled neck feathers. The folded wings were fastened to the sides, and when he turned his head to look at one of his men I saw the spread tail feathers fanned out over the nape of his neck.

Caius had drawn our men up in two ranks, at attention, and I flattered myself they looked as right as Romans ever had. Each wore a plain bronze helmet and a breastplate of hardened leather. A sword belt and a skirt of leather straps studded with iron hung from every man's waist. Beneath his armour, each wore a plain white tunic that reached to just above his knees, and breeches of soft leather. On their legs they wore greaves and on their feet heavy, hobnailed, sandalled boots. Each wore a heavy cloak of homespun wool, and each held a spear and a heavy shield, the Roman soldier's scutum.

Ullic dismounted from his wagon and approached, letting us see his dress. He was swathed in a huge, red cloak, trimmed with animal fur. Barbaric jewels glittered on his breast and his legs were covered by long breeches, criss-crossed with leather bindings. His tunic was belted at the waist by a thick cord woven with what looked like gold, and both tunic and breeches were the same red as his cloak. The man was utterly splendid — and barefoot. He stopped three paces from where I stood with Caius and looked us both up and down, from head to foot.

Caius was wearing a toga-like cloak, and I suddenly wished I had worn mine. But then he looked more closely at my clothes and I felt better. I was wearing a suit of finely worked leather that, in spite of its luxurious appointments, still managed to retain a military appearance. On my left arm I wore an arm-guard of solid silver, laced with thongs — a decoration, but a useful one, since it protected my arm against my bow string. The Chief eyed this, then ran his eyes along the ranks of our men. His eyes were bright blue and his beard and moustache were black, shot through with grey.

He looked again at Caius and finally broke the spell of silence. He spoke, his voice the rumbling sound of water in a cavern. I understood not a word. He raised a hand and snapped his fingers and Cymric stepped forward from the ranks of Celts and came towards us. Ullic spoke again. Cymric looked into my eyes as though we two had never met, and then turned to Caius.

"The King says, 'Let us talk.' "

"King?" Caius replied, blinking in surprise. "I did not know he calls himself King!"

Ullic raised an eyebrow and Cymric rattled on in Celtic. The King frowned slightly, seemed to consider this, snapped out a word or two and then turned away and walked towards the temple.

"Come!" Cymric beckoned to us both. "Leave your men here."

Caius turned to our soldiers. "Hold your ranks!"

Outnumbered as we were by four to one, we did as we were bidden and followed Ullic, who stopped to allow us to catch up. We walked in silence right into Stonehenge and I realized that, apart from Ullic, Cymric and Caius, none of the six hundred or so men gathered outside had said a single word.

We stopped in the centre of the massive temple, and Ullic turned to face us. It occurred to me that I had never been at such a loss for words, not even with the Emperor Theodosius, and then it struck me forcibly that I had seldom been in the company of such a man as this. The surprising word that came to me was regal; this man truly was kingly.

"So, Roman!" He was glaring, narrow-eyed, at Caius. "You are surprised that I am a king. Why?"

He spoke in Latin. Caius looked at me in surprise, and then turned back to him. I did not know the temper of this man, but I hoped Caius would be forthright.

"We —" Caius's voice was husky. He cleared his throat angrily and spoke again, this time with his own voice. "We once had kings in Rome. We threw them out, abolished them."

"You abolished them? Why?" His voice was soft.

Caius looked him straight in the eye. "They were unworthy. They used their kingly power to subjugate the people."

"To subjugate the people. That is good." A pause, then, "*Your people subjugate the world, Roman!*"

Caius considered that. "That is true."

"But that is different? When did you last have kings, Roman?"

"Long ago."

"Before the Empire?"

"Before the Republic."

"But before the Empire?" His voice was rich with sarcasm.

"Aye. Long before."

"And you found them unworthy because they tried to dominate you. So you got rid of them. What was it you said? You . . . abolished them. And then you turned around yourselves to dominate all men."

It was well put. Caius had no answer. I decided I was well out of this. The big Celt spoke again.

"Roman, you have set out in the past four years to establish yourself as a force upon my borders. Why?"

Caius shrugged his shoulders. "My name is Caius Britannicus. Call me that, or Britannicus."

"Why? Do you dislike 'Roman'? You have not answered me. Why are you setting up a military force upon my borders?"

"We were unaware that you had borders. Or that our Colony was close to them!"

"Colony? What is this, this Colony? Are you trying to anger me, Roman?"

This "king" was being nasty with a purpose; I felt sure of it. And I felt that Caius knew it, too. If he felt anger, he was concealing it well.

"Have you ever met a king before today, Roman?"

Caius's response was curt. "Several. I liked none of them. They were all petty tyrants. Every one."

I winced inwardly, gritting my teeth. Tension was knotting my stomach.

"And I? Am I a tyrant? Have you heard stories of my tyranny?"

"No, I have not. I had not even heard of your kingship, as you know. What do you want of me?"

"Much, Roman." Ullic was eyeing Caius steadily. "My people tell me you are training an army on my

threshold. Why? What, or whom, do you look to conquer now?"

"Conquer?" Caius's fists clenched by his sides, and I
could now see the anger seething in him. He glanced at
me, looking grim, and then turned his eyes back to Ullic
defiantly. "We look to conquer nothing. We seek only to
defend ourselves!"

"Against whom?" Again the sarcasm in Ullic's voice
was heavy, but now Caius seemed determined not to
respond to it.

"Not against whom, King Ullic, against what, you
should ask."

His voice was as condescending as it could have been.
In response to his tone, Ullic's voice was lower, more
menacing.

"Against *what*, then, Roman, do you arm yourselves?" Caius said nothing. "Answer me, Roman, and
take care." His voice was soft now. "I do not like liars."

Caius told me later that the moment of truth that
comes to each man had caught up with him then. Something inside him, he said, quailed, and he was deathly
afraid to say the words he suddenly knew to be true. He
had to clench his teeth and swallow to quell a surge of
vomit in his throat, feeling like a small boy caught with
a guilty secret. He knew what he had to say. He knew
the truth.

"I am no Roman!" It came out as four toneless, dis-
connected words. I could not believe what I had heard.
As for Ullic, he looked at Caius sardonically, his right
eyebrow climbing high as Caius's own was wont to do
from time to time. Then he moved his eyes slowly down
the toga-draped length of the man facing him.

"Your pardon, Caius Britannicus! I cannot think how I could make such a mistake. How I could think you Roman?" He bowed slowly from the waist. "But, if you are no Roman, what are you? You're no Celt!"

"I am a Briton, as are you!"

Ullic laughed, a roaring bark of laughter. "A Briton? You? Boudicca was a Briton, man! So was Caradoc — Caractacus, your people called him! They and their people lived only to fight the likes of you! They were Britons! You are a foreigner. An invader!"

Caius's response was immediate and vehement. "Not so, King of Pendragon! I am a Briton, born and bred of generations born here in this land. True, my name is Roman, and my loyalties, the facile ones, have been Roman — until now! And true, no Celtic blood flows in my veins. But I am of Britain by my name, Britannicus; and I am Briton by birthright!"

Ullic folded his arms in front of him during this outburst which could hardly have surprised him more than it did me, and leaned his back against one of the great stones that stood behind him. His eyes were fixed on Caius.

"Huh!" he said. "All right, for the sake of argument, I will call you Briton from now on. The *original* Britons were a tribe of Celts, you know. Your people all but wiped them out completely. But I will call you Briton, for now. You have yet to tell me why you train an army at my door! What is it that you seek defence against?"

Caius answered him squarely. "Against the end of the world."

"The end of the world." I heard amusement in Ullic's tone this time.

"The Roman world." Caius corrected himself.

"I must be dull of wit today. Explain that."

I found myself nodding my head slowly in agreement with Caius, willing him on.

"The Roman's day is over," he said. "The Empire cannot survive much longer. It must fall. Soon."

Ullic shook his head, pityingly. "But how can this be, friend Briton? Rome is Eternal. All the Romans tell us so!"

Caius shook his head. "No. Rome is finished. The day will come, soon now, when the hordes outside will venture in. Rome no longer has the strength to keep them out."

"And? So? How does this end the world?"

I looked at him in disbelief. Was he being humorous? Or could he really fail to see beyond the fall?

"When Rome falls, the world falls, King Ullic." Caius spoke slowly and with great deliberateness. "The law ceases to exist. The army is no more. The cities starve. Their citizens go wild. There will be nothing to protect this land of Britain from invasion by people who will make the Roman invaders seem like children at play. Not a thing. Except the strengths her people build themselves. That is why we have moved onto your borders. We didn't know you had borders, but we do know that we can hold the land we have, and we can defend it against marauders for as long as we have to."

Ullic was silent for a space of minutes, staring Caius in the eyes. Slowly, he turned his head to look at me, and I was aware that I had not spoken since we met. And then he turned back to Caius and smiled, and he was transformed from a figure of menace to man of great appeal and charm. It was astonishing. He held out his hand to Caius, and, mystified, Caius shook with him.

"Caius Britannicus," he said, "you may well be the first of a new race. The non-Celtic Britons. Defend your land, and you defend my back. Defend my back, and I'll protect yours, too. Cymric! Send out the signal to prepare a feast! Our meeting here is done. Now we must tell the others what we have achieved."

Seconds later I heard the blowing of a horn and then the sounds of cheering. I was in a state of shock, as was Caius. I felt an idiotic smile painted across my face as Ullic stepped across to me, his hand outstretched. I shook with him, feeling the giant strength in his mighty fingers.

"Publius Varrus," he said, "we will have to change your name. You should be a Celt, with the love of iron that you have."

"King Ullic . . ." I rasped, my voice dry from tension.

"Ullic will do. The 'King' is for display. I will be King again later. Now is the time for eating . . ." He stopped, staring across my shoulder. "Britannicus, you train your men too well. They still stand at attention. Will you not allow them to stand down?"

"In a moment. Tell me, Ullic, why did you toy with me? It's obvious you knew the answers to your questions before you ever asked them. Was this fair?"

Ullic was smiling broadly now. "Fair? You mean just? Britannicus, I did not know you! I had to take the measure of the man. Varrus I knew about. But not Caius Britannicus. You hold your counsel closely to yourself. And so do I. Thus, if I were to know you, I must meet you face to face, and at your distinct disadvantage!" He grinned a giant grin. "I have met Romans whom I truly did not like, you know."

Caius smiled back at him, and I felt relief flooding over me like cooling water.

"We can be friends, I think, Sir King," Caius said through a smile.

"We will be friends, I know, Sir Briton!" He placed an arm on each of our shoulders and led us out from among the stones of Stonehenge into the brightness of the morning sun.

I allowed our men to break ranks and stand down as soon as we emerged from the temple. Ullic's men had already lighted fires and were preparing food. I saw casks being unloaded from the wagons and heard voices raised in song. A party of Druids had joined the gathering and their white robes gleamed in the strong sunlight.

The remainder of the day was spent in feasting. There were footraces and contests of all kinds, including a demonstration by our men of Roman drill, swordplay and spear-throwing. The Celts were throwers, too, as well as archers, and the championship went to one of them, a skinny stretch of a man who threw a Roman *pilum* fifteen paces further than his nearest rival.

As the sky began to darken, a great fire was built up of logs the Celts had brought with them on a cart, for there were no trees on the empty plain. One of the Celts produced a stringed instrument much like a Roman lyre and began to play, and a Druid priest stepped forward and sang to the sound of the strings. His voice was magical — clear, vibrant and possessed of enormous strength. We were enthralled when, at one point in the song, everyone else joined in and the music soared to a great crescendo, dying off suddenly to leave the Druid's voice shining alone. They sang in their own tongue and none of us could understand a word, but we had never heard such beauty coming from human throats. Again the Druid reached that certain point, and again everyone joined in.

"What are they singing?" I asked Ullic.

"A song about our land — our mountains and our lakes."

"It's magnificent. I must see your mountains some day."

"You will."

"That Druid sings too well to be a priest."

He looked at me and laughed outright. "Too well to be a priest?" He guffawed. "That's why he *is* a priest, man! It's their art! Druids are trained from boyhood to protect the history of our people in their songs. They *are* our history, Varrus . . . the Druids are our *history*! They are our pride, our bards, our singing joy in life, man. That's why they are Druids. That's why they ARE!"

I was somewhat taken aback by the force of his contention. "You mean they know your legends? All of them?"

"Nay, man! Not legends. History!" The singsong lilt of his liquid Celtic language had infiltrated his Latin heavily, making our Roman language musical — no simple feat. "Legends are what you people have. A legend is a story told by strangers, changing form as it is passed from mouth to mouth down through the years until the people that it happened to would never recognize it. Look here," he said, "let me try to explain to you. Each time something great, something momentous, even something funny happens that is worth recalling, one of our Druids sings it as a song. And then that song is learned, word upon word, perfectly, and passed on. It is intact, you see. It does not change — the details never vary. That is the sacred trust of the Druids. They are the bearers of our history.''

"But . . . All of it? How many songs are there?''

He shrugged. "Who knows? Thousands, I should think. Thousands and thousands, maybe.''

"How then can men remember all of them? A man's mind cannot hold so much!''

"Rubbish, Varrus! Who knows what a man's mind can hold? Have you ever met a man whose mind was full up?''

"No, I don't think I have.'' I smiled at the thought. "And yet, thousands of songs, you say?''

"Aye, and hundreds of Druids. They don't all sing the same songs, you know. There are some great songs every Druid knows, but each has his own that he is taught in boyhood, perhaps even some he made up himself, that he will teach to others, passing them on. It is their art, you see.''

I shook my head in wonder and listened once again to the song; the voices rose to one more crashing climax and then were still.

It had become quite dark, and another Druid now stepped into the firelight, bearing his own instrument. A silence fell, and he began to sing. There was a ghostly, fragile beauty to the song he sang, and as it went on, verse after exquisite verse, I found myself lost in the texture of the melody. He varied the strength and power of his voice widely, now soft and plaintive, now alive and strong, now angry, suiting his facial expressions to the mood. And then I noticed the faces of these men who sat and listened, enraptured by his song, and was astounded to see many weeping shamelessly. As his voice finally died away, the silence that ensued seemed unnatural; no one spoke, moved or applauded.

Ullic rose to his feet and stepped into the firelight. He looked around him at his men and mine and began to speak. As he did so, Cymric, our official interpreter, seated himself between Caius and me and translated for us; I saw many more of Ullic's warriors doing the same for our men. He spoke to them as an equal, but with great authority. He told them the details of our meeting at Stonehenge and went on to say that, from this day forth, we were no longer to be known as Romans. We were Britons, born in this land like them, proud of this land and ready to defend it against their foes and ours. He told them that if and when the legions were withdrawn, there might be numbers of them left behind, and that, if these should turn to banditry, we were prepared to fight them, too, Romans though they might nominally be.

We had talked long that day, he, Britannicus and I, he said. The alliance that we formed between us now was to be no mere alliance of convenience. We were to seek true brotherhood, and if our people chose to intermarry, such marriages would be welcome. This was news to me, and to Caius, I could see, but I found myself admiring the vision of this man Ullic. He was no fool. He told his men that we would send our soldiers to their mountains, to train their people in the Roman ways of fighting, and that they in turn would teach us their Celtic ways. And he ended by asking them to welcome us as brothers and neighbours to this new land of Britain, soon to be free of foreign Roman rule.

As soon as he had finished, one of his men leaped to his feet and burst into a song that was taken up by everyone before the second line. It was obviously a song of welcome and of celebration, and its stirring tune swept us along. When it ended, they cheered us, and just as I was beginning to feel that we should reciprocate in some way, Caius stood up and walked to the fire. I wondered what was in his mind and what he would say, but I would never have believed, even after his outburst of the morning, that he would say or do what he did. He stopped in front of the fire and looked at the faces watching him expectantly.

"Thank you!" he said. "Today, I stopped being Roman." And then, in front of them all, he stripped off his beautiful toga and threw it on the fire. There was an astounded silence, and then a roar of approval, in the middle of which Ullic stepped up and draped his royal cloak around Caius's shoulders. Caius thanked him, smiling, and held up his arms for silence. When it came, he cried, "Any of my soldiers attempting to do what I have just done will be court martialled immediately." There were cheers and laughter and whistles from our men. He waited for silence again.

"Seriously, my friends. It is a foolish man who does not learn from history. Roman weapons and armour are the best ever devised for waging war. We will keep them. Perhaps we will change the colours. I like this red." He indicated the cloak he was now wearing. There were more cheers and shouting, and a new cask of ale was hauled into the firelight. Before it could be opened, however, Ullic spoke again, lifting his voice high.

"Drink and make merry all you want tonight. But I want to be on the road before daylight! Thyrrwygg, it is your duty tonight. See to the sentries!" He waved and quit the fireside, beckoning to Caius and me to join him.

"Caius," I said, shaking my head in wondering admiration, "that was inspired, burning the toga! How does your mind work? I could never plan something like that."

He just smiled at me and squeezed my shoulder. It was years later that he told me the gesture had been totally unpremeditated. He enjoyed inspiring awe as well as the next man.

Within the hour, I was sound asleep.

XXXII

It often used to seem to me that Bishop Alaric had a God-given, almost mystical ability to anticipate our celebrations in the Colony and then to pre-empt them with other news of greater moment. He did it again on this occasion, arriving at the Colony before us so that he was there on our return and bringing news that quite eclipsed our own. Magnus Maximus, self-styled Emperor of Britain, Gaul and Iberia, was dead. The revolt was over. Theodosius was in command again.

To give him his due, Alaric restrained himself until dinner time, keeping his momentous news to himself until we had had an opportunity to exult over our own. When he did deliver his information, after our meal was complete, the news stunned me.

"How did he die?" I asked Alaric. "Was it the Frankish horsemen?"

He shook his head. "No, Publius. Theodosius himself had him executed. The news has just arrived. What did you last hear of him? Maximus, I mean."

"That he was installed in the Germanic lands and hoping to claim Illyricum. That must have been two years ago," Caius answered.

"At least." Alaric nodded a head that was noticeably whiter than it had been the last time I saw him. "Last year he invaded Italy, and Valentinian fled to Thessalonica to escape him. He had lived in dread of Magnus since Magnus killed Gratian, the other silly co-emperor, in Gaul. With Valentinian gone, Magnus crowned his own son co-emperor, to rule with him, making four emperors again. Folly! But he was a real threat, and they took him seriously. Not only Valentinian but Theodosius, too, recognized the boy.''

"Four emperors again." Caius's disgust was palpable. "God! This is obscene!''

"Aye. Anyway, Magnus divided his armies and struck back into Illyricum again. Both armies met defeat. Magnus was taken. They killed him out of hand.''

Caius's face was suddenly filled with concern. "Both of Magnus's armies beaten? What about his son? Does he still live?" I knew Caius was thinking of Picus, who might have died with either one.

Alaric shrugged his shoulders. "No one seems to know. It is presumed he fell. But I do have news of your son, Picus.''

"Picus!" Caius's voice was avid. "What of him? Is he alive?''

Alaric laughed. "Aye, Caius, he is alive and well. He rides with Stilicho.''

Caius's sudden frown matched my own. "Stilicho? Who is he?''

Alaric shook his head ruefully. "What, do you people hear nothing here? Stilicho is the brightest star remaining in the Empire's battered crown. A brilliant young general. Picus is one of his protégés, it seems. I heard their names linked together only a week ago, up in Glevum, though no one present tied Picus's name to yours.''

Caius grunted. "No, they would not — not now. I am too long gone to think of. Yesterday's soldier." I saw pain in his eyes. "Tell me more about this Stilicho. My son is his friend, you say?"

"One of his best cavalry commanders is what I heard."

Caius was mystified. "But how can that be?" he asked, frowning, "Picus was with Magnus. He *left* with Magnus."

"Aye, but he also *left Magnus*." Alaric's smile was kind. "Picus is his father's son, Caius. It did not take him long to see through Magnus and his posturing hypocrisy. We can only assume that, having seen the error of his ways, he surrendered to Stilicho and was pardoned. Stilicho is a very clever man, or he would not be where he is today. He would recognize Picus immediately for what he is, and he would want to retain the services and the loyalty of such a man."

Now, belatedly, the rest of what Alaric had said registered in Caius's mind.

"Cavalry?" he asked. "Did you say cavalry?"

"Yes, Caius, I said cavalry." The Bishop was smiling widely now. "You asked me earlier if Rome was training horsemen. Well, she is. Legions of them. Heavy cavalry. Heavily armed and heavily disciplined. Your son, according to the talk I heard, is one of the key figures in the new techniques of horsemanship."

"Picus? He's but a boy!"

I heard the paternal pride in that statement, and smiled to myself as Alaric asked, "How old is he?"

"He must be twenty-three, or twenty-four."

"Then he is no boy, Caius. Stilicho is only twenty-four and already he commands the Household Troops of the

Imperial Court in Constantinople. The word is that he will be named Commander in Chief of the armies within the year."

"Commander in Chief? At twenty-five? Has Theodosius lost his mind?"

"No, only his favourite niece, Serena. She is wed to Stilicho."

"Oh God!" I groaned. "Imperial patronage!"

"No, Varrus, not so — not quite." Alaric held up his hand to prevent my next outburst. "The troops who serve with Stilicho say he is the finest military mind since Alexander."

"Huh!" I reserved judgment. "Stilicho. That's a strange name."

"He is half Vandal."

Caius's interruption was explosive. "Half Vandal? Another barbarian! Being half Vandal seems to me much like being half with child."

His relief at knowing Picus to be well was making him sound most unlike himself, and Alaric's next words were gently chiding.

"Caius, I have never known you so querulous before. Do you feel well?"

"Quite well, thank you. The Commander in Chief a Vandal. I'll be damned!"

Alaric smiled at me. "If you die in this mood, my friend, you might be."

I was grinning broadly, hearing Caius reproached, even thus mildly, at his own table.

"Thank all the Saints that Picus is doing well, Caius," I said, "and don't be such a critic. If he's as good as they say, he might recall our talks of Alexander and teach some decent tactics to his chief, Stilicho."

Stilicho. The name stuck in my mind. I felt excited by it, but not threatened. Somehow, I felt, this was a name to conjure with.

The news of Magnus's defeat and death was timely. I imagined the demoralizing effect it would have on Seneca when I told him of it. Now the status quo in Britain would revert to what it had been before the revolt, and the Imperial Procurator of South Britain would be hard pressed to explain his long absence in the light of the evidence I intended to furnish to the returning imperial forces of Theodosius. I had to wrestle with myself to resist the temptation to tell Caius what I had decided to do about Seneca, but I knew that there was nothing to gain by doing so except argument and opposition. I held my peace and immersed myself that evening and most of the following day in the excitement caused by the outcome of our journey to Stonehenge.

It was clear that all our lives would be changed from the moment of that meeting, and there was a spirit of wild optimism among the Colonists for days after our return. For the first time, we had genuine allies who were prepared to protect our interests in return for our support in their own affairs.

I rose early on the morning of the second day after our return and slipped out of the villa before anyone was awake, having told Luceiia the night before that I was riding to Aquae Sulis that day. It was not a complete lie, for my destination lay only five miles south of that town. By the time dawn broke in the morning sky, I had covered more than ten miles, and my horse was eating up the remaining distance on the straight, solid road that ran for miles without a bend.

In spite of my early start, it was long after mid-morning by the time I arrived at the place where I had arranged to meet Tertius Pella. He was there, waiting patiently with one of his men, concealed within the trees that grew right to the edge of the road. We exchanged brief greetings and he led me away from the road and into the forest, along a track rutted by the wheels of farm carts. Only when we were well concealed from the sight of anyone passing on the road did we rein in to talk.

"How is our prisoner?" I asked.

"Safe and unharmed, I am sorry to say, save for a few bruises and chills."

"Did you have any trouble?"

"A little, not much. One of our men was slightly wounded, no more than a deep scratch. He'll be fine in a week."

"What about the others?"

"What others? Ours or theirs?"

"Theirs, of course."

He grinned at me. "Three of them died. We left the five survivors trussed and gagged. If anyone passes by the townhouse, they will be found and rescued."

I did not like to think of the alternative. "And Seneca, how long have you had him?" I asked.

"Six days. He would probably say six *long* days. We've managed to make them highly unpleasant for him. You wanted him confused, disoriented and afraid. He is totally as you wished on all three counts."

"Good. How far from here is he?"

"Two miles," he said, pointing. "One mile straight in

and another mile along a deer track to the little clearing."

I pulled a package from my tunic. "You've done well, Tertius. Your men will be well rewarded. Now we have to think about timing." I turned to his companion and held the package out to him. "Take this to the commander of the guardhouse at the garrison in Aquae Sulis. Tell him you were given a silver piece to deliver this to him. Here it is." I flipped him a silver coin, which he dropped into the scrip that hung from his side. "The message tells him that the missing Procurator, Claudius Seneca, may be found in this place. There is a map to guide them, too. As soon as you have delivered the package, make your way back to the Colony, but make sure no one knows where you are going and be sure that you are not followed. Is that clear?" He nodded. "Good. It should take you an hour, perhaps longer, to reach the garrison," I continued. "It will take them half that long again to organize a search party, and then another hour to make their way here using the map I drew for them. From this point, they should be able to find their own way to the clearing. In the meantime, Tertius, you and I have to finish our job and then be gone from here by the time they arrive, which should be before mid-afternoon, so let's get on with it."

Tertius swung his horse back onto the path and I followed close behind him, leaning low along my horse's neck to avoid the lower branches of the trees that hemmed us in.

We left our mounts some distance from the clearing and walked in, and I stopped on the edge of the camp they had set up. It consisted of two leather legion tents, a trestle table with a folding chair and a fire-pit. The fire was burning brightly, giving off flames that were almost invisible in the clear air. I could hear the sound of running water from a stream somewhere off to my right.

Beyond the tents, a massive old oak tree dominated the clearing and dwarfed the two men beneath it. One of these, the guard, whose name was Randall, was dozing against the trunk of the tree. The other, Seneca, stood naked by a thick stake that had been hammered into the ground. He was blindfolded and shackled at the ankles, and the chain of his shackles was threaded through the lower of two large iron rings fastened to the stake. His wrists were manacled in front of him and a taut rope, threaded through the upper ring, held his arms stretched downward. Above this ring, not passing through it, a second rope was tied to the first and looped upwards over a thick branch above the prisoner's head. By loosening the one rope and pulling on the other, Seneca's guard could dictate the position of his bound wrists.

I stared at Seneca for a long time, filled with revulsion, savouring the moment and the promised vengeance I would take for Phoebe. He looked terrible. His hair was matted and unkempt and his cheeks were heavy with sprouting, dirty-blond beard. As I looked at him he slumped and then pulled himself erect again, straightening up as far as the taut rope through the ring would allow him to. He could not stand completely erect, and so his back was bent. The guard was under instructions to yank him to his feet if he tried to lie down. As I looked at him, I was conscious that the sight of anyone else in that condition would have moved me to pity and to anger at his captors, but I had Phoebe's sweet face in my mind and was able to stifle any feelings of compassion that might have stirred in my breast. I motioned to Pella to lean close to me and I whispered in his ear, "Has anyone spoken to him?"

He shook his head and whispered back, "Not a word since we took him six days ago."

I nodded and waved him forward, and he walked into the clearing, heading towards the table in front of the tents. Seneca's head came up quickly at the swishing sounds Pella's feet made in the long grass, but he made no sound. His guard heard it, too, and straightened up slowly, nodding to me in recognition. I held my fingers to my lips, reminding him to stay silent.

In the meantime, Pella had bent down and released the tension on the rope that held the prisoner's arms stretched downward. Seneca felt the release immediately, but before he could react to it, his arms were already being dragged above his head as Pella hauled on the other rope. A moment later, Seneca hung by his wrists, high enough that he had to bear his weight on his toes. He howled like an animal but Pella ignored him, concentrating on tightening the knot that held the tension on the rope. When he was satisfied that it would hold Seneca correctly in position, he crossed to the table and picked up something that lay there.

This was the worst part. I resisted the urge to interfere at the last moment and forced myself to stand immobile as Pella went up to the prisoner and laid the metal-tipped lashes of the scourge he held gently across Seneca's shoulders, allowing them to slip down and off under their own weight. Seneca moaned as he recognized the feel of the lashes, and opened his mouth to scream. As he did so, Pella stuffed his mouth with a filthy rag. I closed my eyes against what was to happen next, but made myself open them again immediately. This next step was necessary, as an earnest of what was to come.

As Pella stepped back and swung the lash up and around, Seneca drew his finely muscled body into a bow shape in a vain attempt to avoid it. He was even bigger, stronger than I remembered. The scourge swished through the air and exploded into his writhing torso, and he screamed, in spite of the gag in his mouth. I turned aside and vomited into the grass, shuddering, unable to believe that I had planned this in cold blood, or that I was permitting it to happen. When I straightened up again, wiping the saliva from my chin with my sleeve, Seneca hung unconscious, blood trickling from a score of welts around his whole upper body. I swallowed hard.

"Take that thing out of his mouth and remove the blindfold."

As Pella moved to do so, I crossed to the table and sat in the chair, so that Seneca would be looking at me when he regained consciousness. I picked up the scroll that lay on the table and unrolled it.

"Did you find his seal?"

"Aye, he had it around his neck on a gold chain. Here!" Pella tossed Seneca's seal to me and I laid it beside the scroll and the stick of wax. There was nothing more to prepare.

"Throw some water on him."

Seneca struggled back to consciousness, fighting against the shocking coldness of the water that hit him and the brightness of the sun that wounded his eyes after six days of tightly bound darkness. I watched him become aware of my presence and fight to gain control of himself, then saw him fight again, in vain this time, to bring his eyes to focus on me. For long moments neither of us spoke, and then I broke the silence.

"Do you know me, Seneca?"

I could see him struggling physically for words, trying to control the violent shuddering that racked his wretched body. When he finally answered me, his voice was cracked and dry-sounding and his eyes peered at me almost sightlessly as he held them shut against the brightness of the afternoon.

"No," he whispered. "Who are you?"

I made my voice hard and toneless. "I am an old, grey-bearded man with a limp. Does that remind you of anyone?"

He shook his head sharply, as though trying to dismiss an unwelcome thought. "No. Who are you?" he asked again.

"Come, Seneca, you know me, surely? I had a friend in Verulamium. A bright-faced young woman with red hair. Her name was Phoebe. She died while she was a guest of yours. Don't you remember? You told Antonius Cicero about it."

He was squinting hard against the sunlight, twisting his head and trying to see my face more clearly. He rubbed the right side of his face against his right arm, trying to dry the moisture that was trickling into his eye, and this time, when he spoke, his voice was much stronger and his courage was starting to return.

"Damn you," he cried. "What madness is this? What do you want of me? Who are you? I don't know what you're talking about!"

I pressed on, maintaining the same hard, hectoring tone.

"You do not remember Antonius Cicero? He was Legate of the garrison at Colchester. He died because he was loyal to Theodosius when all others were rebelling with Magnus. Do you not remember, Seneca? You told him about Phoebe's death. Surely you must recall? You told him that the man you sought, the grey-bearded cripple, had escaped you. You had found his whore. But the whore died without telling you anything, and you were vexed. You cannot have forgotten that, surely?"

Now he said nothing. His eyes had narrowed and his face grew cunning. A trickle of new blood seeped down from beneath his right armpit, where one of the lashes had bitten deep. The way he was hanging emphasized the great white "V" on his chest. I stood suddenly, feeling the chair fall back behind me, and strode around the table to confront him. His eyes widened and then clenched shut as I approached. I balled my fist and punched him on the breastbone.

"Look at me, whoreson, look at me! I'm the one who carved you and spoiled your pretty nose!"

His eyes snapped open, though I couldn't tell whether they yet saw or not, and then he lunged at me, and as he failed to reach me he spat, swift as a serpent, in my face. Then he began to scream, stringing obscenities and curses together in a chain that would have shocked even Plautus. But through all of it there was a theme. "Who are you?"

I wiped the spit from my face and waited for him to be quiet. Finally his stream of venom dried up.

"Who are you?" he whispered again.

"Your nemesis," I answered him. "To you I have no name, other than Death and Vengeance, hence my 'V' upon your chest. Do you recall my friend here?"

I indicated Pella with a nod and he stepped forward, to where Seneca could see him clearly.

Seneca glared at Pella, then shook his head. "I don't know you."

"No, you don't, but you knew my son, in Aquae Sulis six years ago. He was five years old. Five. And you killed him, you demented, perverted whoreson, along with four others, and thought yourself safe. But you were seen. And now it's time to pay, with your sick life, you festering sore!"

"Caesarius Claudius Seneca, you have a choice to make," I interrupted, drawing Seneca's wide-eyed gaze, now alert and fearful, back to me. Even still, he continued to glance sideways towards Pella through all I said from that time on.

"Listen, and do not interrupt. If you do, Pella will silence you again with his lash." I picked up the scroll and began to read:

"Mine has been a life in which few could take pride. I have abused my power since I was old enough to do so. I have killed wantonly, in person and through others hired to do my will.

"I have also abused my position here in South Britain. Angered at Theodosius, and mindful of my own future prospects, I chose to aid and support the ambitions of the usurper known as Magnus Maximus, self-styled Emperor of Britain. In order to do this, I secreted funds from the revenues collected on behalf of Theodosius and used those funds to equip and provision Magnus and his armies.

"In so doing I was the direct cause of the death of the Legate Antonius Lepus Cicero, Commander of the garrison at Camulodunum. Loyal to his Emperor, he marched against Magnus and died.

"As soon as Magnus had declared himself, I withdrew into hiding, and have remained in hiding ever since that time, awaiting the outcome of Magnus's venture, and knowing that if he failed I could emerge as a loyal officer who had taken his affairs into concealment to protect them.

"Now I am brought to judgment for a crime that I had not even considered to be worthy of remembrance; a faceless woman, murdered in my search for the man who mutilated me. She lived in Verulamium and her name, I know now, was Phoebe. It is in memory of Phoebe that I accuse myself and stand condemned by my own seal and hand."

I raised my head and looked at Seneca. "There is your choice," I said. "You may either sign this, or refuse to sign it. Either way, it will be found beside your corpse."

His face had the pallor of death and his eyes were wild. "You are insane," he whispered. "Do you really believe I would sign that thing?"

"Tertius Pella here is hoping you will not," I answered him, "because if you refuse, he will flog you to death and enjoy every swing of the scourge. Thirty lashes. You will not survive them, nor would you wish to." I saw him flinch at the thought of thirty lashes. The one he had already received had made a major impression on him. "I, on the other hand, am prepared to offer you a fighting chance for life. Not that I hate you less than Pella does. We could quarrel, Tertius and I, over who loves you least."

I paused, waiting for him to react to what I had said. He stretched upwards, seeking some relief from the agony of his hanging position, keeping his face expressionless.

"If you refuse to sign," I went on, "as I have said, you will die under the lash. That is as certain as the death of Phoebe, whom you killed. If, on the other hand, you choose to sign the confession, you will have an opportunity to live. Not much of an opportunity, but more than you have allowed others. I will give you a sword and we will fight. Should you kill me, you will be free to go, that is if you can kill Pella too, for I think he might dispute your going. Victorious, you will have the document and satisfaction for your scars. If you die, however, and I intend to kill you with great pleasure, your confession, signed by your hand and bearing your seal, will be found beside your corpse as a final and unimpeachable condemnation richly deserved. I have already sent word to the garrison at Aquae Sulis. They will be here, looking for you, in a short time."

There was a flash of something in his eyes, but I killed it.

"There is no other way out for you, Seneca. Not even if the soldiers were to arrive early and save your life. They are no longer yours to influence. Magnus is dead, months ago, and the news is known. Britain has already reverted to Theodosius." I let him think on that for a time, then, "Well?" I asked. "Are you ready to decide?"

"What if I were to sign? You would kill me before I had finished."

Rage surged in me, and I turned away from him to quell it. I turned back only when I had controlled myself.

"That would make me no better than you, Seneca, and I am a better man than you in every way. But what if I did kill you? It would still be better than being flogged to death by Tertius Pella. Once you are dead, your confession can no longer hurt you. For once in your rotten life, Seneca, you are going to have to trust someone to be more honourable than you are. Had I wanted simply to kill you, you would have been dead days ago. I want to kill you sword in hand, to beat you and to know you know that you are being beaten by a grey-bearded cripple." I nodded to Pella. "Cut him down and take off those shackles."

Pella cut the rope and Seneca fell at my feet.

"On your face," I commanded, prodding him with the point of my sword. He rolled and lay face down as Pella undid his leg irons. "Now, roll over." He did so, and I held the point of my sword at the base of his throat until his hands were freed. When he had finished, Pella went and fetched a length of rope and knotted it in a noose about Seneca's neck. I nodded to him and he hauled Seneca unceremoniously to his feet.

"Choose now," I said, fighting to keep my voice emotionless. "Sign or be flogged."

From some deep well inside of himself, Seneca had found new resources to sustain him. The look he threw me was almost a defiant sneer, and, in spite of my hatred for him, I felt respect for his hardness stirring in my gut.

"I may sign," he said, quietly, "but where is the sword I am to fight with?"

I looked at Pella. "Give me your sword."

His face went black as a thunder-cloud. "No, by the Christ, I will not! If this whoreson has my sword at all it will be between his cursed ribs!"

I spoke to the guard who had been standing quietly,

watching what was happening. "Randall, give me your sword."

The guard unsheathed his sword and handed it to me. I took it and stuck it in the ground, about five paces in front of the table. Having done that, I paced out ten long steps and stuck my own sword in the ground, after which I retraced five of those steps to stand between the two swords. "There," I said. "No advantages to either of us. Tertius Pella will tell me when you have signed fairly. After that, we fight and you die."

This time he did sneer. "Your courage is wondrous, cripple. I have not eaten properly, or moved about in six days."

I shrugged. "Weep if you want, Seneca. You are fortunate to have even this chance."

He pursed his lips, seeing no mercy in my eyes. "So be it," he said. "I will sign." He moved forward to the table and took up the stylus I had placed there beside an open jar of ink. Pella moved with him, not allowing the rope around his neck to slacken too much. "Bring me a firebrand," Seneca said. Pella glowered at him and then at me. I nodded to Randall, who went to the fire and picked up a burning stick and took it to where Seneca stood reading the scroll.

Seneca motioned with his head for the guard to come closer, and when Randall had approached him, our prisoner smiled, a smile of frightening charm, considering his case. "I will hold the parchment," he said. "You melt the wax on to it." He watched the wax dripping to form a pool and then he imprinted the cooling puddle with his seal. "There," he said. "And now my name." He dipped the stylus into the ink and signed his name with a flourish. Even from a distance, I could see that his name was clearly legible. Tertius Pella examined the scroll and nodded to me.

"Good," I said. "Now undo the rope, Tertius, and stand away." As he started to obey me, I walked towards my sword.

As soon as the rope was clear of his head, Seneca sprang forward and snatched up the other sword. He crouched, panting, staring at me with a feral grin on his lips. "Now, cripple, you die!"

I looked at him, stark naked, his phallus dangling between his legs, and I felt invincible.

We circled each other warily for a spell, each taking the measure of the other, and then came together in the middle of the circle we had described. Our swords met with a clang as each of us slashed brutally at the other, hoping to finish the matter at one blow. There was no technique here, and no need of it; neither of us had a shield. This matter would be settled by strength, swiftness and chance. I watched his eyes, looking for the message of his next move, and he almost had me, because he moved in again to the attack as swiftly as an adder and with no warning. The point of his sword flashed within an inch of my face as I threw myself backwards and away from him with no chance of a counterstroke. He followed me, fast, his sword poised to stab, and there was nothing laughable now about his nakedness. I was aware only of his ferocity and of the fact that I had underestimated him in every way. I had looked for the weakness and cowardice of the bully, and for the effeminate inadequacy of a limp-wristed homosexual. But where I had imagined weakness, I found strength and bitter determination, and I quickly lost all feelings of invulnerability in my scramble to stay away from his sword.

He actually laughed aloud as he pursued me, and my limp felt more pronounced than it had in all the years since I had acquired it. Again his point slashed across my chest, missing, yet fanning me with its closeness. He came again, and I backed away, waiting for him to commit to his next move. He rushed; I stepped aside and swung at him and missed, and he kept moving forward. Forward, to where Randall, the guard, stood watching with his arms folded on his chest. The swipe of the treacherous blow that followed took all of us by surprise. Randall fell backwards, clutching at the gaping wound in his throat that sprayed his life's blood up and around his falling form like a cloud.

Before I could move or react, Pella flung himself into the fray with a vicious oath, drawing his sword and plunging at Seneca, who seemed still off balance after his killing blow at Randall. As Pella's hurtling body came between us, depriving me of a clear view of Seneca, I saw Seneca twist and dodge, and then Pella was rigid, drawing himself up onto his toes, his entire body expressing outrage and violent death. I heard the grating thud of the blow that killed him and the scraping sound of Seneca's blade plunging home through his breastbone. Like a cat, Seneca moved forward, braced one foot against Pella's sagging body and kicked the corpse free of his sword.

Astounded by the turn things had taken, I was conscious of my mind screaming "No!" and of both of my companions still kicking and squirming, although both of them were dead.

Now Seneca faced me alone, and he was laughing, his

eyes shining insanely with the joy of battle and of killing. "Two gone, Greybeard," he said. "Now, before you die, will you tell me your name?"

I settled my feet squarely and braced myself to meet him head on. "I told you earlier," I snarled. "For you, my name is Death — Death and Vengeance." He sprang at me again, watching to see which way I would evade his charge, but I stood my ground, leaned forward to take his weight and stabbed hard, feeling my blade go deep in the killing thrust. His chin snapped forward onto his chest and his eyes flew wide, and for a space of heartbeats I held the whole weight of him upright on the end of my sword. I felt a savage exultation flow from my head to the muscles of my straining forearm. "Vengeance," I whispered. "Vengeance and Death."

I jerked my arm back hard, wrenching my blade from his chest, and watched as he fell, first to his knees and then forward onto his face. I stood there above him for a long time, looking down. He did not jerk or squirm, and he still breathed, but I knew I had my vengeance. I raised my arm again to strike off his head, and suddenly found I had no wish to strike one more blow. I opened my hand and let my sword fall to the grass, and then I looked around me at the slaughter-ground. The soldiers would be there soon. I brought the scroll from the table, rolled it up loosely and stuck it between his right arm and his chest, feeling as I did so the flaccid deadness of his muscles.

I wiped my hand on my tunic, turned on my heel and walked away to where we had left our horses, leaving the clearing with its carnage behind me forever.

XXXIII

In due time, I confessed my sin and was shriven by Bishop Alaric, but I never did tell Caius or Luceiia what I had done. Not that I had any shame of my actions, but I had no pride in them either, and I decided that no purpose was to be gained by spreading the knowledge among those I loved. It would be sufficient that their lives were the safer for my removal of Seneca. The how and the when of his treachery and his demise would be known soon enough. The catalyst that brought about his death had no need to be named.

The good Bishop went on his way eventually, and life in our Colony resumed its normal pace. We continued to be isolated from the rest of Britain, to a very great degree, and I did not find it too surprising that the news of Seneca's quietus should fail to reach us. His family, I surmised, would have gone to great lengths to conceal his perfidy from the eyes of the people. In the meantime, our crops continued to improve from year to year, and Ullic aided us greatly by decreeing that each of his people who came to visit should bring a stone to raise upon our walls. This made a major difference to the pace of our building activities, for there was much traffic between his land and ours. Soon our masons were working mounted on scaffolding, so high were our walls, and the old hill fort inside the citadel had become a permanent camp, housing our growing army in stout log buildings.

Our governing Council had seen some changes, too. All of its members now lived in the Colony and met together once a month. None of them was selected for his timidity, so we had some stormy sessions, but by and large our lives went on peacefully.

On one of my first visits to Ullic's kingdom in the mountains, he and I discussed strategy in the event of Saxon raids. His men would guard the entry from the river, and he would keep outposts overlooking the main road from the north. We, for our part, would police the approaches from the east, south and south-west. Anyone threatening from the west itself would have to cross his lands. I was content.

And marriages had been celebrated between his Celts and our Britannic Romans. Only a few, but they happened. Life was good to us.

On a rainy evening in March, in the eighth year of my stay in the Colony, I sent my daughter Victoria to bring Caius to the smithy. She was his favourite, his first-born niece. As a child, unable to pronounce his name, she had called him "Uncle Cay." Quintus Varo had been calling him Cay for years, but now, given new currency by the love of a child, the name stuck, and he had been called Cay by the family ever since.

He came into the smithy with his hand resting on her seven-year-old head as they walked together. I was waiting for him, Luceiia by my side, standing at my workbench. I stepped to greet him and surprised him mightily by throwing my arms around him in a hug and swinging him off his feet.

His eyebrows were arched high when I put him down, and he threw his sister an eloquent look of long-suffering tolerance. "Thank you for that, Publius," he said with dignity when I'd put him down. "Now, will you explain this summons? And this greeting? Victoria tells me you had something 'portant for me." He smiled indulgently as he repeated his niece's pronunciation.

"Of course, Caius," I said. "You shall have an explanation. Let me see, now." I pretended to think about it. "Luceiia, why did I ask Cay to come here?" She said nothing, and merely looked at me indulgently. I snapped my fingers. "Aha! I remember. Cay, I want you to meet someone."

He looked around. The smithy was empty, save for the three of us. My daughter had gone.

"To meet someone. I see. And where is this someone?"

"Here."

He spoke gently to me, humouring me as he would a madman. "Publius, my friend, we are alone in here, you and Luceiia and I."

"Not so, Cay," I said, smiling. "There is another here."

"Really?" This was a languid drawl. "Where? Where is he?"

"He's a she, Cay. A female. A lady."

"A lady. Well, in that case, where is she?"

"Over there," I nodded towards the back of the smithy.

"Where? I see no one."

"Then approach! She is there, Cay."

He started to protest, and then he saw her. He looked back at both of us, smiling uncertainly.

"Go on," I urged him. "Move closer!"

Mystified, he did so, staring in perplexity.

"She" was a statue, a female figure, two feet high, large-breasted, ample-bellied, abundantly buttocked and faceless. A rough-sculpted, iron woman standing on a plinth of solid metal that rippled from her footless legs in a puddle.

"Who is she, Varrus? What is she?" There was wonder in his voice, for he had never seen the like of this.

"Coventina is her name, Cay. She's Celtic," I told him. "The Celtic goddess of water. She is a water nymph, and her spirit has lived for centuries in every body of water in this country. She's the reason all these Celts throw coins and offerings into pools. I call her the Lady of the Lake."

"The Lady of the Lake." And then he saw it and swung towards me. "Of the lake! You mean . . .?"

"Aye, Caius. I mean!" I could no longer control the great grin that spread across my face. "She's made of iron from the skystone. I smelted it last month."

His eyes grew wide. "Last month? And you said nothing? All this time? How could you? And you, Luceiia, how could you let this go by?"

Luceiia shook her head, looking at me. "Do not blame me, Brother. I knew nothing of this until now. My secretive husband sent for me only a short time before he sent for you. Until that time he had said nothing, not even a hint."

I smiled and shrugged, saying nothing again.

Caius looked mildly confused, then. "But why a statue, Publius?"

"Why not?"

He looked again at the Lady. She was crudely made, but still, she had a certain beauty.

"Indeed, why not?" he said. I joined him, gripping his shoulder as we looked at her together.

"What else could I do with her, Cay?" I asked him. "I didn't want to end up with a simple ingot, after all. Seven years of effort deserves more of a symbol than a metal ingot. And yet I have no urgent need to use the metal. Some day I will. Some day I shall find the perfect use for it, but until then I thought to leave her in your care. I promised you that if you left me to my own time, you should have iron from those stones. So, until I find a better use for her, she's yours."

He ran his hand over her, feeling her substance. "The Lady of the Lake! Why doesn't she shine, Publius?"

"She will, Cay," I assured him. "She will. The lustre is there in the raw metal. She will shine bright, some day, when I have found the perfect use for her."

"What does this mean, Varrus?" His voice was hushed.

"What does it mean?" I sucked in a great breath and touched the head of the statue, caressing its cold, solid hardness. "I don't know what it means, Cay. Maybe it doesn't mean anything, apart from the fact that my theory was right. Then again, it means that in spite of what your mind tells you is impossible, stones full of iron do fall from the sky." I was rubbing the ball of my thumb against the smooth surface of the Lady's face, and I felt the smile on my own face as I added, "It means, my friend, that God still has some secret wonders that He chooses to hide from men."

"Aye, that it does," he whispered. He reached to pick her up.

"Careful, Cay," I warned him. "She's heavier than you think. Here, let me help you."

Between us, with Luceiia leading the way, we picked her up and carried her with difficulty across the yard and into the house. We placed her in his *cubiculum*, on a table by the window.

"I'll be back in a minute." I left him alone with her and returned shortly, carrying the skystone dagger. I placed it on the metal plinth on which she stood.

"There!" I said. "Like unto like! Let them feed on each other."

"And now, Publius?" Caius's voice was soft. "Will you make swords from your Lady of the Lake?"

"Swords?" I answered, shaking my head slightly. "No, I think not, Caius. Not swords. But perhaps one sword. I believe this lady may have one great sword in her."

THE END

PROLOGUE

The sequel to The Skystone, *entitled* The Singing Sword, *also by Jack Whyte, will be published by Viking in 1993.*

The excerpt that follows is the prologue to the continuing saga of Publius Varrus, Caius Britannicus and their Colonists.

387 A.D.

The tribune recognized the first signs from more than a mile away, just as the road dropped down from the ridge to enter the trees: a whirlpool of hawks and carrion-eaters, spiralling above the treetops of the forest ahead of him. With a harsh command to the centurion behind him to pick up the pace of his men, the officer kicked his horse forward, down the track, unconcerned that he was leaving his infantry escort far behind. The swirling birds clearly meant death; their numbers meant that they circled above a clearing in the forest; and their continuing flight meant that they were afraid to land — afraid not of men, but of wolves. The tribune lowered the face-protector of his helmet to guard himself from whipping twigs and took his horse into the trees at a full gallop, sensing accurately that all danger of ambush or opposition was long gone.

He heard the wolves fighting among themselves while he was still far distant from them, and he kicked his horse to even greater speed, shouting at the top of his voice and making the maximum possible noise to distract them from their grisly feasting. He had little doubt about what they were eating.

By the time he'd burst into the clearing, the wolves had indeed left their eating and were crowded together, bellies low to the ground, snarling and slavering as they faced the newcomer. He put his horse at them without hesitation, drawing his short sword and slashing at them from the animal's back, leaving his horse to use its hooves in its own battle with the wolves he knew it hated. The snarling fury of the wolves quickly reached a crescendo and then began to include yelps of pain and fear as horse and rider laid about them. Soon one, and then all of the lean, grey scavengers broke off the fight and fled to the protection of the bushes surrounding the clearing.

When they had gone, out of sight among the bushes and safely beyond his reach, the tribune looked around at the scene he had ridden into. The clearing was dominated by one massive, ancient oak tree that had an arrangement of ropes and pulleys strung across one of its huge branches. One of these ropes reached to a ring through a heavy stake that had been set into the ground. The condition of the ground around the stake — the grass trodden flat and dead and scattered haphazardly with piles of human excrement — showed that someone had been confined there for many days. The bodies of three men lay strewn around on the dusty, blood-splattered ground, two of them clothed, the other absolutely naked. Flies swarmed everywhere, attracted, like the birds and the wolves, by the smell of fresh, sun-warmed blood. The two clothed bodies had both been badly bitten about the face by the wolves, particularly the younger of the two, a blond man whose neck and throat had been slashed by a sword almost deeply enough to decapitate him.

The naked man lay face down, his left arm extended and ripped open on the underside, close to the shoulder, where one of the wolves had been chewing at it. There was another clear set of tooth marks on the body's right thigh, although the bite had not been ripped away. The only blood visible on this corpse was pooled beneath it. Incongruously, there was a rolled parchment scroll pinned beneath the outstretched arm of the naked body, and he idly wondered what it contained.

The sound of his men approaching at a dead run brought the tribune's head up. They broke from the tree-lined path into the open clearing, hardly even breathing hard, and drew up in two ranks facing him. Before they had even completed their formation, he ordered them to spread out and chase away the wolves hiding in the undergrowth, offering a silver *denarius* for any wolf killed. The soldiers scattered enthusiastically to the chase, and the tribune nodded to the centurion, directing the man's attention to the parchment and indicating that he wished to look at it.

When the man handed it to him, the tribune examined it closely, holding it up to his eyes before breaking the seal and reading the contents. Watching this, the centurion's face remained inscrutable. The tribune read the entire document with a perfectly emotionless expression and then went back to the beginning and read the whole thing again. He felt the centurion watching him and looked back, asking if the man could read. The centurion's answer was terse and negative, and the tribune informed him that the parchment was a demand for ransom, and the naked corpse was that of Caesarius Claudius Seneca, Imperial Procurator of South Britain, who had been missing for months. The procurator, the tribune pointed out, had obviously escaped from his bondage beneath the big tree where the ropes and tackle and human excrement showed he had been kept confined. Obviously, he had managed to kill his captors, who had apparently grown careless, before being killed himself.

At that point the centurion, whose gaze had drifted to the naked Seneca, frowned slightly and then pointed before moving quickly to kneel by the body. Narrow-eyed, he slipped his fingers underneath the chin, pressing gently with finger and thumb beneath the points of the jaw where, against all reasonable expectation, he discovered a very faint but quite regular pulse beat. Claudius Seneca was alive. Two minutes later, the soldiers had been recalled and four of them were hard at work, fashioning a litter from spears and leather tents. By the time the litter was ready and the small procession had set out on its journey back to the barracks at Aquae Sulis, the spa town the local Celts called Bath, no one was even aware that the tribune had quietly folded up the parchment of the scroll and tucked it securely and quite safely out of sight beneath the metal of his breastplate.